"Are you going to kiss me?"

The question was so soft that at first Mark wasn't sure he'd heard it.

"You keep staring at my lips, but you're not doing anything. Are you going to kiss me?"

He *was* staring at Isabella's lips, staring at them but not quite seeing them. He focused on their rosy fullness. "Do you want me to kiss you?"

Her skin flushed and he could tell she wanted to look away, step away—instead she stepped closer, her eyes dropping back to his mouth. "Yes." She said it firmly, but then hesitated. "I know I shouldn't want you to. I've known you hardly half a week."

He ran a finger across her cheek. "It feels so much longer, as if I've known you forever." And it did.

He knew he shouldn't kiss her. She was right about that. And he certainly shouldn't kiss her here, where anybody might see.

He stepped closer, his fingers slid down and cupped her chin, bringing her face nearer.

And he kissed her.

Romances by Lavinia Kent

What a Duke Wants
Taken by Desire
Bound by Temptation
A Talent for Sin

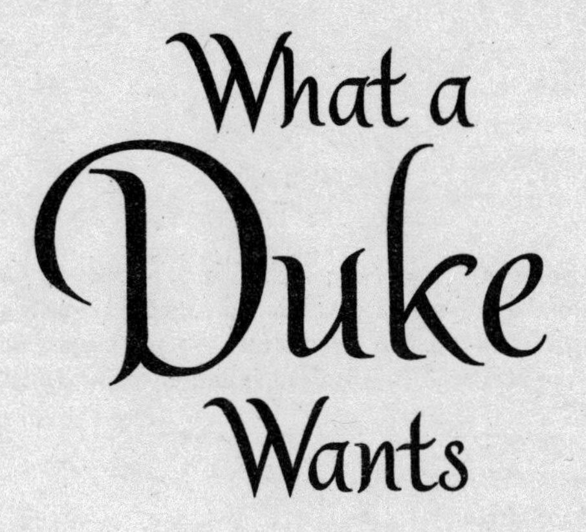

LAVINIA KENT

AVON
An Imprint of HarperCollins*Publishers*

This is a work of fiction. Names, characters, places, and incidents are products of the author's imagination or are used fictitiously and are not to be construed as real. Any resemblance to actual events, locales, organizations, or persons, living or dead, is entirely coincidental.

AVON BOOKS
An Imprint of HarperCollins*Publishers*
10 East 53rd Street
New York, New York 10022-5299

ISBN 978-0-06-198631-4
www.avonromance.com

First Avon Books mass market printing: October 2011

Printed in the U.S.A.

10 9 8 7 6 5 4 3 2 1

What a
Duke
Wants

Chapter 1

Middleham, England, June 1821

"Who covers a cock?" The voice whispered through the darkness. "I've never even dreamed of such a thing. Who does he think he is to make such demands?"

Mark lifted his head away from the rough wood wall of the stable. Retreating here had been the one way to avoid the unending wailing that had pervaded the inn. He normally didn't mind children, but the steady crying echoing since his arrival had been mind numbing. Sleep had eluded him since his uncle's death six weeks ago, but this noise threatened even what little rest he normally managed. Retreating to the stables had been his one hope of closing his eyes in peace for even a few minutes. The smell of the horses was far easier to bear than the noise.

"I can't even imagine how you'd put a hood on the creature. Do you suppose you just cover the head or does one have to cover the whole thing?" The soft voice drew closer.

It was distinctly husky, distinctly feminine, and definitely an improvement over the yowling of the infant.

He peered into the darkness of the yard. A narrow silhouette drew closer. Her soft patter continued. Whom was she addressing? And what was this nonsense about covering a cock? A slow smile spread across his face as he slowly imagined what she must be talking about.

A young woman. A dark stable yard. Plenty of fresh, clean straw.

There could be only one possible explanation.

And covering the whole thing—that brought quite the picture to his mind.

Staring more closely at the silhouette, he tried to determine her proportions. If he wasn't going to be able to sleep, perhaps he should be seeking some other form of entertainment. She looked well proportioned enough—but not too slim. It was hard to tell under the flowing cloak. What was she trying to hide wearing a cloak in this heat?

The voice still contained the soft wispiness of youth. And her walk . . . There could be only one explanation for that wide-hipped sway—only one type of woman practiced that stride.

"Hooding the cock . . . and babies. The man clearly doesn't like babies. It's all just too much to think about. And where does it leave me? Traipsing about the yard when I should be tucked in my own bed. Mrs. Wattington was displeased enough to pay for a second chamber and now I don't even get to use it."

Mark stepped partially out of the shadows and waited for her to become aware of his presence. He'd be all too delighted to let her know that his cock didn't need any hooding. Hopefully her face was as agreeable as her voice. Its low huskiness was causing distinct stirrings in his lower body. He hadn't taken his pleasure in the weeks since his uncle's death.

He stepped forward. "You shouldn't be alone out here at this hour."

Her head jerked up, her whole body tensing. There was a sharp intake of breath. Giving herself a little shake, she stepped forward. She peered into the darkness, her eyes gleaming in the moonlight.

She was taller than he'd realized. She must have been hunched over.

Shadows still hid most of her face, but her eyes squinted, and he could tell she was trying to see him in the dim light.

She paused, but then answered carefully, with only the slightest quaver to betray her nerves. "He told me I wouldn't be alone."

That was strange. "Who told you?"

She paused again and he could almost hear her thoughts forming, see her seeking reassurance. "The duke's man."

Bloody hell. That was all he needed. Mark felt his desire wilt. It was bad enough Divers and the other servants wouldn't let him pull on his own pants, but this was too much—sending a woman to him. Had they counted how long it had been? There were some things a man wanted to do on his own, and choosing his own woman was one of them. It was bad enough Divers mentioning his need to marry at least once a day.

"I don't know what they told you," he began. "But I assure you that my cock needs no hooding." Were they that afraid that he'd catch some disease—or did they think he'd picked up something in his army days? That was more likely. They'd not want word out that the mighty Duke of Strattington was spreading around the nasties. He wasn't having any part of it.

"Oh, then you are the one?" Her shoulders relaxed and she stepped forward. "I did think it was odd to cover the cock, but are you sure you won't get in trouble if you don't? The man sounded very firm that it must be done. He said the duke would be most displeased if it wasn't." She moved closer, still squinting to see his features.

She smelled of powder and something else—something soft, almost milky. He couldn't decide if it was arousing or not. It was certainly not a smell he associated with doxies, but then—he looked about the stable yard—there probably had not been much choice in the hamlet. In fact, he was surprised his men had managed to find one at all. Perhaps they'd sent for one. He wouldn't put anything past Divers.

He wished she'd open her cloak. It was hard to determine much when she was swaddled up like an infant. He wasn't about to fall in with his servants' plans, but it would be nice to think they believed he had some taste and standards. They didn't think he had many—not like those his uncle and cousin had demonstrated. He never knew which coat was correct or which bottle of wine to request. And the manor house—he would never have thought to decorate it in the fashion they'd chosen. Simple, strong furniture was his preference, a good chair a man could sprawl in—not that dukes were allowed to sprawl.

He dropped his gaze back to the woman. Would she be simple or overly ornate?

As if in response to his thoughts, the moon suddenly eased from behind the clouds, spreading a gentle light across the stable yard.

Candle flames. Her hair was like candle flames.

She raised her face to him, the light outlining features as fine as any angel's, her skin as clear as—

He needed more sleep. There was no other possible reason for the multitude of words that sprang to his mind as he stared down at her. "What's your name?" His question was more abrupt than he'd intended.

"Isabell—" She swallowed the remainder of the word, still nervous. "I mean Miss Smith. My name is Miss Smith."

He shouldn't even have asked. Women never answered honestly. "Not something more creative, something French, perhaps?"

"French?" Isabella tried to keep the fear and weariness from her voice as she spoke. Her brain must be quite muddled, for nothing the man said was making sense. Little Joey's wailing and her own worries had left her nearly witless—why else had she given her true name? "Why would I be called something French? I am a good English girl."

"Isabelle is lovely, but I'd always been told a woman could make more money by being French. Are you sure it's not Yvette? I've always had good luck with Yvettes. Or maybe Mimi? I could be quite fond of a Mimi."

He really must be mad, or else she was so tired that her ears no longer worked. She should be more afraid, but that would have required more effort than she had strength left. It was two days since she'd seen the man in the blue coat. Perhaps he had not realized she had left Appleby. No one would believe she would willingly head for London. No, that would be too simple. Her followers were still about, just better hidden.

She tried to peer into the darkness again. If only she could see the man's face maybe she would know if she'd ever seen him before.

"Not Mimi? How about Colette?" He kept his banter going.

Colette? She was definitely not a Colette. Perhaps he thought she was a lady's maid. Some of them pretended to be French. She cuddled Joey closer to her chest. If he started to yell again she'd scream like a banshee herself. "No, it's Miss Smith, plain Miss Smith. And it's Isabella, not Isabelle." She should not have said the last—particularly when her pursuers might be so close—but the words slipped out before she could bite them back.

"I suppose that will have to do then. Why don't you take off your cloak?"

She certainly didn't need the cloak, but it offered a sense of security and kept Joey shrouded in darkness. It was staying right where it was.

If only she could see his face—she didn't think she knew him—or that he knew her. She'd never been acquainted with the Duke of Strattington's household. The man sounded well-bred, but there was clearly something wrong with him. Would the duke's men have sent her out to walk with a lunatic? It truly was tempting to scream along with Joey next time he started up. First, the duke's man had pounded on her door, waking Joey just as he'd finally begun to drift off to sleep. Second, he'd demanded that she take the baby out to the stable yard so he couldn't be heard. Third, he'd given some long story about how she'd be safe because he'd sent a man out to put a hood on the rooster so it wouldn't crow and wake the duke in the morning.

She began to sway from side to side again, trying to keep her small charge quiet. She didn't really wish either of them to begin screaming. It would require too much energy. This whole mess was sheer nonsense, the duke's sheer nonsense. "No" was all she said.

"No? Didn't they tell you to be more agreeable?" His voice became gruff.

"All they said was I didn't need to worry because there was a man out here hooding the cock and that he'd be sure I was safe. Have you ever heard such tomfoolery?"

"So you don't require a hood for the cock?" He sounded relieved.

Her shoulders ached. Her feet were sore. She hadn't slept since four-thirty this morning—or was it yesterday morning? It must be after midnight, probably after one, maybe even two. "I must admit it would be nice if he was hooded; I could just go to sleep and not have to worry, but it's rarely the cock that wakes me."

Isabella rubbed her chin over Joey's downy curls. He was sure to wake her before the first ray of sun eased past the horizon. Ever since his gums had turned red and the drooling had progressed he'd been up long before morning light. She glanced down at the top of his head, peeking out from under her cloak. He was a dear thing—and such a distraction from her own problems. It wasn't his fault that his gums were sore. A new tooth poking through was reason for anyone to cry.

As if sensing her glance Joey tilted his head up and stared at her from eyes she knew were large and blue. The boy was her one comfort in this whole unending mess. The light was dim enough to conceal the brown flecks that had begun to appear in them this past week. His mother would be sorry. Mrs. Wattington was so hoping for a blue-eyed, blond angel, and it didn't seem likely that little Joey was going to comply.

Placing her lips against the soft, dark fuzz of his hair, Isabella hummed softly. Another minute and he'd be asleep and she could return to the inn and try to take her own rest. At least Mrs. Wattington was not an early riser. The party would not leave the inn before ten-thirty or eleven at the earliest. It made for short days of travel, but with Joey involved, that was for the best. The poor lad was not a good traveler even when his gums were not swollen.

His eyelids drifted down.

Isabella added a sway to her bob, and walked forward again. He was almost there.

He gave the mild sigh that indicated sleep was truly upon him. His tiny fist kneaded against her throat as his body went limp. Once more across the stable yard and she'd be able to head back. She counted each step slowly, waiting for some small sign that he was truly asleep.

Suppressing her own sigh, she fought the urge to roll her shoulders back. All she wanted was to put Joey down and to close her own eyes. They ached from the long hours she had forced them open. One more second and she'd be free to seek the safety of her own bed. One more second and. . .

A loud, impatient cough came from a foot away.

Damnation. She'd forgotten the man. Her brain was truly not working as it should. It had been months—if not years—since she'd let her guard down, and now she couldn't even remember the stranger she was standing next to.

Joey opened his eyes, stared at her, and scrunched up his face. Her whole body tensed as his mouth quivered and then the wail began.

Mark's mind was still stuck on her not being awakened by the cock. If she was in his bed he had a feeling that was just what would be waking her. Images of her red-gold hair spread across his pillow filled his mind. He could feel the soft curve of her buttocks pressed tight against him. His fingers ached to pull the supple curve of her waist toward him. He closed his eyes, letting the picture form. Maybe he'd keep her, even if his men had found her. There surely must be worse things.

He opened his eyes.

And. . .

The damn girl had passed him and was walking away. She was engaged in that hip-rolling walk again, though. She must mean him to follow. He was having second thoughts about the stable and the straw, however. He'd engaged in enough such encounters during his army days to know that straw was never as comfortable as one would suppose. It had an annoying habit of sticking one at just the wrong moment.

Should he follow? She'd begun to hum and he'd almost swear that she'd forgotten his existence. Probably she practiced some feminine wile designed to send him into hot pursuit. She evidently did not know that dukes were never required to pursue. No, they had men to bring them their prey. He snorted softly.

She didn't even turn her head.

This was not the way he intended to play the game.

He coughed loudly.

Her neck stiffened.

Her head turned toward him. It should have been too dark to see, but there was no mistaking either her despair or her glare. Her head fell forward again as if staring down at her own breasts.

And then the noise began. A scream filled the yard, echoing off the cobblestones and beating against his ears.

A baby.

What kind of doxy came with a baby?

"Now you've done it." If her voice had sounded young and sweet before, now it echoed with tones he hadn't heard since the schoolroom.

It was all he could do not to drop his head and murmur, "Yes, ma'am."

And the baby. As she turned to face him there was no mistaking what lay cradled against her chest, what had caused her to hunch before. The wailing was coming from her breast. A small, angry red fist shook itself loose of the cloak and waved frantically through the air.

The night was evidently not going to end the way he desired.

If it wouldn't have been less than manly, he'd have turned and run—fast.

"You have a baby." They were not the most intelligent words he had ever spoken.

"Yes." Her reply allowed that she might truly consider him an idiot.

"Why are you out here?" That was slightly more sensible.

"Because I love to stroll while the sweet stench of manure perfumes the early hours of the morning."

No, she was neither pleased with him, nor thought he had a brain in his head. "It was a sincere question.

I would have thought you'd stay safe in the inn with such a sweet child. Surely he should have been abed hours ago."

"Are you trying to be a fool? I am out here because I was ordered out by your master, the duke's man. A man who clearly has even less going on between the ears than you. What other type of man would send a woman and infant out into the cold—and don't you dare tell me that it's not that cold—because the duke must get his sleep and no screaming child can be allowed to disturb that? And that doesn't even begin to address his plans to cover the cock."

Mark pulled his shoulders back. Divers must have spoken to her, and not kindly. Still, it was not the done thing to allow one's servants to be insulted.

"I am sure the man had his reasons for his behavior. You must have not understood."

Miss Smith stepped toward him. A second fist had joined the first in waving through the opening of her cloak. Her mouth started to open, but then she shut it. Palpable weariness spread from her. She bent her head until her chin disappeared within the folds of her cloak. A soft, pleasant hum whispered out. She turned from him and began to walk away with that enchanting sway—a sway that had a very different meaning now that he knew what she held. She walked all the way to the door of the stable. Her posture stiffened and he could tell she was deciding whether to face the dark interior or to turn back toward him.

She turned.

And strolled, and swayed.

She drew level to him. He could see she was biting tight down on her lip. "I am not mistaken. I know exactly what that man said."

She walked past him again and turned sharply on her heels when she reached the inn. The child was quieting and her sway was becoming more of a march.

She passed him again and said, “He evidently believes that having a livery more grand than any I’ve seen gives him rights over us lesser beings.”

Yes, it had definitely been Divers.

She reached the wall of the stable.

Came back again. “All I can say is that Strattington must believe he’s quite the duke, to expect that babies and roosters will fall silent for him.”

Mark watched as she passed. He wished he could explain the true problem to her: he still wasn’t quite sure he believed he was a duke at all.

Chapter 2

She knew she was saying too much. Isabella wished she could stay quiet. Her whole life would have been so much simpler if only she'd been able to keep her lips closed. Of course she'd never been able to and it didn't seem like she was going to start now when her thoughts felt soggier than toast soaked in tea.

Slipping a glance out of the corner of her eye, she debated whether the man was angered by her words. He was every bit as much the duke's man as the one in the fine braid who'd sent her out into the night. She must remember that. His shoulders had drawn back at her last whispered outburst, but he didn't seem unduly distressed. His lips were more tightly pressed than previously, but it was hard to be sure. If only he'd step out of the shadows. The night was dark enough that even with the dim light of the moon full upon him it would have been hard to see. If he stayed hidden beneath the eaves of the stable it was nigh impossible.

At least he seemed unrelated to her pursuers. He had not tried to grab her or whispered her real name from the shadows. He had not demanded that she turn "it" over and then disappeared before she even knew what "it" was. If the fatigue did not kill her, then the constant worry would.

She turned back to him, her tone sharper than she intended. "What's your name? You didn't say. It was rude to ask me and not supply your own." She couldn't go on thinking of him as "the man." It was only proper that she learn his name. She probably didn't need to add the bit about his lack of manners, but once again her lips were moving faster than her brain.

The wall of the inn loomed before her and she turned neatly, a bit of extra rock-and-sway as Joey wiggled slightly against her breast. It wouldn't do at all if he began to scream again. She still had some hope of making it to her bed for at least an hour or two. She needed rest if she was to decide the next step in her life. Perhaps Joey would slumber late in the morning and she'd have a chance for a bit of extra sleep herself. If Mrs. Wattington heard there was a duke at the inn she'd probably delay her own departure, and Isabella might even manage a waking hour without Joey attached to her hip. She wasn't sure she even knew how to stand upright without him anymore.

"Do you always ask questions and then not wait for the answers?" The man's voice spoke out of the darkness.

Pins and needles, she'd forgotten him again. If she didn't get sleep soon she'd forget her own name—Miss Isabella Hermione Masters. She should have used her middle name once she'd run from her brother's home, but somehow she'd never been able to see herself as a Hermione. She could even have taken a new name. Mary Smith. That would have raised no questions, brought no curiosity.

"Are you even listening?" The man spoke again.

She slowed her pacing and turned toward him.

Joey's head was limp against her bosom and it seemed he'd finally drifted off again. "I am sorry."

"You're sorry? We've been acquainted for all of five minutes and already I've the feeling those words don't pass your lips very often."

Isabella would have commented on his rudeness if she hadn't been so aware of her own. "I fear I am just a bit tired from watching Joey—not on my best form at all."

The man nodded. That much she could see.

"So do you want to know?" he said.

"Know what?"

"My name. You did ask."

She wanted to sag against the building and close her eyes for a week—that was what she wanted. She wanted not to worry anymore. She was so tired of worrying. "Yes, of course."

"It's Mark Smythe. That's why I was surprised by your name."

"I never thought you could hear the Y but when you say it I know it's there. Why is that?" Gads, she was rambling. Tired, and rude, and rambling. It was amazing the man hadn't just turned and left. Of course he still needed to cover the rooster. He might have implied he found the matter as unnecessary as she, but it was his job.

She bobbed her hip a bit, feeling Joey settle even more comfortably against her.

"I suppose I was brought up to say it that way. I've never thought about it, but I've always been taught the importance of that Y."

"I can't believe we're standing in the yard in the middle of the night discussing whether *Smith* sounds different than *Smythe*."

"I would admit it was not how I imagined I'd be spending my evening either—none of the possibilities I considered came close to this." He stepped forward and she could feel his glance upon her. She shivered at the intensity of that gaze, automatically dropping her chin into the folds of her cloak. She didn't know him. There was no way he could recognize her. So why did he stare so intently?

She hadn't feared being recognized in nearly a year. It was seeing her pursuers again that had her in such a state. She'd thought she'd lost them in Norwich when she'd taken the position with the Wattingtons. And she was drawing nearer to London. She had promised she would never go back.

Still, Mr. Smythe was a servant—just like her. There was no reason to be afraid.

She peeked up at him.

His hair was dark, very dark. She'd assumed it was the shadows that had kept him hidden, but as he moved into the moonlight she could see that almost everything about him was dark—his hair, his eyes, his clothes. His skin was less so, but still of a deeper hue than she was accustomed to. Few men had skin the sun had so clearly touched, but then ever since she'd been in service she'd dealt only with footmen, butlers, and porters. The grooms and laborers hardly ever came up to the nursery floors, and she rarely ate in the kitchens with the rest of the servants. She wondered how far the color extended.

"You're staring." His voice drew her from her reverie.

"It's simply hard to see. I don't think I've ever had such a long conversation with a man I couldn't see."

"Will it disturb the child if I light the lamp?" He

gestured to a tin lamp hanging from the eaves above the door. "I would admit to my own curiosity about you. It's not often a women comes to me speaking of cocks, particularly not one with a babe in arms."

"A cock." She whispered the word to herself. *Is that what he'd thought?* She felt a deep flush of color rise in her cheeks. She dropped her face back to Joey, deep in the folds of her cloak. "I meant that you were supposed to put something over the rooster's head so that he wouldn't know when the sun was up."

"Oh. I'd forgotten about that."

"You'd forgotten what you were sent out here to do?"

"Yes—well, no. That wasn't my task."

She glanced about, trying to see if there was somebody else in the yard. "Then who was supposed to do it?" It was a bit unsettling to realize she didn't even know that much about who she was talking to. "You are one of the duke's men, though, aren't you? One of his men?"

"I do travel with Strattington's party."

That was not quite a straightforward answer, but she was simply too tired to make proper sense out of it.

She glanced up at the lantern, considered. She didn't know him—he couldn't know her. She'd never met the Duke of Strattington, why would his servant recognize her? "Yes, you can light it. He's well covered and once he's asleep light doesn't wake him—not as long as I keep moving. We could be under the noonday sun and he'd slumber on." Unless some fool decided to pound on the door the moment he fell asleep.

There was a brief spark and then a moment later the lantern glowed with light.

Isabella stepped back, hoping her mouth had not fallen open. He was beautiful. Mr. Smythe was simply beautiful. It was not a word she normally applied to males above the age of six, but she could think of no other that fit as well.

Perhaps *magnificent*. He was certainly that as well. Magnificent.

That was a word you could use for a man.

His dark hair lit golden at the ends under the flickering light and his shoulders— She couldn't even think of a word to describe his shoulders. They were far broader than she had realized, and the close-cut tailoring of his coat left little to the imagination. If she hadn't been holding Joey she was afraid she would have reached out and caressed the soft wool. Even with Joey her fingers longed to reach out and stroke it—stroke him.

Trying to hide her response she turned away, bobbing Joey with more vigor than necessary.

"Do you get tired of holding him? I imagine it must pull on your arms after a while."

Mark didn't know why he'd said the words. He'd never thought about the weight of a baby before and wasn't aware that he'd been thinking about it now. What he did know was that he wanted to see her face more closely. He should have thought about lighting the lantern sooner. He'd considered her face angelic in the moonlight, but in the full light of the lantern she was much more interesting. She still had the balanced purity of an angel, but there was something more, some flicker of life and fun that he couldn't quite define. She was tired, her eyes shadowed and her shoulders drooping, but he knew with a deep certainty that if she smiled her whole demeanor would change, that she'd glow brighter than the lantern.

He was being fanciful again. She was a woman, simply a woman. A pretty one. Perhaps even a beautiful one, but he'd had more beautiful women chasing him since his cousin's death a few years ago, when he'd become his uncle's heir, than he could even begin to count. The finest diamonds in London had allowed that they would receive his intentions—his honorable intentions—most favorably. And there'd been other women, older women, more experienced women who'd made it abundantly clear that they didn't care if his intentions were honorable or not—in fact they often preferred the latter.

"Yes, I must admit it can get tiring carrying Joey. He's gained so much weight in the last few weeks that I can barely believe it. He weighed almost nothing when I first came to care for him two months ago."

That brought his head up. "He's not yours then?"

She chuckled softly. "No, I am only the baby nurse. His mother is Mrs. Wattington. This"—she turned the baby so he could see the fat, scrunched face peeking out from her cloak—"is Master Joseph Wattington. We're heading to London to meet his father and attend the king's coronation."

Her laugh had died as the sentence progressed. There was something she was not happy with. What woman would be unhappy about a trip to London for the coronation?

The baby was not hers.

The thought filled his mind. He'd never been a man for fooling with the servants, but she wasn't his servant and how was a man to resist the delightful blush that still stained her cheeks? He was sure it had arisen when she'd whispered the word *cock*. He'd forgotten all about his uncle's ridiculous habit of shrouding every bird around lest one wake him early from his slumbers. Mark would never have required such a thing, but clearly the servants were still acting on their own idea of what a duke should be.

He shook his head lightly. He had to get over these thoughts of what a duke should and shouldn't be, and whether he could ever live up to the ideal. He knew exactly what a duke should be. He'd had years of observing first his grandfather and then his uncle in the role. Even if he'd never thought to occupy the position he knew how a duke behaved.

He'd never thought to be a soldier either, but he'd done well enough at that during those horrible years in Belgium and France. Nobody could have been prepared for what he'd experienced during that time, but he'd survived.

If he could survive that, he could survive being a duke.

"You seem very lost in thought." Miss Smith's quiet voice drew him back. "Do you think the duke is asleep?"

"No. I am sure he's not." Mark answered without thought.

"Oh."

"You sound disappointed. Do you really care about Strattington's sleeping habits?"

"It's just that I don't dare take Joey back until I am sure the duke is soundly asleep. I am afraid he'll fuss a bit when I put him down."

Mark could not resist. "You're afraid the duke will fuss?"

"Oh don't be funny. I am much too tired for that. Of course if I do bring Joey in and the duke is asleep and Joey screams and the duke wakes up and—"

"Do you always worry this much?"

She breathed out a long sigh. "No. I don't worry nearly enough most of the time. I suppose it's being so tired and knowing there isn't a right thing to do."

"I am not sure I understand."

"If I bring the baby in and he wakes the duke and Mrs. Wattington hears, she's likely to dismiss me. She's been through three baby nurses already. I was actually hired by her husband to be her companion, but when the last nurse left she handed Joey to me. I think she thought I was too young to be her companion. I am surprised she kept me at all—although I think that's only because she knew she had this trip to make and she didn't want to risk having to care for Joey herself. On the other hand, if I don't bring the baby in and stay here with him all night then she's likely to fear I've endangered his health and dismiss me for that. I am not sure there's a way to win."

"Well, if you say she doesn't want to travel alone with the child, then it seems rather unlikely she'd dismiss you before you reach Town. I can't imagine this is a good place to find a new baby nurse." Mark glanced at the few small buildings that stood across the road from the inn.

He glanced back at Miss Smith. She did not seem reassured by his answer. "I am not sure that's any better. I'd rather not be looking for employment in London."

"I would think it's an excellent place for a young woman of qualification to find a post."

"If I had a reference—I am not sure Mrs. Wattington would write me one if she could claim I'd been lax in my responsibilities. Granted I am not sure she'll give me one anyway. I rather believe she dislikes me."

Mark paused, catching himself before he offered to

write her one himself. He didn't think she'd appreciate knowing he was the Duke of Strattington and that, however unwittingly, he'd caused her to be walking the stable yard. "I am sure the duke will not mind if you take the young fellow in. He is not an unreasonable man."

She made a noise that sounded very much like *hmmphf.* "That is not the impression the man inside gave me. I think I am better off here. Do you think if I sit Joey will stay asleep?" She glanced longingly at a bale of hay set against the wall. "Oh, I don't know why I even ask you. I know better. If I had his cradle I might be able to put him down and rock him, but if I am just still he'll never stay settled. Better to keep walking than to have him screaming again."

"Would you like me to carry him for a while?" For the second time that evening Mark didn't know where the words had come from.

"You?" Isabella could not have been more shocked. Not even the other housemaids offered to walk with the baby. It was always a struggle to even get one to sit with him while he slept. Bribery was often involved. In fact, one of the reasons that Mrs. Wattington disliked her so was that Isabella had once suggested that she hold Joey.

Still . . . she peered at Mr. Smythe's strong shoulders. She reckoned he could carry her back and forth across the yard—she rapidly shut her mind to the images that gave rise to—surely he could manage one small baby. "Do you know how?"

"There's a *how* involved?"

Her face must have shown her dismay because he reached out and ran a finger down her cheek, tracing its curve. Her face turned toward his touch. She turned it back.

"Yes, I know how to carry an infant," he said. "It may not show to look at me, but I've five younger sisters. I grew up carrying the youngest of them about like she was my own."

Isabella knew she shouldn't surrender the child. If anyone saw them she'd be sure to be dismissed. But who was going to see them walking about in the middle of the night? "Are you sure?"

He walked over and stood before her, looking down into her eyes. Could any man be as trustworthy as that gaze implied? There was such temptation to trust him, to lean upon him, to— Isabella didn't know why her mind kept following such tangents. It had been years since she'd trusted anyone. She'd worked hard at suppressing that side of herself. From the time she'd taken her first position she'd known such thoughts only led to trouble. "Perhaps you could hold him for a moment or two. It would be so lovely to sit."

"I promise not to drop him or run off with him, and should we be attacked I promise to protect him with my very life. I was in the army, so you know I mean it," he said, his face serious.

She knew he meant the last as a joke, but something in his tone told her it was more than that. He held out his arms and she placed Joey in them, arranging him with care, pretending not to notice how firmly muscled Mr. Smythe's arms were beneath his coat.

Lifting Joey to his shoulder, Mr. Smythe began to walk with an awkward bob and sway. He looked like he was attempting some odd acrobatic feat. The smallest of giggles escaped her lips.

He stopped at the sound. He looked over his shoulder at her, and the corners of his mouth turned up. "I was hoping to get you to smile. I was right."

"Right about what?"

"You're beautiful to start with, but when you smile you become one of the most bewitching women I have ever seen."

Her smile dropped. When he'd said *beautiful* she'd been unhappy, but accepting. *Bewitching*, though, that was dangerous. She had no desire to be bewitching—not anymore. *Bewitching* meant she was memorable and that was something to be avoided.

Joey started to grumble and Mr. Smythe lifted him to his shoulder. The movement emphasized his powerful lines and Isabella found both her attention and her eyes drawn to— No, she would not look there.

In an effort to distract herself from thinking about his body parts, she turned away and went to sit on the bale of hay. At least she meant to sit. In truth it was more of a collapse. The moment her back touched the wall she felt herself slide into a comfortable mound of woman. She even pulled her feet up under her skirts and tucked them beneath her. Relaxing felt so wonderful. She closed her eyes and let herself revel in not moving.

Before she'd run away from her brother's house she'd thought that resting was a waste of time. Now she knew far different. There was nothing as wonderful as closing one's eyes even for the briefest of moments.

"I'd have taken the baby sooner if I'd known it would please you that much."

She opened one eye and looked at him. "I must admit that at this exact moment I feel perfect. It's been rather a long day."

"Did you start your trip early?"

"No, but the packing required hours of work. Mrs. Wattington is not exactly sure what she'll need for the events surrounding the coronation and so it seemed her entire wardrobe must be packed. Normally I just stay in the nurseries, but I was pulled into service helping to fill her trunks. Joey does not need much."

"I'd always heard babies required a pile of belongings."

"No, not if there's a ready breast or milk cow."

He glanced inquiringly at her, his eyes dropping down. "Do you think he's hungry now?"

"Oh stop it. Mrs. Wattington did have the sense to make sure all the inns we were stopping at had cows. She says that the newest wisdom is that a mixture of cow's milk and pap will fatten the baby better than anything else. I believe she just didn't want the added expense of bringing a wet nurse along. Stop looking at me like that." She pulled her cloak tight over her breasts.

"A man can only dream."

She closed her eyes again and ignored him—and how strangely safe she felt. At least Joey was quiet. She would be thankful for that and the moment of rest it gave her. It wasn't like there was any danger of falling asleep. She'd barely slept since she'd first seen the blue-coated man again, and seen the way he stared directly at her.

Mark glanced across at Miss Smith. Her eyes had been closed for a good ten minutes now, and he believed he'd heard a gentle, rumbling snore. He peeked down at the baby. His eyes too were shut tight, and he gave no indication that he'd be opening them again anytime soon.

There was an empty spot on the hay next to her. She surely couldn't object if he sat for just a moment beside her. Lifting the baby higher, onto his shoulder, he tried to lower himself beside her.

The baby, Joey, she called him, began to squirm.

His nose scrunched. His eyes squeezed tight into slits. His mouth began to open.

Mark could hear the squawk before it even sounded.

He rose quickly and began to pace the yard again.

He should wake her. It was time for him to find his own bed. He would assure her again that the duke would make no complaint should Joey happen to wake.

She might not believe him.

He stopped and stared down at her, shifting from hip to hip to keep the child quiet. She looked so peaceful, so beautiful—so exhausted. If he woke her she might spend the rest of the night walking with the baby. And he doubted Mrs. Wattington would let her sleep in the carriage.

Whereas he could doze the day away riding in his uncle's fine carriage, as well sprung a vehicle as had ever been created.

He stepped away from her and returned to his pacing. He'd been right about that smile. It lit her whole being and most of her surroundings. A man would do a lot for a smile like that. And for that devilish glint in her eyes. A glint that led a man to wonder. A glint that gave a man plenty to consider as he marched back and forth.

Now he just had to figure how to meet up with her again, how to make her smile again.

Chapter 3

The twisted body lay on the floor before her, the neck bent at an impossible angle, blood pooled about the head. More blood marked the back of her hand.

Isabella bolted upright, the scream caught in her throat. Her eyes remained closed, the image printed across her inner lids.

Should she flee?

It was the first thought that filled her mind every morning. The first thought that had filled her mind for more than three years. She drew air into her lungs until she thought they'd burst and released it slowly.

A soft sound whispered at the edge of her thoughts—and then a louder cry, a scream.

She swallowed once, suddenly afraid of what she might see.

Opening her eyes, she peered through the dim light. The tiny garret. Her own bed.

It was Joey, crying—again.

Another dream-haunted morning, no different from any other.

She turned her head, relieved to see that light was creeping over the horizon. It was early, then, but not too early. Sleep still held at the edge of her consciousness. Despite her dream, it had been weeks, if not longer, since she'd felt so rested, slept so unencumbered by her troubles. She stretched once in the comfort of her bed—and stopped.

Her bed. A moment of fear took her.

It was not simply another morning.

She hadn't come to bed. The last thing she could remember was leaning against the stable wall, her eyes sliding closed as she watched Mr. Smythe's long legs pace. It had so felt wonderful to be free of Joey's weight for however brief a time.

Joey.

She sat upright, her gaze sliding around the room, following his angry cry. A small bootied foot waved above the edge of his cradle. He was there.

She slipped her bare feet onto the warm wood floor. Her own stockings lay draped over her half boots at the foot of the bed. The rest of her was still fully dressed, although her cloak lay piled on the tiny garret's one chair.

Joey was also clothed. He stopped whining and smiled brightly as she walked toward him, clearly eager to be lifted and held. His small arms reached out to her. He squished as she picked him up, his behind more than a little damp.

Mr. Smythe had carried her up to bed—and carried Joey as well. How he had managed that feat she was not going to question, or question how he'd known where her room was.

It was over and done. She was safe. Joey was safe. She would simply be thankful.

Laying Joey on the bed, she quickly stripped off his wrappings and wiped him down with a damp cloth. He giggled as the cloth ran over him and she couldn't resist blowing a kiss against his pudgy belly.

When you looked down at a smiling baby the world could be perfect for a moment. How could anything be wrong in the face of such joy and innocence?

Of course it was only for a moment.

She sank down on the bed beside him, wishing she could remember what it was like to care about nothing but the excitement of noticing your toes for the first time. Last night she had said she didn't worry enough. That was not strictly true—not anymore.

Four years ago, at the age of seventeen, she hadn't worried about anything—not really. Oh, she'd worried about dresses and bonnets, and smiling at eligible men now that Masters had finally let her come to Town, but none of that was real worry. And then her brother had suggested that she marry Colonel Foxworthy. She still got a shiver down her spine when she considered it. It hadn't seemed awful at first. Foxworthy was wealthy, with a position in society. He wasn't even that old or awful to look at—and she knew that women were not tied to their husbands once they'd produced an heir.

Then he had touched her. Just the lightest of strokes, his gloved fingers across her bare arm, hardly a touch at all, but it had sickened her to her core when she'd seen the look in his eyes.

She could never. It was impossible.

She'd tried to tell Masters she couldn't possibly marry the man and only then had come to understand there was little difference between a suggestion and a command. She had given up protest and formed other plans. If only she had fled right then. Fled when she first knew she couldn't marry Foxworthy. Instead she had turned to Violet, to her sister, for help—longing for someone else to save her.

Yes, she should have fled that first moment, that

first day—then none of the rest of it would have happened.

A clock chimed from some lower floor. There was no time to think about her past. The present was what mattered.

It grew later by the moment and soon Mrs. Wattington would come looking for her and Joey. It would not do at all if they were not yet ready.

She glanced down at her own bare feet and reached for her stockings, pulling on one and then the other. She tied the garters tight, trying not to imagine other hands, large, long-fingered hands, engaged in the opposite task—trying not to imagine what it had felt like when *he'd* touched her, when he'd pulled off her stockings, sliding them down her legs. Her garters tied much higher than she had ever realized. She was glad that there was nobody but Joey here to see her, because she knew her cheeks were the color of a fresh tomato. Hopefully a quick wash would cool them.

She shook her head, trying to clear Mr. Smythe's image from it. She didn't have time for such things, no matter how safe he'd made her feel.

Made her feel safe. That was rubbish. She had barely met the man. It was pure coincidence that she'd slept soundly last night. It had nothing to do with him.

Nothing. She'd been tired and he'd been there when she needed somebody to lean on. There was no more to it than that.

She quickly slipped her feet into her half boots and buckled them up. Grabbing fresh clothing for Joey, she bundled him up and headed down to the kitchens to find some milk. It was amazing that he hadn't started to scream again already. The boy was not patient when it came to his feedings.

* * *

"And what were you doing last night?"

Mark turned away from the washstand toward the grizzled voice, pulling on a shirt as he did so. Douglas had been his batman during the war and had been in his employ ever since.

"I was sleeping," he answered. "What else does one do at night?"

Douglas said nothing but his mouth twitched, the scar that marked his face from lip to cheek curving.

"Well," Mark tried again. Douglas had known him far too long. "What else does one do at night—here?" He gestured out the window at the small huddle of buildings and the stable yard.

"Sleep would have seemed the obvious answer, but given where I sleep"—Douglas gestured to the pallet set at the foot of Mark's bed—"I would ask again—what were you about last night?"

"I don't know why I even try to pretend with you. You could have been sleeping in the cellars and somehow you'd still know. You might have been able to sleep through that brat's infernal wailing, but it kept me up most of the night." Now that he'd met Joey he felt bad calling him a brat—but that boy could scream.

"You've slept through cannon fire—as have I—and a little crying wakes you?"

Mark sighed. "You know I have not slept well since my uncle's death and—well—"

"Becoming the duke." Douglas moved away and started to throw shirts into a bag. "I can't say I'd want it. Where is that bloody man Divers anyway? Isn't it time for him to come wiggle you into your jacket for the day?"

"Dukes do not wiggle. We are fitted into our clothing."

"I see that hint of a grin. You can't hide it from old Douglas. What did happen last night? You've not smiled like that since before this whole blasted business began."

"You cannot possibly be planning to wear that coat," Divers said as he moved to select another from the selection laid out on the bed.

Blast. Mark had not even heard the man enter the room. He knew that a good servant was not supposed to be seen or heard, but he'd never taken it literally.

"And"—Divers turned to Douglas—"I'd appreciate your not using such language. We must all remember our positions in this world."

Douglas looked like he wanted to spit, but he held his tongue and contented himself with glaring at Mark.

Mark tried to slide toward the door. "I was just going to stretch my legs. I will be back before we leave and you can shove me into the coat of your choice then."

Divers gave him that look that spoke clearer than words that Mark's desires were unacceptable. He could only wish he hadn't inherited the valet along with the duchy. Although without Divers he'd have even less idea what he was doing. Douglas's advice was rarely suitable for his new position.

He tried again. "I'll be back in just a few minutes. Nobody will know."

"And what if you do meet someone? A marriageable lady perhaps, or, even more fitting, her father. You will need to do your duty soon, and it would be a shame if you were to miss your chance because of an improper coat."

Divers was undoubtedly correct, but Mark was

equally sure that a duke should not be cowed by his valet.

"I will be back with time to change before we leave. It is unlikely that I will run into anyone of import at this hour of the morning, not to mention this place." He stepped through the door, trying not to pay attention to Douglas's wide grin.

Isabella stopped in the doorway and stared into the stable yard, porcelain feeding bottle in hand, Joey cradled in her opposite arm.

It was a far different place in the bright, early morning sun than it had been the previous night. Still, something was not right. There was a tickle on the back of her neck as if she were being watched—again.

Was Mr. Smythe here? No, she didn't see him. She glanced quickly about. Nothing seemed out of place.

When she'd first fled from London she had always felt eyes following her. She had become expert at examining her surroundings for anything strange or unfamiliar. It was a lucky thing she had, too. Several times she'd managed to avoid her brother's man as he sought her—at least she hoped it was her brother's man. She did not want to think of the alternative. If it was Masters who sought her it would be unpleasant, but she was of age, twenty-one. Her life was her own.

She glanced about the yard again. Everything was as it should be. Her fears were for naught.

As she calmed herself, a fine carriage pulled up to the inn, a very slightly more battered coach behind it. They must be the duke's. There was some temptation to stay and watch them being loaded, but she forced her feet around the corner and found a seat on a bench under a large apple tree.

The apples were still smallish and green, but they gave a crisp scent to the air.

She leaned back and, setting Joey comfortably on her lap, gave him his bottle, her thumb lifting and lowering over the top hole to release droplets of milk. The small teapot-shaped bottle was remarkably effective for controlling how much milk she dribbled into Joey's hungry mouth.

She closed her eyes and tried to enjoy the light breeze. The day was going to be a hot one and it would seem even hotter enveloped in Mrs. Wattington's coach, with every window covered to be sure that no sun hit the woman's ivory complexion. She could hear bees buzzing and the soft gurgle of the baby as he sucked hard on the bottle's neck; reflexively she lifted her thumb from the hole in the bottle's top, releasing more of the milk. The usual sound of the inn and stable supplied a busy background.

She was headed back to London. She'd sworn she'd never return, known she could never return without being forced to face the reality of those memories again.

When Mrs. Wattington first told her about the journey to Town she'd almost quit on the spot. But she could no longer afford to be so headstrong—not when the blue-coated man was searching for her and positions were so hard to come by. She could not leave without a reference and she could not get a reference without staying. She was truly caught. As long as she kept her head down and concentrated solely on Joey she should be fine. Nobody noticed the servants.

Still, the impulse remained to flee. She'd changed positions six times since leaving London and could not regret a single time. It was only occasionally that she allowed herself to long for that normal, quiet, steady life that could never be hers, that life of home and hearth.

The girl she'd been would never have longed for anything so simple. She drew in a deep breath remembering the headstrong girl who had fled the city with only a pocket full of coin and a couple of hasty letters of recommendation written by a family friend. Did she consider Lady Smythe-Burke a friend? The lady had certainly saved her when Isabella had been certain her goose was cooked—and Isabella had adopted a version of her last name as thanks. Lady Smythe-Burke was a true leader of society and Isabella would never understand what had driven her to seek the lady's help on that horrible day when everything had gone so wrong.

She pushed the memory away, focused on something else.

Lady Smythe-Burke said *Smythe* with exactly the same intonation as Mr. Smythe. Perhaps that was why Isabella had picked up on the Y. The thought caused the corners of her mouth to turn up. It was hard to imagine a more unlikely pair than Mr. Smythe and Lady Smythe-Burke. Lady Smythe-Burke was all starch and corsetry. Isabella had sometimes wondered that Lady Smythe-Burke could bend at all.

Now, Mr. Smythe—him she could picture bending in all sorts of interesting ways.

"I didn't think to see you again." As if conjured by her thoughts, his rich honey voice sounded a foot before her.

Her eyes popped open and she stared up into deep brown eyes. How had he gotten there? She'd been listening to the surrounding noises and she still hadn't heard him. Had she been so distracted by her thoughts? She needed to be more careful.

The sun was behind him and it cast his frame in stark silhouette. As he leaned toward her she could almost read his face, but as he stood back, swinging a booted foot onto the bench beside her, only the tips of his curls shone in the sun, the rest was shadow.

For a second she inched away from him, caught by some unexpected air of power and authority, blocked from the sunny fields and bustle of the inn. Inhaling deeply, she told herself that it was only her imagination. He had no bad intent, no desire to separate her from the rest of the world. He was no different now than he had been a second ago when she first opened her eyes, certainly no different than he'd been last night in the stable yard, no different than when he'd carried her to her room, removed her stockings. She felt heat rise in her cheeks at the thought and turned her face away.

He laughed then and swung his leg back down, taking a seat beside her.

"I've not made a girl blush like that in many months—and certainly not without words."

She didn't know how to reply. The temptation grew to tell him she was a woman, not a girl, but she could imagine too many replies to that. And if she made a comment about his abilities to do things without words—well, the answers to that were even worse.

He turned his face and stared toward the inn. "I am not sure how much redder you can grow. I overheard one of my sisters once discussing that redheads shouldn't wear pink, but I must say I find it a most becoming color for your skin. I am not looking, but I imagine you're glowing even more now."

"Don't you have anything else to do besides pick on me? Surely the duke needs you to help prepare for the journey."

He chuckled again. "No, the duke is delighted to have me right where I am."

"I find that hard to believe." She knew she sounded prickly, but could not help herself. Something about the man set her nerves on edge this morning—and that was even before she started to think about his fingers and her garters. At least he distracted her from her thoughts.

"I am sorry," he said softly.

That brought her face around to him. "For what?"

"I seem to have somehow gotten off on the wrong foot and I am not sure why. I only meant to sit beside you for a moment and be sure that young Master Joseph had let you sleep through the rest of the night. He seemed to settle well into his cradle, but I could not be sure."

"No, it must be me. I don't know quite what bothered me." She looked down at her hand, still holding Joey's bottle. Sometimes it was best to admit the truth. "I think I must have been embarrassed and I did not even realize it myself until I took affront. I've never had a man remove my stockings before."

"Never? No footman or young gentleman?"

"Never. Although some have tried."

She could sense he wanted to ask more, but didn't have the words. She slanted a look out of the corner of her eye. There was something between them—something more than a now drowsing baby and the smell of freshly cut hay.

Chapter 4

Damnation. It wasn't bad enough he was thinking of seducing the servants, now they were virginal servants. When he'd first seen her he'd even wondered if she was the same woman he'd talked with last night. She'd looked far different in the morning light, her dark gray gown pulling the color from her face and that fabulous hair bound tightly back, all the life and vitality of the night before missing.

And then she'd blushed and smiled—that bewitching beauty filling her again.

He was tempted to ask if a man had ever removed anything besides her stockings—and he wasn't thinking about her gloves. There were a great multitude of things that could be done without removing stockings. In fact there were very few activities that did require their removal. His mind filled with an image of her for a moment, standing before a fire, smiling, dressed in nothing but her stockings.

It was no wonder Douglas had sensed something different.

Mark shifted away from Miss Smith; his thoughts were affecting parts of his anatomy that had no business rising up on a sunny morning—at least not in a public inn yard. And not in front of an innocent, although that glance from the corner of her eye wasn't innocent at all. Even when she looked pinched and gray she looked as if she'd seen a piece of the world.

He crossed his ankles and stared firmly at his boots.

"Does the duke give you his castoffs?"

Her question startled him. "What? Why?"

"Your boots. I've rarely seen finer."

He kept his eyes locked on his feet. She was right. He should have considered the matter. Not that he had a lesser pair here. He could have asked Divers to procure another pair, but that would have raised questions he didn't want to answer—not even to himself. His breeches and shirt were undoubtedly too fine also. At least he'd slipped out without his brocade jacket. He glanced at his sleeve. He paid little attention to such things, but snowy linen of such tight weave was not something he imagined his grooms had access to. "Yes, sometimes—I take what I am given." He sounded far gruffer than he meant to.

"I am sorry. I didn't mean to give offense. I sometimes speak without thinking. I thought I cured the habit over the last few years. I am afraid I was quite dreadful as a girl."

"I can't imagine that." Although, in truth, he could. He found it charming. It was good to have somebody besides Douglas—and occasionally Divers—speak their mind to him. In the scant time since he'd inherited the duchy nobody ever said anything they didn't think he wanted to hear. At least they didn't say it with words. Both Divers and his porter were more than able to give him a look that let him know he was getting it all wrong. And he wasn't even going to think about the house steward.

He felt himself with her, his real self, not the duke—there was no need for pretense.

Miss Smith didn't answer his statement, but stared toward the stable where the owner's wife was trying to lead a milk cow toward the trough.

"Do you think she's getting more milk for the child?" he asked. "Will he need to eat again soon?"

She smiled briefly, her cheeks rounding. "They had quite a bucket of milk in the kitchen. I can't imagine they'll need more soon. But I gather cows need to be milked when they need to be milked. And as for Joey, it's hard to say. He often takes a good long nap after his morning feed and then wakes hungry and unsettled. In the afternoon he's more likely to play and smile for a while."

What was he doing sitting here discussing milk cows and infants? He had to admit little interest in either. He should have left the moment she told him that she'd never had a man untie her stockings. She was trouble he clearly didn't need. "Do you know where you're stopping tonight?"

She hesitated. "I believe we're traveling to The Three Feathers in Ripon."

"That's not far. I am surprised that you don't go on to Boroughbridge."

"Mrs. Wattington doesn't like to journey too far in one day. She finds travel tiring."

Mark looked up toward the sky. "It's strange. I am realizing the duke may have said he was planning to stop in Ripon."

"Really?"

"Why so surprised? Perhaps the duke does not like travel either." It was true, his uncle had never left London unless forced.

"It's just that Mrs. Wattington was complaining that The Three Feathers was not the type of place she felt was up to her standards—not a true coaching inn. Apparently there were no other choices. I would not have expected the duke to be willing to stop there."

His uncle would never have stopped in such a place, that was certain. His uncle had traveled with his own bed linens and mattress, his own silver and china, and more staff than most London town houses. He could have camped in a cave and still lived like a prince, but it would have offended his dignity. Mark had no such qualms. He'd spent years traveling with the army. Nothing could be as bad as those years. "The duke assumes that everything will be rearranged to his standards."

Miss Smith glanced down at her hands, twisting her fingers. "So I might see you again this evening."

"You might." He leaned slightly toward her. She smelled of lavender soap. "You just might."

Her eyes flitted back up, and her tongue wet her lower lip. Then her eyes fell again.

His glance could not leave that glistening lip. He waited.

Her eyes rose again to meet his.

He could feel her breath against his neck, his chin, his mouth. He leaned closer.

She didn't move toward him, but neither did she retreat.

Her gaze did not waver. He could see a million questions in her eyes—and a million answers.

All the trouble might be worth it.

Was her mouth as soft as it looked? Did she taste as sweet he dreamed?

He bent forward that final inch, parted his lips slightly.

Joey chose that moment to open his eyes fully. He looked from one to the other, his fists waving frantically.

Mark found his glance forced down to the wiggling child. He saw that nose wrinkle, watched the tiny lips open as his whole face grew into one loud wail.

Miss Smith was on her feet with the child bobbing on her hip before Mark could even close his mouth.

Bloody hell. He'd been wrong. This was definitely not worth the trouble.

Dukes should stick with ladies of title, or opera dancers—not pretty nursery maids.

He turned to stomp off toward his coach.

He paused to turn back only once. She was entering the inn's kitchen, walking with that magic sway.

"I'll see you tonight, then," he barked, stepping out of sight behind the coach and doing his best to ignore Divers's glare from the doorway.

How many times could one child spit up? Isabella longed to lean against the corner of the carriage and close her eyes to the whole mess. Mrs. Wattington was doing just that in the opposite corner. She'd made one comment to the effect that Isabella must have fed the boy something offensive and then she'd turned her face to the wall and closed her eyes. Loud snores had been her only contribution since.

Poor little Joey had finally fallen asleep himself and now lay cradled in his basket on the bench beside Isabella. A pail of stinking rags lay at her feet.

It felt like the worries of the last days had taken physical form, everything striving to defeat her. Since the moment she'd left Mr. Smythe in the stable yard that morning, nothing had gone right.

Oh, needles and pins.

Isabella wasn't even sure whom she was cursing. She'd learned a few more explicit expletives while in service, but had long ago decided it was far better not to voice them—or even think them. Her habit of speaking without thought might be mostly cured—except when *he* was around—but she could just imagine Mrs. Wattington's face if Isabella ever released even a quiet *damnation* after dropping something on her foot. No, it was far better to avoid actual curses altogether.

Oh, dogs and cats.

This time she knew exactly what she was cursing. She was cursing little Joey for being so difficult and so lovable. She didn't know how she was ever going to manage to leave him—only that she was. She cursed Mrs. Wattington for not showing more interest in caring for her own baby. She cursed *him*, she cursed Mr. Smythe, for appearing now—now, when he was the last thing she needed. And she cursed life itself for being so unfair. She cursed the life of her past when she'd had everything and not known it. She cursed the brother who'd forced her to flee from that life. She cursed Colonel Foxworthy, whose death had been the final reason for her flight, whose death still haunted— No, she refused to think about that.

She cursed the man in the blue coat—whoever he might be. And she cursed her new life. Cursed that she'd never appreciated how hard it was to work. Cursed early mornings and late nights. Cursed cold baths in well-used water. Cursed the pail of smelly rags. She was so tempted to kick the thing over with her foot.

But mostly she cursed London, wonderful, horrible, stinking, lovely city. She had spent most of her girlhood longing to be there, longing for balls, and gowns, and stylish bonnets, and titled young lords who would fall instantly in love with her beauty and ask for her hand in marriage.

She closed her eyes and remembered the dream, the wonder, the enchantment and hope.

Then she opened them wide and stared about the slightly worn carriage, breathed in the smell of baby spit.

She knew the difference between fantasy and reality.

This was reality.

Reality was that she was speeding toward London and with every mile that passed she became more convinced she could not return, more sure that somehow she had to escape.

"Why don't you just tell her who you really are?" Douglas asked as he glanced through the pile of correspondence that had just been delivered. They'd been at The Three Feathers for barely a quarter of an hour and Douglas already appeared as if he'd been working for days.

"Why don't you give that to my secretary or whoever in that bunch of dour-faced gentlemen that follow wherever I go is responsible for it?" Mark answered, trying to shrug out of his jacket, the stiff embroidered brocade fighting his every move. He didn't even want to consider how many people were actually in his traveling party.

"Is that your way of telling me to mind my own business? You should know by now that is a hopeless cause. And I will be passing this all on to Mr. Downs, but it never hurts to have a good look first, keeps everybody on their toes."

"How did I end up with the only batman in the whole army whose real goal is to be a barrister's clerk?"

"You're still avoiding my question. Why don't you just tell her who you really are?"

"I haven't said there's a *her* and even if I had, what makes you think I am hiding anything?"

"The *her* is tall, but slight, and has red-gold hair. You should stick to the shadows more if you don't want to be seen. And you haven't told her who you are because you're taking off your coat instead of adding another ring. If she knew you were the duke you'd be putting on the finery, not taking it off."

Mark gave up the battle of the coat and sank into a chair—as well as he could sink with his cravat still tied tight and the blasted coat stuck halfway down one arm. "You always did see too much. I would dismiss you if I weren't afraid I was going to be begging you to rescue me from my coat within minutes."

"You could call for Divers. It is his job."

"Then he'd want to know why I wanted it off—even if he'd never actually ask. He'd bring up marriage, as well. I swear the man thinks marriageable virgins are just waiting to throw themselves at me if only I wear the right coat." Mark shot Douglas a piercing glance. "And he'd probably have me dressed in something even worse before I knew what was happening. I swear that man wants to starch and iron my nightshirts."

"That calls for some comment on stiffness, but I'll pass until you answer my question."

"Get this coat off me and I'll answer you anything," Mark answered.

Douglas moved behind him and with a few quick yanks the coat was gone.

Mark dropped his head and stared at the floor. "I don't really know. I certainly didn't plan to hide who I am, but she didn't realize and then it would have embarrassed her to find out—and then—"

"You like having somebody who treats you like you used to be—"

"Yes. Even you act differently now—at least some of the time. Owning half of England wasn't supposed to be so bloody unpleasant."

"Don't know why you thought that. Ownership is always a burden. It's why I am happy the way I am with only myself to care for."

Mark had always rather thought that Douglas also cared for him, but he made no comment. "You are right, I am afraid." He nodded at the pile of correspondence. "I suppose I am going to have to deal with all of that."

"I would reckon only about half of it will need replying to and of that Mr. Downs will take care of most and only ask for your signature—but . . ."

Mark rubbed his temple. He knew that *but* all too well. He waited.

"But I rather think you should ask him about the leases on the properties in Wales. There is something not quite right."

And of course Douglas would be correct. Douglas was always right when it came to those little *buts*.

It would be one more headache that the duke would

have to deal with—if he wanted to be a good duke. And he did.

He stood and walked to the mirror, mussing his hair as he went. He stared at himself and yanked his cravat free.

"So are you off to see her?" Douglas asked as he went to sift through the papers again.

"I am simply planning on a walk."

"If you say so—Your Grace." Douglas let the last words linger in the air.

Chapter 5

"I saw the duke today." Isabella watched as Mr. Smythe's shoulders straightened at her words. She'd come out as soon as she'd spied him from the window. She might have known him little more than a day, but already he seemed a friend. Luckily Joey was finally asleep again and one of the maids was happy to watch him for a few minutes.

"You did?" He did not turn and look at her as he spoke.

"Yes, he looks a bit like you. Oh, don't get me wrong. You are completely different. He walks like he can't bend his head to see his feet. Granted, given the cravat he was wearing it's no wonder."

Mr. Smythe still didn't turn toward her. "Where did you see him?"

"Out the garret window. Maybe I should say that I saw the top of his hat when he left this morning." She tried to make a joke, wondering why Mr. Smythe suddenly seemed so somber. "I wouldn't even have known it was him if Mrs. Wattington hadn't said so. She's quite put out that she hasn't met him yet. It seems he keeps to his rooms once he arrives and is not interested in visitors. Mrs. Wattington hinted to his staff that she would be more than happy to keep him company if he grows bored and needs genteel companionship, but she was most pointedly ignored—at least that's what she says. It has put her in quite the foul mood." Isabella tried to shut her lips. Her words were rambling and Mr. Smythe showed little interest. His mood seemed distinctly odd.

"Does talking about the duke upset you? Is there a problem between you?" If he wasn't going to say anything she would tackle it head-on.

"Why would you think that?" he snapped.

Isabella just laughed. It was so nice to worry about somebody else's difficulties. She imagined that was the reason she'd been eager to see Mr. Smythe again despite the risks and the favors she'd have to do for the maid who watched Joey. She'd seen a man in a blue coat in the taproom when they'd arrived today. It was why she'd been peeking out the window when the duke arrived. Both her fingers and toes were crossed that it was not her follower. Surely many men must have blue coats, mustn't they?

"I am sorry," he said after a moment, drawing her from her thoughts. "I do have a sometimes difficult relationship with the duke. We do not always want the same things."

"And I would imagine the duke mostly wins."

Mark laughed at her words, a bit of his usual lightheartedness returning. "I would say the duke always wins."

"That's too bad. He should listen to you more often. I find you quite sensible."

"I am not sure he would agree with you. Can I tell you a secret?" He leaned toward her.

She stopped breathing as she stared into his dark

eyes. His breath brushed along her cheek. "Anything," she whispered.

"It's why I like being with you. I don't have to think about the duke when I am here." His eyes dropped to her lips.

She was not going to lick them. She was not. "That's why your mood shifted when I mentioned him."

He looked back up to her eyes. "Yes, I don't want the duke to have anything to do with our meetings."

"If that's what you want." Was he going to kiss her? It felt like the moment. Should she lean in closer? No, it had been only a day. She couldn't want his kiss yet, could she?

He stepped back suddenly and strode to the center of the yard, looking up at the windows. He scowled as if he'd seen something unpleasant. "I will need to go back in soon. The duke will be missed."

Isabella wasn't sure that made any sense, but she didn't wish to talk about the duke anymore. She pushed herself off the stairs and dusted the back of her skirt. One nice thing about the dull gray Mrs. Wattington demanded that she wear was that she could sit where she wished and not worry about dirt. She grinned to herself as she imagined sitting on the coarse wood steps in a delicate silk ball gown. She'd have left half of it behind trapped by splinters.

"Something amuses you." Mr. Smythe stepped back toward her.

"I was just thinking how quickly life can change."

"It certainly can."

"It makes it hard to know what to wish for. All the things I wanted when I was younger seem so silly now."

"You make it sound like you're an old hag. You can't be more than twenty."

"Twenty-one actually, but I feel much older."

"Yes, you are quite ancient."

She took a step nearer to him. "Sometimes I do feel it. There are so many things I wanted that I imagine I'll never have now. I think giving up dreams makes one old."

"That's much too serious a thought for such a moonlit night."

She reached out, hesitated, and then, unable to stop herself, unable to control her desire to touch him, traced a finger down his cheek. "Yes, I know, but somehow you seem to be the only one I can talk to. I've known you less than two days, probably spent less than four hours together in your company, and yet I feel I can tell you anything."

"As if you'd have deep, dark secrets to tell."

If only he knew. Isabella let her hand drop. In a matter of days they'd be in London, back to the scene of her crime. She wasn't sure if the man in the blue coat she'd seen today was the same one she'd seen at the beginning of her trip, but her gut told her that he was. If that was true she had to leave, and soon. If only she knew how. If she continued to London she might be able to blend into the crowds and disappear, seek new employment.

She swallowed and tilted her head back to stare up at the stars. "You'd be surprised. We all have secrets. Don't you?"

He was quiet and she wasn't sure he was going to answer. He pulled in a lungful of air. "Yes, I would have to say I do."

"It would be easier if we didn't. If we could just be who we are in this minute."

The next night Isabella peered about the stable yard nervously. It was too early for Mr. Smythe to be here. If he followed the pattern of the last two nights, he would probably not appear until full dark. Unfortunately she might not be able to get away from her duties then.

She glanced about the still-busy stable. It was amazing how similar they all looked. Normally she found comfort in a crowd. With people about she just felt safer. Today, however, her nerves had the best of her. It wasn't just the blue-coated man. There was something else wrong and she couldn't quite put a finger on it.

She edged back from the bustle and took a seat on a bench, wishing there was one against the wall where nobody could get behind her. Despite how brief their actual acquaintance was, waiting for Mr. Smythe felt like a natural piece of her life—a very pleasant piece.

Only not today. Today she wanted to be upstairs with Joey. He'd fallen asleep the minute they arrived and the other maids had required only minor bribes to watch him for a bit. She'd snuck down the stairs eagerly, avoiding Mrs. Wattington's room and . . . and then the feeling had overtaken her.

Something was not right.

This was something different than her normal unease, a slow creep of dread deep in her stomach.

She shook her head to clear it. The cause of her feeling didn't really matter. In fact the feeling didn't really matter. She should leave before her troubles found her. Leave Joey—and Mr. Smythe.

It was going to be harder than all the other leavings had been.

And there had been a lot of other leavings.

A cry came from the other side of the yard. Her head jerked up to see a groom yelling at a stable boy as a horse stomped down on his foot.

Somehow she had to get away and head in a new direction. Standing up, she began to pace. Her mind ran in circles without finding an answer. If she'd been a man she could have slung a bag over her shoulder and hiked down the road seeking a place to sleep in return for a strong back. Unfortunately it was not a strong back men were after when they offered a woman a place to sleep.

There was only one easy way for a woman to make her way in this world, and that life held no appeal.

But what other choices were there? If she left her position here she'd have no character reference, and without a reference—

She swallowed at the thought. No, she was not that desperate.

She could write to Lady Smythe-Burke. Surely the lady would help her out again. But would it be in time?

"Miss Masters?"

Her head jerked up at the voice—and the name it spoke. It came from the door of the inn, came from behind her.

She turned slowly.

He was there, the deep blue of his coat marked by a week of travel.

She tried to find her voice. It stuck deep in the recesses of her throat. Her lips formed words and she sucked her stomach in hard, forcing air out. "Are you looking for someone? I haven't seen another woman here."

He stared hard at her, small dark eyes glinting against pale skin. "No, I think I've found just who I am looking for."

"The Duke of Hargrove requests your company for dinner, Your Grace." Divers stood across from Mark and glared.

A man's valet was not supposed to glare at him contemptuously no matter what he was wearing. "What on earth is he doing here? His estates are on the other side of the country." Mark glanced out the window at the dirty stable yard.

"I imagine he is traveling to the coronation as well, Your Grace. I could not say why exactly he is on this road," Divers answered.

Mark hadn't really meant it as question. He was well aware of why the other duke was here. Half of England was traveling to London. Hargrove had probably been visiting with someone before heading to Town. The question had really been *Why now?* Why, when he was about to go down and meet Miss Smith? He'd actually borrowed a coat from Douglas for the meeting. It was a little loose about the body, but it should have helped prevent Isabella wondering about his station in life. It was not a coat to have dinner with another duke.

"May I help you change?" Divers's lips were firmly pressed together.

Mark nodded and within minutes he was brushed and smoothed and dressed in black silk.

Miss Smith was correct. His cravat was so tight and high that he couldn't see his feet. And he wasn't even going to think about trying to move his shoulders in the jacket. He glanced at the window one more time. Miss Smith would probably be waiting for him.

He wished for a moment that he could pull off the coat and go to her. Instead he turned and headed for the door. He would see what favor Hargrove desired.

"He's not coming."

Isabella jerked around and stared up at the man who'd come through the inn door, her nails biting into her palm. She couldn't remember ever seeing him before, but he was clearly addressing her.

She should have gone in long before, but she'd stood frozen ever since the blue-coated man had addressed her. She could only hope the other maids would forgive her.

"I don't know what you're talking about," she answered the new man, backing against the wall. Why hadn't she done that before? Blue Coat had seemed ready to grab her before another coach had pulled into the yard. He'd disappeared in the milling crowd before she could decide what to do. Could he have sent this man to take her? He certainly looked strong enough. He was not young, probably approaching fifty, but he had a broad, capable look about him. A deep scar marked one cheek.

She should have run, or gone to hide, but still she stood motionless. Unsure if she was safer here in plain sight than she would be retreating to the quiet corridors of the inn's upper floors.

"The man you're waiting for." The man spoke again, waking her from her shock. "Strattington is having dinner with the Duke of Hargrove. He's not coming."

Isabella let the remarks sink in slowly. He was not here to apprehend her, not with Blue Coat. He was with Mr. Smythe. "The duke is having a meal with Hargrove and Mr. Smythe's presence is required?"

"Yes." The man was certainly not verbose.

Isabella did not move away from the wall. The thought of entering the inn still chilled her. Blue Coat might be waiting to catch her in private—there would be fewer questions if no one saw her taken.

She was safer here.

And now all she wanted was a few minutes with Mr. Smythe, a few minutes of make-believe in the midst of everything else, a few moments of pretending to be safe. "Did he ask you to tell me?" she asked.

"No."

"Then . . . ?" If Mr. Smythe wasn't coming she should leave. She glanced nervously toward the door.

The man sighed and sat down on the steps. "He probably wouldn't want me talking to you but—Mr. Smythe—was busy and I couldn't just leave you waiting." He glanced about the yard. "This is not a good place for a woman at night."

It almost sounded a veiled threat, but somehow she knew his words were just what he said. The tension in her shoulders eased. She would be safe while he was with her. It was not the same as it was with Mr. Smythe, but it was something. "Do you work for the duke like Mr. Smythe?"

He opened his mouth, looked at her, and then closed it. She didn't understand why it should be a difficult question.

"I am employed by the duke, yes," he answered after a moment.

That should not have been so hard to answer. What

about the duke had his employees grasping for words? "And the duke required Mr. Smythe's presence this evening?"

The man suddenly smiled, his scar creasing his cheek. "Yes, Strattington required Mr. Smythe's presence. He most often does."

"Oh." There was not much else to say. "I guess I should go in, then." She hoped her fears did not sound in her voice.

The man nodded. Isabella began to head up the stairs back into the inn when he spoke again. "Let me walk you up." He stood and held out his arm. "You make him happy, you know. You probably shouldn't, but you do. I know it's only been a couple of days, but he is different. He needs more happiness. He has a difficult time with—the duke. They are too closely related."

She paused, then with only the slightest worry took his arm and let him lead her to the door. Nobody would come close to her if she was with him. "If you are to walk me up you must tell me your name. I feel at quite the disadvantage." She moved close to him, hoping he would not see anything odd as she hid behind him, trying to avoid being seen. Her fingers tightened about his arm. She could not help wishing it was Mr. Smythe's.

He looked down at her, his eyes kind, but questioning. "Just call me Douglas. It's what His Grace does."

Had three hours really passed? Mark wished he'd simply ignored duty and ignored Hargrove's invitation. Hargrove was not an uninteresting man, but he was a long-winded one. Mark cared about Parliament and fully intended to take his seat, but Hargrove's endless discussion of petty minutiae was wearing him down. He smiled and tried to ask an intelligent question about the agricultural horse tax. Hargrove grabbed on to it and began to expound again.

Miss Smith would be gone by now. She never stayed long and he doubted she'd waited more than fifteen minutes when he had not appeared. The brightest spot in his day, the only moments when he felt himself, and they were past before they could begin.

Hargrove was still answering his question and Mark could no longer even remember what it was. Had he actually asked about timber duties? What else could he say? Something about the coronation, perhaps? He noticed that any mention of it brought out opinion. Was the king spending too much? Would Queen Caroline dare to come? What would be served for dinner that night?

The last question brought as much discussion as any other.

"You seem to have drifted off. Strattington? Am I going on a little long? My mother always said I could talk from now until Judgment Day and not grow tired," Hargrove said with surprising perception, wiping his mouth with a lace-edged handkerchief.

"No, of course not. I am merely trying to consider what you have said in light of my new responsibilities." He rested his head upon his hand.

"Is that your father's ring?" Hargrove stared at the large ruby upon his finger. "It's rumored to be one of the clearest rubies ever mined."

"Yes."

"I remember when your father brought it back from India. I think the king offered him a title in return for it, but he would not sell."

"I've always believed that to be only rumor. My father loved the king, as did my uncle. If the king had asked for the ring I am sure that one of them would have gifted it to him."

"It must be difficult taking over from such a great man as your uncle. He was so perfect in fulfilling all that was expected of him. He set us all an excellent example. I know your cousin William admired his father greatly."

"Did you know William? I must admit I had not seen him for several years before his death."

"We were—were close. I was only a few years ahead of him at school. We had been the best of friends since then. His death was a great tragedy."

"Yes, it was. I certainly never expected to inherit." Mark hoped that was not saying too much.

"Life is strange. And you got his valet, too. Excellent man, Divers. I tried to steal him once." Hargrove seemed to give himself a little shake. He dabbed his mouth again. "Now tell me about your journey. Has anything eventful happened? Have you met anyone interesting?"

Mark had the feeling that Hargrove was asking about something specific, but he could not imagine what. And he was not about to mention Miss Smith, though she was the only interesting person he'd met since becoming a duke.

He glanced at the clock, wishing he could turn back its hands. He would not see her tonight—not unless he snuck into her room. The thought held a certain appeal.

Chapter 6

Isabella sat on the back stairs of the inn, tapping her boots against the step below her. This was the first inn without a view to the stable yard and she hoped Mr. Smythe would find her. She shouldn't be out at all, but she didn't want to even think about not seeing him for another night.

Blue Coat had stayed hidden today and she hadn't once had that chill on the back of her neck that made her feel watched. It was the only reason she hadn't fled, but it didn't make her feel any safer. It almost seemed more dangerous now that she didn't know where Mr. Blue Coat was, if he was still following her.

Had he returned to London? Was she actually safe for now? She tried to pretend that she was—it was easier than giving in to her fears. She wrapped her arms tight about herself in the gesture of a young child.

When she'd fled from London after Foxworthy's death she'd had a list of possible employers from Lady Smythe-Burke, a wonderful recommendation for Miss Isabella Smith, and a small purse of coin. Now she had an even smaller purse of coin and that was all. Mrs. Wattington would never give her a reference if she fled with no notice.

Did she need to leave? Perhaps Blue Coat had decided that she wasn't Isabella Masters.

No. Not a chance. He knew just who she was.

She squeezed her hands tight and tried to think about her situation, forced herself to consider the actual possibilities.

The blue-coated man might be working for her brother, Masters. If that was the case, the outcome would not be pleasant, but it would not be as dire as . . . Her mind could not complete the thought. Her brother no longer had power over her. He might still force her home, but despite everything she doubted he'd imprison her in his home. They might have disagreed those last couple months before she ran—he might have been ready to force her to wed Foxworthy—but deep in her heart she believed he'd only done what he thought he had to. If only she knew what else he might believe he had to do. What if he felt obligated to bring in the law?

And what if Blue Coat was not working for her brother? She wrapped her arms tight about her body as a chill took her.

She had killed Foxworthy.

She was a murderess. There was no going back.

It might have been an accident, she might have had no choice, but he was dead and she was to blame. The memory of his body lying across the cold stone of the floor came back to her with all the horror and disbelief contained in the moment it had happened.

She had done that. She and no one else.

And she knew what happened to murderers.

Her fingers shook. She wrapped them even tighter about her arms. Thinking about Foxworthy always affected her badly. And that was without the added worry of trying to understand who her pursuers were—and what they might want.

She fluttered her lashes quickly, trying to dry them before tears could form. She did not want Mr. Smythe to see her cry . . . He was her one spot of comfort in the midst of the mess her life had become.

Would she still be here? Had she come at all? After his failure to arrive the night before, he would not be surprised if she stayed in her room. He paused at the back door of the inn, his hand flat upon the rough wood.

He was nervous.

The thought caught him off guard. He was never nervous. He'd faced cannon fire without feeling this tightness in his gut. He swung the door open and stepped out onto the stairs, the boards creaking beneath his boots.

She was there.

Her eyes opened wide as if he'd given her a fright. Was she as nervous as he was?

Her hand shook slightly as she brushed at her skirt and stood.

"I wasn't sure you'd be here," he said.

"I am." She sounded breathless.

"Yes, but . . ." He let it hang, not wanting to mention his failure to show the night before.

Her gaze moved from his booted feet up his thighs and belly to reach his face. More than his gut tightened. She hadn't looked at him like that before.

He wanted to reach out and touch her, to draw her close.

Her words stopped him. "You didn't tell me you were related to the duke. Why would you not?"

* * *

"Related to the duke?" His features were in shadow, the inn's lamp lighting him from behind, but she could hear the confusion in his voice—and something else, that magic something that made her troubles seem so far away. "You think I am related to the duke?"

"I don't know why you try to pretend. I met a man last night, Douglas—he came to tell me you were dining with the Duke of Hargrove—and he told me of your relationship."

He looked perplexed for a moment as she drew close enough to see him more clearly in the dark. He opened his mouth, shut it, opened it again. "Douglas."

She nodded.

"He didn't tell me that he'd spoken to you."

"Should he not have?"

"And he said that I was related to the duke?"

"Not quite. He said something about a close relationship and troubles. I thought about it and decided being related was the most probable answer. And, as I said the other night, you look a little like the bit I saw of him."

"The tops of our hats are the same?"

"No, I think it's your height and general coloring. You don't stand like he does though—all stiff and straight, like a poker. I wonder if it was bred into him?"

"Like a poker?" He sounded quite affronted.

"I am speaking without thinking again, aren't I?" The sudden feelings of safety Mr. Smythe brought with him had loosened her tongue along with her nerves. "I should have realized he's your employer and perhaps even family. What is he, some type of cousin?"

He pressed his lips tight for a moment. "We're rather closer than that."

Mr. Smythe was illegitimate. Oh, raspberries. She hadn't even thought of that. Hadn't even considered the possibility. She should have, but she hadn't. Her thoughts had been on her own troubles. "I am sorry."

Now he just looked confused. "You're sorry?"

"You keep repeating what I say as question." She was glad they seemed to be moving beyond his relationship to the duke. There were some things there was just no good way to talk about. "You look much nicer than he does." Oh, she shouldn't have said that. "Someday I am just going to sew my lips shut."

"Now that would be a shame." Mr. Smythe stepped down a couple of steps until they were face-to-face.

It was the perfect moment for a kiss.

The wonder of anticipation filled her. She hadn't realized she was longing for his kiss, but suddenly it was all she could think about. She leaned a little further.

The desire for his mouth upon her own was more powerful than anything she could remember.

A few years ago she'd kissed more than one man and enjoyed every single one. Kisses had been fun and flirtatious. They held the possibility of risk, but of only the most minor variety. And she'd certainly never needed them, felt that she couldn't survive without them.

Unfortunately what had been true of Miss Isabella Masters, lady of the *ton*, was, however, not true of Miss Smith, nursery maid.

A kiss that for Miss Masters was light entertainment could spell disaster for Miss Smith. Her teeth bit into her lower lip. Maids and governesses could be dismissed over a kiss—in fact, not only could be, but probably would be.

So was he worth the trouble a kiss might bring?

And did she have any choice? She did not believe she could live without knowing what his lips felt like.

Surely she deserved a single moment of happiness. Surely she deserved the kiss she needed before she was forced to flee, forced to leave him behind.

She stepped closer, felt the heat of his body against her breast. She raised her head slightly, tilted her neck to the perfect angle, looked at his lips, inhaled, letting her own lips part, moved her gaze to his eyes, and back down—waited.

And waited.

She could feel his glance upon her, knew her invitation was not subtle.

He stared down at her lips and suddenly she knew it would be now, that moment when a well-behaved girl would step away, but. . .

She didn't realize he was the duke. It was such a relief. Douglas had talked to her and kept his secret. He would have to find out exactly what the man had said. Mark stared down at her softly lit face, so sweet and trusting, though he always had the feeling that she could do anything at any time.

But was he really so stiff? He must be getting better at being the duke than he'd imagined.

He would admit to feeling different when dressed and combed. There was something about being fastened into stiff brocades and expensive silks that made one change. His shoulders went back further. His chin rose just that tiniest of bits. And his eyes—he supposed he even looked at the world a bit differently when he was the duke.

When he was the duke.

It seemed an odd way to think about it, because he was the duke all the time, but he just didn't feel it. Someday he supposed it would grow around him, become part of him, but right now it seemed like something he put on along with his coat, like something his valet kept locked away and took out when it was time to dress each morning.

But right now, right this second, this moment, he was anything but the duke. He was simply a man, and only a man.

She moved closer to him. He could feel her breath against his cheek, feel her gaze upon his mouth. She could not possibly be aware of the invitation she was sending, an invitation it was beyond his power to deny.

"Are you going to kiss me?"

The question was so soft that at first he wasn't sure he'd heard it.

"You keep staring at my lips, but you're not doing anything. Are you going to kiss me?"

He *was* staring at her lips, staring at them but not quite seeing them. He focused on their rosy fullness. "Do you want me to kiss you?"

Her glance darted from his mouth up to his eyes. Her skin flushed and he could tell she wanted to look away, step away—instead she stepped closer, her eyes dropping back to his mouth. "Yes." She said it firmly, but then hesitated. "I know I shouldn't want you to. I've known you less than a week—hardly half a week."

"Has it only been that long?" He ran a finger across her cheek. "It feels so much longer, as if I've known you forever." And it did.

He knew he shouldn't kiss her. She was right about

that. And he certainly shouldn't kiss her here—on the inn steps—where anybody might see.

He stepped closer, his fingers slid down and cupped her chin, bringing her face nearer.

And he kissed her. Light. Gentle. The perfect first kiss for his innocent girl.

Her lips were tender and a little dry. He licked them for her. She tasted of mushroom gravy. The inn must have served it for dinner that night. It almost made him laugh—but only almost.

Laughter would have been impossible as she leaned into him, her lips pressing against his with greater pressure, her firm breasts rubbing against the linen of his shirt, her arms coming up around his neck, pulling his head down, her—

It was definitely not her first kiss. That fact filled Mark's mind and then faded as the desires of his body forced away all thought.

His hands wrapped about her waist, lifting her into fuller contact. His tongue swept along the crease of her lips, pushing its way in. She opened her mouth to him, welcoming him in. She was as fully in the moment as he—then she pulled back. Her hands slid down his shoulders to push against his chest.

"No." She was breathless, but firm. There could be no mistaking that she meant the word.

She didn't mean it at all. Isabella wanted to lean in to him, to lick him, devour him, have him devour her, to grab her moment; wanted to push her common sense, her troubles away. When she was with him all her worries faded to nothingness. She felt a strength she'd never known before—as if she could do anything.

Only. . .

She forced air into her lungs and tried to bring her mind around to the *no* her lips had formed so perfectly. She pulled back far enough to stare into his eyes. They were nearly black with passion—and tenderness. It was almost enough to have her lean into him again.

Only—they were standing on a public stair.

Only—the lamp was bright above them.

Only—the lady's maid who was sharing a room with her and Joey had agreed to watch him for just an hour while he slept.

Only—somebody could appear at any moment.

They were all good reasons, sensible reasons, and she needed to be a sensible girl if she wanted to survive. She needed to act with reason as well as passion. She had put her wants, her needs aside before—she could do so again.

Only—he looked so good, so kind, so everything she'd ever wanted, ever dreamed could be hers.

She started to lean against him again, tilted her chin up—caught herself and stepped back.

"No." This time she did not sound so sure.

"Are you a tease?" He said it flatly.

"No." She glanced up toward the light, feeling his eyes follow her subtle movement. She smiled at him, just barely, just enough to let him see her own wants. Her sister had told her nothing drew a man as fast as a woman's desire.

"Ah, there is that. Should we go someplace else?"

"I need to get back to Joey."

He reached out and placed his fingers beneath her chin, drawing her glance back to his. He stared at her for several moments. "Tomorrow, then?"

"I don't know." Another little smile. She would keep her options open.

"What don't you know? If you can get away? If we can find a place to meet? Or you don't know that you want to do this?"

"If I say 'I don't know' again I'll feel like an indecisive idiot," she answered, licking her lower lip, drawing his gaze. "Well, I don't know the answer to the first two questions. I never know what Mrs. Wattington will want or how Joey will be feeling. It's the third question I am not sure about. What exactly is 'this'? A kiss? I think after thirty seconds I know that I could kiss you for hours. But I know that men want more." Her voice dropped very low. "I know I want more."

She watched him swallow, saw the tendons in his neck draw tight. His eyes closed and then opened again.

He stepped back suddenly, turned, and walked away.

She held her breath for a moment, until he pivoted and walked back toward her. Then he paced away again. He repeated the pattern several times before coming to stand before her. "If all you want is kisses I can be happy with that. Well, not happy precisely, but contented. You are right, a man does want more, but a man also controls those wants."

There was a slight tap from the interior of the inn and then the maid who had been watching Joey popped her head out. She gazed down the stairs, looking beyond Isabella.

"Is he waking then?" Isabella asked.

"No, he's still resting like the baby that he is, but I need to lay out my mistress's dress for tomorrow and I didn't wish to leave him alone." She stuck her head out further. "I thought I heard you talking to someone."

Isabella turned her head, following the maid's gaze. Mr. Smythe was gone. "I was," she said. "One of the duke's men. He was advising me on what the roads should be like tomorrow."

The maid gave a snort and stepped back into the inn. "A groom, I suppose. You need to be careful with them. They're only after one thing."

Isabella did not reply, merely following the maid back in and up the interior stairs to the attic room they shared.

The problem was she wasn't sure what Mr. Smythe wanted. Well, he did want that, but he did seem to be considering something more besides. Somehow she had to find out just what—and quickly.

And then there was herself, what did she want? What did she need?

Mark stood in the shadows and watched Isabella slip back into the inn. His body was still tense with both arousal and the nearness of being discovered. If there was one thing he knew about maids, it was that they never kept quiet. If he'd been caught kissing Isabella the whole inn would have known of it within the hour and probably half the surrounding town as well. It was bad enough that Douglas probably knew. The blasted man knew everything.

Mark glanced up at the dark windows above, looking for the familiar silhouette.

Isabella had been right to step back, to step away, to draw a halt to it all.

Still, he wished she hadn't. His lips still longed for

the feel of hers beneath them, soft, sweet, willing.

Only how willing was she, and did he care? Could he be content with kisses? Could he risk more than kisses? If he seduced her did he need to tell her who he was first? Surely it was the only honorable thing—and yet his whole being cried out against letting her know that he was the duke.

So he was back to the original question: Could he be content with kisses?

He never had been before. He couldn't recall ever willingly entering into a relationship that would consist only of kisses—not that this was a relationship. It was more of a dalliance. Still, she was right. A man wanted more, needed more.

So why hadn't he said that or even just walked away?

He still could. It would be the easy thing, the sane thing, to simply instruct the driver to travel a normal distance tomorrow instead of these shortened drives that Mrs. Wattington demanded. If he did that, perhaps even added an extra few miles to the day, he would arrive in London as expected, rather than late. It surely couldn't be a good thing to be late for one's king—and yet he'd been willing to risk it.

For kisses.

Was he truly willing to risk royal ire for kisses?

Isabella's mind danced with the glory of Mr. Smythe's kisses. It had been years since she'd been so lost in the wonder of a moment. All things suddenly seemed possible. She almost skipped as she headed up the stairs to her room.

"We want what you took and we want it now." The whisper came from behind her as she was halfway up the stairs.

She froze, the breath leaving her.

Then fear set in. She had to get away. Before she could turn and run she felt her arms grabbed and held tight. A large male body pressed against her back, forcing her against the stair rail. The scent of old sweat filled her nostrils.

Her entire body froze. Last night she had been scared to enter the inn. Tonight it had not even occurred to her. Her thoughts had been of nothing but Mr. Smythe and his kisses. How could she have been so foolish?

"Don't turn, and don't say anything," the voice continued. "We want what you took from Foxworthy. Give it to us and we'll let you be. If not, I am sure that many would be interested in what happened to the colonel and his papers."

"I don't know what you're talking about." Isabella tried to hold her voice even despite the terror that was fast taking over.

"Don't give us that. You have until we reach London."

"I don't know—"

"I am sure you do know what happens to those who commit murder—they hang."

Isabella's heart jumped to her throat. They knew. They knew what she'd done. How?

"But—" Even as she spoke Isabella felt herself thrust forward, her feet slipping beneath her as she fell to her knees on the hard wood of the stairs, splinters slipping through her skirt. She turned quickly, but there was only the clatter of boots and the swing of the door into the taproom.

Chapter 7

Hang. She could hang.

Isabella had always known that, but hearing it said aloud made it all too real, too immediate.

It was more than she could bear to think about.

She turned over, pulling the covers up high, glad that the sun was finally peeking above the horizon. The night was over. Joey still slumbered safely in his cot, unaware of the troubles that plagued her.

What did the whispering man want? She forced herself to remember that horrible day—not Foxworthy's death, she always ran from that memory, but the aftermath. She'd been intent on finding the false papers that declared her brother guilty of treason. After the way Masters had treated her she almost hadn't bothered, but her sister's happiness had been tied up in it all as well.

She remembered sweeping all the papers off the top of Foxworthy's desk and stuffing them in her reticule. She'd dumped everything on her bed at Masters's house and fished out the needed papers, turning them over to Violet.

It would not make sense for the whispering man to be after those papers. Why would he want papers proving Masters was innocent of treason? Why would he want papers involving Masters at all?

There had to be something else. She tried to remember what she'd seen as she tossed things aside. There'd been other papers, but it truly had been rubbish, if she remembered correctly. A couple of unpaid bills from a tailor, an IOU from a game of hazard, some lady's florid love letters written in purple ink—they had at least been educational, if a little strange in tone—and some scraps of paper used to scribble sums, nothing that was worth anything.

The IOU perhaps?

No, it had been for less than fifty pounds.

Perhaps the scribbles were a secret code? She could have built quite a drama with that as the plot. If that were the case, however, Foxworthy would probably not have been using them to blot spilled ink.

The love letters? Love letters could be used for blackmail, but surely she would have remembered if there had been anything truly scandalous in them. The most exciting thing about them had been the bright purple ink.

Could she have missed anything? Probably. But what did it matter now? The papers were tucked away at Masters's house, if they had not been thrown away. The maid who had cleaned up after she left might very well have seen them as rubbish and tossed them aside. For that matter Masters might have just thrown all her belongings into the streets.

There was no hope there. She didn't know what they wanted and even if she did, she'd have no way of retrieving the papers.

There seemed to be no possible solution but flight and even that did not seem possible. If only she had somebody to help, just one person on her side.

Could Mr. Smythe be that person? What would she need to do to make him so?

"Do you see this? How am I supposed to travel with wrinkles in my skirt? I told you yesterday to be sure everything was ready. I cannot believe you pressed this at all. What did you do last night, flirt with stable hands? It's almost ten, time for us to be on the road. I will be forced to travel looking no better than a servant." The woman who said the words was as young and sweet-looking as any Mark had seen the last month—or at least since he'd kissed Isabella last night. The voice, though—the voice could have belonged to a fishmonger's wife. Hell, it could have belonged to the fishmonger himself.

The poor maid to whom the comments were addressed bent her head and mumbled words of apology.

The woman was having none of it. "I don't care what time we arrived or how many other tasks you had to do. You should not have slept until my clothing was ready. You're lucky I don't dismiss you on the spot. If I did not have such a tender heart I'd leave you in this godforsaken little town and just be done with it. The kitchen maid could do a better job than you."

"Thank you, Mrs. Wattington," the maid whispered. She turned to go.

Mark's head came up. This was Mrs. Wattington, Isabella's employer? She didn't look old enough to have a baby. He'd pictured a full-figured merchant's wife, not this slip of a girl. Still, based upon the voice, appearances could be deceiving.

"I did not dismiss you." Mrs. Wattington reached out and grabbed the poor girl by the collar.

He stepped forward reflexively. His boot bumped

into a coatrack, causing it to smack against the wall.

Mrs. Wattington turned, her mouth open, ready to berate him—then she stopped. Her eyes swept from the toe of his polished Hessians to the well-shaped felt of his hat. A slow smile spread across her face.

She stepped forward, lowering her eyes and then raising them in a gesture surely designed to enchant. She repeated the move. There was temptation to ask if she had something in her eye.

"Forgive my boldness," she said, stepping even closer. "I know it is not done to speak without proper introduction, but I fear nobody in this hamlet has the manners to accomplish even such a simple task so I must take it on myself. I am Mrs. Wattington, wife to Mr. Henry Wattington. Perhaps you've met my husband. He travels only in the best of circles." She batted her lashes again.

"Strattington, at your service." Mark gave the barest nod. He was tempted to cut her, his uncle probably would have. A duke would never speak to such a—a— He didn't even have a word to describe such an obvious social climber.

"The Duke of Strattington, I thought it must be you. Poor man forced to dine alone each night because there is not suitable company along the road. I would have thought there would be more people of our class coming to London for the coronation, but alas, I seem to always be forced to dine with only myself for company."

If she moved her lashes any faster he'd be able to feel a breeze.

"Personally I find no company better than my own." There, that sounded like a duke.

"But food is always better shared."

What was there to say to that? He certainly did not intend to eat with the woman. "I find myself occupied the next several nights. Perhaps you should see if the Duke of Hargrove is free. I am told he is now traveling this road also."

It was an evil thing to do to poor Hargrove, but the other man was sensible enough to travel at a decent speed and must be far ahead of Mrs. Wattington's meandering pace. Mark certainly was not going to miss a chance to spend time with Miss Smith in order to eat with Mrs. Wattington.

"Excuse me. My carriage is ready." He nodded a last time to the woman and strode through the door without looking back.

Eleven hours later Mark had only one thought. *The hay was not fresh.* He walked through the inn's stable and pulled in a deep breath. Normally he would not have stabled his horses in such a place, but there was not much choice in the village that Mrs. Wattington had chosen as their stopping point.

The woman must really hate to travel.

His ears still rang with the sound of her voice as she'd berated the maid. And he'd been sure she was about to strike the poor girl when she'd grabbed her by the collar. He wasn't sure what he'd have done then. He'd stepped forward without thought, only knowing he hated the abuse of authority. He hated the thought that Isabella worked for such a woman.

Mrs. Wattington had changed soon enough when she'd seen him, however. The saccharine voice that had leaked from her lips then might have been even worse than the tone she'd used with the maid.

Being the duke was not always a pleasure.

Would he ever stop thinking of it as being the duke and start thinking of it as being himself?

He remembered his uncle's humorless stare and doubted it. He was learning to act the duke, but he doubted he'd ever actually manage to be the duke.

There were some advantages, though. Mrs. Wattington had let the maid go with hardly another glance once she'd seen him. If only he could protect Isabella as easily.

He strolled to the stall holding his gelding and stared at the great horse. Achilles had been with him since before France and while the horse had not come to war with him, he owed the horse far more than his life—he owed him his sanity. Achilles listened without judging, something very rare in Mark's life since the death of first his cousin and then his uncle—even Douglas judged him. He'd seen it in the man's eyes often enough. He whistled quietly and Achilles wandered over, almost as content with a scratch as a carrot.

The horse kicked at the straw beneath his feet, impatient for more attention.

The straw was not fresh.

The thought returned and with it the true motivation behind it. It was true that he would not normally have housed his horse, or any horse, in such conditions, but he accepted the realities of life. The straw did not trouble Achilles. Mark smiled as the horse nudged him again. No, the truth was he'd been thinking about Isabella—and not just about the need to protect her.

Achilles shoved his face harder toward Mark and Mark gave him one last good rub between the eyes.

He looked out the door at the nearly empty yard

and then back at the equally empty inn. It was impossible to imagine a tryst of any kind in such conditions. He shook his head at his own thoughts. Isabella had not indicated definite willingness for any further relations and, if he was honest, if she did he would not care where they were. The condition of the straw would not matter in the slightest if she was smiling up at him.

And damnation, he should not be having such thoughts anyway—the rule was kisses, kisses only. He could not afford more than that.

A noise near the door drew his attention.

Isabella shivered as she stepped into the yard. She hadn't been sure she would come until the moment she stepped out the door. It had been the hardest day of her entire life as she pretended that nothing was wrong when all she wanted to do was run and hide. Only she didn't know where to hide. The one thing that she did know was that she had to do something.

And so she was here, creeping through the darkness looking for the one thing that made her feel safe, Mr. Smythe. If only she could find a way to keep him with her forever, to feel safe forever.

She stepped toward the stable, her eyes darting around. "Are you in there, Mr. Smythe?" Isabella was relatively sure it was Mr. Smythe she had seen entering the stable, but she would hate to be mistaken and end up with the duke. There was something so similar about them, but it had definitely been Mr. Smythe's loose-hipped walk. She didn't know what she'd say to a duke besides "Yes, Your Grace." Once she would have known how to flirt and what to say, but not any longer. Flirtatious gestures were not taken well when coming from a servant—or perhaps they were taken too well.

Which was ironic given that she was trying to decide if she could persuade Mr. Smythe to help her by flirting with him. She was steeling herself to try almost anything. Only somehow it was all different with him. She didn't need to think and plan, although she did intend to try a couple of the things her sister had told her about. She'd seen Violet spin men in circles until they didn't know which way was up. Could she do the same?

Could she make him help her, make him stay with her?

Pulling her cloak about her shoulders, she moved through the dark doorway. There was a light farther back, near the far stalls. It must be Mr. Smythe. Drawing in a deep breath, she considered. She released her cloak, let it slide open.

The first step was to make him want.

The second was to make him want more.

The third was to test what he was willing to do.

The fourth was to make him want even more.

The more he wanted, the more she held back, the more he might be willing to help her. She hadn't decided just what she wanted yet, but she could figure that out once she knew he was on her side.

It should have felt cold-blooded, but when she thought of Mark cold didn't enter into it.

Mark. It was the first time she had allowed herself to call him that in her mind. After their kiss last night it felt strange to think of him as Mr. Smythe or even just Smythe.

A shuffling from behind had her turning. "Mr.

Smythe?" It was too soon to say his Christian name aloud.

All she saw was darkness. She shivered, peering into the darkness.

"Mr. Smythe," she called out again.

No answer.

Could she gamble that Mark would help her, protect her, if—if she slept with him? That was what she was considering, wasn't it? She was thinking about more than simple flirtation.

She swallowed as she let the thought form.

No, she wasn't sure that she could go that far. It was too risky and she had always wanted to wait for love. Surely she could persuade him to help without actually seducing him.

Besides, what would happen if she failed? She shivered to even consider the possibility. If she had sex—she forced her mind to form the word; if she was going to consider it she had to at least think it—with Mark and then he abandoned her, what then? She would be even worse off than she was now.

And what was the best thing that could happen?

She doubted that he would leave the duke and take her away, but could he be persuaded to give her the money she needed, or perhaps to even find a place for her to stay?

That was the most likely scenario, that he would give her money. The idea was distasteful, but perhaps necessary.

No, she was not going to think that way. She wanted to be with him, to feel safe—not just to take his money.

Another sound brought her thoughts back to the

moment. Her head jerked up and she stared more deeply into the darkness. And then she felt it, that prickle on the back of her neck, the sensation of being watched. Was somebody there? A movement near the inn caught her eye and she peered in the blackness. A cat. It had to be a cat.

Since the meeting with Blue Coat and the Whisperer—were they one and the same?—she acted like she needed eyes in the back of her head, always glancing about. It was only when she was near Mark that she let down her guard.

Mark. Was he the answer to her problems? The thought surfaced again.

A step sounded in the dark stable, a definite step, a definite movement toward her. She stepped back into the stable. "Mark?" Her voice shook with nerves.

There was a man. It was hard to see. Was he coming her way?

She edged back. He couldn't see her, identify her, could he? Between her cloak and the darkness of the stable she must be nearly invisible.

"Mr. Smythe, please answer. Are you in here?"

And then there was the sound of footsteps from within, slow, steady steps she already recognized.

"Yes, I am here. Why don't you come in and meet one of my friends?" His voice was so calm, so reassuring.

She glanced back at the yard. There was nothing there. It must be her harried imagination.

She gave herself a little shake and focused on Mark's words.

A friend?

That gave her pause. He'd never wanted to introduce her to anyone before, and with her probably silly, but ever growing, fears, she wasn't sure she wished to meet anyone new. Maybe it was Douglas? Perhaps Mark thought they needed a proper introduction, although he hadn't seemed happy that they'd talked before.

And why now? Why when it would interfere with her plans? And that wasn't even considering the possibility of danger. She glanced back at the stable yard.

"Are you coming, Miss Smith?" Mark's voice called out from the dim stable.

Isabella pushed her shoulders back and entered. Mark was alone. What was he talking about, a friend? All she could see was a great black stallion. Well, not quite a stallion—some things were more apparent when one drew closer. "You wanted me to meet someone?" she asked.

Mark smiled, one of the warmest smiles she'd yet seen cross his face, and the sense of safety she'd come to depend on settled about her. "Yes." The horse leaned over the edge of the stall, setting his head on Mark's shoulder and nuzzling at his ear. "This is Achilles. We've been friends since I was a boy."

He wanted her to meet his horse? Isabella found her own smile spreading to meet Mark's. She'd never been introduced to a horse before, at least not since Masters bought her first pony. "He's very beautiful, quite the charmer. Was he in the army with you?" She strolled over and laid her hand on the velvet nose. Achilles snuffled against her.

"No." His voice was gruff.

"Oh, you had another horse? Did something happen to him?"

Mr. Smythe stopped at that and turned back to her. "No. Do I look like I had the wherewithal to buy a cavalry commission?"

Not knowing why he'd taken her question so badly she looked about. "No—I suppose it's merely that I found you in the stables—and then there's Achilles, whom you've had since you were a boy. I assumed you knew your way around a horse. I never did understand how the army worked, or the navy for that matter. I suppose I was always more interested in dresses and pretty bonnets. Even during the war I found the whole matter dull. I suppose I was still too young to really understand, or at least to want to."

Her words seemed to calm him.

"So you weren't cavalry?"

"No, I was infantry—right in the thick of it all." He too lost his smile, but he did not seem displeased, only somber. "My poor mother worried endlessly, convinced I'd never make it back or that if I did I'd be missing a piece. I can't say she was wrong to worry. From all I saw I probably should have suffered some wound. I was grazed a few times, but my luck always held."

"Does that mean no interesting scars?"

His eyes flicked over her as if judging the intent behind her words. "No, no interesting ones from the war. A mark across one shoulder and another across the small of my back, hardly more than scratches. If you want interesting scars you'd have to ask about the time I jumped from the vicarage roof."

She pressed her lips shut tight, lowered her face, and tried to look innocent. She was not going to ask. She was not—at least not yet.

Mark stepped toward her, letting the subject drop. "I was worried you might be scared. I know not all women like horses."

"I started riding when I was in short skirts, although my pony would barely have reached Achilles' thighs. I would admit it's been a few years since I've been mounted, but I imagine there are some things one never forgets."

At that Mark gave her the strangest look, his glance focusing first on her lips and then moving down her body. His eyes flared with heat and she could read intent in his gaze.

Her mouth dry, she swallowed and tried to answer his look.

Chapter 8

Her gaze stayed fastened on his eyes as she tried to understand what he had reacted to. It took only a moment for comprehension to arrive. *Since I've been mounted.* Oh. She had not meant that at all—although she would have if she'd thought of it. She could not remember another instance when everything she said seemed to cast other allusions—at least when she didn't mean it to. This seduction thing was easier than she'd anticipated.

Only did she mean to seduce him? She didn't know what she wanted—only that the closer she got to him, the closer she wanted to be.

"Where did you get him? He is so beautifully formed." There, that should delay a moment—she didn't want this to move too quickly. She needed to be sure what she planned, what she wanted. Men could talk about their horses for hours. It was only too bad he didn't have a curricle as well. That would have filled up conversation for the rest of the night.

Instead of answering immediately Mark looked away and hesitated. After a moment, he answered. "He was a gift from my father. He gave him to me about a year before he died. I am not sure I would have survived his death without Achilles." He gave the horse a hearty pat. "I suppose that sounds silly."

Isabella remembered the rag doll she'd poured her sorrows out to when both of her parents died. No, talking to a horse didn't seem silly at all. "No, I'd love to have a creature to talk to who was just there for me."

"Have you never had a pet?"

"I had a pony when I was very small and I did love him, but it was always clear he was for teaching me to ride and that was all. I would love to have a cat, but it doesn't work with being in service. I never know where I will end up and so many homes have hounds."

"Yes, I would admit that I have hounds myself. It would take some work to get them to accept a cat."

"You have hounds?" Did that mean he had a home of his own as well? That would work well for her. There was so much that was unexplained about the man.

Mark had caught the drift of her question. She could see a desire to backtrack in his glance. Should she let him get away with it if he changed the subject?

Violet had always said the key to manipulating a man was to never let him know what you were about. She walked away, looking for a place to sit. Now if she could just get him to talk, really talk.

She wanted to know everything about him—but how much of herself was she willing to share in return?

She'd had a pony as a child and learning to ride had been considered important. Mark didn't know why he felt surprised. Many governesses had genteel backgrounds. He didn't know specifically where a nursery maid or baby nurse fit in the great scheme of things, but it was easy to believe the same might be true. He examined her closely, trying to discern the truth. Was she some poor gentleman's daughter cast out to fend for herself? It seemed very possible. She did speak like a lady, and while her clothing was clearly that of a servant, there was something about her carriage that said she'd once been used to better things.

If Isabella had been a lady it might change things. He wasn't quite sure how, but he was sure that it would. He needed to know more.

And she'd asked about his dogs. That had been a slip on his part. Telling her that he now owned a pack of the sleekest hounds in the country would only raise more questions. He thought of Pumpkin, the dog that had slept in his room when he was a boy. Pumpkin had come from the best of bloodlines, but an accident with a trap as a pup had left him unable to run with others. His uncle had been ready to shoot the dog when Mark had begged to be allowed to raise him. With great reluctance his uncle had nodded his approval—as long as he never had to see the beast again.

"I've always had a dog or two about. My family always laughed at how I attracted strays. I always seem to be caring for one more creature. I am surprised that I've never had a cat, now that you mention it." There, that did not answer the question about the hounds, but gave her enough that she should be satisfied.

She shot him a look that told him she knew exactly what he'd done and was deciding if she should let him get away with it. Her nose wrinkled as she looked down at the straw. He could see that she wanted to sit, but did not find the slightly rancid smell appealing.

She moved to a tack chest and set aside the objects on top. "Tell me more about Achilles, then. He is such a fine beast. He must have wonderful bloodlines."

"I didn't know it was proper for young ladies to talk about bloodlines."

"I am hardly a young lady." She sank down on the chest, spreading her skirts about her. A look of relief crossed her face and he could picture her day spent running up and down stairs at Mrs. Wattington's request. He should have found her a seat or a bench as soon as she appeared. He'd have to remember that in the future. Offering to rub her sore feet was unfortunately out of the question—for now.

"You seem very much the lady to me." And that was true.

She smiled, uncomfortably, at his words. "Whatever may have been true once is no longer. I am a servant. There is no going back. I should not say even that much, but you do make me wish I could confide all."

He leaned against a stall across from her, the darkness creating a private world. "Why don't you share your secrets? I am very good at listening."

Her teeth worried at her lower lip as she stared straight at him. The light from the stable's single lamp cast long shadows upon her face. "I ran away—years ago," she said after a moment.

It explained much about her, but why had she run away and why had her family not come looking for her? "I imagine your parents must be worried about you after all these years. Have you corresponded with them at all?"

"My parents died when I was very young. My older brother was my guardian until I reached my majority."

"Well, if you're no longer in his charge, why don't you go back? Surely what you ran from can't be that terrible."

Her lips clamped shut, but then her eyes tilted up a bit at the corner. "I think it's time for you to answer a question for me. There are things I want to know."

Mark pulled in a deep breath and let it out. Achilles mimicked his gesture in a much grander manner and they both laughed, breaking the tension.

Isabella leaned forward, her lips pouting deliciously. "So tell me, what do you do for the duke?"

Would he answer her? Mr. Smythe—she reverted to the more formal—was the only man she could remember meeting who had not instantly made her aware of his station in life. Every man from footman to gentleman seemed to place tremendous importance on what he did in life—or in the case of the gentlemen, great pride in how little they actually did. Mr. Smythe had never made any mention of his life beyond saying that he was with the duke's party.

If she even was to consider seducing him she needed to know more.

He took a couple of steps forward until he stood above her. Leaning forward, he rested an arm on the wall behind her. "I've just told you I was in the infantry."

That was true. He had mentioned it, but he had not been detailed. But then, even while she ignored the war, she had noticed that the men who had seen the worst of battle were the ones who said the least. It was the men who had done little more than polish their own boots who had the longest stories to tell. "Yes, you mentioned that you were in some very unpleasant places, but surely you must have mustered out years ago. How does that answer my question?"

"I suppose because I don't feel I've done much

since leaving the army. Life was so intense while I was there, every decision mattered. It is as if I lived in a brilliant oil painting and now I am stuck in a pen and ink drawing. Life is not the same. I did manage my father's estate for several years right after I got out, but it was a very small estate, and in truth my mother could have managed it just fine without me—as she did for all the years I was away. The duke offers me new opportunities."

That all made sense, but she was left with questions. If he'd managed his father's estates, then what had the duke been doing? Why would an illegitimate son manage them? And his mother? If she'd been the duke's mistress, then what was she doing anywhere near the estates? There was something here that did not make sense at all. Isabella closed her eyes and tried to remember everything she'd heard about the Duke of Strattington. Mrs. Wattington had been quite prolific on the subject since speaking with him that morning. The duke had recently inherited from an uncle. That meant the duke's father must be a younger son and that would explain the small estate. The current duke had never been expected to inherit as he'd had a cousin of about the same age. But then the cousin died in some type of hunting accident.

The new duke was traveling to the coronation, although he was still in mourning, but would return to his estates immediately after. And he looked very handsome in the severe black he wore to mark his mourning, although Mrs. Wattington rather thought he'd look handsome in anything and didn't understand why the duke bothered with mourning when he'd barely known his uncle. Mrs. Wattington had managed to share all that information in the space of three breaths. Isabella rather thought it had taken her longer just to think it.

She looked up to find Mark staring down at her, his eyes focused on her lips. Yes, she had been lost in thought for too long.

"Are we done, then? Or do you have more questions?" Mark leaned toward her, his intent clear.

She edged away, but not too far. "You still haven't told me what you do for the duke."

"I thought I had. I manage his estates." He reached forward and ran a finger across her lips.

"You're his agent, then?" She tried to focus on his words. An estate agent would be good. They made a handsome living—and they had wives.

No, she was not going to think about that.

Mark's fingers stopped at the middle of her mouth and plucked at the lower lip. It felt so good. Thinking of anything but his fingers grew difficult. It was so much easier to feel than to think, so much easier to let thoughts of what she wanted, what she needed, slip away.

"His agent. That would be one way to look at it." His finger teased her again.

It was all she could do not to lean forward and lick. There was something else she needed to ask. Something else important. Oh yes, the mother. Why was his mother living on the estate? She tried to find the words—which would not have been easy at the best of times and was nigh impossible as Mark stared down at her, his own lips parted, his breath a tangible force between them.

She tried again to focus her thoughts, but all she could think was how dark his eyes looked in the shadows and how tiny points of reflected light flickered in them. She wanted to lean forward and examine them more closely.

"Are you going to kiss me?" he asked.

She might be in a daze, but Isabella could not mistake his repeating her question from last evening. It would be dangerous, not as dangerous as the inn's steps, but still, anyone could come in.

She wanted to, though. Oh, how she wanted to.

She reached up, tangling her fingers in his dark curls, mussing them hopelessly. "If you walked around with your hair like this no one would ever believe the duke trusted you with his estates."

One corner of his mouth curled. "No, I daresay they would not."

She pulled him closer. "Do you want me to kiss you?"

"I want whatever you are willing to give me."

He was honest. It reassured her, made her feel even safer. When she was with him nothing bad could happen, all her worries fell away.

He would never betray her.

No, she had to be more careful. Betrayal came when one least expected it. "I think it will be kisses for now. I can't say I'd want to do more than that in a stable."

He chuckled. "You are always so honest with me. I can always trust you to tell me the truth."

The truth. He thought she was telling him the truth? Well, she was—just not very much of it. It brought back her thought of a moment ago. Betrayal came when least expected.

She raised her lips, parting them as she moved,

eager to avoid any further discussion. It would be easier to become his lover than to tell him the full truth about herself.

Mark felt her lush lips touch his and gave a silent prayer of thanks, both for the wonder of her lips, but also because he didn't have to say anything else. If she kept asking questions, at some point he was going to have to actually lie—or trust her with the truth. And he was not yet ready to see the change in her face when she realized who he was. So far his own feelings of being separate from the duke had protected him, but that could last only so long.

She was soft. He'd thought that before, but now the feeling overwhelmed him. He was only touching her lips, but he felt enveloped in comfort—complete. His lips moved against hers, pressing them even farther open. Her breath filled his mouth and his own swept out in reply. Her aqua eyes opened wide and she stared up at him. He could feel her surprise—and her joy.

His tongue swept out and licked along her lip line, not seeking entry, but enjoying the fullness of the curve.

Before things could progress further, Achilles kicked hard against the wall of his stall. He stuck his large head over the top and stared at Mark. It was clear Achilles knew who he believed should be the center of all attention.

Isabella began to laugh, her whole body shaking with the emotion. "All males are the same."

"I beg your pardon?" He turned his glare from the horse and back at her.

"Oh, don't look at me that way. Can you say that

if I were focusing all my attention on him, you'd react any different? I didn't think so. Now I want to hear more about you. Where do you live when you're not traveling with the duke?"

He focused on her lips again. More distraction was called for.

He bent his head. There would be no more questions tonight.

Chapter 9

"You careless tramp." Mrs. Wattington's words echoed through the interior of the carriage. Isabella didn't know what she'd done to deserve the *tramp*, but the slap that turned her head with its force was very clear indeed.

Isabella could only stare and blink, her body shivering with the shock of what had happened.

Mrs. Wattington had hit her, hit her.

The thought echoed through her mind.

The perfection of the previous night—and now this. Touching her cheek gently, she winced. Mrs. Wattington was much stronger than she looked.

They stared at each other for a second, and then without another word Mrs. Wattington turned her face back to the wall. Isabella wanted to say something, to retaliate in some fashion, but knew she mustn't.

She dropped her hands to her lap, squeezing them tight. Then, with a deep inhale, she turned to Joey, comforting the small, screaming boy. He ceased the yell immediately, smiling sleepily up at her.

His belly felt better and that was his only concern. He closed his eyes and drifted off.

Leaving her with a mess of stinking baby vomit and

an employer who wouldn't even look at her, although perhaps that was for the best.

Isabella pulled some damp rags from the pile at her feet and started to dab at the cloth-covered seat. She hardly dared look at Mrs. Wattington's skirts. They were more than dabbled with sour-milk baby spit-up. They would smell for days, even with a proper cleaning. Did she dare try to clean the sodden dress?

The decision was taken from her. Mrs. Wattington rapped hard on the roof and the carriage stopped.

"Out." The woman's command was clear. Isabella was obviously not needed if Joey was asleep. She stepped out, and Mrs. Wattington's personal maid replaced her.

The fresh air was wonderful and Isabella tried to hide her relief as she climbed up on the box beside the driver. He stared at her cheek for a moment before starting the team. She could only wonder how red it glowed from the slap.

She'd never been struck before, not by her older and very strict brother, not by any of her previous employers, not even by Foxworthy—and she'd killed him for what he'd tried to do to her. She wished she could say that to Mrs. Wattington. Picturing the woman's face as Isabella said the words was almost worth the slap.

Of course she could never say such a thing—not that she'd really have meant it. What had happened with Foxworthy had been an accident.

Again she forced the picture of him lying on the floor from her mind, forced herself not to think of the men who now chased her, who threatened her.

Staying with Mrs. Wattington was fast becoming even more of an impossibility. She'd never known of an employer to become kinder over time. One bad thing always led to another.

Which left Mark. The time they had actually spent together could be measured in hours, not days, but she felt as if she'd known him her entire life.

She could even imagine marrying him, being his wife—and wouldn't that be the answer to her problems. She could marry him and disappear, become a proper matron far from those who sought her.

There would be no need to flee, no need to leave him. She would simply become someone else.

When she'd first had the barest thought of the possibility flit at the edge of her mind last night she'd dismissed it, but it kept coming back, growing.

If they were so happy together after less than a week, think how happy they would be after months, after years.

Only they didn't have years, or months, or even weeks. They only had now.

They had no time for anything.

Unless she risked it all.

Could she do it?

She was convinced he would want to marry her if only they had time—but they didn't. She would need to persuade him—fast.

They were made to be together. Everything she knew about him drew her, even if she didn't know that much.

They belonged together.

Swallowing, she put the thought into words.

She wanted to marry Mark.

Now all she needed was to do what was necessary.

She'd watched her older sister charm enough men to know how it was done, to know how much a glance from under lowered lashes could do, how the simple sway of a hip or brush of a breast could entice beyond reason.

It was the only way.

It was a great gamble.

How much risk was she willing to take? Her hand stroked her swollen cheek as she looked out over the fields they sped by, the carriage racing toward London.

She was almost sure that Mark would wed her if they made love.

But almost was only almost.

Was she going to come? Mark stood on an almost identical set of steps to the ones where he'd first kissed her, and stared into the twilight. This inn could have been built on the same plan as that one, heavy stone walls on an all-too-squat square frame, shutters half closed with peeling paint, thirty paces to the stable—dry now, but probably terribly muddy in the spring. The straw had been fresher at the last place. That he knew.

Damnation.

What was he going to do about her? He couldn't keep acting like a courting boy. Even if he kept his needs in check she'd head off in her own direction once they reached London and then what would he have accomplished?

Did he need to accomplish anything more than a few stolen kisses?

Should he not just look at this as a couple of days of foolishness? He'd amused himself while he traveled and that was surely an accomplishment in itself. The only thing lost was a few extra days in Town before the coronation. The king might not be pleased, but he also might not even notice. What was one duke more or less? It wasn't like they were even acquainted.

Double damnation.

He knew better. King George would be very aware that his newest duke was missing. The note that Mark had received from the king made it clear that he was expected to be there. The king made no allowance for Mark's mourning period and he certainly wouldn't so that Mark could have a few days of flirtation along the road.

A few days of flirtation, a little play, that was all he wanted.

Wasn't it?

Isabella rubbed again at the red mark across her cheek, succeeding only in making it redder. The sting of the blow still caused her hand to shake. She dipped a cloth in cold water and held it to her skin, hoping the mark would fade.

Pressing the cloth tighter she tried not to think, not to remember.

She would forget the whole day if she could, Joey's illness, the slap, and Mrs. Wattington's quiet fury, the constant threat from her pursuers. No. She was not going to dwell on things she could not change.

Mark was the only answer.

She tried to focus on the kisses of the night before, to remember the pleasure of that moment, the anticipation. It had been a moment full of danger for her, the danger of discovery, but when she was with Mark it seemed unimportant. She trusted he would keep her safe. It might be naïve. In fact she was sure it was, but she could not shake the feeling.

He clearly wanted her. Those kisses and the physical reactions of his body were very clear.

She pulled the cloth away from her cheek. It could go either way right now, either fade completely or turn to purple and yellow.

It was redder than ever.

She had prayed for fading. Too often she'd seen the victim held responsible for her own misfortune.

And it was hard to imagine trying to seduce Mark when her face was swollen and red.

Glancing out the dark window, she made her decision.

It was now or never.

Mark heard a rustle behind him. She was here.

He turned as she eased out of the half-open door. "I am sorry I am late. Joey didn't want to settle and I didn't dare leave until he did. I'll need to go back shortly. He's not feeling well and the scullery maid who agreed to sit with him is very young. I've told her to find me quickly if there is any trouble. I wouldn't have come at all except that I didn't want you to worry."

She kept her face turned from him the whole time, almost as if she were looking back into the inn.

"What's upset you? You don't seem quite yourself."

Her shoulders drew back, tight, and then she gave herself a little shake. "It will sound silly, but I've been certain that something awful is about to happen. Rather like that chill you get when somebody is supposed to have walked across your grave."

Mark knew that feeling well. He also knew that it was accurate far more often than one might suppose. "Do you think Mrs. Wattington suspects us? Is there something else that you worry about?" If Mrs. Wattington knew, he would need to protect Isabella even if it meant telling her the truth, losing her forever. Once she knew his station, then he would be the duke and she only the maid. Everything would change.

Isabella glanced at him quickly and then turned away, her posture still. She was clearly considering his words with care. "No, I don't think she knows. I would know if she did. She is not a subtle woman. If she suspected she would not hide it. This is more like the feeling when you catch a movement out of the corner of your eye, but when you turn you can't see anything. I am probably just imagining it."

"Then why does it have you so upset? Why won't you look at me? What aren't you telling me? Have I done something? Are you worried about our kiss? Worried I'll want more? Of course I want more, but I would never push."

"No, it's not that." She still didn't look directly at him. Instead she walked past him into the shadows of the yard.

He turned and followed her. Even when she wasn't carrying Joey her hips had a delicious sway.

She stopped in the middle of the yard and turned her face up to the sky. She twirled once, her skirts billowing wide.

"What are you doing?" he asked.

"Remembering."

"What?"

Stopping, she turned to him, her face hidden in the dark. "A few years ago, when I ran away, I went through a great unpleasantness. I felt that everything was going wrong. It seemed that things only got worse. My life was not at all what I had wanted and I believed I was truly trapped. I felt like I would pay forever for the mistakes that I had made."

"I've had days like that—weeks like that."

"And then one day I looked out the window at the falling snow, big fat, heavy flakes. They were so beautiful and the world looked so new. I felt like I could begin again. It might not be the life I had planned, but it would be as good a life as I could make it. I promised that I would take joy in every minute that I could. But more than that I promised to remember that every minute is fresh, different than the one before. There is always a chance to start again. Indeed we have no choice but to start again every minute of every day. I look up at the moon now and remember that nobody has ever seen it look just the way it does at this moment."

"I've never thought about that. But what has you feeling the need to remember that right now?"

"Do feelings need reasons?" She started to step away.

Damnation. He reached out and caught her beneath the chin. "Who did that to you?"

It was easy to guess the answer. Something caught in his chest as he examined the deep purple mark marring one cheek. He didn't know whether to pull her to his chest or to go and find whoever had hit her and pound him into the ground.

She blinked and he knew she debated what to say, that she wanted to deny the bruise that marked her cheek, to pretend it did not exist.

"What does it matter? It is nothing. A bruise is a tiny thing in this world."

He took her hand and pulled her back toward the

inn. "Come, let me see it in the light. It does not look a little thing to me."

Trying to stop, she dug her heels in. "No, it is nothing."

"Then come and let me see." He paused as they reached the door. "Nobody will see us, if that is what worries you. Everybody is down in the taproom. Come."

Her lips were pulled tight, but she allowed him to lead her up the stairs and through the door.

She stopped as they crossed the threshold and stared about. "This must be the best room in the inn."

"I imagine it is."

"Then it must be the duke's room. I can't imagine he's in the taproom." She started to pull back through the door. "I'll go back and check on Joey. I can put another cool cloth on my cheek. There really is nothing for you to be concerned about."

"Don't worry about the duke. He's not of concern right now." And oh, how he meant that. Nothing mattered except Isabella and the fact that somebody had dared to hit her.

"How can you say that? This is his room. We could be discovered at any moment."

Mark wished he could explain that he'd sent all the servants away an hour earlier, saying he wished to be alone. He'd done that each night since meeting Isabella, and while they might still find it strange, they no longer found it surprising that His Grace wished to put himself to bed. He had not been disturbed once in the past week. It seemed unlikely that he would be tonight. "Come, let me light another candle and look at that."

She started to speak, but then her shoulders sagged

and she came toward the table obediently. He lit an extra candle and stared at her cheek. It was starting to yellow just across the top of the bone.

He ran a finger over it softly.

She cringed at the contact.

"Tell me what happened. And don't lie. I will know if you do," he commanded, like the duke that he was.

"I don't see how." She sounded like a belligerent child. "Mrs. Wattington did it. I don't think she meant to, though."

He had been right. "I fail to see how she did that by mistake. I can almost see the fingerprints. Do not even try to tell me that the carriage hit a bump or came to a sudden stop." He remembered the fury with which Mrs. Wattington had gripped the maid's collar. Isabella could not continue to work for such a woman. It was unthinkable.

Turning to stare directly at him, she reached up and placed a hand over his where it rested against her cheek. "No, she hit me, but I think it was more instinct than intent. Joey spit up all over her quite suddenly and she just swung. I should have been more careful, positioned him better."

"You do not believe that." His own fury was growing.

She pulled in a long, slow breath, her breasts rising against the ruffle of her gown. "No. She meant to hit me. She was mad to have her dress ruined, but I truly think she did it without thought. She would never want to leave a bruise that could be remarked on. I do not believe she would find it ladylike."

"That I do believe." He remembered the look Mrs. Wattington had turned on him before realizing who he was.

Isabella squeezed his fingers. "It really is nothing. It will fade by morning."

"I doubt that. I think it much more likely you will be purple and yellow for a week." He had to find a way to protect her, to remove her from this life she was living. He had to show her that he could protect her.

"Don't say that." She tried to step away, but he held her cheek still.

They stared at each other for a moment. He moved slowly, giving her ample time to step away. His hand slid down her face to tilt her chin up. Her soft breath lightly caressed his face.

He could feel her eyes drop to his lips and back. They were caught again in that magic moment before—

—and then it was during. His lips skimmed hers, hardly more than the brush of a butterfly's wing.

She should not be doing this. It was too soon. She needed to be sure he would care for her afterward. Her plan had not been for—well, it had been—but she'd imagined that they'd talk first, that she'd have more time to decide, to be sure.

Did she know what she was doing?

Did it matter?

She leaned closer.

This was part of her plan—seduction. How would she get him to marry her, to take her away from London and to safety if she didn't ply her feminine wiles? Only—her reasons for kissing him had little to do with her future and much to do with her present desires, her desire to touch him, feel him, know him.

Pressing her lips tightly against his, she brought

her hands up to his neck, stroked, buried them in his hair. He felt so good, made her feel so secure. When Mark touched her it seemed the world would be right, that all her fears, all her mistakes were meaningless.

He tasted of tobacco and brandy—sweet and smoky.

She'd forgotten how magic his kiss could be, how it could fill one with wonder and passion, peace and anticipation.

She ran her tongue along the opening of his mouth, impatient for more. She pulled him closer, moved herself until her breasts were pressed tight against him. For the first time in years she longed for a ball gown, for something low and thin, something that would cover and entice all in the same moment.

His hands were on her waist now, lifting her to her toes, bringing their months into perfect alignment.

She could have kissed him forever, letting the passion and momentum grow second by second. The sweep of a tongue here. The gentle nip of teeth. The dance and play, every action inviting a response. This was no possession but a master fencing duel. Each sought control, but each enjoyed the game too much to want to win.

She sighed into his mouth.

Then she felt his hand upon her breast—and froze. She forced herself to relax but it was too late.

He was pulling back, staring at her, his eyes full of consideration.

Oh, she loved that look—loved him.

Could she possibly love him this quickly?

It would explain her sudden desire for marriage as well as safety. Never since fleeing from London had she even considered the possibility. Marriage . . . after

Foxworthy it should have been a frightening thought, but with Mark she could think of little else.

It would grant her freedom and safety. Who would ever imagine that Miss Isabella Masters would become Mrs. Smythe, estate agent's wife? And surely once married she could just stay at his home in—well, she didn't actually know where his house was, but it must be somewhere near Strattington's main estate.

Now the only task was to make sure that he wanted her—forever.

She let her lower lip plump out, and leaned toward him.

Chapter 10

Mark stared down at her passion-darkened eyes. Whenever he believed he had seen her at her best she surprised him. The more he came to know her, the more beautiful she became. He could not remember ever seeing a sunset as beautiful as her kiss-swollen lips and flushed cheeks—but it was those eyes, shining blue around deepest black, that moved him, that spoke to some part of him he had not known he had.

Even the deepening bruise did not detract from her beauty—although it did spur him on.

He needed to persuade her to trust him, to let him take care of her. She could not stay with Mrs. Wattington. She needed to be with him.

He needed her to be with him.

She leaned closer to him, her mouth quivering, and his gaze dropped. It was hard to see anything beyond her need—and his own.

There was no way he could resist her. He had been fooling himself.

She was meant to be his.

He should have realized it before.

There was one way he could assure her safety, wipe the worry from her eyes, take care of her.

He would make her his mistress, support her as she

deserved, love her as she deserved, filling all her nights with passion and her mornings also. He would cover her in diamonds and emeralds, parade her before his friends. He would care for her as no woman had ever been cared for.

A duke should have a mistress.

He didn't know why he hadn't thought of it before.

Glancing farther down, he stared at her breasts, heaving beneath the heavy linen of her gown. He would be sure she was always dressed in something thin and low-cut, no more servant's attire for her.

The blue of her eyes drew his attention back. Maybe sapphires. He'd been thinking emeralds because of her hair, but with her eyes it should be sapphires, large sapphires.

He should tell her the truth. He could not take her if she did not know—only he wanted her to want him as a man, not a duke. If he told her how would he ever know that she had chosen him and not the duke?

He wouldn't.

He leaned closer. "You do know that I'll care for you, take care of you always, don't you?" he said as he drew his finger across her collarbones just above the neckline of her dress.

He would care for her always. The words filled Isabella with a far different warmth than the heat his fingers evoked. Her few doubts dissolved like a morning mist. He cared for her.

It should not be hard to move him from caring to marriage—marriage and safety.

Her plans slowly formed again, fighting against the passion that filled her.

She looked up into his mink brown eyes and let

her dreams evolve. She lowered her gaze to his lips, lifted it back to his eyes, watched his own gaze follow. There was such power in desire.

Her thoughts of love a moment ago no longer seemed so improbable. She'd been ready to dismiss them as mere physical attraction, the desire to be held by a handsome man after all these years. Now, with a few words, her world changed.

Marriage.

A home.

A family.

He cared for her—was that a man's way of saying *love*?

She leaned back toward him and kissed him with all the passion of which she was capable. Her lips pressed hard, her breasts even tighter. Her whole body was one big tingle, one large ache needing to find release. She moved her lips over his, devouring, wanting, seeking—finding.

His tongue met hers, tangled with hers, pushed its way back into her mouth. She felt his desire to take over and fought back. She ran her hands beneath his coat, slipped them over his shoulders, ran them down across his chest, let them find their way between the buttons of his shirt, reveled in the silk of his skin. The desire to taste that flesh, to know his scent, his being, became almost uncontrollable.

Her fingers moved faster, but she could not give up his mouth. That intimacy was greater than any she had ever known.

This seduction thing was much easier than she had ever imagined.

His breath grew still each time her fingers moved; she could feel her power over him.

How daring could she be?

She slipped the first button loose.

And then the second. The third.

Her fingers moved ever lower and his breath grew ever shallower.

His lips moved then, down her chin to that most delicate spot where neck begins. She'd never noticed that spot before, never even considered that it existed. But now, as his lips explored it, she felt as if her whole being centered there on that wonderfully sensitive bend of skin and bone.

She didn't know how she continued to breathe. Her dress was tight about her, her breasts pressing against the constricting fabric, her nipples rubbing with near irritation.

And then there was freedom. She felt her dress slip, without even being aware that his hands had been at her ties. Some small part of her brain sought to protest, but it was a very tiny bit. Far greater was the longing, the desire.

This was what she wanted. This was what would get her what she needed.

She ran her fingers up his chest, over his shirt, deep into the silky glory of his hair. She pulled his face back, wanting to see, to know.

She sought answers.

What she found was passion.

His eyes were dark, and full of desire. His lips swollen from her kisses.

"You are so beautiful," he murmured. His gaze dropped low and her own glance followed.

She gasped. Her dress hung about her waist, her corset pushed down, one strap hanging off her shoulder, so that only her chemise covered her. If it could be called coverage.

Her nipples were sharp points, thrusting hard against the thin white fabric, their dark rose hue clearly visible.

She should have been shocked.

And she was. But the shock was that she saw herself as he saw her, saw the beauty, saw the glory.

She glanced up and met his gaze again. Holding her gaze in his, he reached out and ran a finger over the upward thrust of one nipple.

The sensation of that barest touch was unbelievable, the rasp of the fabric making her whole body jerk.

She saw the slight movement of his mouth at her response, felt his pleasure in hers.

He pinched her then, catching the peak between finger and thumb, squeezing with tormenting slowness.

She was going to die. There could be no other outcome to such pleasure, no other ending to the need that filled her.

She wanted to run, to scream, to do something to release all that grew within her.

But all she could do was watch, watch his eyes as his fingers moved. She would have thought his glance would be on her breast, on what he did, but he kept his gaze on hers, catching every piece of her response.

And then. . .

Then he bent his head, still holding her eye, and brought his lips toward the nipple he so tortured. She watched as he drew in a deep breath—and then blew. Then his mouth was on her, wetting the fabric, grinding it against her. He sucked. He laved. He twirled his tongue about her. He owned her.

And still he watched her face, watched her reaction, her passion.

He drew back and she almost cried, almost begged.

He smiled. He knew her thoughts. Not all the power was hers.

And then he moved to her other breast.

His tongue once again wetting, moving, laving.

She found her own hand rising to the other, now neglected breast. His gaze finally dropped from hers, his full attention caught by her fingers as they caressed her own breast, tugged at her own nipple.

His hands came up to her shoulders, slipped beneath the fine linen of her chemise, pushed it down in one quick movement.

She heard a rip, but it did not matter.

All that mattered was the look in his eyes as he gazed down at her naked breasts.

God, she was beautiful.

He thought again of telling her. It seemed wrong not to, but—but how could he take the risk that she would look at him differently? All that mattered was the warm passion in her eyes. He could see her insecurities, her innocence, her trust.

Damn it.

He had to tell her. How could he not tell her when she looked at him as if he were her whole world, as if she would believe anything he said? He could not betray that look.

"Isabella, my Bella, there is something I must tell you."

It took a moment for her eyes to focus, for his

words to be understood. She smiled, slowly, from under lowered lashes. "You've never called me by name before—Mark." She breathed his name as if it were a sacred word.

This should not be so hard. She would be thrilled to learn his position, to know that he truly could take care of her, to understand that she need never worry again. He could live with not knowing if it was Mark she wanted, not the duke. He would do what was right. "Isabella." He said her name again. "There is something you really must know."

"What could I need to know now?" Her eyes clouded and she crossed her arms across her breasts, those magnificent breasts. "You don't have a disease, do you? I've heard whisper of such things. Is that why you thought I needed to cover your—your cock when we first met?" A shiver shook her.

"You do not need to fear. I have never had such problems. I have always been careful."

She did not look fully convinced.

"Ah Isabella, you do amuse me, make me happy. But I assure you I need no covering—not there."

She wrapped her arms tighter. A shiver shook her again.

The air was warm. There was no need for her to feel chilled, although he could feel shivers coming on himself.

"Do you doubt me? Do you wish to examine me for pox?"

"No." Clearly the question startled her. "I am just a little shy. It is all so real suddenly."

He reached out and laid his hands over hers, squeezing them gently, and then drawing them down. "You are beautiful. You should never feel the need to hide yourself from me. I wish I could put it to words how I feel when I look at you. You make me believe in God and all his plans. The perfection of your breasts could not exist except by design."

She blushed. The sheer rosy pink spread up over her chest and neck until it highlighted her cheeks.

"I think that's blasphemous," she whispered.

"I am sure some would find it so. But how can relishing beauty be wrong?"

She grew even redder and tried again to cover her breasts.

He looked down deliberately, let himself stare. He took in every detail, every freckle, every shade of cream and pink. Then he looked up and met her gaze evenly. "Does this feel wrong?"

Chewing on her lower lip, she looked unsure. "It feels strange, certainly. I am not sure about wrong. Can something that feels so good not be wrong?"

He chuckled. "Why the assumption that what feels good is wrong? You strike me as a woman who takes the time to relish the little moments in life. Can you not equally appreciate the—the bigger moments?"

"I don't know. I've never been in this position before."

"That is very clear."

He had to stop teasing her or she was going to be redder than the ripest tomato.

Her hands pulled loose from his and he went to grab them again, but instead of covering her breasts she lifted them from underneath, raising them toward him like an offering.

"I understand so little of this," she said. "I've never before understood what it is about breasts that drive men wild. I still can't say that I understand." She moved one thumb, flicking it across the nipple. Her gaze never left his. "I must say I do like it, though."

He was going to explode, right here, right now, like a schoolboy caught in a dream. He was going to explode. He'd seen plenty of women, been seduced by the best. But he could never remember anything as erotic as her hesitant voice as she whispered those words, as her fingers moved over herself, as her eyes grew large at each sensation she aroused.

"I do love when you look at me like that," she continued. "You do make me feel we truly will be together always."

Always. The word gave him pause even as the slow movement of her fingers over her plump flesh drew him on.

She'd never felt like this before. They were such simple words and did not begin to encompass all that she felt. There was such strength in this moment. He would do anything for her, anything to keep her fingers moving, to keep her eyes on his, to keep open the moments that were to come. No man had ever looked at her like this—like he wanted to devour her and treasure her in the same instant.

For the first time she understood why her sister, Violet, had taken lovers. A woman could surely grow addicted to this, to the power of desire.

Desire. She'd been warned about it since she was in short skirts and never understood its danger. Now it surrounded her, almost physical. His desire for her—and hers for him.

His kisses had not been enough, a lifetime of them would not be enough. His touch had not been enough. When his hands had moved upon her breasts, when his lips had suckled at them, it had been the most amazing feeling. And yet it was not enough.

There was something more. She could see it in his gaze, feel it in the ache that began between her legs and rose, filling her.

She knew the basic mechanics of the situation. His piece fit into hers. She even knew about what his looked like. Several of the maids had owned dirty drawings, and of course she'd seen Joey's and several other young boys' over the last years. She had a feeling, though, that was not what she would be dealing with. Violet had books—books she was not supposed to look at. But she could not believe that this would be like that. Surely much of what she'd peeked at was impossible.

But this was more than mechanics. This was emotion—and commitment. He'd said he would care for her—did care for her.

That was not the same as proposing marriage, but she knew men were slow at such things. What came out of their mouths was rarely the same as what went on in their minds. Normally the words were meant to persuade, to reassure, while their minds ran far in the other direction.

Any woman in service knew the difference between what a man promised and what he delivered. She'd seen far too many maids promised everything by a man who disappeared or pretended to forget as soon as the event was over.

The event.

She was going to do that, here, now.

Her gaze left Mark's and flitted across the duke's parlor. It was not a grand room, the furnishings hardy and well used. But it was far finer than she'd known for years.

There was no bed. Did they need a bed? Did she want to do this without a bed?

It suddenly seemed tawdry.

She was thinking too much.

And then she met his gaze again. The desire was there. The need was there. But there was more. There was that— Oh, she didn't know a word for what she saw. She wanted to say *love*, but she was not so foolish. But there was something.

"You seem nervous." His voice was raspy.

"Yes."

He reached out and trailed a finger over the curve of her breast, not touching the peak, but outlining it. He swallowed, hard, as he touched her. "We don't have to do this. I promised I would be content with kisses."

"You want more, though. You want this."

He smiled at her words, his glance filled with irony. "I am a man. There is not a man alive who would not want you, as you look now, your lips swollen with kisses, your breasts tight from my touch, your hair mussed about your shoulders—and—"

"And what?" What more could he have to say? His every word convinced her more and more.

"And the innocence that shines from you, your uncertainty, your need to be kissed until you are blind with desire, kissed until you cannot think the thoughts I see spinning through your mind, the knowledge that every experience, every move, every feeling will be the first that you have felt. You drive a man to do things that he should not. Gads, I am not a man for fine words, and listen to me. You bewitch me, Isabella. You have from the first moment I heard your voice, saw your face."

All she could do was stare at him. Her hands were still on her breasts. She knew her mouth gaped open. How could she resist such honesty? This was a man who held nothing back from her.

This was the man she would marry. She didn't care if he could provide for her—although he did promise to—and she rather thought he could.

All she cared was that she had him.

He was a man she could trust.

She reached out and placed a hand on each of his shoulders, drawing him toward her.

Chapter 11

What was he waiting for? Mark was not a fool. No man would refuse what she offered. Far better to explain things later. Then it would be impossible for there to be any misunderstandings between them.

She would be his, would have to let him care for her. There would be no chance that she would stay with Mrs. Wattington.

And besides, no rational woman could be upset that he was a duke. She would be pleased.

He knew he was justifying his own actions, that he was finding an excuse to do what he wanted, but there was no way he could resist her, no way he could risk losing her, losing this.

He leaned into her embrace, letting her pull him tight. His lips found hers, felt them open beneath him, her tongue as eager as his. He forced his hands to the back of her waist, not allowing them to go where they wished. She might be eager, but he would keep this slow, keep her with him every step of the way.

And he would allow her to stop—this must be her choice as well as his.

She was not so controlled. Her fingers tangled in his hair, seeking to draw him closer than was physically possible.

He ran his hands down her backside, cupping her buttocks and lifting her until her legs separated, bending up to wrap around his waist. A simple shift of hip and she was where he wanted, positioned over him, only layers of fabric separating them.

She drew back, her eyes wide. Staring at him she shifted, feeling him with her body, her mind trying to comprehend. She swallowed, but did not pull farther away. She moved again, experimenting. Her hands slipped down his neck and came to clasp tight about his shoulders. She leaned back, pushing the apex of her thighs farther against him.

He gasped as she rubbed herself against his full length.

She smiled her delight at his response.

He longed to pull her to him again, to kiss that mischievous smile, but his hands were holding her to him. Glancing about the room he spotted the table and stepped toward it.

Her mouth opened at the bump and grind of the step. A light laugh escaped her.

How could such passion be such fun? He'd never before felt this mix of need and joy, delight.

Reaching the table, he settled her upon it. She glanced back, startled, and then dropped her hands from his shoulders, bracing them behind her.

He slid his hands down her hips and legs until he reached her slender ankles. He started to slide his hands back up, inside her skirts. Someday soon he would cover her legs in silk instead of coarsely knitted wool. He closed his eyes and for a moment saw her only in those fine silk stockings and rosetted garters. Pulling in a deep breath he opened his eyes again. The reality of her was so perfect he had no need for fantasy.

He slid his fingers upward, past her knees, up to her thighs. He was close, so close. His body throbbed with urgency, while his mind cautioned patience.

"Stop." Her single word held him.

She couldn't mean it. But he had promised himself he would not push past her desires.

His fingers stilled, but only with the greatest of efforts.

"You want me to stop? I thought you wanted this."

The smile she gave him then revealed a far greater understanding than he would have believed. She might not know the act, but she certainly knew how to be a woman. "Yes, I want you to stop. Just be still."

He obeyed, waiting.

"I want to feel you first. You mentioned I could examine—examine it."

"What?" His heart missed a beat.

"I don't want this hurried, rushed. If I am going to do this I want to know it all." She leaned forward and traced a single finger down the front of his breeches.

It was a gesture full of seduction, of temptation, but more than that—he looked in her face and saw . . . curiosity.

She was caught in passion, filled with it, but she wanted knowledge. He swallowed. Straight seduction he could have handled, but this?

"Stop." It was his turn to say the word.

"Am I doing something wrong?" Her hand pulled back and her eyes mirrored uncertainty.

"No, I just need a minute or neither of us will be happy with the outcome." He drew in a deep breath and counted slowly to himself, then he reached out and took her small hand within his own, squeezed it once in reassurance, and brought it back to its original position.

He gasped as her hand traced his length. Her eyes were wide. Her gaze met his and then moved lower. Her fingers moved back and forth, outlining him.

He was going to die. Or else he already had. The sensations she sent through him were beyond words.

And the look on her face.

Her fingers suddenly moved up to his waistband, catching at one of the buttons of his fall. Her glance came back to his. She chewed on her lower lip and then slipped the button free and then the next. He could almost feel her caution and her inquisitiveness.

He took the opportunity to draw in another breath. He could not be sure he had breathed the whole time she had touched him.

And then her fingers were beneath the fabric, stroking his length.

"Your skin is so soft. I didn't expect that."

He couldn't say a word, couldn't do more than swallow as she ran her hand over him again, her fingers pausing to figure out his shape, to understand the movement of his skin over the hard strength beneath.

When her fingers wrapped all about him a tiny cry leaked through his lips.

Her mouth formed an O and then she ran her hand up him again, a grin growing as he jerked in response.

The smile that formed across her lips spoke of innate seduction. She might not know what she was doing, but she knew she did it well.

She leaned forward so that her other arm was free. She quickly worked at the remainder of the buttons until he was bare before her.

She gulped, glanced up at him and then back down.

"I didn't believe the pictures. I should have."

Not knowing what to make of that he put it aside for later—much later.

She moved her hand again, watched his body clench in response.

That was enough. He reached forward and caught her hand, stilling it. "My turn."

Placing a hand on each of her thighs he pushed her skirt up, inch by inch. Her arms dropped behind her again as she leaned back.

Her muscles were tight and he sensed that not all of it was anticipation. He slowed his movements yet again. Bending forward he blew softly on her bare breasts. Playing a little longer would have its own rewards.

He opened his mouth, caught her nipple between his teeth, felt her squirm and cry out under her breath. "I can't wait until we can do this every night, every day, until we are wed."

His jaw tensed, almost bit hard. He had not heard that. Had she really said that? Could it have been his imagination?

All he could feel was shock—and then greater shock as after only the slightest of taps the door to the hall swung open wide.

She felt his body tense. He pulled back, his face still.

She couldn't believe she had said that. She refused to—and then—scratch. Tap.

The slight noise drew her gaze from Mark's face. She glanced over his shoulder and clenched in horror as the door pushed open. An unknown maid walked in, a large snifter of brandy in hand. The maid pulled up short at the sight of them, her face paling. "They said you were out," she murmured as she began to back out of the room.

Isabella shut her eyes tight, prayed that when she opened them she would not be sitting on a table half naked, staring at an open door. Squeezing her eyes as tightly as she could, she formed the picture she wanted to see when she opened them again. One. Two. Three.

She should have been more specific in her wish.

She was not staring at an open door. Now she was staring at not only the chambermaid but at the maid who had been watching Joey, and behind her—behind her was Mrs. Wattington.

Isabella's whole body went cold. It felt as if ice had formed in her veins. She wasn't sure she'd ever be able to move again as each muscle in turn froze solid.

Joey's thin wail pierced the air. He sounded as desolate as she felt.

It was Mark who moved her legs together, brushed her skirts down over them, and turned to stand in front of her, blocking her fully from view. She could only hope he'd somehow managed to fasten his breeches. She didn't know whether to laugh or cry at the thought of him standing exposed before Mrs. Wattington.

There was silence.

It was a second that seemed to last for an eternity.

Isabella waited for Mrs. Wattington to say something. She always had something to say. Why silence now?

Mrs. Wattington's gaze was not on Isabella, however. It was firmly set on Mark. Isabella could only pray again that he had fastened himself up.

Mrs. Wattington pursed her lips so tight that Isabella was sure they would fuse. Stepping into the room, she started to say something and then stopped. She stepped back for no reason that Isabella could understand, her delicate pink complexion growing white.

Finally she spoke, addressing Isabella. "Joey has awakened unwell. My maid fetched me when you could not be found. See to him, then attend to me in my chamber." She nodded to Mark with utmost and unexpected politeness and left the room.

The maid stared for another moment and then turned and fled.

Mark stalked to the door and slammed it shut. He stood facing it for a moment and Isabella could feel him try to gather himself. He turned slowly, examined her more closely.

"I am sorry. That was my fault. I should have locked the door. It never occurred to me that anybody would enter without being bidden. Do you want me to have the girl dismissed?"

"Oh no. That would never do. She was only doing her job." Isabella thought that one dismissal for the day was enough. She had no doubt what would occur when she went to Mrs. Wattington's room. She was only surprised that she would be allowed near Joey first.

Joey. She would focus on Joey, allow him to be the only thing she thought about

"I must check on Joey. I do hope he is not ill. It would be so dreadful if he were sick here, so far from home." She slid from the table and tried to pull up her corset and bodice.

"And, of course, the first thing you think of is Joey, not yourself. Oh, come here. Let me take care of that." Mark pulled her over and fastened her bodice with great skill and speed. She did not wish to consider where he had picked up such mastery.

"Thinking of myself would serve no purpose. What is done is done." She stepped back from him and smoothed down her skirts. If she just kept moving she would not have to think. If she did not think she did not have to accept that any of this was real.

He caught her as she started to move toward the door, his lean fingers caressing her cheek. "I will make this right, Isabella. We will talk later—reach an understanding."

The door closed behind Isabella with a light click.

Mark walked to the window and stared out into the darkness. He'd been a fool. Had she really mentioned marriage? Even now he was not sure, his mind so blurred by the aftermath.

It had been wrong to seduce her, no matter how willing she'd been. It had been even worse allowing them to be caught. He'd been practicing seduction for over fifteen years now and had never come close to being caught. Well, there had been one time in Lord Besley's library, but the lady involved had made it very clear that the risk was part of the thrill for her.

He was trying to distract himself.

He had created this situation—or had he? Could she have planned it, arranged for them to be caught, attempted to force his hand? He considered—and rejected. No, she had been as shocked as he was, perhaps more so, by the intrusion. And it would not have fit with what he knew of her character.

Bloody hell, harming Isabella had never been part of his plan, not that he'd had much of a plan. There were enough shadows in Isabella's eyes without his adding to them.

Why had he ever brought her to his rooms? He could have examined her cheek somewhere else. And why had he bloody well not locked the door? He hadn't even bothered to take her to the bedchamber. If they'd been in there he would have heard the door open. The bloody maid would probably have just left the brandy on the table, for that matter. It wasn't like the bloody bed needed to be warmed at this time of year. Bloody, bloody, bloody hell.

Pressing his face against the glass he wished it was as cold as a December day. He needed something to clear his wits and tell him what to do.

Oh, he knew what to do. It was what he'd wanted to do anyway. He'd set Isabella up as his mistress. He'd promised to take care of her and he would.

He couldn't even pretend it would be a hardship.

He'd wanted her to have a choice. He'd wanted to be her choice, or at least he told himself he had.

He pulled back to look at his face reflected in the dark glass. If he'd truly wanted to give her a choice, wanted to put her first, he would have told her everything before. He hadn't wanted her to have a choice. He'd just wanted her to think that she did. He hadn't been willing to take the risk—and now all might be lost.

Had she really mentioned marriage? Would she ever forgive him if she had? Once she realized who he was, and she must have by now, she'd understand that marriage was impossible. She would be pleased by what he could offer her. What woman would not be? Every woman wanted beautiful gowns and sparkling jewels.

So why did his gut remain knotted? Why did he dread seeing her face now that he was the duke, not simple Mr. Smythe?

He put the thought away. Mrs. Wattington still needed to be dealt with. He walked toward the bedroom and considered which finery to don. If he was going to act the bloody duke he'd better dress like the bloody duke. And he had a certainty that the bloody duke was required for this interview.

Bloody, bloody hell.

Isabella paused outside Mrs. Wattington's door. Her hand was shaking and she refused to reveal even that much. Her chest hurt with the effort of holding her breath steady. At least Joey was fine.

All the boy had required was a new wrapping of dry cloths and a good cuddle and he'd been just as happy as could be, completely unaware of all the trouble he'd caused. She'd given him an extra hug and kiss as she left him, confident that it would be her last. Missing him would be just one more pain to add to her others.

There'd been the smallest of temptations to pretend that he was ill. Under those circumstances she was sure that Mrs. Wattington would keep her on until the crisis was past. That, however, would not have solved anything.

Looking down at her still quivering fingers, Isabella knocked and then hid them in her skirts.

Mrs. Wattington opened the door quickly. The shock of it caused Isabella to step back. Mrs. Wattington never opened the door. She always called for Isabella to enter—unless she'd been expecting someone else.

Isabella stepped into the room, keeping her eyes firmly fixed on the floor.

"You think you're the smart one, don't you?" Mrs.

Wattington snapped before Isabella was even over the threshold.

The smart one? Isabella had spent the last hour thinking what an idiot she was, wondering how she could have risked it all for so little.

Awkward silence continued for a moment and Isabella realized that Mrs. Wattington expected an answer.

She raised her gaze to the height of Mrs. Wattington's hands. "No, ma'am. I don't feel very smart."

"Proud, then. I can't believe I let you near my dear, sweet Joey. I do hope you haven't corrupted him already." Mrs. Wattington's hands clenched tight, the knuckles white with stress.

The baby wasn't more than three months old! Isabella doubted her corrupting powers were anywhere near that powerful. And if she was so bad an influence, why had Mrs. Wattington sent her take care of him before coming to her? "I am sorry, ma'am."

Mrs. Wattington turned from her in a swirl of skirts. "If it weren't for His Grace I'd have had you out of here an hour ago. As it is, I can't believe he had the nerve to ask me to show kindness and understanding. What right does that man have? He obviously was not thinking clearly—didn't seem like a duke at all. I should have known better than to hire a girl of your age—too young by far. Only got one thing on the mind, you do. I knew I should have taken someone with more experience. If only my dear Henry hadn't persuaded me you'd be a good companion. I'd heard from my maid that you'd been seen out with a man, an attractive man—but this, I never dreamed of this. You probably had this planned from the start."

His Grace had intervened? Mark and the duke must

be closer than he'd let on. Isabella sincerely doubted she was more than a year younger than Mrs. Wattington. And as for planning it from the start—yes, her whole goal had been to be caught with a groom in the duke's chamber of an inn far too close to London. This was exactly what she had wanted. She had to bite her tongue until she tasted blood to keep from spitting out the remarks.

"I am sorry, ma'am." She knew she was repeating herself.

Mrs. Wattington whirled again. "I don't know what His Grace expects me to do. I can't keep you. I certainly can't write you a reference. It's all fine for the man to say he'll take care of everything, but that doesn't tell me what to do."

He'll take care of everything. Those sounded like Mark's words. For a few moments after she'd left the room, Isabella had dreamed that he meant marriage. It was what she'd been brought up to expect. When a well-bred girl was caught in a compromising situation it meant only one thing—marriage. Of course she was no longer that fine young lady. The same rules did not apply to nursery maids as to daughters of the gentry.

"I will just have to let you go, no matter what he thinks or does. I don't see what else I can do. And for that matter I don't see what His Grace expects to do—at least not that he'd speak to me about. I can think of plenty of other things he'd have in mind. Although I can't imagine you'd still hold any appeal for him now that he's had you. Men lose interest very fast."

The woman was bitter. Isabella wasn't sure that it was because of her, or— Her mind suddenly caught up with Mrs. Wattington's words. "What do you mean His Grace has had me?"

"Oh don't be so coy. Had his pleasure on you. Tupped you. Do you really need me say more?"

"But—His Grace—Strattington—I never—"

"Don't be a cow. I saw you with my own eyes, as did half the inn. Are you really telling me that his breeches were down and your skirts were up so that he could put a cool cloth on your face?" Mrs. Wattington glared at Isabella's cheek. "That is what he claimed, by the way. He seemed to expect that just because he is a duke I'd pretend I hadn't seen what I saw, that I'd let you continue to care for my innocent Joey."

Isabella's belly filled with rocks, almost dragging her knees to the floor. A moment ago she hadn't believed this could get any worse. Now she knew better. "The duke, you say? Strattington himself?"

"You are clearly a wanton. I had no idea you were also an imbecile. Yes, Strattington. How many other dukes have had their way with you today?"

Isabella dropped her gaze to her feet. She wasn't sure if her mind was whirling like a child's top or frozen in place. "That was Strattington?"

"I do believe the shock must have dimmed your wits entirely. Now go. I expect you gone quickly—within the hour if possible. I will not pay for another night's lodgings. No matter what His Grace thinks there is nothing else to be done. It would be most unwise for you to try and talk to him. He will forget about you by dawn. I hope I am clear."

Isabella couldn't think at all. Her life had dissolved about her once before, but nothing could have prepared her for the cold that filled her now.

She couldn't look up at Mrs. Wattington as she left the chamber.

Chapter 12

Wages. She hadn't even asked for her wages. Not that Mrs. Wattington would have paid her anyway, but she should have asked. It would have been the sensible thing to do.

Sensible. Not that anything she'd done in the last day—the last week—could be described as sensible.

Isabella sat on her bag by the side of the road and waited. She didn't even know for what. Morning light was finally filling the sky, but it brought no joy. She'd just left the inn last night and started walking—walking into the darkness.

Her feet hurt, her legs also. She didn't know how far she had walked before the sun came up, but it could not have been far enough. The few coins in her bag weren't even enough to jingle. The innkeeper's wife had given her enough bread that she wouldn't starve, at least not today.

And now she couldn't move. She needed to go farther, but her feet seemed determined to stay put.

She'd heard of brave soldiers who after the battle was done were unable to move. That was how she felt now.

Mark was Strattington.

Her entire being hurt with that knowledge, immobilizing her. She had dreamed like a fool and once again the world had come to knock her back where she belonged.

It had been so naïve to let herself begin to believe that she might care for him, might love him. She had let herself believe because she wanted to, because it made everything so much easier—and this is what it got her. Nothing. Less than nothing.

Mark was Strattington. Why had he not told her? Had he been intent on seduction from the start? But wouldn't a duke have stood a better chance at persuading a companion and nursery maid than an—an estate manager?

Ashes. Her mouth tasted like ashes. She'd heard that expression once, but had never realized its truth. Even after Foxworthy died she had not known that lost dreams had a taste, a flat, bitter one.

Knowing that Mark was laughing at her, had never cared for her, certainly wouldn't marry her, was so painful that it felt like a silk cord cutting into her neck, cutting off her air.

No. Mark had never existed. He had been a creature only of her dreams, her wishes.

It was the duke who laughed, Strattington, if he thought of her at all. If she thought of Mark by his title it hurt less. She could live with the duke laughing at the trick he had played on her, cursing only that fate had interrupted his ultimate seduction.

That humiliation was part of why she had walked away from London, back the way they'd come. It would have been unbearable to have him pass her on the road, to know that he might laugh, if he even saw her at all.

But maybe he would stop, maybe he would call to

her to get in, take her sore feet upon his lap and. . .

She bit down on her lip as hard as she could. Had she learned nothing? Surely she was not still so naïve. She had to stop dreaming, dreaming was for the young and innocent. It had been a long time since she'd been either of those things.

The pounding of hooves sounded down the road, coming from the direction she had just trudged.

Mark was coming for her. Her heart missed a beat before her mind took over.

Mark wasn't coming. Mark didn't exist. Strattington would never come for her.

And a woman didn't need to be caught alone by the side of the road. She snatched up her bag and hustled over the fence and behind the hedge, ducking low as she went. She bent lower as two men on horseback came up the road at a fast trot—one of them wearing a blue jacket.

It was too late to flee.

She huddled lower, glad for the dull color of her dress. She wished she could fade into the low bushes. They paused on a low rise directly opposite her on the road. The one in the blue coat looked around.

"We must have missed her," he said to his companion. "She can't have come this far."

"Maybe the innkeeper was mistaken in her direction. I don't see why she should be heading back the way she came."

"I've been searching for Miss Masters for over a year now. I should have grabbed her the other day. I would have taken her sooner, but she was doing the work for me, heading to London. Masters will only pay if we actually produce the girl. Let's try another mile or two and then visit the nearby farms. She won't get away from me now." Blue Coat kicked his heels and was off. His companion followed.

Isabella stayed on the ground, her arms wrapped about her knees.

"What do you mean she's not here?" Mark questioned the innkeeper.

"She left sometime just after full dark. That is really all I know. I would suggest that you speak to Mrs. Wattington," the innkeeper replied, his brow coated with sweat.

"I will do just that." Mark turned and pounded up the stairs. He had been very specific last night in his talk with Mrs. Wattington. Nothing was to happen to Isabella until he'd had a chance to make his offer. He would be most displeased if his instructions had been disregarded.

He passed his own chamber and swept up another flight of stairs. Standing before Mrs. Wattington's door, he paused.

He had never felt as much the duke as he did at this moment. Displeasure, indeed. He swore his glance would freeze said lady where she stood. He raised his hand, dropped it, and strode more softly back down the stairs.

The duke did not pound. He sent someone else to do it for him.

It took the barest of moments to have Divers heading back to Mrs. Wattington's door. As he glanced about his own chamber, his eyes fell upon the table that had caused so much trouble. He set his chair beside it deliberately, moving all the other chairs to the side of the room.

He sat and waited.

There was a light tap on the door.

He waited. This time nobody would enter without his call.

The tap repeated and he bid his guest enter.

Mrs. Wattington entered the room, back stiff. "You wished to see me, Your Grace."

Mark stared at her, lifted one brow, made it clear she should have waited to be addressed. His uncle had always used a monocle at such a moment. He would have to have Divers procure one. "I have been told that Miss Smith has left the inn."

Mrs. Wattington raised her gaze to his face and then quickly dropped it again. "I believe that is correct, Your Grace."

"I thought I was quite specific that I wished her to remain."

"Yes, Your Grace."

"And did you not understand me?"

"I am sorry. She left on her own."

"So you did not dismiss her?"

Mrs. Wattington looked at him again. "What else was I to do? I could not let her continue to care for my innocent child."

"So you disobeyed me?" He rested an arm on the table, tapping his fingers slowly.

The woman did not answer for a moment. He could feel the consideration in her gaze. Finally she ventured, "You seemed quite emotional when you spoke. I believed you would have reconsidered by morning. A gentleman does not wish to be confronted by his mistakes. I thought it wise to remove her."

He stopped tapping. "You thought to choose for me how I would feel in the light of day? You trusted your own judgment over my very clear words?"

Mrs. Wattington swallowed, visibly. "I was merely trying to do what was best."

Mark stared back at her, letting his gaze wander from her toes to her hurriedly brushed hair. He made no bones that he found her wanting, somebody to be easily dismissed. "So you deliberately chose to ignore me? That is what you are saying, yes?"

Her glance fell to her hands, hands that were very tightly clenched. "It is just that you seemed so—so overwrought, not rational, not befitting a duke at all."

"Not befitting a duke. Hmm. Tell me, Mrs. Wattington," he asked, "does your husband like London? Was he looking forward to attending events around the coronation, making contacts? It is such pity that he received no invitations."

"Oh, but he did. My husband wrote and told me that—"

"I am sure when you arrive, you'll find that you were quite mistaken. I don't believe he will be received anywhere—at least not if you are accompanying him." Mark had no idea if he actually had such power. His uncle would have, but he was not his uncle. Still, he imagined that the eligible Duke of Strattington would be quite desired by those with unmarried daughters, and that was power in itself. Divers certainly went on endlessly about the choice of bride he'd have once he put his mourning aside.

"What do you . . ." Mrs. Wattington's voice trailed off as her understanding caught up with his words.

"You had best hope that she is unharmed when I find her or you will find yourself unwelcome anywhere outside of your own home and perhaps even there—I do not know how understanding your husband is."

"I, well, I—that is . . ." Mrs. Wattington did not

know what to say. She turned to leave, but the slightest of coughs had her feet frozen in place.

There was a bee buzzing outside the window. Mark turned his glance and watched it throw itself against the glass before heading off in another direction. He pushed himself to his feet and walked to the door leading to his bedchamber. Not befitting a duke, indeed. He stopped for a moment, without looking at Mrs. Wattington, who stood frigid. "I will trust you can find the door—that I do not need to have you shown out."

Divers stood just inside the bedroom door. He did not even pretend he had not been listening. "So it is true then?"

"Yes, it is true. I was caught at an indelicate moment with Mrs. Wattington's companion."

"I heard it was her baby nurse."

"I believe Miss Smith has served in both capacities."

Divers did not say anything, but continued to pack neck cloths into a trunk.

"You have something further to say? Please speak freely," Mark said.

Divers pressed his lips tight, but then turned and spoke. "It is simply not fitting to your station to be seducing the servants. You need a wife and an heir. If you need more, you should take a proper mistress and be discreet about it. There is a house near St. James."

He pushed aside the reminder that his behavior was not fitting for the mighty Duke of Strattington. He never wanted to hear that again.

The information about the house, now that was good to know. He had planned to buy Isabella a house, but if there was one waiting, so much the better. "Did my uncle . . . ?"

"It is not my place to discuss what happens in private. I am sure you would not wish me talking about your affairs." Divers turned back to the packing.

Mark could only snort. "At this moment I am sure you would only be one of many—but yes, I value my privacy."

"Then you should learn to lock the damn door." Douglas strode in.

"I was wondering when you'd arrive and say your piece." Mark turned to Douglas.

"I'll hold my counsel for the moment. I imagine you're itching to be off after the girl."

"You're not . . ." Divers let his words trail off.

"You just said I should acquire a mistress." Mark didn't know why he felt the need to answer.

"But you don't know anything about her. She might be a criminal for all you know." Divers gave up all pretense of work. "I heard a man making inquiries about her, about Miss Smith. There is clearly something going on. And the way she ran—that can only mean one thing."

"Oh be quiet, man." Douglas turned on him before Mark could. "She's a young girl who's lost her employment and has every man for three miles wondering if her titties could possibly be as wondrous as described. I don't blame her for leaving as fast as she could."

"Are they really wondering . . . ?" Mark could hardly bring himself to ask.

"Yes. But that is not why I am here. I need to leave you. The more I ask Mr. Downs about those leases in Wales, the stranger the answers become. I am off to do some investigating of my own. I'll rejoin you in London. Unless you don't think you can track the lass on your own."

Mark had been about to question Douglas further, but the last stopped him. "Don't worry, I'll find her. She'll be with me again by nightfall."

She was still shaking. Even after she'd been sitting in the mud for half an hour in the ever-increasing heat, Isabella's hands would not be still. And the knot in her belly . . . She would not even think of that—it had arrived long before the man in the blue coat. From the moment she'd realized who Mark was it had sat there, eating away at her innards.

It was hard to believe she had been such a fool, on so many fronts.

Forcing her mind to the more immediate, she blew out a long, slow sigh, slowly rising to her feet. Her gaze scanned the countryside in all directions.

The man in the blue coat worked for her brother. At least she knew now. She was not as scared of her brother as she was of the law. Being returned to him would be unpleasant, but he would not have her proclaimed a murderess. At least she didn't think he would.

She rose partway, stretching the cramp from her legs.

If she did let Blue Coat take her, it would not be the end of the world. Masters's only hold on her was monetary. Although it must be admitted that standing in the mud, wearing one of the only two dresses she owned, with only a few coins in her pocket, she'd do quite a lot for a little money. And Masters would take advantage of that. Masters took advantage of everything. It brought chills to her stomach to think of the things he might make her do—the men he might make her marry.

But what if it wasn't only Masters looking? That

thought was an icy breeze sucking the breath from her body.

Her gut told her that the man who had grabbed her on the stairs at the inn was not the man in the blue coat. The man in the blue coat spoke only of her brother, not of the mysterious "it" he demanded she give to him.

The mud squished beneath her shoes as she sat back down, resting on her heels.

The man who'd grabbed her knew about Foxworthy.

He had threatened her with a noose.

She could be tried for murder if she didn't deliver him the mysterious "it." And soon he would know she was running from London, not acting as directed. What would he do if he did catch her?

And what was the "it"? She ran through the list of papers she'd taken again. IOU. Love letters. Bills. Meaningless scribbles. It still made no sense.

The knot in her belly grew larger, filling her chest. It was hard to breathe.

There was so little she could do.

Hooves sounded again. There was another horse coming down the road.

She tried to shrink herself even farther behind the hedge.

Her fears that it was her mystery pursuer grew as she realized that the rider was coming from the direction of the inn.

It was not the man in blue returning.

She couldn't see much beyond the fact that it was a single rider in a dark coat. As with the man in blue, he paused on the rise and looked about. He muttered to himself, the words almost indistinguishable. "Slut . . . duke . . . have my head . . . London . . ."

Had Mark sent him to find her? She held her breath until he pounded off down the road.

No, it was more probable that he'd heard about her and Strattington. The whole inn had been abuzz when she'd left. Several men had made her offers as she'd crept out into the night. She pushed that thought away, as she had so many others.

Her last pursuer was the whisperer. She was sure of it.

Tightening her fists until nails ground into flesh she tried to breathe, tried to make the knot loosen enough to pull in a single gulp of air. And then another. And another.

One breath at a time, she would survive.

Finally, when she was sure he was gone, she gave herself a shake and stood. She was being silly again. Well, not so silly given that she was clearly being pursued by not one but two groups and at least one of them knew about Foxworthy.

Brushing at the mud on her skirts, she told herself to be sensible. She had no money and no place to go, more immediate worries at this moment than whether she might be sought in Foxworthy's death.

She didn't even know which direction to head—to continue away from London and risk running into Blue Coat or to turn around and head toward Town? Looking one way and then the other, she hesitated.

There was no right answer.

Maybe if she just sat here for an hour or two an answer would come.

As if her thoughts were heard, the pound and rattle of a carriage echoed in her ears. Her knees ached as she tucked back down, heart pounding. She peered through the leaves.

Her heart missed a full beat; the knot eased—slightly.

It was the duke's. Mark had come.

No, not Mark. Strattington.

Even before she finished the thought she stood and began to walk back toward the road.

It was the sensible thing to do, the only possible choice, she told herself. The duke you knew was better than the stranger you didn't.

Mark sighed with relief as he saw Isabella suddenly emerge from the brush and walk down the ridge to the road. She had been hiding from something, but apparently it was not he.

So why had she left without telling him? Did she not trust him? He had told her he would care for her.

She had found out that he was Strattington. He could see it in her unforgiving posture; her rigid shoulders and drawn lips spoke of great anger.

Damn, he should have told her. He would have told her if they had not been interrupted.

What woman would not be happy to find her lover was a duke?

Judging by the way she was stomping down the hill he had found the one.

Fury rose off her in almost visible waves.

Stopping about ten feet from the carriage Isabella waited, glaring at the open window. It was dark in the carriage and he doubted she could see in clearly, but she knew he was here.

The bruise still marked her cheek. He should not have let Mrs. Wattington off so easily.

Mark ran his fingers through his hair, messing the neatly combed waves. Divers would have a fit. He stared back at Isabella as she stood there waiting. She was not coming any closer.

He pushed the door open. She did not move.

With a sigh, he swung out of the carriage.

Still, she came no closer. She stared at him, measured him. He could feel her considering him as a duke and not merely a man.

He stepped forward. "Are you coming?"

Startled at the abruptness of his question. Her lips drew tight, but she nodded. "I have no choice, do I?"

Did she? He didn't know. He could give her money, but that would not assure her safety—and he needed her safe almost as much as he needed her.

She took a step forward, coming nearer. "You came back. This is not the way to London and the king."

It was his time to purse his lip, unsure how to respond to her hostility. "No, it is not. Come."

He stepped back, placing a foot on the step to the carriage. He waved her forward.

She looked straight into his face, but he could see her judge his whole appearance. "I'll ride on the box with the driver. It is more fitting."

Chapter 13

It was a lovely day. Lush green fields sped by on either side. Lazy cows strolled up to stone fences, their mooing lost beneath the rattle of the wheels. The sun was bright, but not too hot. Sitting on top of the speeding carriage, Isabella found the breeze most refreshing. She raised her face into the wind and let it whip by her.

It kept her from crying—or screaming. It was hard to be sure which emotion would win out.

She'd turned her fear to anger when she'd faced Strattington before getting on the carriage, but now. . .

Now she felt like she'd put her whole self in a basket and set it upon the waters only to have it sink.

And it was all his fault.

Her eyes began to water again, and she turned even more directly into the wind. If her eyes teared it was only because there was grit from the road. It had nothing to do with Mark—Strattington. Nothing to do with her fears for the future.

Damn him. Damn him. She would not be reduced to acting like this. She searched for the fury again, and wrapped it about herself like a cloak. Anger was strength—and she would be strong.

Not that anyone would care anyway, not the driver,

not Divers, and not—not Strattington. It was all too clear what they thought. If Douglas had been here he might at least have given her a smile. He'd seemed to like her.

That sounded like self-pity. She pulled in one deep breath, and then another. It was time to show him just what she was made of.

A sudden knock from below startled her. Without so much as a glance in her direction, the driver slowed the horses and pulled to the side of the road. The door swung wide before the groom could climb down and open it.

Strattington stepped into the sunlight. He blinked as the bright light hit his face, but then stared straight up at her.

She stared back, letting the anger build within her, preparing to show him just how she felt.

Strattington pointed into the carriage. "Divers, out," he addressed the interior.

Then he pointed up at Isabella. "You, get down and get in. We need to talk." Without saying another word he stepped away and waited. He really was a duke.

Divers was out of the coach and climbing up to the seat before Isabella could even blink. "Don't think too highly of yourself," the valet whispered as he slipped beside her.

Damn Strattington. Did Mark think he could order her about this way? Yes, he did, and the problem was that he could. And they did need to talk, to settle things between them.

She suppressed her feelings of powerlessness and somewhat slowly, being clear that she was unwilling, she climbed down. She did not immediately get into the carriage but walked back and forth stretching her legs. She did not look at Strattington. He would see that two could play these silly games.

He coughed but she paid no attention.

Snorting his understanding of her actions, he climbed back in himself—and waited.

It would have been nice to make him wait all afternoon, but she needed this settled before they reached Town.

With some reluctance she climbed into the carriage and sat carefully across from him, facing backward. He sprawled on his bench, legs wide, arms relaxed. He appeared not to have a care in the world. She gritted her teeth.

Silence held until the coach began to move. The world passed by quickly outside the window. At least he didn't insist on riding in total darkness like Mrs. Wattington. But there was no Joey to distract her either. Oh, how she missed him.

No. That was self-pity again. She would not think of Joey or her ruined life; her only thoughts would be of Mark's deceit. None of this would have happened if he had been honest.

None of it.

A discreet cough drew her attention and she turned her face to Strattington, willing herself to an icy calm.

"I think you must become my mistress," he said without an ounce of emotion.

Damn it all. He hadn't meant to say it like that, but warmth, or even civility, was difficult with her looking so murderous. Half of Mark's day had been spent working out the perfect words, the way to make her understand that he was not doing this just because he had to. He really wanted her to be his mistress.

Ouch. He could tell by her face she'd throw something if she could. She'd looked as if she might have been crying when he'd called her into the carriage, but now—now she looked like she wanted to chew off his ears.

He moved his legs out of the way. He wouldn't put a good kick past her.

"You want what?" was all she said.

"I think it's a fine idea." Oh, he was sure she could tell how long he'd spent figuring out this speech.

She didn't even answer, just glared.

He tried again. "I think you'd suit me very well."

She sputtered. At least he would take it as a sputter and not a spit. "You think I'd suit you very well. You ruin my life and you think I'd suit you?"

"Well, yes." His conversational skills were clearly on the rise.

"And you think I should just agree?"

"Well, yes." Now he was repetitive.

"Oh."

He hoped she was thinking about it. Her face turned to the window so he could not make out her full expression. He wished her body would relax. She looked like she was sitting on hot coals rather than the soft plush of the carriage benches.

The bruise was beginning to fade, if you called turning yellow fading.

Her chest rose and fell, expansively, as she pulled in one deep breath after another. That was good, it must mean she was thinking about his proposition.

"No." She did not turn back to him.

"No, what?"

"No, I will not be your mistress. I am insulted by the very suggestion."

Insulted? That he had not expected. She hadn't been insulted to be his lover when he'd been only an estate agent. Why would she not want to be the mistress to a duke? *Marriage*. The word whispered guiltily into his thoughts. She had wanted marriage. Guilt touched him and made his tone harsher than he'd intended. "I told you I'd take care of you and you did not protest before. What the hell did you think I was talking about? I think you should think again."

"I thought you spoke of marriage. I thought that was what 'take care of me' meant." The words were out before she could hold them back.

His body stiffened further, if that was even possible—but he did not look surprised. If anything he merely looked tired, very tired. "Dukes do not marry baby nurses, or even companions."

"But I didn't know you were a duke. You should have told me."

"Yes, I should have." He looked away from her.

She was shocked by this admission. "Then why didn't you?"

He relaxed slightly, his back actually touching the cushion behind him. "I liked not being the duke for a while. With you I could relax. You always made me see the joy in the moment."

"You still should have told me."

"Yes." He did not say more.

"I would not have dallied with you if I'd known you were the duke."

"Would you not have?"

The worst of it was that he was probably right. If she had known who he was then she—she might have decided to become his mistress anyway. "I don't know." She answered his honesty with her own.

They were silent for a moment.

"I cannot marry you, you know."

"Dukes do not marry baby nurses." She repeated his words. But did they marry slightly scandalous gentlewomen? What if she told him the truth? But murder was more than slightly scandalous.

"No, they don't. I tried to tell you at the inn before we were discovered. I was afraid I heard you mention marriage in your cries."

"I didn't." *Please, don't add that shame to this.*

"I am rather afraid you did."

"And then everything happened."

"Yes. I realize that I led you on and I am prepared to do what is right."

"By making me your mistress?" He had a strange idea of making things right. Then again, it was a testament to how far she had fallen since that night in Foxworthy's rooms.

"Yes." He turned toward her. His voice softened, but she heard the command in it. "Just say yes."

He was still every inch the duke, even if she had seen a glimmer of Mark in his honesty.

It was anger that had made her say no before. With no money in her pocket and no prospect of employment, no other options presented themselves to her. She could beg. She could walk the streets and deal with multiple men—or—

Or. . .

Could she really do it? Could she be his mistress?

She kept her face turned to the window so that he could not see her temptation. What were her choices, really?

She could return to her brother. Would Masters

take her in even after she had defied him for so long? The fact that he still pursued her rather indicated he would, but it would not be without cost. Masters might make her marry a man even worse than Foxworthy. Was it not better to stay with Mark; at least she wasn't disgusted by him. She might deep down confess to even liking him. She'd certainly liked kissing him. It would be a gamble. But then so was her life.

Could she turn to her sister, Violet? Violet had demonstrated that she would give up anything for Isabella—including the man she loved. Before Isabella had run away she had found herself engaged, if only for a matter of hours, to Lord Peter, Violet's true love. She hoped they were married by now, but regardless, Isabella could not see any way in which asking Violet for help would not hurt her sister. It was Isabella's turn to be selfless. She would not do anything that might cause her sister distress.

What of Lady Smythe-Burke? She had already done enough. Isabella didn't even know why she had helped her flee in the first place. Their relationship was not such that Isabella could impose further. It would be awful if Lady Smythe-Burke was involved and someone called in the authorities.

She did have a friend, Annie Westers, who had helped her out before, but that had always been with covering for small things—not murder. She doubted there was much that Annie could do about this, even assuming she was in Town. Annie might even feel compelled to turn her in.

With some trepidation she turned and looked at Strattington. Looking at him now it was hard to see how she had ever not recognized him as the duke;

his every sinew and line cried out authority. He sat looking straight ahead again, not deigning her with further attention as he awaited her response.

He wore full black again today. He must still be in mourning for the uncle Mrs. Wattington had mentioned. The coat was a heavy brocade, black upon black. She could not make out the pattern in the dimness of the carriage. His linens almost glowed they were so white. And the boots, they were polished enough for her to see the reflection of her own half boots.

It was not his clothing, however, that spoke of who he was. He turned to her, his voice soft but his face unmoving. "Surely you see there is no other choice."

Choice.

She remembered her sister yelling at Masters about women and choices, how they had the right to make their own even if they made mistakes. It was not until later that Isabella had truly appreciated her sister's words.

Did she have a choice now?

She needed to understand. "What will you give me if I become your mistress?"

"Excuse me?" His voice lost its softness, its warmth.

"Oh, I don't mean it like that—or at least not quite like that. I guess the more accurate question would be what can I expect?"

"I would think the usual." He sounded slightly unsure. Could a duke be unsure?

"But I have no idea what the usual is. Do you pay for an apartment? A house? Do I get a staff? Do all my bills get sent to you? How often do you, do you—visit? Do you have other lovers?"

"A house, I imagine, some discreet neighborhood. Divers mentioned that my uncle owned such a house near St. James. I am sure Divers knows how all this is handled."

Divers—she could hardly bear to think of that conversation. She had to turn and face the window again. "You wish to put me in your uncle's house?"

He coughed, slightly, but she did not look.

"Only if it is what you wish," he answered.

What she wished? Since when was this about what she wished? "I do not think I would care for it."

"I will get you a new house then. I imagine the ducal coffers will survive."

"And the rest?"

"Why are you being difficult? It will all be worked out."

Where was Mark? The man who spoke to her like this was not the man she had kissed and certainly not the man she had almost . . . Why, going to bed with him would be like going to bed with a stranger. She might be better off walking the streets. "Why would you want me as your mistress? Surely there are beauties in London who would tempt you more?"

"It is the right thing. I misled you. Therefore it makes sense."

Oh, weren't those the words every woman wanted to hear.

Her eyes were watering and she couldn't blame it on the wind. The sun, maybe? It was bright out. If only the sun were shining in her side of the carriage instead of the other, that might have been believable. "I think I need the details worked out now. If I do this there is no going back. My life will be changed—forever."

"I shall consider the matter."

"Let me know when you are done considering and we can speak again. I will ride with the driver again." It was so hard sitting next to him when her body said one thing and her mind another.

"No." That, at least, was clear—and very ducal.

Why could she simply not cooperate? Mark wished he could kick the bench he sat on. Of course dukes did not kick.

He knew he was not acting well. He even knew why. It had taken a moment for him to realize that he cared about her answer. It would have been much easier if he had not. Caring made him nervous, made his stomach clench up. And that was not even considering the guilt that he felt. It made him all the more defensive.

The problem was he could not even imagine what he would do if she said no. He'd never needed anything as much as he needed her, her smile, her warmth. And the more it mattered, the more he acted the duke. He could not let her know the power she had.

Dukes never let anyone else have the power.

And he hadn't liked that moment when she'd asked what she would get. He trusted that she had not meant it as it sounded, that she was not a gold digger, but still . . . He had become very used to those who looked at him only for what he could give them.

Watching her from the corner of his eye as he stared straight ahead was beginning to give him a headache. He turned and faced her. He could not wait any longer. He needed to know—to know that she was his. He should be more persuasive, he knew that. But he could not bear to think of her on the streets—alone. Even if he gave her money, she would still be alone. "I have considered enough. I do not believe that we need to resolve the details now. I desire an answer."

She paled at his words, but the muscles in her jaw clenched. "As long as you realize that the choice is mine. You would be wise not to forget that. It may not be a good choice, but still there is choice."

He should have known she would only argue more. "You have told me you are a sensible woman."

Her eyes dropped to her hands, which were twisting in her lap. Her lips were stuck tight together.

A part of him longed to lean closer, to draw a finger across their sweet pink curves, to soften them and then her. It would be so easy to tempt her into agreement, to inch near to her on the bench, to slip a foot under the edge of her skirts, to. . .

"Fine." She said the word very softly.

"What?"

"You are correct. I am sensible." Her voice spoke of despair. "If the choice is to be your mistress or starve, I will be your mistress. However, do not think that I do not realize that it is you who creates the choices I have. You have the power to give me another choice if you wish."

She was right. He did have the ability to give her another alternative, to pay her way, to give her a recommendation. Only how would he know she was safe if he let her slip away? She might find herself in even worse circumstances. With him she was safe. "If you believe so."

"So you will not simply give me some funds or help to find a position for me?"

"I have already suggested the position I wish you to fill and you have agreed."

"Fine." She did not look so fine. Her hands were no longer twisting but were clenched tight. She turned and stared back out the window without another comment.

He wished he could explain how he felt, how he needed her, how he feared for her, but the words would not come. He did not know how a duke would say them. Hell, he didn't know how he would say them.

She had agreed. Isabella saw nothing as she watched the passing scenery.

He was right. She did have no choice.

"Why were you being pursued?" Mark's voice interrupted her thoughts. She had believed they were finished.

"I don't know what you are talking about." Did her voice sound normal?

"Divers spoke to a man who could only have been asking about you. I've already set a man to investigate."

She knew she paled slightly. "Call your man back. If I am to be your mistress then call him back. The past does not matter."

He leaned forward, his face softening. He looked like Mark again. "Do you have a problem? I can help you. I am good with problems."

"No. I will be fine."

"Are you sure? A duke can solve almost anything. It's not like you killed a man."

"Just call your man back. I may reconsider my decision if you pursue this."

He stared at her, his eyes filled with consideration. "I will do as you . . . request."

This time it was he who turned away.

She bit down hard on her lower lip, trying to stem the tide of emotions that was rising.

She longed to be numb. Instead she felt as if she would burst apart from the swirl of emotions that filled her.

The worst was that even now she longed to be cradled against his chest, to feel his strong arms about her, to feel that sense of safety that Mark always gave her.

But that was Mark. This was Strattington.

Which brought her to the question at the center of it all. She had been prepared, indeed wanted, to have sex—she forced herself to phrase it bluntly—with Mark out of desire and dreams, but was she ready to do the same with Strattington?

Could she give her body to the duke?

Chapter 14

She was back in London. It had not changed much. Perhaps it was dirtier, more downtrodden, but that might just be her own view after the last years spent in the country. It was certainly gray.

The day was gray—whether it was fog or a single enveloping cloud she could not say.

The city was gray—not even a brightly painted door added color to the view.

Her mood was gray—that might even be an understatement. She verged on black.

The wheels rattled as the carriage sped over the city's cobblestones. Each movement jarred her already aching brain. Her hands twitched with the desire to rub her neck, but she would not show such weakness to the man who sat across from her.

She closed her eyes. Her temples throbbed with lack of sleep and tension. She didn't know whether to attribute it to her anxiety at being back in London, back at the scene of her crime, or to the strange, awkward silence that held between them. She would have thought her agreement to be his mistress would have brought peace. Instead. . .

"Why did you not send for me last night at the inn? I thought that once you had my agreement you would wish me in your bed." She was too tired to attempt to play games.

Strattington turned and stared at her. Oh, how she longed for Mark. The duke must put on formality along with his tight cravats and brocade coats. "I thought that I was doing you a kindness, giving you time to adjust to your new life."

"By leaving me awake half the night waiting?"

"Were you waiting?" Did she detect the glimmer of a smile in his expression? Mark's eyes had glinted with humor and caring. Strattington's eyes seemed to show nothing but the reflection of his surroundings.

"Yes, I waited. Does that make you happy?"

He turned and looked at her fully. "I want what makes you happy. You seem to be missing your usual sense of fun."

Yes, she imagined that she was. What did he expect under the circumstances? "Where do we go now?"

His lips tightened and he turned away again. "I am still considering. I certainly go to my house in Mayfair. I am not sure what to do with you. It would not be seemly for you to accompany me."

The duke really knew how to win a woman over. "I am sure you are correct. That does seem to leave you with a bit of a dilemma, though, doesn't it?"

"I just said it did."

Could you scream at your protector? Provider? She refused to call him master, even if it did seem that it should go with mistress. What did she call the blasted man? He certainly was not her lover.

"I will leave it to you, then," she answered with complete calm.

"That would be best. I am trying to prevent you from having worries." He sounded sincere.

"Thank you," she replied, hiding her emotions.

"I am glad you appreciate my efforts." He nodded.

Forget yelling at him. She was going to strangle him. Or at least kick him—and hard. One of the other maids had taught her exactly where to aim. She wouldn't have to worry about whether he was her lover then.

He considered her a moment before saying, "I do think perhaps it would be best if you went to my uncle's house for tonight. I do apparently still own it and have been informed that it is unoccupied except for the staff."

"Your uncle's house?" Understanding filled her. "You mean his mistress's house. I thought I explained that I did not wish to go there."

"I do not see that there is another choice, no matter what either of us might wish. I would put you up at a hotel, but that would be less than discreet."

Oh, how she wanted to argue. The problem was she needed to be discreet also. She didn't know which would be worse, if the men seeking her found her or if her family learned what she was about to do.

Violet had taken lovers, but she had taken care never to be any man's mistress. She said that it was unwise for a woman to let a man support her outside of marriage, that such situations never ended well. Not, she had added, that marriage offered any guarantee. Men were men and were often beastly.

Isabella glanced over at Strattington.

She seemed to be taking it well—or at least acceptably. Mark had been nervous that she would react badly to going to his uncle's house, but he could not think of another choice. He had not been to London since assuming the duchy and couldn't think of another place to put her. He should probably have considered this before making his offer.

As an unemployed servant she could have been stuck in one of the maid's rooms. For his mistress-to-be that did not seem suitable. And he didn't mean to be thinking of sticking her anywhere, although phrased that way he could think of— Why did his brains seem to depart when he was near her?

He glanced across at her. Her lips were tight and she lacked her usual vitality. The gray gown was overshadowing her beauty.

He wished Divers were here with them—the first time he'd ever had that thought. He'd asked his valet about the correct way of setting up a mistress, but none of the man's advice seemed quite right. Divers had assured him that Isabella would not mind staying at his uncle's house for a few nights—although his tone had also implied it was not her place to question. Divers clearly did not know Isabella.

Mark would have to explain the situation to the man more carefully and seek further advice. He did want to do this right.

Damnation. He was not sure why everything had grown so tense anyway. He had been trying to do her a favor by leaving her alone last night at the inn and she'd taken even that badly. What had happened to the natural ease that had flowed between them? It had been so much easier when she had not known he was the duke. Now everything seemed endlessly complicated, endlessly examined.

Bother. He should be thinking of his coming meeting with the king, and instead his thoughts kept turning to Isabella, wishing she were in his arms.

Something was going to have to change.

* * *

It was not an awful house. It wasn't even particularly bad. The furnishings might have been half a century out of date, and despite having a staff, it looked as if no one had lived here for ages. Isabella didn't know how old the last duke had been when he died. Perhaps he had been too old to keep a mistress. Were men ever too old for a mistress? Isabella added that to the list of things she didn't know.

The hall was cold. Outside it was warm enough to raise a sweat, but in the dark of the hall there was a distinct chill.

She turned in a slow circle and looked around. Strattington had deposited her in the hall, spoken to the elderly porter, and left. Her small bag had been taken upstairs and she'd been directed to a parlor to await her room being made ready.

Only nobody had come for her.

Should she go searching on her own? Her temples were aching again and she desperately wanted the chance to lie down. Somewhere, back deep in her mind, was the hope that she would sleep and when she awoke this would all be a dream.

"Come this way, miss." The dour-faced housekeeper had finally remembered her. "I'll show you to your room. I am sure you'll find it delightful, quite a step up for a maid. It was decorated only a few years ago."

Divers must have talked to the woman. Nobody else would have said she was a maid. Why did the man seem to dislike her so much?

"I am sure it will be lovely," she said to the housekeeper.

"I reckon you'll be wanting a proper meal and a bath."

"Please."

"It may take a while. We weren't expecting you and it's been years since anybody has stayed in the house."

Had Mark's uncle not used the house? "I thought you said it was redecorated recently?"

"I said that we hadn't had anyone staying here—not that the house had not been used. I would think someone in your position would realize the difference. And don't ask questions. Gentlemen like their affairs kept quiet."

Someone in her position. Isabella was too caught by the phrase to worry about the rest of the statement. She lost even that thought when the housekeeper swung open the door to her new bedroom. Isabella could only gape at the chamber beyond.

He hadn't planned on visiting her tonight. In fact, he'd planned on staying away from her until he had new accommodations set. A home of her own would go a long way toward getting him back in her good graces.

He allowed himself a single sigh as he walked up the steps to his uncle's house—well, his house actually. An evening spent with the king was enough to tire anyone. There had been several messages waiting when he arrived at his home in Mayfair. The king had made it very clear that his newest duke had better come calling the moment he arrived. Or at least as soon as his valet dressed him in a coat without a wrinkle—that also allowed no movement—and a neck cloth tied in so many layers that he'd felt like a lady's petticoat. And that wasn't even mentioning the satin knee breeches. Mark hadn't known that they were required anywhere besides Almack's. Divers saw it differently.

The new King George was not actually a bad man, or even a tedious one. He was, however, a demanding one. Mark never wanted to hear so many details about an event again. He simply did not care what types of herbs were going to be sprinkled on the ground before the king as he walked along. The coronation was important, the number of yards of train the king would wear and the number of attendants necessary to carry it were not.

Only a brief conversation with the Duke of Brisbane had kept the evening bearable. Now there was a man who understood with all his being what it was to be a duke.

Mark scowled. He was becoming a grouchy old man and he still had barely reached thirty.

Which was why he was here, standing on the stairs of a house he owned, wondering if he'd be welcome.

He needed her, not the cold woman of the last days, but the warm Isabella who reminded him of who he was, the woman who saw him as a man and not a duke.

Or at least she had. Now that she knew who he was could they go back to the way it had been?

What was he doing here?

Well, Isabella imagined that she knew what he intended, but now? It was well after midnight and she had finally fallen asleep. He had no right to arrive now. Hurriedly she slipped out of bed and pulled on her robe.

Glancing in the mirror, she grimaced. Her hair was a curling mess about her head, and her face—well, yellow had never been her color and her bruised cheek looked like a lemon. How could she even think he'd want to have sex with her when she looked like lemon? A curly-headed lemon.

Not that she wanted to have sex with him. No, she did not.

She was not done being angry yet. It sounded petty even in her mind, but she still felt a cold fury when she thought of how she'd ended up here. She might have some blame in the matter, but she'd wanted Mark in her bed—not Strattington, not the duke.

Was it possible to have one without the other?

The question gave her pause, stilling her anger. Could she find Mark again? If she approached him in the right manner, was Mark still there? Could she have him and not the duke?

That was the question in her mind as she tiptoed down the stairs in her bare feet. The servants had put him in the blue parlor. At a guess she thought that was the front one. There wasn't much blue in the room, but it looked like the carpet might once have been that shade.

At least he hadn't just appeared in her bedroom, in her bed. A shiver took her at the thought and she was not quite clear on its cause.

A fire had been lit. It was true luxury on this temperate summer night, serving to dry the air and add a warm glow to the dark room.

Strattington sat in the high wing chair before it—only he didn't look like Strattington. He looked like Mark. Perhaps there was hope. The dark waves of his hair lay mussed and disarrayed. His cravat hung untied about his neck. She was only surprised he had not removed his coat.

Her eyes must have portrayed her question.

Mark shrugged. "I can't get out of it without help. It's too tight. Silly, isn't it?"

Should she offer to help? It seemed the natural

thing for a mistress to do, but she wasn't sure she wanted to touch him—not yet.

Or maybe the problem was that she was sure that she did? It was too easy to imagine running her hands over his strong shoulders. "It's been years since I wore anything I couldn't manage myself. I can even do my laces if needed." She blushed as she said the last.

He really did seem like Mark again. She would never have made such a comment to anyone else.

"I've gone the other way. Until I inherited I've never had a garment I couldn't manage. Come sit. I need some company."

"Only company?"

The corner of his mouth quirked up. "Yes, only company. Even I know it's not fitting to show up in the small hours of the morning expecting more than that."

The fire did look inviting. Watching him warily, she came and sat across from him. "I thought that was the purpose of a mistress, that you didn't need to worry if things were fitting or not."

"That might be the theory, but I have been informed it is not at all the practice."

"Informed?"

"Well, as I've never actually had a mistress before, I only know what I am told."

"And who exactly is doing the telling?"

It was his turn to act wary. "A man hears."

She smiled slightly at his discomfort. He was not so imposing now. "I would imagine he does."

He sighed loudly and let his head fall back. "And I must confess to being so sick of hearing. I spent the evening with the king and his friends. The chatter that surrounds them would send a magpie screaming."

"And so you came here looking for company? Would you not have been better with quiet at home?"

The ceiling seemed to have an endless fascination for him as he continued to stare at it. "You would have thought so. After the night I've had, going home to my solitary bed in my solitary house should have had immense appeal. But somehow I find myself here."

"Oh." Her heart added an extra beat.

He lowered his face until he looked straight at her. "Do you want me to go? I should have realized I would be pulling you from your bed."

"No. It is fine. Please stay. Should I ring for something? Port? Brandy?"

"Would you think it unmanly if I asked for hot tea and cold water?"

"Not at all, although I would confess I might find it a bit strange."

He had been right to come. He lifted the tea to his lips and took a gentle sip. The water had been gulped down as soon as it arrived. A good drink of water after a night of overindulgence often saved him from a pounding head in the morning. The tea, now, that was just soothing.

As was Isabella. He couldn't remember a more pleasant time than this last half hour spent gazing at the flames and chatting whenever the need took them. The time had been far different from the awkward days they'd spent in the carriage.

He shrugged, trying to release the tension in his shoulders. Bloody jacket.

"Would you like me to help you with that?"

The soft question took him by surprise. When he'd first arrived he'd been ready for her to offer, had even hinted that she should. Now, as sleepy familiarity surrounded them, it seemed more dangerous. "Yes, I would like that," he answered, hoping his voice didn't sound too husky.

She rose from her chair and walked toward him. The belt on her robe had loosened and he could see a hint of skin through the thin linen night rail. It was old and worn. Part of him longed to dress her in something new and fine, but a bigger part was very happy with the way the threadbare fabric outlined her skin.

And then her hands were at his shoulders easing his coat down. The stiff fabric slid easily under her fingers, and he twisted an arm back until he was free. "Ah, that feels good."

"Getting you out was easy. I am not sure getting you back in will be possible."

"Divers manages with only the barest of complaints."

"I am not Divers."

No, she certainly was not. Her robe gaped further with her movements, and he could see one rosy nipple peeking through the fabric. His fingers curled in the effort not to touch. He swallowed, hard.

"You are looking tense again," Isabella murmured as she reached over and stroked his cheek. She had no problem with touching.

He closed his palm about her hand. "That feels so good."

Their gazes met and held.

"I've missed you." She spoke so quietly he was not sure he heard correctly.

Chapter 15

Touching him was heaven. She leaned nearer as he remained in his chair. She should be mad and standoffish—or at least cold. He had forced her into a situation that she had no wish to be in. But, as she ran her fingers over his cheek, felt the scruffy stubble of his beard, it was hard to remember that.

Instead she remembered that this was her own doing as well as his and that his offer was better than any she had expected to receive.

And she remembered that this was Mark.

For the past days she had been so busy thinking of him as Strattington that she had forgotten just how drawn she was to him, to the man. The duke she could do without, but the man, that was something else.

She pulled in a deep breath and considered.

It was not awkward between them at this moment. That had been her greatest fear. How was she to do this thing when she felt so distant from him?

But here, now, this was not distant. This was—possible. Could she take the lead and bring them to the next step?

If she was going to do this, she should set the terms, the pace.

Leaning forward, she let her hair brush across

Mark's face, watched the flickers of his eyes as each strand brushed him. His eyes darkened with desire. His wants were clear.

Her glance dropped to his lips, back to his eyes.

And she kissed him, softly, gently—but with unmistakable intent.

Her breasts brushed against his shirt and she made no effort to pull back. If she waited the mood might change—it had to be now, now while he was Mark.

He tilted his face toward her, capturing her lips more fully, bringing her mouth into deeper contact. His tongue licked her lips and then slipped inward. He shifted, opening his legs and bringing her between them. His strong thighs surrounded her, making her feel both captured and powerful. She tilted her hips forward, bent her knees, brushed against him, felt his reaction deep in her core. He might have the muscles, but she had equal control.

Catching his head between her hands, she plundered his mouth and was plundered in return. His eyes closed slowly. It should have taken away from the intimacy of the moment, but the vulnerability of his expression caught at her. This was Mark. He was not hiding anything from her. Somehow in closing his eyes he had exposed himself further.

Something in her heart softened. This was Mark—he had said he would care for her—and he would.

She smiled against his lips. His eyes slipped open. "You look happy," he said against her mouth.

"Yes, I think I am."

"You have not been happy these past days."

"No, but now I am."

"And I must say that I am too." He tilted slightly, bringing her to sit on his lap.

He pulled his head back and looked at her for a moment. "I was not expecting this tonight. I had planned to wait—at least until I had bought a house for you."

Her spine stiffened and then she forced it to relax. This was all he could offer and she had decided to accept it. "That is not necessary. This is not about money and payment. No, shhh—let me explain." She held a hand up to his lips. "This is about us—about Isabella and Mark. I was willing before you became the duke and I am willing now."

"I was always the duke."

"But I did not know that." She placed a sweet kiss upon his mouth. "Believe me, it was never my ambition to be a well-kept woman."

He kissed her back once, the slight noise of the pucker slipping between them. "Then what was your ambition?"

Could she tell him? Yes—or at least part—the part that had to do with him. "You will laugh."

"I promise not to." He crossed his fingers over his heart.

"I rather thought I'd be an estate agent's wife. I've already told you that I wanted marriage. I was working hard to seduce you into an offer." She ducked her head as she spoke.

His fingers caught her chin and pulled her glance back up. "You thought to seduce me to marriage?"

"I know—it does seem silly now."

Laying a kiss upon her nose he cuddled her closely. "No. It is not silly. I think—I think if life were different I could have seen that life—and liked it. I imagine us growing fat by the fire with our six children clustered about."

"Six?" she sputtered.

"You want seven?"

She reached up and slapped him lightly.

Laughter filled the room and then stilled.

"It was a nice dream," he said.

"Yes, but now we must live with what really is." She rested her face against his shoulder and stared into the flames. The fire should have been ridiculous on this warm night, but it did bring comfort. "I guess it won't be so bad."

Mark cleared his throat. "I have been assured that I am better than not so bad."

She was so sweet when she blushed. "I didn't mean it like that," she said, tilting her face up to his.

Mark cuddled her tighter. He could not believe the warm lump that had risen in his throat when she talked of marriage this time, when he understood her dream. Normally such talk would have had him backtracking as quickly as possible. Perhaps, however, because of its true impossibility Isabella's dreams had cast a spell over him as well. He truly could imagine a life with her at his side, see the two of them raising that impossible brood of children together. A household of redheads would not have been quiet—but it would have been wonderful.

He cleared his throat. This was not what he had come here for.

He did not have time for silly impossible dreams. When he married—and it would be far sooner than he liked—it would be to someone respectable from a good family. Someone who was definitely not Isabella.

"I should go." He moved to slip her off his lap.

She placed her hands on his shoulder. "Don't."

His lungs halted in the middle of a breath. Her fingers squeezed, gripping through the thin fabric of his shirt. He exhaled slowly. "You want me to stay?"

"Yes."

He drew in another breath. "Why? I need to be clear. I want no more confusion between us."

It was her turn to swallow. The muscles in her neck tensed and relaxed. "I want—I want you to stay. I want you to spend the night with me."

"In your bed?"

She laughed. What was there to laugh about?`

"Can I just say I want you to spend the night with me?" she asked. "I have no wish to claim the bed. You'll understand when you see it."

He placed his hand over hers. "I don't care whose bed it is as long as you are in it."

Her cheeks turned pink again, but the corners of her eyes crinkled. "I think that can be arranged."

Slipping off his lap, she stood and, taking his hand, led him out of the room to the stairs.

He could only smile as he followed. After the evening he'd had, he could only believe the gods were finally rewarding him.

What did she do next? Isabella shut the door to the bedroom and went to light another candle. As the light spread across the room she heard him gasp.

"It is quite something, isn't it?" she said. At least the room provided a short distraction from what came next.

"It's purple."

"I think of it more as violet."

"There is certainly violet here, along with fuchsia, and I don't know names for all these colors."

"I am not sure that there are enough names to describe every shade here." She looked about the room. Purple did not even begin to describe it. The walls were pale lavender and the bed hanging the most royal of purples. That would not have been so strange. What made it odd was that there was not another color to be seen. The furniture had been painted, along with the doors and window frames. Even the china was purple.

And the bed—the linens were purple, the pillows were purple, even the lace edging was a delicate light plum.

"Plum—that's another shade," she said as she walked to the bed. At least the coverlet was soft. Reaching out, she brushed a hand across it, smoothing an imaginary wrinkle.

She turned to face him, suddenly awkward. What did she do next?

Her hands played with the tie of her robe, but did not unfasten it. Her teeth worried at her lower lip.

Bare toes peeked from the hem of her gown and she tucked them back in.

Finally she lifted her eyes back to Mark. She didn't know why she was so worried; he was still glancing around the room, his face full of amazement.

It took every ounce of control he had not to stare at Isabella. She was a goddess in the dim candlelight. Her hair curled about her with a life of its own, contrasting with the pale white of her skin. She was nervous, though. He could see it in every hesitant, shaking movement.

She wanted him. He was sure of that. But somewhere in the long walk up the stairs her nerves had returned.

She might want this, but she was unsure of how to go about it.

The problem was that he felt the same way. Not since he was a boy in his teens had he felt this way. After all the practice he'd had in these matters in the past years, it should have been a simple thing.

Only this was Isabella. From the moment he'd met her, nothing had been simple.

"I never knew my uncle was fond of purple. My cousin wore a lavender waistcoat on at least one occasion, but the duke was the most dour of dressers. Even Divers has mentioned it and he never has anything negative to say about my uncle."

"Perhaps it was his mistress who was fond of the shade? It is only to be found in this one room from what I have seen. Everything else is quite regular, almost surprisingly so." Her toes peeked from beneath the hem of her robe again.

"I know nothing about his mistress. I did not even know for a certainty that he had one until I learned of this house after I inherited. I would have supposed he did. My aunt had been dead for many years and he undoubtedly thought that keeping a mistress was part of his position in society."

Her lips curved up very slightly. "Is that what I am—part of your position in society?"

"Of course, what else would I want you for? It has nothing to do with this hair that curls about you like liquid flames."

He reached out and stroked a curl, pulling it straight and then letting it bounce back.

"And," he continued, "it has nothing to do with having lips so full and lush a pink that they look like I've been kissing them for hours, like I want to be kissing them for hours." He ran his thumb over her lower lip, enjoying its quiver beneath his touch.

"Your eyes have grown so dark." Leaning toward her, he stared straight into them. "Normally they are the soft blue of a summer sky, but now the centers have grown large and black like a cloudless night. They have nothing to do with my desire either."

Her breaths grew rapid, one merging into the next. He ran his fingers down from her lips, across the silky skin of her chin, down the long length of her neck. Her pulse was speeding. He pressed his lips to it, to that soft spot between neck and shoulder. "And my wants are entirely unrelated to this spot, this magic spot just made for kissing, this spot where I can feel the life flowing through you, feel how my words affect you."

He nibbled on her neck, enjoying her every little gasp. Sliding his fingers farther down, he enjoyed the smoothness of her skin until he ran into the neckline of her gown. He trailed his finger back and forth just above the tie that held the gown up. It was tempting, oh so very tempting, to give the tie a tug and move things along, but instead he let his hands move sideways, skimming down her arms, past the swell of her breasts. He stopped as he reached her waist, grabbing the belt of the robe.

She swallowed, her neck quivering.

He hesitated, but she did not stop him as he opened her robe and let it hang loose.

He could only stare at her thin linen shift. He'd seen her breasts before, seen them naked, but they were more than worth a second look. He expected he would never get tired of looking at them. Their rosy tips were pressed against the worn fabric, and he watched them pucker beneath his gaze.

Her chest rose and then fell as she pulled in a deep breath.

He forced his gaze up to meet her eyes. Her pupils were even darker now, but he could see the uncertainty in them as well.

"Yes, I am definitely only after you as a reflection of my position in society." He let his gaze drop and then brought it back to her eyes.

"I was going to seduce you, try to make everything the way it was."

"The way it was when I was just Mark Smythe and you were Isabella Smith?"

"Yes. It was so much more—more comfortable then."

"It still can be. Although I must admit that this room makes it hard. I still can't picture my uncle here—not that I want to at the moment. I will have to make finding you a new home a high priority."

"You don't need to. This one is fine. I was being silly."

"You want this?" He gestured about the room.

She smiled and stepped back, edging up on the bed to sit, her gown sliding up her legs. "I would admit that I'd like some fresh paint and perhaps some new linens. I was thinking yellow—a whole room full of yellow—lemon, mustard, butter, saffron—even perhaps a touch of canary. Maybe I could even get a real one. Would you buy me a bird in a gilded cage?"

He moved to sit beside her on the bed and reached out to grab one of her hands, bringing it to his lips. Opening it with care, he laid a kiss upon the palm.

"I think I would buy you anything you wished, Miss Isabella Smith, just to have you look at me like you are now."

"Like I am now? I don't know what you mean."

Another kiss was laid upon her palm. "You look at me like a man and not a duke. In the time since I inherited I don't think another person has done that. Even my mother and my sisters look at me differently now. God, even Douglas is not the same. I rather like being just a man. If I need to have the house painted to look like a giant buttercup to keep you looking at me in this way, then that is what I will do."

He could see her fight for seriousness, but bit by bit humor took her face until she was laughing. She fell back on the bed, tears wetting her eyes, she was laughing so hard. "I am sorry," she said between giggles. "I know it's not that funny, not really that funny at all, but can you imagine the great Duke of Strattington pulling up to a house painted like a giant buttercup?" She pushed up to her elbows and stared at him. "And can you imagine what anyone would say if this was how they knew the duke's seduction went—or that the duke's mistress was too busy laughing to take off her clothes? Not that she knows how to take them off in front of a man anyway."

He stopped laughing.

Chapter 16

Isabella couldn't believe she had said that. Admitting one couldn't even pull off a shift was not seductive.

"I am happy to help you take it off," Mark said. "Or if you'd rather, I could take off my clothing. I do declare this shirt is feeling rather tight."

Even with his jacket off she could see how the fine-woven fabric of his shirt might be uncomfortable. That would never do. "Yes, I do think you should remove your shirt. But"—she glanced over him—"I really think your shoes should go first."

They hit the floor with a thud.

"Shirt or stockings?"

She looked him over. "Stockings, then shirt."

The stockings followed the shoes. He shifted then, so that he knelt beside her on the bed, towering over her.

His neck cloth fell beside her on the bed.

The first button slid open.

Then the second.

The third.

Had his skin been so tempting before? It was hard to remember. She tucked her fingers under the edge of her robe to keep from stroking. Right now she just wanted to watch.

The fourth. There was a light dusting of dark hair on his chest, a small scar on one shoulder.

The fifth. The skin on his chest was lighter than his face, but still darker than she had expected.

The sixth. His shirt slid open revealing his puckered dark nipples. They were so much smaller than her own.

The seventh. The last. He let his shirt fall completely open, but made no move to push it from his shoulders. His eyes met hers. He waited.

Pushing up to her own knees, she knelt beside him. A swarm of butterflies beat in her belly as she reached forward and slid her hands across his tight stomach. The few dark curls rubbed against her palm.

Her own breathing was fast. It felt as if her heart would burst within her chest. And those butterflies—they were ready to beat their wings until they burst free. She slid her hands up, over his hard nipples, and back down, then up again. She swallowed as she pushed the shirt over his shoulders and ran it down his arms. It caught at his wrists. She should have made him undo the cuff links first.

Although she rather liked how he looked with his arms trapped behind him. It was tempting to leave him that way.

She leaned forward and blew, watching the hairs shiver on his chest.

Should she taste?

He was salty. The smell of his soap and a light musky cologne filled her nose. She turned her face, feeling the texture of his skin against her cheek.

He shifted a little and her weight overbalanced, sending them both sprawling on the bed.

He began to laugh again. "I always have so much fun with you."

She tilted her head up to look at him. "Isn't this always fun? Isn't that the point?"

"Not like this. I don't know why, but it's different with you. I can be laughing and playing and be delightfully happy. Oh, don't get me wrong—I am eager for things to move along. But still, this is perfect."

He reached out a bare foot and stroked it along her calf. It was her turn to laugh. She hadn't realized her legs were ticklish.

His foot brushed higher up and she gasped. He smiled, devilishly, and moved in for further attack.

With a quick jerk she slithered sideways, running her hands across his bare ribs. His laughter increased.

And then it was all-out warfare.

Tickle. Rub. Nip.

Her ribs hurt from laughing and her eyes watered with joy—not, she was sure, in an attractive way.

She fell back on the bed, chest heaving as she tried to pull in a full breath. "This isn't at all what I imagined."

"Haven't you ever had a tickle fight before? You must have as a child."

That stilled her. A tickle fight? She couldn't remember anything even close. Her siblings had both been older, and Violet had left home when Isabella was still very young. It was impossible to even think of Masters in a tickle fight. She thought he'd hugged her once or twice, but even that was hard to be sure of. Her family had never been one for physical closeness.

She changed the subject. "That's not what I meant. I was referring to my planned seduction. I think the only part that has gone as planned is that we are both in my bed."

"I thought you refused to claim it as yours—the bed of purple passion, that is."

"Can't you be serious for a moment? Seduction is supposed to be serious." She rolled over and leaned up on her elbow.

He stared up at her. "Why?"

"Because this is my whole life. I am changing everything. It should not be a joke. This might be fun, but I cannot forget everything in my life will change because of this."

The smile dropped from his face. "You are right. This is serious, but it is also fun. It should always be fun. Don't forget that, Isabella. We can be as serious as you like, but we should both have a good time." He brushed a hand over the thin fabric covering her breasts.

She swallowed at the look in eyes. How could sheer silliness change to passion so quickly?

His gaze focused on her mouth and her face was drawn toward his.

It started with a simple brush of lips on lips. Soft and dry. Almost the kiss she would have given a friend after a long absence. But only almost.

No friend would have tempted her to open her mouth, to let her tongue slip out, to taste, to sample—

—and then to devour.

It happened in the blink of an eye. One moment there was curiosity and innocence, and the next, flames.

Lips ground against lips. His hands swept through her hair, holding her head captive. His tongue ran around her lips and she opened them to him, wanting to taste him, to feel him, to drive him on.

His hands slid down over her shoulders, down to her breasts. He pulled back a moment, looking deep into her eyes, and then with a simple twist of hips he was over her, on top of her, his hips grinding into hers as he fitted them together. His breeches and her gown were still between them, but her body only knew what it wanted—and wanted now.

Her hands locked around his head, his hair was silk, thick and alive, but still silk. She could have spent hours running her fingers through it, but that would have kept her from feeling the rough nap of his beard, the sweet fullness of his lips. She didn't know where to touch next, where to taste next.

Her whole being was caught on the wonder of skin on skin, on the glory of touch.

She felt him glide her gown and robe down her shoulders, over her arms. She replied by rubbing herself against him. He felt like warm velvet. And smelled like . . . leather, musk, a hint of cigar—and something else, something she could only define as him, as Mark.

And then there was no thought, only touch and sensation.

There was fire, and light, and glory—oh yes, there was glory. Isabella had never realized that all these sensations could exist at once, that her whole body could be nothing but feeling.

Her head fell back against the pillows as she sucked in a great breath. The other afternoon had been wonderful—at least until the interruption—but it had been nothing compared to this.

Mark stared down at her, his gaze firmly locked upon her breasts. His eyes were black with desire and she could feel the movement of each deep breath filling her chest. Reaching out, he ran a single finger down the side of her breast, following the full curve. Each inch of flesh he traced quivered. She had not known she was so sensitive there.

His movement became a series of circles, each one smaller and nearer to the center. Then he stopped and started on the other breast. In a moment she would be begging him to hurry.

He smiled as if sensing her thoughts. He brought his finger to his mouth, dampening it, and then finally traced her tightly peaked nipples, one at time. He blew after each touch; his hot breath on her damp flesh was almost more than she could take.

When he bent forward and took her breast into his mouth, her hips rose off the bed in response. She needed to move, to react. Her hands stroked down his back, fingers kneading into hard muscle.

She was so beautiful, so perfect. Mark buried his face between her breasts. He would have been content to die right here, right now. Life could get no better than this.

Her hands came around his shoulders, massaging him, urging him on.

He was wrong, life could get better—and better.

Keeping his lips moving over her breasts, he used his hands to slip her robe and gown farther down. She raised her hips so he could slide the fabric to her thighs. He nuzzled his way along the curve of her breasts and across her softly rounded belly. She shivered as he blew into her navel before beginning further downward exploration.

"What are you doing?" Isabella's voice was hesitant.

He lifted his head to stare up at her. "What do you think?"

"If I knew, then I wouldn't ask."

"Then why don't you wait and find out?"

Her breasts brushed the top of his head as she rose up on her elbows. "Are you sure that this is how it's done? I am sure this wasn't in any of the pictures."

Pictures? That caught his attention, which, given what he was doing, was quite a feat. He lifted his head and looked up at her, giving himself a sightline right between those delicious breasts. Maybe he should move back to them for a while. He might have missed tasting an inch or two, and she did like it when he— Mark shook his head. Pictures—he was going to ask about pictures. "Who showed you drawings of such things?"

She blushed. It was quite something, given his current position, to watch the color spread up toward her face.

"Well," she said. "Nobody exactly showed me—well, there was a footman who tried, but what he had were just nasty. I stayed with my older sister once and she had some books that had belonged to her late husband. They were beautiful Asian books with gilt covers."

"Beautiful books with gilt covers. And that is, of course, why you looked at them."

Isabella turned even redder. "Well, it was in the beginning. It was tempting to find out what they were—my sister did have them just lying on a desk—and then they were irresistible. Nobody tells girls anything. I'd lived in the country so I knew the basics of how things worked—but not with people. I had no idea there were so many possibilities. Do people really do all those things?"

He was lying with his head almost between her legs and they were having a discussion—a serious discussion. Mark would have laughed if—well, if it had not simply been so wonderful. And given the nature of their discussion, perhaps it was not quite so surprising. "If they are similar to books I have seen, I would have to say I think people, men and their mistresses, do most of those things. I have to admit I have seen some that do not seem either possible or pleasurable. I have never wanted to tie myself into a knot." It was time to turn back to the matter at hand. "But you say there were no drawings of this?" He blew across her belly, causing the red curls to dance. "I find that surprising." He blew again.

"Well, if you would tell me what you were going to do"—her voice shook as he blew lower—"then I would know for sure, but I think most of the books—well, I don't remember exactly, but I don't think that . . ." Her voice trailed off altogether as he used the fingers of one hand to separate her folds.

"There weren't any pictures of a man simply admiring a woman, of him gazing enraptured at her most intimate places?" He ran his thumb over her, noting how she quivered at each spot. Ah, there was his target. He moved his thumb again, watching how her whole body jerked and moved.

"No, I don't think there were any pictures of men just looking."

"Then they must not have been very good books. I can tell you for a certainty that men do like to look, even if that is all they can do."

She squirmed beneath his touch, trying to find either escape or ease—it was impossible to tell which. "But you do intend to do more than look?"

"Yes, I certainly do. Although you are so pink and pretty—and wet. It drives me wild to see how much you want me, want this."

He started to lower his head.

"If only you would tell me what this is, then I would know for sure that—" Her words stopped completely as he made contact.

He had chosen his target well. He could feel every muscle in her body tighten as he found that hard nub with his tongue.

She had never even imagined such a thing. Isabella felt her world dissolve in the midst of sensation. Mark's mouth, his tongue, controlled her. As the feeling grew and tightened she pressed herself up on her elbows so that she could look down at him. She expected to see only the crown of his head, but to her shock she found him gazing up at her.

Their eyes locked. She could see his pleasure in her desire, see his eyes glow with delight as each twitch of muscle revealed her ecstasy to him. And then it was too much.

She tried to hold herself up, to meet his gaze, but as her whole body clenched in ultimate pleasure she could do nothing but cry his name—and then collapse.

She lay there, almost numb, as he slowly kissed his way up her belly, around her breasts, and finally up to her lips.

She could taste herself in his kiss.

His skin was damp with sweat, and tension still held his muscles tight. He might have enjoyed her pleasure, but it was clear that he had not found his own.

"Mmmm," she murmured against his mouth as she turned on her side toward him.

"What?"

"That was wonderful. I don't know why it wasn't in Violet's books. It clearly should have been."

"Everyone has their own tastes."

"I must say I like this one." She leaned forward and kissed him lightly.

"I do too," he answered.

"Only—only there were other pictures, pictures of women doing something very similar to men. Is that also to your taste?" It was her turn to trail kisses down his neck and chest, pausing to lick at his hard brown nipples, so different from her own. "And do you think I'd like it?" She reached the waistband of his heavy silk knee breeches. "I thought you were going to undress first. How did I end up naked while you are still covered?" She pouted up at him, but ran a finger over his hard arousal.

His whole body jerked in response. Catching her hands in his, he pulled her up toward him. "Yes, I would confess a taste for that, but not now. Now I have something different in mind. Something much more usual, but still I trust pleasurable—for both of us."

Trying to pull her hands free, Isabella grinned at him. "I do trust it will require you to remove your breeches. I still maintain that your not being naked is most unfair."

"If you will be still for a moment, my wiggling wench, I will see what I can do about that. I do believe it was my task to strip for you and despite some distraction"—he licked his lips and grinned back at her—"I am more than willing to comply."

He released her hands and she fell back into the pillows, rolling onto her back to stare at him.

* * *

He felt like a lusty schoolboy. He had almost disgraced himself while pleasuring her a moment ago, and as her glance swept down him to fasten on the bulge in his trousers, he had to fight the need again. The scent of her musk wafted about him and he finally tore his eyes from her to stare at the deep purple of the wall beyond. It was almost enough to grant him control. Keeping his gaze firmly from her, he started to undo the buttons of his breeches.

Her soft sigh finally drew his glance back. She was staring at him, her lips parted. He swallowed hard as her gaze rose to his. Her pupils were huge in her eyes, the light blue almost black with desire. Undoing another button and another, he forced himself to think of nothing except her eyes, her desire. He would make this good for her if it killed him.

And at this moment he feared that it might.

"I don't remember it being so big," she whispered.

He couldn't help himself, he laughed, and laughed hard. "You are priceless, my Bella. Did your sister's books have words? That response could have been scripted."

She looked startled at his laughter and then joined in. "I can see why you would say that—even I know it is what every man wants to hear—but really, imagine it from my point of view. It seems unbelievable that that is supposed to fit into me." Her gaze skimmed down her own body to the juncture between her legs, the damp curls like fire against her white skin.

He fought for seriousness. It was hard when she brought him such constant delight. "Does it scare you? You did not seem scared before."

"Not really. A little, I suppose. A girl is told of the

pain and not the pleasure, and it is hard to reconcile the two. I will be happy when it is done."

Her words from earlier came back to him. "Even though it will change your life forever?"

"I can't believe we are talking—now. This is not at all how I thought it would go."

He was kneeling above a naked woman he'd been longing for for well over a week, his cock was so hard it might burst at any moment, he was fighting to hold himself back at every second, and he was willingly asking if she was sure she wanted to do this. "No, I can't say that this moment is how I imagined it either."

She pushed up on her elbows, raising her breasts toward him, letting her knees fall open. "Then perhaps we should proceed—assuming that you do plan to proceed."

He laughed again, but moved between her legs as he did, kicking his breeches aside. "Yes, I do have very definite plans."

Moving over her until he was pressed against her entrance, he looked down into her eyes, seeking any sign of hesitation. No matter how he wanted this, wanted her, he had to be sure it was mutual, that it was really what she wanted.

She lifted her hips, rubbing against him.

It was all he needed. He positioned himself, slid in with firm thrust, felt the barrier and then—heaven. There could be no moment more blessed than this.

He heard her gasp, saw her eyes widen, felt her whole body draw tight—and then she relaxed, not completely, but enough.

He pulled back, slid forward again.

Her glance moved down to their juncture and then back to his face. She shifted her hips a little, then again, tightened herself around him. Then she smiled, a full-face smile of joy. "That was not so bad at all. In fact"—she shifted again—"I think I could come to like this."

Now wasn't that just what a man wanted to hear from his mistress? He bent forward to kiss her on the lips, before straightening his arms and finally allowing his body to get down to business.

He lost track of all but the pleasure then, the thrust and recede. He heard her gasps, saw her face tighten, her mouth open, heard her call his name, and then in a final deep thrust he let himself go, let her name escape from his own lips as he gave in to the moment of endless color and darkness.

It was hard to even think. Isabella's entire body felt like it had melted into the bed. She was no longer a virgin, no longer untouched. And she didn't feel one bit different. Oh, there were some aches in places that she'd never ached and she certainly knew some things that she hadn't twenty minutes before, but she'd expected to be more changed.

She'd come to bed a girl and expected to leave it—well, to leave it a mistress.

Instead she was still just Miss Isabella Hermione Masters.

She rolled onto her side and peered at Mark. He was flat on his back, eyes closed, a sheen of sweat on his brow and chest. She ran her fingers through the light hair covering his breast. That was different. Twenty minutes ago she would have thought before taking such action. Now it was reflex. And a rather nice reflex. He opened one eye and smiled at her.

She smiled back, and then stopped. Her eyes were

drawn to an ugly mark across the top of one thigh.

She reached out and traced the heavy scar, the red ridge hard beneath her fingers. "The war?"

"No, my own foolishness. I think I mentioned a scar from jumping off the vicarage roof. I landed on the iron fence. I am lucky that I didn't do more damage. It is very close to areas I would hate to have impaired."

"I would say we are both lucky, then." She stroked up his leg, along his belly, and up to his chest, ignoring his sudden stirring.

"Do that again," he said.

She flattened her palm, rubbing it all along him. "Like this?"

"I feel like a big, lazy cat being petted. I'd purr if I knew how."

"Hmm, that sounds almost like a challenge. Can I make a duke purr? I would admit it's a possibility I'd never considered." She leaned over and laid a kiss just above his right nipple. "You taste salty."

He rolled onto his side and, placing a finger under her chin, tilted it up so that he could kiss her on the lips, softly, sweetly, but with definite intent.

There was power in that intent—both for her and for him.

She'd never realized that sex involved power. That was another difference that twenty minutes made.

For instance, she already knew that if she let her kiss trail down his chin to that point where chin and neck merged, if she nipped him there, not hard, just a nip—then— Oh yes, that was exactly the response she'd expected.

She nipped again. Slightly harder.

Chapter 17

She didn't want to open her eyes. The bed had shaken when Mark rose a few minutes before, but she was not yet ready to move. Even through her closed eyelids she could tell that dawn had come, but she was sure it was still early, too early. Rolling onto her stomach she burrowed her face into the pillows.

Was there anything mistresses were supposed to do the morning after? She'd never heard of anything, but then it wasn't like she'd ever heard much about being a mistress. She stretched in the bed, reaching for each corner with a limb. A large bed was a rather wonderful thing. She couldn't remember ever before being able to reach out without a foot or hand going off the edge somewhere.

Her whole body was sore in the most wonderful of ways.

Maybe being a mistress wouldn't be so bad.

And something smelled like coffee.

Coffee brought to her bedroom in the morning, now that would be almost heaven.

Had Mark gone down to fetch it?

It didn't seem like something a duke would do, but then after last night it was hard to think of Mark as a duke. A duke would surely never do half the things they'd done last night.

She stretched again, and with supreme effort she rolled over to look at Mark. He was not a quiet riser. Did he have to slam every drawer in the chest? She opened her eyes.

And blinked.

Divers stood at the dresser, opening and closing the drawers with little clear purpose. Mark's clothing wasn't there, was it? She didn't remember him bringing anything yesterday and there hadn't been anything in the drawers when her own meager bag had been unpacked.

Divers slammed another drawer shut. "Will that be all, Your Grace? The king is expecting you within the hour."

"See if there is any marmalade. I do not care for the currant jam." It was Strattington's voice that answered.

Careful to keep the covers wrapped tight about her breasts, Isabella rolled over toward the voice. Yes, it was definitely Strattington. The carefully cut black coat and flow of white linen and lace left little mistake. She wished she could pull the covers over her head. It was difficult to go to bed with one man and awake with another—even if they did share the same body. And that was not even adding in Divers.

After spending years in service Isabella was accustomed to sharing a room, and on many occasions a bed, with another maid, but never with a snotty valet. It was impossible to imagine a more miserable way to wake each morning than to Divers's lean face. He'd looked down on her during that first meeting at the inn when he'd awoken Joey and he clearly was not pleased to be here now. He was slamming the drawers on purpose. She was sure of it.

That brought on another thought. That first night at the inn—it had been Mark who had demanded she take the baby out to the stable yard. Only Mark had already been out in the yard.

Divers turned and glared at her, shutting another drawer hard. "I've put away a few days' linen, Your Grace. I will bring anything else needed when I am summoned. I imagine you will need me each morning that you spend here." He did not make it sound like he expected to be called often.

"That will be fine, Divers." Strattington turned, in all his ducal splendor, and saw her watching him. "Ah, you're awake, Bella. I fear I must be off to do my duty to the king. Divers will give you a purse of coin. I am sure that you have shopping to do. I do not imagine your current gowns will meet your new needs. You may have the accounts sent to me, but there are other baubles and things you will desire. I am sure that Divers can instruct you on the best place for a woman in your position to shop. He does seem to know everything."

A woman in her position. Last night she had not felt much different. Now she felt a hundred years older.

She was the duke's mistress, not Mark's lover.

She thought she'd learned that lesson already, but evidently he'd fooled her again.

Mark existed only in the dark of night—and in her mind. Strattington was the reality.

Her reality, and she'd best not forget it.

She glanced over to Divers, who pulled out a small purse and dropped it atop the dresser with a clang.

* * *

She was worth more than she'd expected, or else Mark was a very generous— Damn, she still didn't have a word for what he was to her. She'd go with *provider* for now. It didn't feel right, but it certainly was what he was.

She weighed the purse in one hand and then shifted it to the other—none of this felt right.

Last night had been almost magical, far better than she'd expected, but this morning didn't even reach mundane. It might even be considered awful.

She hefted the purse again. She'd been desperate for money for months, if not years. Why then did finally having a pocket full of coin make her feel—feel dirty? A simple purse had turned a night of wonder into something tawdry, something very tawdry.

She was a whore.

Mistress might be a far better term, but she had never been one to hide. She might run from trouble, but she was always honest with herself. She had known what she was doing, she had just not been prepared for how she would feel afterward.

She was a whore.

Dropping the purse on the dresser, she sighed. At least she was a very well-paid whore.

Her plain gray dress lay draped over the back of a chair, ready for her to wear. Running a hand over the sturdy fabric, she found herself comforted by it. She'd hated the simple dresses when she'd first acquired them. They were ugly and would have fit a cow as well as they fit her. She'd once asked another maid about having them fitted and been laughed at. It had not taken long for her to understand that looking frumpy and invisible was a valuable accomplishment.

Not that it had helped her with Mark, he'd seen through her plain dresses without a second glance.

What did she require as a mistress? Her sister had always had the most deliciously enticing dresses, dresses that could appear appropriate, but were anything but. She remembered a dress that had swirled about Violet, making her appear to be dressed in a fine spray of mist. The dress had covered her completely and yet left one believing she could be naked at any moment. Isabella had been so envious of that dress as she'd worn her own demure, maidenly, high-cut pastels.

Now she could wear things like that. She was probably supposed to wear things like that.

Violet's modiste would probably be delighted to make dresses for the Duke of Strattington's mistress. Only that would be dangerous. She could not risk the possible contact with her family. That could only lead to disaster.

She grabbed up the purse again, squeezing it tight between her fingers. The bag lay heavy in her palm. It would make a worthy donation to an orphanage. Wouldn't Strattington be surprised to know her thoughts?

Of course they were only thoughts. She was a practical woman.

Mark gazed across the room at the Duke of Brisbane. How did the man manage to stand perfectly straight and still look like he was lounging? The morning of waiting upon the king had been endless. The whole matter seemed to consist mostly of nodding at whatever nonsense was recited. Even the Duke of Hargrove was looking distracted from the proceedings. It was all more talk of the coronation—more discussion of train lengths and who would wear what color. Who would ever have thought that a king would spend time discussing which colors those who stood near him would be allowed to wear? Hints that it was inappropriate for Mark to wear black, despite his mourning, had not been subtle. Apparently he would choose to wear a deep teal blue if he were actually a loyal subject.

Could a man be hanged for treason for wearing the wrong color?

Suppressing a sigh, he resolved to leave the whole matter up to Divers. The valet had to serve some purpose. Going back to the days when Douglas had supplied all his needs would have been delightful. His quiet companion was far better than Divers and his dour glances. Divers had not been happy to be summoned this morning. He'd seen it as far below him to wait on Mark with Isabella in the chamber.

But Mark had been loath to leave her before she awoke.

Isabella, his Bella. She was a beauty and the shortened name suited her.

A yawn took him, and was quickly swallowed. He would need more sleep this night if he was not to drowse before the king.

He looked across the room and saw Brisbane watching him. The other duke raised a brow. Mark had not hidden the yawn well enough.

Isabella stood still as the long yards of fabric were draped about her body. It would be her first new gown in years and the prospect should have filled her with joy. Only what good was a fabulous gown when she had nowhere to wear it? Even coming to the modiste's she hurried from door to carriage and back again, her face veiled.

Could she go on like this? She honestly wasn't sure. Every night as she curved beside Mark's warm body it didn't seem so bad. She felt like his lover—even as she reminded herself she was not. She worked hard to hold herself in reserve, to not allow her emotions to become involved—and then he'd come in looking so tired and worn, and he'd smile at her.

The things that smile did to her, the convictions it made disappear.

"Are you unhappy with the fabric? I find the color quite wonderful on you." Yvette, the modiste, spoke, her mouth full of pins.

"No, it is very nice. I was thinking of something else."

"Now what would be bringing that frown to your face? With a protector like yours you should be smiling for days. Handsome and generous."

Protector. That was the word she'd been looking for. Mark was her protector. It was a better word than any she had thought of. When she curled against him in the early hours of the morning, when he pulled her onto his chest and her nose tickled in the hair on his chest, she did feel protected, feel that all was right with the world.

And then daylight came.

Daylight and Divers. She always made sure to pull on a shift sometime in those predawn hours. There were some things she did not want seen by any man but Mark.

Only he wasn't Mark in the morning. He was Strattington.

It seemed strange that even after several days she could not see them as the same man. She'd grown used to the change, but she still could not reconcile it. Mark plied her with kisses. Strattington left her with purses—and with Divers.

"You are frowning again. Are you sure I am not sticking you with pins? I would hate for you to have any complaints," Yvette said.

Mark had suggested she call herself Yvette that first night at the inn. Somehow she did not imagine he'd had the plump, graying modiste in mind. Although her accent was quite delightful.

Isabella smiled and tried to find a response. "I am just wishing I had somewhere to wear the dress. It seems a little grand for dinner at home. I had something much plainer in mind when I first came in."

"I was instructed to be sure you had a full wardrobe and that is just what I will do." Yvette stepped back and surveyed the yellow silk. "You look like a buttercup. It suits you well, but I would never have considered the color myself. I was quite surprised when you suggested the shade."

A buttercup. It was exactly the thought Isabella had formed when she'd seen the heavy silk. She wondered if Mark would remember. A dress was surely better than a whole yellow house.

That did bring a genuine smile to her face.

"Be sure you don't keep His Grace up too late. He'll never find a wife if he doesn't look his best. He must secure the succession. We wouldn't want the bloodline to be polluted." Divers shut the bedroom door with a slam as he left.

She was growing to hate Mark's valet. It was bad

enough having to deal with him in the morning, but he'd taken to stopping by at odd hours—and always with a snide comment. Isabella wished Douglas would return from whatever errand Mark had sent him on. Douglas might have been quiet, but he never made her feel worthless the way Divers could with a single glance.

And he went through her belongings—daily.

Did he think she was pocketing the coin that Strattington left each morning? Well, she was, but she was smart enough to keep it either on her person or tucked away at night. When the time came she wanted to have options. Life had taught her the necessity of preparation.

Pacing back and forth across the room, she tried to keep thoughts of the past from her mind. This was her life now. It might not be what she wanted, what she wanted now, but it was hers.

It was the waiting for Mark that was hard. With a small sigh, she settled into her chair and stared at the door to the chamber. It would make more sense to wait for Mark in the bed. He never arrived before midnight and always came straight to her, his intent clear.

Waiting in the bed would, however, have made her feel even more of a harlot than she already did.

Wives waited in bed for their husbands to come home. She knew that, but somehow it didn't seem at all the same. If she waited in bed her whole life would devolve into what happened there—not that it wasn't wonderful. It was. Mark was endlessly considerate and imaginative. A woman could not have a better lover.

The front door of the house creaked open. The sound was unmistakable, the loud click and light scratch on the marble floor below. The soft tread of footsteps across the hall, mumbled words to the porter, another click as the door was shut and the key turned for the night, and then she heard him on the stairs.

Running her fingers through her hair, she glanced down at herself—at the red velvet robe and thin linen night rail. The modiste Divers had taken her to had tried to persuade her that lace and translucent silk were what she needed, but Isabella had held firm. The linen might be so thin as to hint at what was beneath it and the robe was very close in color to scarlet, but they still seemed like clothing a decent woman might have worn—clothing that Miss Isabella Masters might have worn. If Mark wanted her in black and gold lace he could buy it himself.

The handle of the door turned. She blew out a long breath, releasing the anger and worry that had held her all day. These moments, these hours, would not be touched by the rest. She knew she was foolish, but the smile she greeted him with as the door swung open was real.

Now, just now, she was simply Isabella, his Bella. "I am so glad you are finally here. Can I help you with your coat?"

"Not quite yet. I have a surprise for you."

What could the man have gotten her? She hoped it wasn't jewels. Jewels with no place to wear them would only make her situation more apparent. She put a smile on and rose to greet him. "I do love surprises."

"I do hope you like this one. I am afraid Divers will never forgive what it has done to my coat."

His coat? Her question faded as a soft meow echoed from his pocket and tiny furred ears poked up.

* * *

"Are you coming to bed?" Mark rolled onto his side and glanced at Bella as she sat staring down at the sleeping ball of fur. Who would ever have thought that a piece of fluff would bring her such joy? He'd only bought the kitten because the boy standing on the corner with the box had looked so tired. It was only chance that he'd even looked out of his carriage at that moment.

And Bella had seemed a little blue recently. The easy grins and laughs that normally filled her seemed to come less frequently every day. He'd wanted to cheer her and as he'd gazed into the box of kittens he'd remembered her desire for a cat.

He'd tossed the boy a shilling without another thought.

Bella's smile as she'd taken the small creature from him was even better than he'd imagined.

In fact, life was far better than he had ever expected. Stretching out on the bed, he waited for her, and his further reward.

"In a moment. Do you think he'll stay asleep?" Bella's voice echoed slightly in the darkness. She rose, moving in front of the window, the light from it silhouetting her through the thin fabric of her shift. When had white become so enticing? He could not see her smile, but he knew it was there. She was such a contradiction of seduction and innocence. One minute she seemed like she knew exactly what she was doing to him and then she'd blush and look like she was hardly out of pigtails.

"I believe he is a she. And I have no idea."

"I do hope she's not lonely. Perhaps I should put her in the bed with us."

Now that was not happening. "I am sure she'll be fine where she is. I'd hate to crush her in my sleep."

"You are right. I hadn't thought of that."

"Are you going to name her?"

Bella stopped, placing a hand beside him on the bed. Then she grinned, the smile he had been waiting for. "I do think I'll call her Duchess. Every duke needs a duchess." She climbed up beside him.

He could only grin himself. These nights with Bella made everything else seem possible. They had been together less than a week and already these nights were the highlight of each day.

And it was not merely the sex. Oh, the sex would have been enough to keep him happy—and he would have been most unhappy without it—but it was talking to Bella that he looked forward to the most. When she greeted him each night with her soft smile he felt something inside him loosen, something tight that he put on each morning with his cravat and let loose as her small hands eased the jacket from his shoulders. She would pour him a glass of brandy and no matter how late the hour they would talk—sometimes about the most mundane things, should she replace the pillows on the bed with something of a different shade or should she redo the whole chamber at once? Sometimes she asked about his family, consoling his sadness that neither his sisters nor his mother were making it to London for the festivities. On other nights he would discuss the news he had heard that day. To his surprise, she too was much more interested in current politics than in the king's wardrobe.

"Thank you for the kitten." She snuggled up beside him. "I've been missing caring for Joey these past days and Duchess will give me something to do, something to love."

He pushed aside the thought that she could have loved him. She'd been missing Joey. That must be why she'd seemed sad and worried. It was as simple as that.

He wrapped an arm about her, drawing her closer. "I am glad I could make you happy."

She kissed him lightly on the cheek. "Thank you."

She made no further move, but there was no hurry. There was great comfort in knowing what was coming without having to plan each move—not that he normally minded the planning, but he could definitely see the attraction in keeping a mistress. Having a wife must be like this too.

Where had that thought come from? He pushed it aside and turned to Isabella, running a finger down her upturned nose. "You're being quiet now. No political questions tonight?"

"Will you think me silly if I confess to just enjoying listening to you talk? I do care about politics and what is happening. In fact the more I learn the more I care, but mostly I just like listening to you. It may be the best part of my day."

"The best part?" he questioned, leaning over to lay a light kiss upon her lips.

She giggled on cue. "You know what I mean." She rubbed her hips against him. "Some things are just without compare, and therefore should not be compared."

"You're saying all the things a man likes to hear."

"Should I try doing all the things a man likes to do instead?"

Her lips began a slow trail down his chest and he did not bother to answer.

Chapter 18

It was a very small life, very safe and very contained. Isabella walked around the walled garden behind her house. Her house. Her world. She had left it exactly twice in the week since she had returned to London with Mark. Two visits to the modiste, that was her world.

That and this house. She had begun to claim it as her own, recognizing that she needed to claim something in order to survive. It was strange how the meaning of that word could change from day to day, even from hour to hour. Last week as she'd stood along the roadside, hiding from the men who sought her, survival had meant coin in her pocket and avoiding those who would drag her back to London, those who knew of her past, of her crimes. Two weeks before that, survival had meant rising at dawn to feed Joey before he could awaken Mrs. Wattington.

Sitting down on a bench, she stared at the high walls of her home, her prison.

What did survival mean now? It meant not leaving the house, not being seen more than was necessary. It meant keeping Mark happy—although that did not seem to be a problem. It meant not giving in to Divers's dour glances or the pinched lips of the housekeeper. Surviving meant trying to keep the pieces of herself together.

It meant persevering—alone.

This was not a life she had been raised for, that she understood. Even as a servant there had been a certain level of respect, and satisfaction when a job was well done. And friends. It was not until now that she realized just how important the light chatter of a chambermaid could be, realized that even if it was annoying to share her bed with a snoring lady's maid, it was still companionship.

Here she had no one, nothing.

Only Mark.

Mark and this house.

Mark should have been enough. He talked to her, he laughed with her, and he loved her—if only in the physical sense.

"Merrreow." The kitten danced into the yard, her short gray tail held high. She'd yet to master a proper meow, but Isabella delighted in her singing call.

"Trying to tell me I am not alone, are you? How could I forget about you, my Duchess?" She scooped up the cat and buried her face in the soft fluff.

"Merrreow." It was not much of an answer.

"I am sorry for ignoring you, but sometimes I just long for a person to talk to during the days. The maids make me feel a disappointment and I am not even sure why. It's like they don't want me here." She rubbed her nose in the fur again, earning herself a light swat.

Grabbing the small paw, she pulled slightly. "Don't do that or I'll think you don't like me too. Oh, do I sound like I am feeling sorry for myself?"

The kitten batted at her again.

"Do you think I should leave? I am safe here, but

how long can I go on like this? I have money now, so that is no longer an excuse." She pulled a deep breath into her lungs and held it. One week with Mark had earned her more than she'd earned in the previous year. She wondered if he had any idea how much was left on her dresser each morning—and how insulting she found it. But still she grabbed the coin and placed it in her pocket or under her pillow at night.

Because money was survival. It gave her mind the freedom to dream of something different, of that small cottage with a garden.

It gave her the chance to believe she had choices.

Only they would be choices without Mark. Whenever she pictured that small cottage he was sitting in some corner of it, or outside splitting logs. A duke splitting logs. She was clearly demented.

But did she want her dream if he was not in it? Could she be happy without him?

"I would miss him if I left, you know," she said.

The kitten looked up at her wide-eyed.

"You do think I am feeling sorry for myself and that it is not attractive."

Duchess struggled to be free and Isabella placed her back on the ground. Pulling a gulp of air into her mouth, Isabella puffed out her cheeks and blew out an extremely rude noise. There was some small advantage to always being alone. It was wonderful not to constantly monitor one's actions.

Standing, she shook out her skirts. The deep blue silk shimmered about her, tempting her to twirl in circles.

Why not?

Bowing to a narrow beech tree, she began to dance, Duchess chasing after the swirling fabric. The king's coronation was in two days and she imagined herself at one of the private balls being held the night before. Dancing had always been one of her favorite things. During the few balls she had attended before running away she had danced with anybody who asked her. There was such joy in the precise movement, in the bend and curtsy, the intricate footwork that placed one in perfect position with one's partner. It was hard dancing with an unmoving tree and a chasing kitten, but she made adjustments and ended in a great twirl, laughter flying from her. The cat looked up in confusion.

It was with some disappointment that Isabella finished her imagined dance and curtsied politely to the beech.

Maybe Mark could take her out someplace. There must be someplace that mistresses were allowed to go, mustn't there? It would be far different from Almack's, but she could adjust—just as she had to dancing with a tree and a kitten.

That would need to wait until after the coronation, however. Mark had returned later and later each night as the king demanded more from his courtiers. Her job for now was simply to help him relax and forget for a few hours all that awaited him in the day.

She twirled again, letting her skirts bell about her. She would not be disappointed in her isolation. She scooped up Duchess again and placed a kiss upon her nose.

She would go out. It was early enough in the day that nobody fashionable would be seen for hours. Mark, or rather Strattington, was probably watching the king's stocking being pulled up.

And if nobody was out, then nobody could recognize her—her pursuers could not spend their entire lives looking for her. She would go and buy ribbons and bonnets and pretend that it was all just great fun, pretend that she was the girl she used to be.

Why did being king mean that you required a room full of people in order to dress? Mark kept his face placid as the king's corset was pulled tight. Really, there were some things that should be kept private. Although, as Mark attempted to shrug his shoulders in his tight, wrinkle-free jacket, he had to admit that even with only being a duke his life had changed and things that had once seemed preposterous now seemed normal. He might allow only Divers to help him most days, but that was far more than he'd ever had before. Douglas might occasionally have helped with his uniform coat or pulled off his boots, but it had been the exception rather than the rule. And he'd certainly never had to wait for Douglas in the morning before he could begin to dress—nor had Douglas shown up when he'd had a woman in the room.

He'd almost screamed at Divers to get out the first morning he'd appeared at Isabella's bedside. The top curve of one of her breasts had been visible above the coverlet and he'd seen the man's eyes drop to it—not that he could really blame him. It was only Divers's calm look that had kept Mark from action. Divers had clearly seen nothing out of the ordinary in his being there and it had forced Mark to realize that this was just one more piece of being a duke. He hadn't liked being forced to don the mantle before he'd even put his feet on the floor.

Being king must be like that—you simply adjusted to what must be. Although the king had been raised knowing he was going to be king. He'd never had the unexpected duty thrust upon him—well, taking over the regency might not quite have been expected, but King George had seemed rather willing. Mark was not sure he would have taken the duchy if there had been any choice involved.

"I am glad to see you here." The Duke of Hargrove strode toward him. "I always value another sensible addition to our company."

Mark nodded. He could not say that he was happy to be here.

"And how was the remainder of your journey? I heard there was some commotion about a girl, a maid. I do hope it did not affect your journey."

Had the gossip about Isabella already spread through London? "My travel was quite satisfactory. Thank you."

"And the girl? What happened to her?" Hargrove asked.

Before Mark could ask why Hargrove cared, the Duke of Brisbane's voice spoke from behind. "Have you been fitted for your coronation costume yet?"

"I'll talk to you later." Hargrove strode away.

"Not a friend of yours, Brisbane?" Mark asked.

"Let's just say Hargrove and I tend to take different sides on almost everything, from voting in Lords to choosing our lovers."

Mark was not going to pursue that. "And what do you mean, *costume*? I must have seen it. I would admit to losing track, given all the swags of fabric that have been held against me in the last weeks. In truth I leave that all to my valet. He knows far more than I have any wish to."

"You have not seen it or I believe you would have

remembered. You must ask your valet about it. Given your normal somber style of dress, I would imagine he is hiding it from you."

"Why would I remember my coronation attire? I am sure it is grand, but I must confess it all seems unbelievable to me." Mark gestured down at his own dark coat. "I am still in mourning, but have been informed that there are many different shades of black and that I must know when it should be adorned with gold embroidery along with all the rest. I do not see the need to embroider so many layers of black when they do not show unless carefully examined."

Brisbane sighed softly. "I will begin with the easy question. If you had paid any attention you would realize that we are all to be dressed as Tudor nobility for the ceremony. Do you really believe that you would not have noticed a pair of bright puffed pantaloons, a properly padded codpiece, and a jacket with sleeves too broad to fit through a doorway? And the hats. I will not even begin to describe the piece of grandeur that will sit atop my head."

"Tudor?"

"You really have not been listening these last days, have you? That is something else you will have to learn. It is all very well to think about something else—someone else—but you must still pay attention and consider. The king has spent twenty-four thousand pounds on his coronation robes alone and we do not even begin to figure the cost for the raised walkway to Westminster. I understand his need for pomp and show, it is a very valuable tool, but he does not consider how the people will feel about the cost. There has been outcry at his expenditures before and still he pays no heed."

Mark's mind was still reeling from the thought of a Tudor costume. Damn right, Divers had been hiding it from him. He wouldn't—although of course he would. An important lesson in life was learning when an issue was worth raising to a high level of importance. A Tudor costume was no more than a few hours of embarrassment. There would be some discussion of the padded codpiece. He did not need padding.

"Your mind is wandering again," Brisbane said. "You must learn to keep your ears open and think at the same time. Our mutual aunt, Lady Smythe-Burke, assures me that you are more than worth the time and effort. Now, what do you think of this matter of blocking the queen from the coronation? He may have tried to divorce the woman, but she is still queen. And do keep your voice down. There are some answers you do not want to reach his ears." Brisbane's glance went to the king.

It felt wonderful to be out in the air. July was hot. It was one of those moments she was glad to be a woman. The thin blue silk of her skirts not only twirled well, it was also light. Being dressed in a wool coat, waistcoat, and high linen shirt would have been unbearable. She glanced at a man on the other side of the street. And boots. Who would wish to wear boots when the weather was like this?

She was young. She was fed. She had a place to sleep—a quite wonderful place to sleep. And she had money in her pocket, a great deal of money. It was preposterous that she had let herself feel morose because Mark was not the same in the morning as at night. Her sister had told her that the way men treated you before and after was subject to great change—although the one time she'd seen Lord Peter sneaking from her sister's rooms in the early hours of the morning he had not looked stiff and forbidding. He'd looked like he should be whistling.

She knew just how to put that look on Mark's face. Last night she'd stood before him in nothing but her stockings and she'd seen that look. Of course the likelihood of Divers arriving bedside before they were properly awake did put a damper on those thoughts in the morning. One more thing to think about after the coronation. She could not mention it to Mark when he was expected to be dressed for the king each day—but afterward—afterward might be a whole different story.

Oh, look at that bonnet. Isabella strolled across the street toward the most magnificent creation she had ever seen—feathers and froth in the most delightful shade of peach. It should have been ridiculous, but it was simply, simply wonderful. She'd have no place to wear it, but what did that matter? She'd be happy sitting in her own garden in such a flight of whimsy.

Pausing before the window, she stared at the hat, imagining herself in it. She had just decided that she would indeed purchase it when a voice called from across the street. "Isabella Masters. You stop right there. I know it is you. Don't you dare try and leave."

Chapter 19

Standing across the street, her striped gown dancing in the breeze, was Isabella's best girlhood friend, Annie Westers. Isabella glanced from side to side, searching for some possibility of escape. There was none.

She pasted a smile on her face and stood waiting as Annie darted across the street. "It is you, Isabella. Where have you been these past years? Both your sister and brother would only say you had gone to the country for a rest. I knew better. You hate the country." Annie leaned in close. "You didn't have a baby, did you?" she whispered.

Gaping in shock, Isabella didn't know what to say. She'd been scrounging to find words before Annie's question. Now she was simply speechless.

"I guess not. I should have realized, given that you are as thin as always. I just couldn't think of any other reason you'd stay away so long. Did you elope? Marry somebody most unsuitable? Do tell me that he's gorgeous, at least. A handsome footman? But if that's the case, why are you back? Did he die? That would be tragedy, of course—although it would be wonderful to have such an adventure and then come back to society afterward with no one the wiser."

"No, I have not married—and I no longer hate the country."

"That's too bad—the not marrying a beautiful, but now-deceased footman part. I've always been rather fond of the country myself. Do you think we could leak a rumor about the footman? That would explain your being away and be almost as much fun as marrying the footman."

A pounding headache was beginning to form behind Isabella's temple. Annie had never been quiet, but she had never been such a chatterbox. A part of Isabella was delighted to see her friend in such fine form, but this was not the moment for it.

"I am rambling, aren't I?" Annie's face took on a slightly dejected look. "My husband claims I have started to speak endlessly and I fear it's true. The problem is that he never speaks at all and I hate the awkward silence. I am glad that he is so busy with the king and the coronation. It is so much easier to be alone when there is no one there than when there is another person in the room."

Isabella considered the mornings when Mark turned into Strattington and nodded. "Yes, it is. I was not aware you had married. You didn't even have a beau before I left. Who did you marry?"

Annie reached out and grabbed her hand. "Lord Richard Tenant. I would have thought you had heard, but perhaps not. And, I have a child, a son. I have no idea where you have been, but it must have been the far corners of the earth not to have heard of my marriage. I had the match of the season two years ago."

"No, I have not heard anything." It all felt quite unbelievable.

"Oh, do tell me you are not doing anything besides

admiring that delightful bonnet. I have been debating buying it for days. Do come and have tea with me. My husband will not be home until late tonight and I must have company. I will even promise not to talk too much."

"I really should not."

"Oh, but you must. I need someone to talk to, someone I can trust. I know it's been years since we've seen each other, but that does not change the fact that we have always held each other's secrets tight."

Could she talk to Annie? It seemed an impossibility, but it was true that Annie had never revealed her secrets to anyone, not even when she'd run away from Masters the first time. It was hardly more than a schoolgirl prank now, but still, Annie had held her tongue when it had been the riskiest thing either of them had ever done.

"Yes, I'll come with you—but you must keep our meeting quiet. I do not want anyone to know."

"Where is she?" Mark paced back and forth across the parlor of Isabella's house. At least Douglas had returned from investigating the leases in Wales. It was good to have his friend back. "She's always here when I call."

It was true he was hours earlier than expected, and that he had not sent her a note telling her to plan for him early, but still she should be here. It was a mistress's duty to be here. He needed her. She was the one good thing in his day.

A day in which he'd actually worn tights and pantaloons. He shuddered just thinking of the experience, and that had only been at his tailor's premises. He could not even imagine that he was going to wear them parading in public—and *parading* was the word. He'd be walking on a raised platform following the king. The whole of London would be staring at his shins. At least he hoped it was his shins they'd be staring at. He told Divers that he was not wearing a codpiece of that proportion, but who knew whether the man had actually listened to him?

"I am afraid I couldn't say," Douglas answered. "But then I don't suppose you expect me to. I am not sure quite why you brought me with you. I could have told you my dull tale of farmland and cows and sheep later. I've never come calling on a mistress before."

"I've never had a mistress before."

"So why do you now?"

"I've never been a duke before."

"So you chose Miss Smith to be your mistress because you're a duke? For no other reason?"

Mark scowled at Douglas. He was not going to answer that question. "So where is she?"

"Do you want me to ask? I am sure the housekeeper or the porter would know. Or I could send a message to Divers. The man does seem to know everything. He may still be busy with the tailor, however." Douglas gave him a knowing smile.

Sinking into a chair, Mark added a scowl to his sigh. The deep pillows of the seat rose about him. A man should not be reduced to worrying about pantaloons. And certainly not a duke. He had estates to run, politics to argue—and a king to please.

He nodded to Douglas. "Ask the housekeeper. I should have set a guard on her. I don't like the thought of her wandering around alone. She's not used to London. I'd hate for her to get into trouble."

Douglas left and returned a moment later. "She

went shopping—before the noon meal. They were expecting her home a while ago, although she did not leave a time. She may simply have stopped for ices or taken a walk in the park. It is a beautiful day."

So where was Isabella now? He glanced at the clock. It was far past the time she should have returned from any shopping expedition, even if she had taken a long walk. He didn't know whether to worry or to be angered.

A duke would be angered—although, of course, he would not show it.

A man, now. A man could worry.

Douglas came and stood before him. "You seem concerned. Is there any reason to believe she is not simply taking her time? I cannot imagine what harm could befall her. You never worried about your sisters when they were late."

"It is simply not like her."

"Do you know her well enough to know what is like her?" Only Douglas would dare ask such a question.

"I know her well enough."

Douglas glanced about the parlor, his eyes stopping on the open door to the hall, and the steps leading up beyond it. "Yes, I would reckon you do."

"Oh, just spit it out," Mark said. He could see that Douglas had more he wanted to say.

"It's not my place, Your Grace." If Douglas was calling him Your Grace it was not a good sign.

"I've said to just say it," Mark said. "I am very aware that even if I dismissed you you would not leave. I am stuck with you for life, it appears, so say what you mean."

Douglas pulled in a deep breath, his chest filling

visibly. "It is just, I think you are concerned that she does not wish to return." He glanced about the room again. "She seemed a nice girl, not the sort who would end up here."

"By 'here' you mean with me."

"In these circumstances, yes. I did not see her as the type to be happy being kept. It seems somehow dishonorable." He caught Mark's eye. "But then I am not a duke."

"She is happy. I did not force her. This is what she wants."

"If you say so, Your Grace." It was clear that Douglas held a different opinion.

"I could not let her just go off on her own. It was duty to do the honorable thing and care for her."

"And this is honorable?" Douglas shut his mouth. It was clear he knew he had said too much.

"What else could I have done? Her employer beat her. I could not leave her in such a situation or risk what might happen if I just let her wander off on her own. And it's not like I could marry her."

Douglas pinched his lips together and did not reply.

Mark turned away and strode to the window, pretending that he was not staring down the street looking for her. "I will go out, to my club. You can wait here, as you take such an interest, and let me know when Bella returns."

Drawing his lips even tighter, Douglas nodded.

Pulling his coat together, Mark turned and stalked from the room.

Was Bella unhappy? The thought once planted began to root and grow. Damn. He'd let himself believe that she was just missing Joey. He was doing everything a protector was supposed to do—and more. She could not be unhappy.

He refused to feel guilty about not giving her the letter of recommendation and letting her go off to find new employment. This situation was better for both of them—not just for him.

The street was quiet as he exited and he could not resist one final glance down it.

Where was she?

"And so I married Lord Richard." Annie bit into a cake and settled back into her chair, comfortable in her own parlor. "He courted me, made me believe that I was all he had ever wanted, that he was ready to displeasure his brother by marrying me."

"His brother?" Isabella asked.

"I would have thought you would know. I was betrothed to Lord Richard's elder brother, the duke, practically from birth. It was such an old-fashioned thing and my parents never mentioned it so I assumed it was forgotten. Nobody betroths their children anymore. But then, shortly after you left, my father started making noises. He started to think it would be desirable to have me married off and to a duke."

"You have lost me." Isabella reached out for a cake and sank her teeth into the scrumptious morsel. Chocolate cream exploded into her mouth. She leaned her head against the back of her chair, curling her feet up beneath her. Tea with cakes and crumpets, a comfortable chair, the release from keeping perfect posture at all times—oh, she had missed this. It might not be the wisest way to be spending her time, but she needed these minutes of being her old self, of pretending that the world was right.

"I was prepared to be courted by the brother. I had not decided if I would marry him, but then at our first dinner at his house I met Lord Richard—and lost my heart. He was everything I had ever wanted. He could have been the hero in one of the dramas we wrote as children. And it was not just his appearance, although he can still make me breathless with a look, it was him. He was kind and strong and noble and— I could go on for hours. If you read my diary from that time you would see that I spent pages discussing just how perfect he was."

Isabella grabbed another cake. She was sure she could order them from Mark's cook, but they would not have the same magic that they had in this moment. "If he is so perfect, why do you seem so unhappy now?"

Taking two more cakes, and eating one with great speed, Annie answered. "Just before our son was born, I found out that he'd lied to me—not about who he is. It would be easier if that had all been a lie. No, he lied about wanting me, about loving me. Apparently his brother, the duke, has decided to never marry—some nonsense about losing the only one he could ever love. Oh, I know I sound cold, but his desires were no reason to do what was done to me. The duke went to my father and explained the situation, assured him that my son would still be the heir to the duchy and that a proper settlement would, of course, be made upon my marriage to Lord Richard. If they had just told me, I would have understood and could have decided what to do.

"But instead Lord Richard seduced me, convinced

me that I was the true love of his life. I was with child when we wed, sure that all my dreams had come true. He let me see heaven and then . . . I almost lost the child when I found out." Annie's words trailed off into gentle tears.

"That is horrible, but how do you know that he didn't love you? Doesn't love you? Just because he was acting at his brother's behest does not mean he does not love you."

Annie lifted her eyes and stared at Isabella. The deep pain she felt shone in those eyes, as did a knowledge far deeper than her years. "I know. Trust me, things were made clear to me. I would tell you all, but it would serve no purpose other than to make us both angry. And besides, if you have not married there are details that I should not be sharing."

"I may not be married, but I can assure you that there is nothing you could say that would shock me, Annie."

Annie pulled her feet up under her, following Isabella's example. "Did you know that I am not Annie anymore? My husband does not like it. He prefers Georgiana or Georgie. Annie does not fit with his idea of what Lady Richard Tenant should be called. When he first called me Georgie I took it for affection. Now I just think he does not care what I like."

"I've become Bella instead of Isabella. I haven't decided how I feel about it. Most times I do not mind, and in the dark of night it can be wonderful, but it does feel like being molded, turned into something I am not." Isabella licked at the cream on the edge of the cake. The wonder of the afternoon was fading as reality intruded.

"That is exactly it. It makes me feel that who I am,

who I was, is not good enough. I wish I could go back to who I was before."

"Do you? I am never sure," Isabella answered. "I know that things were simpler then, and that I was happy, or at least more content most of the time, but I like who I've grown into. Going through hard times has made me mature, made me be less silly. I think I am a better person now than I was when last we met."

"Do you? I've spent most of the last years on Lord Richard's estates with my son. I did feel happy and worthy while I was there. I could spend all day playing with my baby. It is only here, in London, where I feel I serve no purpose."

Isabella leaned toward her. "Then why don't you go back to the country? Does your husband demand your presence here?"

Annie—or rather Georgie – laughed, but not happily. "I long to go back. And no, I think Lord Richard would rather I left. We barely speak—except that I am always talking, but he never hears so that does not seem to count. It is clear he is uncomfortable with me in the house. I believe that is why he is hardly ever here. But, and it is a big *but*, I have decided that I want another child, and that does seem to necessitate us both being in the same location—even if it means I must leave my sweet baby in the country for a few months. Now, enough about me. Tell me what you have been doing. I know you are trying to avoid the subject, but this is I. You can tell me anything and I will not tell anyone. I may talk a lot these days, but I have never revealed a secret. Come now, I have told you all but the most intimate details of my life."

Could she do it? Isabella had never talked to anybody about what happened, not a single soul. Her sister had been there at the end and must have some idea—and Lady Smythe-Burke knew that something had happened—but Isabella had never actually said the words to anyone. "Do you have any sherry to go with the cakes? Or is that too forward a question? I think I need more than tea if I am going to talk."

"Let me call for it."

They were silent for a minute, a good silence that filled the space by itself. How had she survived so long without a girlfriend to talk with? These few minutes had filled her with a warmth that ran clear down to her toes.

Annie—Isabella could not think of her by any other name no matter how she tried—poured generous glasses when the sherry arrived and lifted hers into the air. "To us, may we always be able to talk—no matter what."

"To us," Isabella said, mirroring the gesture. Then she put the glass down.

She was going to do it. With all that had happened today and in the last week she needed to.

"I killed Foxworthy." There, it was out.

Chapter 20

Annie stopped her glass halfway to her mouth and stared. "You stabbed him? I wouldn't blame you, but I don't believe you."

"No, no—or at least partly no. I didn't stab him. I pushed him and he fell and split his head open, but I assure you he was most dead."

"But he was stabbed. Everybody knows that. The knife was left sticking right out of the middle of his chest."

Pulling a large swallow into her mouth, Isabella let it sit and burn for a moment. "I know—I have heard that—but I was there. There was no knife involved."

"Perhaps you just thought he was dead. Maybe you didn't kill him." Annie sounded hopeful.

"No. I have wished that myself, but he was dead. I have no doubts about that."

They were silent again and this time it was not wonderful and full.

The wind whistled outside the window and Isabella turned, shocked at how late it had gotten. She should be going, but who was there to miss her? Mark would not come by until late, probably very late, with the coronation little more than a day away. But now there was Duchess. "I should be going."

"Nonsense. You have just begun to talk. I will not grill you about why you killed Foxworthy. I know your brother was trying to force you to marry him—and I know what a toad he was. I would imagine that he forced you to it."

"If only all the world were as understanding as you. I did not mean to kill him. It was an accident, but as you do not wish to talk about the intimate details of your marriage, so I do not wish to remember that time. How it happened would not matter. I killed him and that really is the end of the situation."

"It certainly is not the end. You have barely begun your story. I don't even know yet where you went or what you were doing. You must tell me more—at least a little."

Isabella glanced out the window again. A stiff wind was growing. The thought of going out and calling for a hack to take her back to her empty house was not pleasant.

"I've been in service. Can you believe that? I've been a governess, a companion, and most recently a baby nurse. Did you ever imagine to see me with a baby?"

"Actually I did."

Annie's words caught in Isabella's throat. She'd always assumed the same. It was other people's children she'd had a hard time picturing herself with, not her own.

Suddenly Annie leaned forward, a grin spreading across her face. "I've the most wonderful idea."

Isabella remembered that expression well. "What?" she asked with some trepidation. Annie's plots did not always end well.

"You can be my companion. Richard was just

saying that he wished I had somebody to talk to so I wouldn't bend his ear so constantly. Who could be better than you?"

"But I don't want to stay in London. As long as I am here I fear that somebody will find out about Foxworthy. And—"

It was so hard to explain the rest of her situation. Confessing to murder should have been the hardest part of this, but somehow it was even harder to tell Annie that she was now a courtesan—even if she was a duke's mistress.

"Well, that's perfect. Nobody is talking about Foxworthy anymore. I can't believe anybody even cares. And as soon as I am with child then we can move back to Richard's country estate and spend our days sitting in the garden or walking by the lake. And if you have experience being a baby nurse and a governess so much the better. Oh dear. That did not sound like I meant it to. I would never consider you a servant, Isabella."

"But I am one—or at least I was. Now . . ." She pulled in a deep breath. "Now I am the Duke of Strattington's mistress."

Annie laughed. "Oh, what nonsense. You almost had me believing you. But you, you would never do such a thing."

Isabella sank back in her chair. Life could always take you by surprise. "You believe that I killed Foxworthy with little more than a raised eyebrow, but you don't believe that I am Strattington's mistress? Whyever not?"

"Well to start with, if you've been in service how would even meet a duke? I've never known baby nurses and dukes to mingle, or is that the newest fashion?"

"Actually you'd be surprised how many young men seem to make their way to the nursery with a roving eye. It's something to keep in mind if you ever do have that child you long for. But, as it happens, I met him on the road to London. Travel can relax many of the normal boundaries."

Annie leaned forward again. "You mean you really are a duke's mistress? How absolutely wonderful. That is even better than running off with a handsome footman."

"You are being silly—and this is my life. There is nothing wonderful about the situation I have found myself in." Well, there were plenty of wonderful points, but she was not going to discuss those with Annie.

"I am sounding like a silly fool," Annie said. She leaned back and hooked a foot around a leg of the chair. "I hate that I've become this way. Ever since things went wrong with Richard, I chatter and indulge in silly gossip, things I never used to care about."

Isabella made no comment.

"But you must stay for dinner. There is something else I need to talk to you about. I am sure your duke won't be back until late and—"

Suddenly the door to the hall swung open wide. "Well, well, who is this, my dear sister? I did not know you had a guest."

Isabella's eyes widened as the Duke of Hargrove strode into the room. He stopped and stared at her a moment, the strangest smile playing about his mouth. She could only hope he had not seen her at one of the inns they had stopped at. Mrs. Wattington had pointed him out to her once, but why would he have noticed her?

* * *

Mark resisted the urge to count the strokes of the clock. It was late, too late, and Douglas still had not sent him notice that Isabella had returned. He glanced at the cards he held, almost certainly a winning hand, and dropped them on the table, making his apologies. It was too hard to concentrate when he was worried.

And angry.

Isabella had left him. The cold conviction was growing deep in his chest, a small knot becoming ever tighter. It was a ridiculous thought. What possible reason could she have to leave? He gave her everything she could possibly want.

But the feeling would not leave.

He kept seeing her stoic face when she'd first climbed into his carriage on the way to London, her shock when he'd made his proposal. He didn't know what it was she wanted, but it was not what he offered. He remembered her dreaming about that country cottage, with husband and family. That was something he could never offer—even if he wanted to. Yes, he gave her everything, but at the price of her happiness.

"You are looking glum—and that was not well done." The Duke of Brisbane spoke from behind him.

"I am sorry."

"A man of our stature always finishes the hand. To throw your cards in implies that you cannot afford to lose. It can lead to all types of mistaken conclusions—and it is just bad manners."

"I was winning. I just lost my taste for the play." He turned to face Brisbane.

"That is even worse. If you are winning you must

finish the hand to give others the opportunity to regain their losses."

"But I would only have taken more of their money."

Brisbane raised a brow and gestured to two empty seats. "Do you have time for a drink? Tomorrow night will be filled with all the pre-coronation balls and soirees—and then the next day . . . Did you ever see your costume?"

Mark could not suppress a shudder at the thought. "Yes."

"I imagine yours are at least somber, if not black. The joy of mourning. I am going to look like a peacock. I don't think even our grandfathers wore such colors with their long powdered wigs. We will look like a parade of tropical birds as we stroll along to Westminster."

"That's a polite way of putting it."

"That is part of the art of being a duke—saying exactly what you think, but without giving offense. Unless, of course, you mean to. That is a far different story." Brisbane draped a knee over the armchair, but somehow still retained the appearance of upright posture.

Mark drew a long swallow of the offered brandy. The warm burn down his throat was reassuring. At least some things had not changed. He let his head fall back and stared at the ceiling. "It was so much easier when I was mere mister. Who wants to worry about what one says all the time?"

"I think you were doing it before and just didn't realize it. A duke is actually far freer to say what he wishes, he just needs to say it in the right way."

"I am not sure that I take your meaning."

"If you wish to say something irregular, unpopular, or off-putting, you merely need to inject your voice with enough authority or disdain. If you look down upon someone and peer at them as if they are dirt, you can say whatever you wish. The only one this does not work with is the king." Brisbane pulled out his monocle and swung it in easy loops. "And, of course, you should get a quizzing glass. Ever so valuable."

Mark was about to answer when Brisbane suddenly straightened. "Damnation. You are about to meet one of the few great inconveniences of being a duke. The father with unmarried daughters. Beware, no matter what he says it will lead to a situation where you will be forced to converse with one of his daughters. And, I am afraid, Milton's daughters all look like the horses he so values."

"Brisbane, it is so good to see you." Lord Milton approached, holding out a hand.

"Milton, as always." Brisbane turned to Mark and it was impossible to miss the glint in his eye. "I am afraid I was just leaving, but you must meet His Grace of Strattington. I know you were well acquainted with his uncle. Do forgive me." And then he was gone. Were dukes also given a special cloak of invisibility? If so, Mark wanted to know where his was. He rose from his chair and acknowledged Milton.

"Good to meet you. As Brisbane said, I knew your uncle well. We were in school together. A fine man. Such a pity about both him and your cousin—but good for you, heh?" He gave Mark an elbow nudge.

It seemed rude, the height of rudeness, to comment on death as being good for anyone. Mark almost smiled politely, but then he remembered Brisbane's words. He stretched to his full height—it must be hard being a short duke—and peered down his nose at Milton. "Actually it was most unpleasant. I have never considered death good, having seen too much of it in the war. And you, have you ever experienced a good death?"

Milton took a step away, lost his jovial expression. "Do forgive me. I meant no harm. As I've said, I was friends with your uncle—and your cousin, Lord William."

Mark just continued to glare.

Pushing his shoulders back, Milton tried again. "And how are you enjoying London? It is quite an exciting time with the coronation. I am sure you must have spent hours with His Majesty. I do look forward to the ceremony."

Despite Brisbane's comments it probably would not do to say exactly what he thought of all the pomp and foolishness. "It certainly is different than what I am used to."

"And tomorrow evening? You must have invitations to all the best affairs. Will you be making the rounds?"

"I try to restrict myself to one, perhaps two, parties an evening." He did not want to get back to Isabella too late. His worry over her absence returned to him. It was far, far past when Douglas should have sent for him. It was time for him to go and seek her himself.

"And which will you be attending tomorrow?"

"I thought perhaps Lord Richard Tenant's masquerade." He spoke the words before he saw the trap.

"Oh, then perhaps I will see you there. I must introduce you to my oldest. Caroline was a great favorite of your uncle's. I am sure you would enjoy a dance with her."

* * *

Isabella could only stare aghast as the Duke of Hargrove entered the room. Did he remember her from the inn? Surely not. She looked far different here than she had in her plain gray dress with her hair pulled back. It was possible that she sparked some flash of memory, but she could not have made a true impression on him.

"It is so good to see you, brother." Annie rose with a smooth grace she had not yet demonstrated. "Richard will be so sorry to have missed you. Is there something I can help you with?"

"I was coming to ask that of you. I am not sure why you and my brother wished to host this masquerade tomorrow night—and why you chose not to have it in my ballroom—but still I wish to do what I can." He pulled out a handkerchief, edged in rich plum lace that matched his waistcoat, and lightly dabbed his lip. He turned back to Isabella, making it clear he expected an introduction.

Isabella almost held out her own hand. She didn't know what she would say, but—

Reaching out a hand and laying it on Isabella's arm, Annie smiled at her brother-in-law. "Let me make you known to Miss Bella," she glanced about the room, "Miss Bella Crumpet. I have been looking for a companion, on Richard's advice, and have decided upon Miss Crumpet."

"I am pleased to meet you, Miss Crumpet." Hargrove looked anything but. "There is something familiar about you. Have we met before?"

He couldn't remember her. He couldn't. Had they met sometime previously that she did not recall? "I do not believe so, Your Grace."

"Probably not, then. I am sure you'd have remembered."

"Do forgive me, my lord, but I must be going. I am sure you and Lady Richard have much to talk about." Isabella eased toward the door.

"You will be by first thing tomorrow, will you not, Miss Crumpet? I do have plans that I need your help with." Annie moved to intercept her.

"Surely you do not plan to put the poor girl to work on your masquerade on the first day?" Hargrove stared at Isabella coolly. She was tempted to wipe her nose to be sure there was not a blob of chocolate cream upon it.

Annie squared back her shoulders. "That, I believe, is my own business." She turned to Isabella. "You will be here?"

"Yes." Until she decided what she was doing she would hold tight to the one friend she had.

She should have taken Annie's offer of a carriage. While it was still several hours until full dark, the streets had taken on the quiet feeling of a forest before a storm. London could never be still, but it seemed everyone moved with silent purpose.

Passing the shop with the bonnet she had so loved earlier, she paused for a moment, distracted by the perfection of the foolishness. She was about to turn away when a man's reflection joined her own. He was only an inch or two taller than she, but the width of his shoulders almost doubled her own.

"You've caused me quite a lot of trouble, Miss Masters," he said, moving to block her escape. She knew that voice. It was the man who had grabbed her on the stairs at the inn, the last rider who had followed after the man in the blue coat. She had been found.

She started to turn, but his hand gripped her arm, forcing her to stillness. "Just keep looking at the hat. I am sure you would look quite fetching in it." His fingers wrapped tighter.

"I don't know what you want," she replied, keeping her eyes locked on his reflection in the glass.

"I don't believe that. Why would you have taken it if you didn't know what it was?"

"Will you just tell me who you work for, then perhaps I would know?"

"Come, come, Miss Masters, you can do better than that. We have been quite patient with you, but I want it now."

Isabella closed her eyes for the briefest of seconds. "I really don't know what you want."

The man's fingers dug into her arm. She was sure to have bruises in the morning. "Just hand the papers over—you must have them by now. I can't believe you don't have them with you. Do I need to drag you into an alley and search you myself?"

"I'll scream."

"I don't think you will. You cannot have attention drawn to you now, can you? If you scream I will simply say that I apprehended you, that I remembered seeing you fleeing from Foxworthy's after his murder and wanted to bring you to the authorities. Do you wish to hang?"

Every nightmare she'd ever had seemed to come true in that one moment. "I will deny I know what you are talking about. It is years later. Who would believe that I had anything to do with such a thing?" She widened her eyes, trying to look even younger than she was.

"The man I work for will make sure that interest is taken. Do not force him to such measures. He was no fonder of Foxworthy than you, but he must have the papers that you took."

"Papers? What papers? I truly am not sure what you mean. I would admit to grabbing some things from his desk, but I was only after letters regarding my own family. There was nothing else of any import. And I certainly do not have them with me."

The man loosened his grip slightly, considering her words. "Then why did you take them?"

"I was just grabbing what I could. I didn't have time to look for exactly what I needed."

"Assuming that you speak the truth—and that is not my decision to make—where are these worthless papers that you grabbed?"

They were in her room at Masters's house—or at least that was where she had left them. Should she just say she had destroyed them, tossed them in the fire to burn? The man met her gaze in the window, staring deep into her eyes. It was impossible not to believe that he would know if she lied. "I don't know. It was years ago. Why did you not ask me then?"

"It took a while to find out who you were. We thought it was your sister, Lady Peter St. Johns, who had taken them. By the time we realized it was not, you were gone. We might still be looking for you if we hadn't followed your brother's man."

Even with her fear Isabella stopped at those words. Lady Peter St. Johns. Violet had married Lord Peter then. For the first time Isabella felt some sense of relief. At least that had gone right. Her leaving London had allowed Violet to marry the man she truly loved.

The relief did not last long.

The man's fingers tightened again. "Do not play with me. My employment depends on my getting those papers. I suggest that you find them and fast. You have until tomorrow."

That was impossible. "With everything going on with the coronation, that is not enough time for me to retrieve them. I left them behind when I left London. Even if I tried to get them nobody will be receiving until after the coronation."

He considered. It was clear he did not like to give ground. "Three days, then. The day after the coronation. But do not think to run. You will be followed, and the next time my employer will not be merciful"

Then he was gone. A crowd hurried by and he disappeared along with them.

Isabella was left staring at the hat. It did not seem so enchanting now.

Chapter 21

"Where have you been?" He sounded like an overprotective father, waiting at the door. Mark was glad he wasn't actually waiting at the door. It had been close.

Isabella walked slowly up the stairs toward him. "You are here early."

"Not so early—and where have you been?"

"Does it matter?" She sounded very weary, her face pale.

"Of course it matters. I do not like to be kept waiting." That should have brought a spark to her eyes.

"Should I just remove my dress and get on the bed then?" She sounded serious, not joking at all.

He was tempted to say yes. He might have been worried, but there was still that core of anger burning. She was his. She should not be late without his permission. He hated how he sounded, even in his thoughts, but he could not rid himself of the feeling. "That will not be necessary. You simply need to explain why you are so late."

He turned and stalked to the bedchamber.

She sighed softly and followed. "I went out to choose some new ribbons and baubles. I thought that was the purpose of the purses you leave me."

"You do not like the purses?" He didn't know how he knew that from her words, but it was very clear.

"No. There is not a problem with the purses. I am your mistress. What does it matter how you pay me?"

"I do not pay you. I choose to give you gifts. That is quite different." How had they ended up talking about this?

"If you say so." It was clear she was not convinced. She sounded so tired, so lifeless.

She walked to the dresser and started to pull the pins from her hair. "Have you eaten? I am going to call for a tray."

"Do I need to demand that you tell me where you've been?" He came up behind her and placed a hand on each of her hips.

She removed the last pin and, as her hair fell down her back, leaned back against him. "It really does not matter. I shopped and wandered for several hours without buying anything. I almost bought a hat, but then lost my taste for it. I had a long tea and then I walked in the park and thought about life. I was out too late, I know. I lost track of time as I wandered and considered. I know it was dangerous, but I truly was not thinking about it. I would have returned sooner if I knew you would be here. I did not think it mattered."

"There is more that you are not telling me." He nuzzled the top of her head, his anger dissipating. Now that she was here, in his arms, the world seemed right again—if only she did not seem so troubled. "You can tell me your secrets."

She rested her head back against his shoulder and for a moment he thought she would answer honestly, but then she pulled back. "What more could there be?

Do you worry I have another paramour? A second duke come to sweep me off my feet? I assure you that one is more than enough for me." Her eyes were closed and he could not see her expression.

He did worry. That was the thing. He wanted her to be his, completely—and he wanted her to be happy. He was not sure that he liked either feeling. "I am hungry—but not for food." He let his fingers wander up from her waist.

Her shoulders tensed and then relaxed. Turning in his arms, she laid her face against his chest. "I'll ask for the tray to be sent in an hour. Does that suit you?"

Now his hands moved lower, cupping her buttocks, squeezing lightly—and then harder. He felt himself harden against her soft belly. "That should suit me just fine."

He waited as she tilted up her chin and began to kiss him. Her eyelids were still lowered, hiding her gaze. He wished she would look up, but was afraid of what he might see.

She was crying. In all of her years Isabella could never remember waking with tears upon her cheeks. She slipped from Mark's embrace, easing away from him in the bed. The whole room was in darkness, the candle gutted on the bedside table. Her pillow was cool to the touch and she turned her face into it as tears continued to stream.

She had dreamed the most wonderful dream. The cottage, a garden of flowers, the smell of bread baking—and Mark—and a baby, a small, dark-haired creature who had combined the best of both them. She'd felt the baby in her arms, his gentle weight. She'd felt Mark's hands on her shoulders easing her aches, his soft kiss upon the back of her neck. She'd been so happy, so content. All the desire for family, all the desire to fit in, to belong, captured in one bright moment.

But it was a dream. A dream that would never be.

Her heart ached with the longing for it.

It had been so wonderful and now she was back in her life, back with the whispering man's threats hanging over her.

Careful not to sob, she rolled onto her side and stared at her lover. There was just enough moonlight that she could see his sleep-softened features. His long lashes lay heavy against his cheeks. His lips curved upward in a small smile of satisfaction.

She wrapped her arms tight, fighting the chill that took her. How was she ever going to find the papers she had taken from Foxworthy's house? Was there a way she could return to her brother's house? Could she sneak in? It might be possible. She'd certainly left it enough times without being detected.

Looking about the dark room, she wished that she could stay in this moment, put aside her desire for more—and her fear that she could not even keep this.

If she could not find a way to retrieve the papers, or could not find the papers at all, what would she do? The whispering man was correct that Mark, that a duke, did not need a mistress hanged for murder. Even the accusation would cause Mark to cast her aside.

The thought was too painful. She could not risk it.

It might even be better to hang. That was just being morose, but at this moment, this exact moment, the emotion seemed true.

Despite the whispering man's threats she would have to flee again, leave again.

Could she go to Annie? Surely if she was careful nobody would make the connection. This time she would stay inside, never let her face be seen until they went to the country. She could care for Annie and the child Annie longed for. It would in so many ways be the answer to all her problems. Nobody would seek her there and if she was gone there would be no reason for the man and his mysterious employer to bother Mark. She would never feel the pain of his rejection.

Mark stirred in his sleep, rolling onto his back and reaching out to lay a hand upon her shoulder. His warm fingers gripped her and then relaxed, reassured of her presence.

How could a moment so sweet cut her so deeply?

She started to turn away, but his fingers caught her again.

He opened his eyes. "You're crying."

Denying it would have been pointless. "Yes."

She waited for him to ask why, but he did not. He just stared across the bed at her in the moonlit twilight of the room.

His hand moved from her shoulder to brush a tear from her cheek. He brought it to his lips.

"I thought I could make you happy," he said at last.

"You do." It was not a lie.

"But the situation does not."

"I was not brought up for this."

"And you want more?"

She closed her eyes. The word hung on her tongue—it felt as if she had to physically push it out. The word was honest, but it would also leave him unsurprised when she disappeared. "Yes."

He sighed and stared up at the canopy. "I don't have more to offer."

"I know. I should be content with what I have. It is far more than I would have expected. You are very generous."

"Too generous, apparently. You do not like the purses of coin."

"To be honest I do not think any woman would. It makes the fact that I sell myself to you too apparent."

Turning back toward her, he brushed her cheek again. "I do not feel that you sell, or that I buy. Why can I not take care of you without it being a transaction? I want to care for you."

"If you only wanted to care for me you would have given me enough funds to survive on until I found other employment. I am here because you want me here. Let us be honest. We are always honest in the night—it is only the morning that brings distance and deception. The purses are left in the morning."

"I will have to inquire how these things are handled. You make it clear that I have it very wrong."

She smiled, with only a slightly bitter edge. "I do not know that there is a right way. And who would you ask? Divers again?"

"I don't know who I would ask. Maybe Brisbane?" He said the last as if speaking to himself.

She had not meant to fight. There was a good chance she would leave him tomorrow—forever—and she had not meant to spend their last night bickering. Even when he had seen her tears she had thought it was concern that marked his face. Now she was not so sure. It was the first time that she'd felt so separate from him in the dark of the night.

She dabbed at the tears on her cheek with the edge of the sheet, the embroidery abrading her cheek. The dark of the room lay around them, isolating them from the purple madness. This was their time. The small hours of the morning when passion and caring met. She wiped at the tears harder, willing them to stop. She knew her emotions were not leaving her rational. "Why could you not just give me money and let me go? You've given me more in this last week than I would have needed to survive a year. Why could you not have done this days ago? Before—" She stopped and took a deep breath. "You say you don't pay me, but if the money is a gift, why wait? Why not give it to me before I became your mistress?"

"I did not force you to come to me. I never have."

"Then let me go."

"I am certainly not stopping you. As you've said, I've given you enough funds."

She wanted to leave him. Mark stared at the purple pansies embroidered on the bed's canopy. He could not really see them, but he knew they were there. He had forced her into this situation. He wished he could deny it, but he must be honest with himself. He had wanted her and he had taken her.

He had been very much the duke. Perhaps he was learning far quicker than he had believed.

He tried to ignore the tears that still leaked down her cheeks, tried to resist the urge to wipe them.

He had not meant what he said. He had spoken in anger at the thought that she was not happy. He certainly did not want her to leave.

She was better off with him. He could not begin to imagine all the trouble she could land in if she left. A young woman alone was not safe. And even if she found employment it could be for somebody like

Mrs. Wattington, someone who would abuse her with words and perhaps even hit her.

That was not what he wanted for his Bella.

And she was his.

Only. . .

Only she wanted to leave him. He could see it in each tear that trickled down her soft cheek. He longed to kiss the tears away, but feared that would only make them flow faster.

He stared at the flowers he could not see and awaited her answer.

"Is that what you want, for me to leave?" She followed his lead, rolling onto her back to look up into the darkness.

"It is you who speaks of wanting to leave. I make no such demands."

"So you want me to stay?"

Such a simple question, such an easy answer, but the words would not come. She was better off with him, he could keep her safe—but he could not give her what she wanted, what she needed to be happy. "You need to do what you think best."

She rolled further, turning onto her side—away from him.

The inches between them could have been feet, or yards—but they were as uncrossable as an iron fence. He swung out of bed and went to stare out the window at the silent street. Not even the leaves on the trees moved to distract him. He had hoped for the first traces of daylight, some marker that things would soon begin afresh. There was only black.

He grabbed his pants off a chair and pulled them on. "I shall return home. Divers will be happy not to be dragged over here to dress me in the morning. It will be a very long day preparing for the coronation and I will have events to attend until late into the night."

She did not reply, did not tell him she would miss him, did not tell him he was welcome at any hour.

He grabbed the remainder of his clothing and headed to the door. He slipped through it quietly, closing it with barely a click.

It felt more final than a slam.

He'd never left her before. It felt as if he no longer wanted her. She'd always heard that about men, heard that once the pursuit was over, the challenge gone, they lost interest. She had not expected it to apply to herself.

Granted, she had tried to make it so he would not be surprised if she left. She just hadn't expected it to be so easy.

Not that she thought he would kick her out. Isabella dropped the brush on the dresser and turned to survey the purple room.

This was the moment. Did she stay or did she go?

She wanted to stay. Despite everything, she wanted to stay.

But she could not, not while the whispering man's threats surrounded her.

She did have more than enough money to keep herself for quite a while and Annie had given her a place to go. If she could sneak over to Annie's house and stay out of sight once there, she would be safe. She refused to believe that the whispering man would find her again.

Why was she even debating? She had been over this before. There really was no choice. She would run as she had before.

If she could have trusted Mark with the truth she might have been able to stay, but she did not trust him. If he could not even consider marriage to her now, then how would he feel if he knew the truth? He would never protect a murderess. And even if he did, what would that do to him? She knew how he cared about his station, his duties; helping her could only hurt him.

Her dreams had been false.

Leaving felt like cutting a piece out of herself, but it was a piece she would have to live without.

She began to plan.

"I am so glad that you have come." Annie grinned from cheek to cheek as she led Isabella in through the kitchen door. "I was worried that you would not—and I realized that I could not get in touch with you if you did not. I suppose I could have asked Strattington tonight . . . Oh, don't look at me like that. I am joking. You know that I would never do that. I must guess that you have come to stay, given your method of arrival. It quite confused me when the maid told me the cook said that I had a visitor in the kitchen. That has never happened before. But do come in now and have some tea—or would you like to go to your room first?"

"Tea would be fine."

"I will have someone take your bag up. Come. I have so much to discuss and I find I need your help."

"You need my help?" Maybe Annie's problems could distract her from her own. She would not think of all she had left behind, not think of Duchess. Mark would care for her.

Mark. She promised herself again that she would

not think of him, not consider what she had lost. She would think only about what Annie needed and nothing more.

"Yes, I am afraid I do. I have set up this perfectly wonderful masquerade for tonight and now I find myself in need."

Isabella followed Annie into the parlor and sat. The room was just as pretty as before. The rest of the home might seem lacking in feminine flourishes, but here every delicately arranged flower and figurine hinted at her friend's touch. She took a chair across from Annie, running a finger over the flocked cotton upholstery. Soft green had always been Annie's favorite. "What could you possibly need from me? It is I who am here seeking your help, in your debt."

"What nonsense. We are friends, we help each other. There is no debt involved."

After a statement like that, how could Isabella do anything besides help her friend? "What do you need?"

"I need you to come to my masquerade tonight."

"You what?" That had not come out as graciously as she had meant. "Do you need another maid?"

"Of course not. How could you even think such a thing? I need you to come as a guest."

"But I will be recognized. I cannot risk it. You should not risk it."

"It is a masquerade."

"But when the masks come off . . ." What was Annie thinking? She could never do such a thing. She had come here because she could think of no better hiding spot than heading off to the country with Annie. This was not in the plans.

"That is the beauty of what I need. You can be

long gone when the masks are removed, the dominoes lowered. I only need you to pretend to be me for a few hours."

"Pretend to be you? A few hours?"

There was a tap at the door and the maid entered bearing a full tray, not just the cup and teapot Isabella had been expecting. There were more of those fabulous cakes. Her mouth watered at the reminder of the thick, rich chocolate cream. The memory of the flavor filled her mouth—but her distraction lasted less than a single second. She waited for the maid to leave. "I don't understand. Why do you need me to be you? And how would we ever accomplish such a thing?"

Annie took a cake and smiled, the grin spreading from ear to ear. "I've planned that already, but the friend who was going to help me cannot. Do take a cake. My physician has assured me it is not healthy for a woman to be too thin."

That was far more than Isabella really wanted to know. "So tell me about tonight."

"Oh, yes." Annie leaned forward, her excitement palpable. She lifted her cake but did not bite into it. "I am going to the masquerade as the three Graces. I have the most delightful costume and wig—revealing, but not too much so."

"You're going as the three Graces?"

"Oh, stop. I am going as one of the three Graces, but I have friends who will dress as the other two."

Ah, now Isabella understood. "And one of them dropped out?"

"No, but . . ." And now Annie hesitated.

A *but* was never a good thing with Annie. "Then why do you need me? I can't imagine you want four Graces."

"No, I definitely don't want four—only I do."

"That makes sense." Isabella placed as much irony as she could in her voice.

"I am explaining this badly." Annie bit into her cake and chewed.

Isabella bit into her own and waited.

"I want there to always be three Graces and I don't want to always have to be one of them. I want to be able to slip away if I choose." Annie began to turn red as she spoke.

"And why do you want to be able to slip away?" Isabella was afraid she already knew. There was only one person it was likely Annie would wish to hide from.

"I don't wish my husband to know if I leave."

Isabella closed her eyes. She should ask why, but surely there was only one answer. If Annie wished to hide from her husband, it had to be because there was another man.

She bit into her cake again, but it no longer tasted so sweet. "I thought you were trying to have a child."

"I am." Annie put her cake down, stood, and walked to the empty fireplace. She ran a finger along the gray-lined marble. "I am just not sure with whom."

"Your husband, I would have thought." The cake was beginning to taste like sawdust. Isabella could not believe that Annie meant what she said.

Annie picked up a delicate figurine of a couple embracing. She ran a finger down the line of the man's back. "I thought so too. I cannot pretend to be happy with what I contemplate, but . . ."

If there was one thing Isabella knew, it was that life did not always grant fair choices. She would try not to judge her friend until she knew the full story.

"I still can't believe your plan would work. Even if we wore the same costume surely someone would notice the difference between us." She gestured to her own figure and then Annie's. "We are not exactly the same."

Annie put the figurine down and turned back to Isabella, her soft green skirt swirling about her. "That is the beauty of my plan. With three, or four, of us dressed the same there will always be confusion about who is who. As long as three are visible nobody will question too closely if they do not recognize whichever one is closest to them. Lord Richard will just assume I am the Grace across the room."

Isabella still had her doubts. She wanted to refuse—but how could she with all Annie was prepared to do for her? "Let me see the costumes."

Chapter 22

"I am surprised that she did not slit your throat as you slept." Brisbane spoke quietly, but the words held their own power.

Mark kept his eyes focused ahead, looking only at the king, not looking at Brisbane or inviting others to listen to their conversation. "It is that bad? I asked my valet and trusted what he said. He has never steered me wrong before."

"You trusted your valet." It was said as a statement, but question and irony rang in each syllable. "You trust your valet that your cravat does not make you look a fool. You trust your valet that the stitching on your waistcoat is not too garish. You can even trust him to tell you that your court dress is too simple. But you never ask your valet how to pay your mistress."

"But you do pay her?" Mark was feeling the fool and it was a feeling he did not like.

Brisbane sighed without making a sound. It was evidently one more aspect of being a duke that Mark would need to practice.

"You do not pay a mistress. You keep her. I do not believe coin has ever passed between myself and a woman whose company I enjoyed. It would be vulgar—in the extreme. A man should never be vulgar, unless he chooses to be."

"Then what does she do for coin?"

"All her accounts are sent to you, discreetly."

"What if she needs funds for something small, some worthless trinket?"

"I do not actually know, but I imagine that either the household accounts are exaggerated or that some piece of jewelry you have given her, that she does not care for, may disappear. That is her concern, not yours."

Mark pondered this as he watched the king discuss how to maneuver with a cloak of such length and weight. And warmth. Why the man chose to wear ermine in July Mark would never understand. Why be king if you could not be comfortable? If he were king he'd outlaw neckwear that reached above one's chin.

He was glad he had asked Brisbane about Isabella—not directly, no names had been given. It had been difficult to approach him about the question, but there had been nowhere else to turn. Still— "I am not sure I understand why it makes such a difference. Is it not payment no matter what form it comes in?"

Brisbane nodded to another gentleman across the room. "All I can say is that it matters. And I think it matters for us as well as them. If it's as simple as throwing down a coin or two then you might as well visit a brothel. A mistress is for much more than that—at least mine always were."

Mark did see the sense in that. His relationship with Isabella was about far more than sex.

"I trust I will see you at the Tenants' this evening? It will be an event not to be missed. There will, of course, be other required stops throughout the evening. It will be a nuisance to stop home and change before heading to the masquerade." Brisbane glanced at the king. He rose from his chair like a large cat stretching. "But Lady Richard throws a party not to be missed."

"There's nothing to it," Isabella exclaimed.

"I think the half mask will cover your face quite well," Annie answered. "I wanted to be quite sure that nobody could see our features. I made sure the mask was raised slightly above the eyes to leave them cast in shadow. The lips, of course, I left uncovered, but I did specify that we all wear the same color of rouge—and perfume. Perfume is always important."

Isabella slipped her hand under the many layers of sheer silk. "It is not my face I was worried about." In fact she had not even considered the mask, which demonstrated just how shocked she was by the bodice. "My chemise would show."

"The Greeks and Romans did not wear chemises and neither shall we."

"The other women agreed to this?" It was impossible to imagine any lady agreeing to such a costume. Even her sister, Violet, would have questioned the dress.

Annie picked the dress up and held it against her body, smoothing it over her curves. The single shoulder that held it up was clasped with a silver pin. The rest of the dress—if one could call it a dress—consisted of layers and layers of fine chiffon draped to drift with every movement. If the wind blew, the wearer was likely to be left completely bare—not that there was much wind in a ballroom. "I would admit there was some trepidation, but yes, they have agreed."

"Can you wear anything under it?"

"You could probably wear Roman sandals, but I am considering that we should all have bare feet."

"Bare feet? In public?" Isabella was not sure why this shocked her even more than the slightness of the dress.

"It will make a statement about how free we are feeling, about all the rules and propriety that we are willing to slip off for the evening."

"I've never said I am willing to slip anything off for the evening." Isabella looked at the single silver clasp that held the dress together. No, she was not slipping anything off.

"Oh, don't be silly. I am talking of myself—and my other Cinderellas."

"Why do you call them Cinderellas? I thought you were going as the three Graces. And who are they? If I am going to help with this plan then I should know."

"So you will help? I cannot tell you who they are. I have promised to keep that a secret. And I call them my Cinderellas because they, like you, could never appear at my ball as themselves. Although of good birth, circumstances have forced them from society. I wanted to offer them a chance to attend a ball before the coronation, a ball in all its glory."

"So I am one of your Cinderellas also?"

"I had not planned it that way. I truly do need your help, but I did think you might enjoy the chance to dance and flirt once more, to wear a gown, and drink champagne."

It would be wonderful to dance. She had always loved dancing, the twirling, the patterns, the subtle movement and signal when palm met palm—and this time she would not be wearing gloves.

In truth, it was an opportunity she had never imagined having again. After the last days of worry, all her years of worry, the chance to be carefree for one night was too much to resist. "I'll do it. But are you sure the dress will fit?"

"Trust me. I am sure." Annie grinned. "One of the good things about the pattern is it really will fit anyone."

"I suppose that is true. Let me go to my chamber and try it on."

"I have put you up where the governess would go if we had one. I would normally put you next to me, but I do not want Richard to question anything until it is done."

"What is it that you intend to do, Annie?" Her friend had always been daring, but never had her eyes been lit with such a reckless gleam.

Annie did not answer, but only called for a maid to take Isabella to her room.

A few moments later she was not worried about her friend.

There was a note upon her pillow.

Did you think you could escape us? You have two more days or we go to the authorities with what we know.

Despite the heavy flourish of the masculine hand, the heavy scent of lavender wafted up as Isabella lifted the note with trembling fingers.

This time she was gone. He had told her he did not care and she had taken him at his word.

Most of her belongings still hung on hooks in the

dressing room, or were carefully packed away in drawers, but she had taken her favorites—and the carefully lined-up row of small empty purses could not be mistaken.

She was done being paid.

Mark swept the row into his palm and then tossed them in a fluttering mess onto the bare hearth. The desire was great to throw something else, something that would break with a most satisfying crash, but he held back.

He did not want the servants to know his upset, to know that he could not hold on to a mistress. He would sell this house and all its contents as soon as possible.

Now—now he would return home and dress for the night's events as if nothing in his life had changed. Divers would be pleased not to be called to dress him in the early hours of the morning.

He only hoped that Divers had listened to him and found a costume that did not involve codpieces.

He could find another mistress whenever it pleased him.

Isabella was no different from any other woman.

Only she was. And she had left him.

A low meow had him turning. Duchess lay curled in a small forlorn ball on Bella's pillow. Her wide blue eyes begged him to stay and pat her. He scooped up her small body and cuddled her to his chest. Bella must have felt desperate if she left the cat behind. He'd seen for himself how much Bella loved her.

If he hadn't been a duke he might have allowed himself a solitary tear for what might have been.

Only he was a duke and a duke soldiered on.

Still holding Duchess, he headed home.

* * *

She could not be seen in this. She could not. Isabella stared at her reflection in the mirror. The half mask and blond wig were wonderful. Nobody would ever recognize her in them. Even her lips looked fuller and puffier with the mask ending just above them. And the rouge Annie had chosen—scandalous.

But it was the dress that was impossible. While the right breast beneath the single shoulder fastening was reasonably covered, the other one—well, the truly important parts were hidden, or at least mostly hidden. Bending forward, Isabella tried to decide if they would stay out of sight. It appeared that they would, although the impression was definitely the opposite.

She imagined that men would be watching all night hoping for that forbidden glimpse. At least they wouldn't be staring at her face. She doubted there was a man alive who would recognize her from her breasts—well, perhaps there was one, but she wouldn't think about that, about him.

"It looks wonderful on you," Annie said as she entered the chamber. Her own costume was in place and for a moment Isabella could only stare. Did she look that way too? Each step caused a sway of the hip that bespoke a personal confidence that Isabella had never had. It said, *Look at me, dream of me, I can be all you ever wanted*. And then Annie smiled, slowly, seductively—and Isabella found herself swallowing. In truth it was Annie's regular smile, but when combined with the mask the effect was powerful.

"I am not quite sure it fits." Isabella tried pulling the fabric up over her left breast. "I keep worrying that it will fall."

"It won't, but even if it did you will be wearing a mask—and have three more of us in costume. Nobody would ever know it was you."

"Somehow I don't find that reassuring. I am really not sure I should be doing this." That was an understatement. From the moment she'd found the note on the pillow she'd been determined to flee again. But where? She was very tired of running.

"Of course you should. When will you get another chance? Enjoy this night for all it is worth." Annie stepped forward and arranged a curl. "I will need to go down soon to be sure all the arrangements are finished. And I need to let Richard see me in my costume. My plan will only work if he knows what I look like."

"He doesn't know what your costume is?"

"No, not at all. He has shown no interest. In fact, the only interest he has shown in the masquerade at all is to forward me a list to be sure I invite those he considers politically important. He didn't even discuss it with me. Just handed the porter a list of those I should be sure were included. I'd invited them all already. I do pay attention, but he will never know that." Annie's voice grew quiet at the end.

"How soon after tonight do you think we can leave for the country? I am eager to be gone."

"I can understand that and I assure you it will be as soon as possible—as soon as I know I am with child. I have no desire to linger." Annie turned to the mirror, puckering her bright red lips to check the rouge. "I will go down— Oh, there is one more thing—"

"Yes?"

"I forgot to tell you. Your brother and sister will both be here tonight."

* * *

He'd never shown his legs in public. Mark stared down at his bare calves. What had Divers been thinking?

"You'll certainly have the ladies after you tonight—and that's before they even know who you are." Douglas was clearly enjoying this.

"Believe me, if I have to go in this—this thing, they will never know who I am."

"If that's how you feel why bother to attend at all? Your host will never know. Though I think you need to be there at midnight for the mask removal in order to be polite."

"Blast. You are probably right." Mark turned again. "Do you think I could just pull out my uniform and go as a soldier?"

"You're a soldier now." Douglas nodded at the sword hanging at Mark's waist.

"I was thinking of a few thousand years later. I've never had a fascination for Romans. I much prefer a musket to a sword—even a decent one." He pulled the sword from his belt. "I know I told Divers I didn't want a large codpiece, but somehow this feels like revenge. It's hardly even a toy. I can't help feeling women will be judging me by it all night." He held it out and the flimsy tip bent down. Quickly he shoved it back in his belt.

"Are you concerned about women—or one particular woman?"

Mark did not pretend to misunderstand. "She won't be there. Why should her opinion matter?"

"I was thinking more of later in the evening—or earlier in the morning. I would think you care very much what she thinks of your sword."

Pulling back his shoulders, Mark turned away. "I will not be seeing her then either. She has decided the arrangement does not suit her."

Douglas made as if to pat him on the back, but pulled away at the last moment. "She's probably right. I told you she didn't seem the mistress type."

"But she left—she just left. How will I know that she is fine if I don't know where to find her?"

"Perhaps you should have thought of that before."

"Before what?" But Mark knew the answer—before he had made her his mistress and taken away her choices.

Douglas changed the subject. "Are you expecting to see the king tonight?"

"I could not say. I would not be surprised. He should be in church praying, but . . ." He thought it unlikely that the king would spend the night on his knees—and Brisbane had hinted at the same.

Even with Douglas's continued effort to keep the talk away from Bella, Mark's mind returned to her again and again. He was angry, furious. She should not have left—she should have trusted him, talked to him. He would have listened, not argued. Or at least not argued much.

It was good he would have a mask tonight. He did not want people questioning his scowl.

He grabbed the mask off a table and shoved it down upon his head. Damn, with its furrowed brow it was scowling too. At least nobody would question that. The problem was he didn't know how he'd answer if he was asked why he frowned.

He was enraged, but he didn't know at whom. Most probably at himself.

* * *

Isabella stood at the top of the stairs looking down at the crowd below. She was partially hidden by the curve of the wall. She laid her hand upon the cool marble of the banister, wanting to run more than she ever had before. Masters would be there. And Violet. And Lord Peter. And she didn't know who he was, but chances were her mysterious follower or his employer would be there also.

Tapping her fingers on the banister, she debated—and took a single step forward.

She was tired of running—and even more importantly it seemed that no matter how far and fast she ran she was always found. She had been sure nobody had followed her to Annie's house and yet the note had been on her pillow. She'd considered running to her sister and begging Violet to hide her, but that would be the first place they would look.

A deep breath. Another step.

And another.

The mask was firm upon her face, the blond wig covering her own coppery curls. She should be safe.

Another step.

The light silk of the dress drifted up, partially baring one leg. She hadn't realized it would do that. Think of it as distraction from anyone looking at her face. She doubted even Mark would recognize her knees.

She could see through the grand double doors to the dance floor. There were only two Graces visible. She needed to be there for Annie's sake. Annie had said she would slip out at eleven-ten and it was now eleven-twenty.

What did Lord Richard look like? What costume was he wearing?

How was she to make sure both that he saw her and that she avoided him if she didn't even know what he looked like? She should have asked Annie. It was too late now.

She pulled in a final deep breath, spread a smile across her face, and sauntered into the room, hips swaying.

Not halfway across the room, she stopped and slowly turned. A prickle of awareness made its way up her neck. Her gaze scanned the crowd. What had made her stop? Three King Henry VIIIs. A shepherd with two sheep. Who would come to a party dressed as a sheep? A woman dressed in Arab garb, her belly bare. There had been pictures of such clothing in one of Violet's books. A Viking. Several knights. Two damsels. Far too many Grecian gods and goddesses to count. Or perhaps they were Roman. How did one tell?

Still, nothing to cause her alarm.

She started forward again, and saw him. One of the multitudes of Greeks—although actually he clearly was Roman. A centurion.

Mark was here. The air rushed from her lungs and for a moment she felt faint.

Chapter 23

Why was it always the fear you did not have that came to be? With all the multitude of parties and events in celebration of the coronation, he should not be here. There were, she was sure, at least a dozen other events he could have attended. So why was he here?

Did he know Annie or Lord Richard? Surely Annie would have mentioned something. Or would she have? She had waited until the last minute to mention Masters's and Violet's attendance.

Forcing her eyes from Mark she scanned the crowd again. Her brother and sister were nowhere to be seen. Why was she sure she'd even recognize them? And if she did, why did she think they'd not recognize her? She'd known Mark almost instantly.

Her gaze slid back to him. He was beautiful. The word did not normally spring to mind when she looked at him, but the tight-fitting leather chest piece was a work of art. And his legs. She'd never given his legs enough notice before. She swallowed, feeling heat rise in her chest.

It had been only a day since she'd seen him, but her body cried that it had been at least a week. She put a hand to her cheek, hoping the mask would hide her flush. It was growing very warm in the ballroom. The dozens and dozens of candles that lined the walls and hung from above could take the blame for now. And the press of people—they were what pulled the air from the room, leaving her lungs empty.

As if sensing her presence Mark turned. His glance passed over her, and then returned. He stared at her feet, and slowly his gaze moved up, pausing at thigh, and hip, and breast—and back to breast, up to lips, back to breast. She almost laughed out loud at the relief. Not even Mark seemed capable of looking at her face. Oh, his glance was moving up again. She shifted to turn more of her left side toward him, sloped her shoulder to let her dress gape. His gaze dropped again.

A waltz began playing and he stepped toward her, his eyes still fixed well below her face. She tried to ease back into the crowd. If he didn't recognize her now he would as soon as he heard her speak. Someone stepped behind her and she had to wildly sidestep to avoid the stomach of one of the Henry VIIIs. This one looked far too real and Isabella had no desire for that type of contact.

Turning quickly she ran into a hard, firm chest—at least it was not a chest she knew. Her eyes darted up and stopped. She might not know the chest. She did know the man.

Lord Peter St. Johns, her sister's husband, wearing a devil's horns, but no mask.

He glanced down at her, smiled, and gently lifted her away. With the barest of nods he turned and headed toward a woman dressed in angel's wings, her face fully covered by a sheer waxed-cloth mask. Her face might be hidden, but not her flowing red hair or her curves. It had to be Violet.

Isabella started toward her sister. It would be so wonderful just to be near her. Even if they did not speak, Isabella would content herself with the knowledge that they had been close.

A hand reached out, blocking her way. Strong, tanned hands, a slightly lighter, well-muscled arm. This arm she did know. This man she did know. Almost unwillingly she raised her eyes to Mark. Their glances met for the barest of moments and then he inclined his head toward the dance floor.

The waltz was still playing. It had probably only been seconds since it began, although it seemed like hours as Isabella glanced again at her sister. She could not see her face, but it was impossible to miss the way her body softened and leaned forward as Lord Peter drew near.

Mark coughed, drawing her gaze back.

She looked down at his hand and placed her own within it. The tightening of his fingers bespoke safety, a safety she did not trust. He turned and she followed him to the floor. He placed one hand upon her waist and, still holding the other tight, lifted it high, swirling her out onto the dance floor.

Happiness. She should still worry. She should keep her guard up, but Isabella had always loved to dance and, as Mark held her as close as propriety would permit, she let herself get lost in the music. There would be time enough to fret when the dance ended. This moment she would take and keep, locked deep within. Whatever happened in the future, the warm clasp of his fingers, the perfect rhythm of the music, the feeling of his gaze upon her lip would stay with her.

And then it was over. They slowed to a stop and stood for a moment, silence between them. Did he have as little desire for speech as she did?

"I want to kiss you," Mark whispered against her cheek as he leaned forward, bringing her hand to his lips.

Did he know who she was? And if not, why did he want to kiss her? Was she that forgettable?

He didn't know why he had said the words. Mark stared down at the young Grecian goddess before him. He wished he could see her eyes, but the depth of the mask shadowed them from his view. He'd thought she was Bella at first glance. Her lithe and seductive movement as she edged around the dance floor had seemed too familiar.

Unfortunately that could only be wishful thinking. He'd wanted to find her and let himself believe that he had. There was no way that Bella could have gained entry to a party such as this one. He peeked another glance down at her breasts, not wanting to appear rude. And Bella would certainly never have worn anything like that. Even the clothing she'd bought since becoming his mistress was discreet. For God's sake, her nightdresses were barely transparent.

At least she didn't smell like Bella. The musk she was wearing was almost overpowering.

The breasts were very similar, the same perfect size and delicate shape. Would they taste the same, like salty strawberries? What was he thinking? He'd barely met the girl and he was thinking about suckling her breasts and wanting to kiss her. He'd never been this way with anyone but Bella.

Bella. This was all about Bella. Was it coincidence that he'd chosen a girl who reminded him so much of her? No, he was honest, it was not.

She hadn't answered his statement, which was probably a good thing. Bella or no Bella, a gentleman did not tell a gently reared girl that he wanted to kiss her only moments after meeting her.

"I'd like that too. But where?" Her low whisper called his attention back to her mouth.

He blinked and could only hope his own mouth had not fallen open. She could not have really said that—could she? He looked at her more closely, wishing he could see under the mask. "The terrace? The library? The servants' hall?" He glanced about. "Behind that large potted tree?"

"Do you know the way to the servants' hall?" She kept her voice so quiet it was hard to hear.

Damn. He had no idea. He'd never been to Lord Richard's house before and it certainly wasn't a question he could ask. In fact, the only place he could find with some certainty was the terrace and it was unlikely to be empty given the lovely weather. The potted tree was starting to hold real appeal.

"Should we explore?" She offered her hand.

He paused, surprised at the guilt that suddenly ate at him. He should not be doing this. He should be thinking about Bella.

Only Bella had left him.

He placed her hand upon his arm and headed toward the high open doors leading out to the terrace, the scent of night jasmine leading him forward.

What was she doing? Isabella wanted to stop and run, but her feet kept moving. How dare he be hunting for another conquest when he had only left her bed that morning? It didn't matter that they'd fought, didn't matter that she'd run. He should not be doing this.

If he did realize who she was—she didn't think he had, yet—then she did not want him to connect her to Annie. She had spoken as quietly as she could, investing her voice with an exaggerated upper-crust accent she had not used since she first fled London.

Her lips were dry. Her whole mouth was dry. Was she really going to do this?

There was no way she could resist one last kiss. It might be unwise, it was unwise, but she could not leave now.

They stepped out onto the terrace, the hot summer air cooling rapidly as twilight fell. The crowd was almost as tightly packed here as it had been on the dance floor. She spotted several couples peering about as if looking for their own darkened corner.

A faint breeze blew across the yard, causing an almost audible sigh from everyone. Isabella started to turn toward it when she realized several of the gentlemen were staring at her. She dropped her gaze. The wind had lifted the panels of her dress, revealing her leg to midthigh. Clenching her fingers, she fought the urge to pull everything back together. Instead she lifted her chin and met each gentleman's eyes in turn. She pursed her lips, ran a hand down her side, pulling the fabric tight.

"Let's go back in." Mark was not pleased with the attention she was getting.

"I am only letting them look." She kept her voice pitched low, as quiet as she could manage. "There's never harm in looking." In truth, she was suddenly feeling very powerful. It was amazing what feeling desirable could do—desirable and in control.

That was why she'd said yes to Mark, invited the kiss.

She wanted his lips upon her own one more time—but also, she wanted to feel wanted, wanted to know that she was something special. She might be angry that he was looking for another so quickly, but when the other he chose was she it caused a tingle to run the line of her spine. Out of a ballroom full of beauties in scant dress, he had chosen her.

"It is not looking I am interested in—either mine or theirs." He sounded firm, but his arm was pulling her from view.

She leaned closer to him. "I rather thought you liked looking. I can't believe that it was my sterling wit that drew you before I had even opened my mouth."

They entered the ballroom again, avoiding the dance floor. He pulled her closer as couples swirled by. "Would you like to dance again?" he asked.

It was a hard decision. Years, if not decades, could pass before she had another chance to dance. "Would you be disappointed if I said yes?"

"I cannot promise you more than another dance without raising gossip."

"Ah, but that is the joy of a masquerade. How will anyone know how many dances are with me, and not them?" She tilted her head toward the edge of the floor where the two other Graces stood a few yards from each other. It was lucky the terrace had been crowded. She'd promised Annie she'd stay in sight until twelve-thirty. Forgetting her friend because of Mark would be very poor form.

Mark laughed, a low rumble deep in his throat.

"I hadn't even noticed them. I thought you were a goddess."

"Is it a letdown to find yourself with only a Grace?"

"Not at all." He looked across at the other two. "It's strange, you look identical and yet I feel no desire to sweep either of them into a dark hall."

Was it really her he was drawn to? It seemed impossible, but then it seemed impossible that he did not know her when she had known him instantly. Again her mind told her to flee, but she held tight to his arm. "I am awaiting that dance."

"I do believe a new one is starting." He led her out onto the floor.

This time it was a simple country dance, fast, but precise. And fun. So gloriously fun and carefree.

Her breathing was heavy by the time the music stopped and she let him lead her toward the refreshments table. She didn't care what was offered as long as it was cold.

Champagne. She'd only had champagne once before. Accepting the fine crystal glass, she raised it to her lips. Cold. Bubbles. The sharp tang. Another sip. She drained the glass. Mark offered her another.

She shouldn't, but this was not a night for shouldn'ts. It felt as if the bubbles were filling her brain, making each moment more wonderful than the last.

He leaned near her, his breath brushing her neck. "I want to kiss you more than ever. I want to taste the wine on your lips, feel your pleasure in each new experience."

She pulled back, stared at him. His face was almost hidden by the scowling mask. Only his lips, soft and full, lay revealed. "Do you speak to every woman in that fashion? You must have quite the reputation."

He ran his thumb across her bare palm. "No."

She wanted him to say more, to whisper more sweet nothings—but who was he whispering them to, to Isabella, or to a stranger at a ball? She took another sip from her glass, playing for time. She didn't know what she wanted—or she knew, but wasn't sure it was what she should do. "I don't believe you."

"You should. I never lie."

She knew better than that. She would not be in this situation if he'd told her he was a duke from the start—not that he'd lied exactly. She glanced at the clock. Soon Annie would be back and it would be time to leave. Her Cinderella moment would be finished. "Let us dance again."

"If that is your pleasure." They slowly walked back toward the dance floor.

A portly man slid in front of them, a slight wobble to his stance. "I think it's my turn to escort the lady. It's unfair to hold on to the pretty ones."

"Forgive me, sir," Mark answered, "but I do believe you are speaking of my wife. Have care what you say." His hand dropped to his belt. "This sword may be only a toy, but I assure you I can have very real steel in hand by dawn."

His wife? Why had he said that? Why did it send a quiver of hope straight to her heart?

The man turned and left without another word.

"Sorry about that, it seemed the easiest way to get rid of him. And as you said earlier, nobody will be able to connect us later. Even I may not recognize you in the morning." Mark turned and looked at her, his lips drawing tight. "You're not married, are you?"

"Would I have told you I was willing to kiss you if I was?"

"I would hope not." He did not sound sure.

She was about to assure him that she had never wed when she suddenly remembered who she was supposed to be. Annie most certainly was wed. What of the other two? If only Annie had told her something more. Surely at least one of them had remained single. She refused to lie. "No, I have never married."

"You sound sad."

"Is it not every woman's dream to marry?"

She had meant the question facetiously, but Mark replied in utmost seriousness. "In my experience, no. Many women seem to marry out of duty or desperation, not desire."

There was great truth to that. She had seen many women in her time in service who had accepted a ring because they saw no other option. From the time she had been little, however, Isabella had always dreamed of marriage and family. It was her sister who had tried to avoid the state. Although Violet seemed quite happy with Lord Peter now. "Will it be off-putting if I say that I had always hoped to marry and have children? I can think of nothing I would like more."

"I will wish that for you, then. You do seem the type who deserves to have her dreams come true."

"But not with you."

Oh dear, that had shocked him. She was forgetting where they were, forgetting he did not know her—or at least claimed not to. It was odd. She could say things to him that she never could have if they were face-to-face, but she never could have said them at all if she had not known him so well. It left her feeling there was no clear path.

He chuckled, clearly trying to make her words a joke. "No, not with me, unless you're the daughter of an earl. I've been informed I must not marry lower than that."

"How about the granddaughter of an earl?"

"Hmm, perhaps with impeccable character. Someone well loved and respected by all of society."

It was her turn to try for humor. "I did just agree to kiss you behind a potted palm. I am afraid that does rather cry against impeccable character."

"I am glad we are back to the kissing. I would not want you to think I had forgotten."

"You've danced with me twice, walked with me on the terrace, and fetched me champagne—and you are a man who is not thinking of marriage. No, I was not worried you had forgotten the kissing."

"I am afraid that we can no longer hide behind the tree. The spot has been taken."

Surely not. "Oh dear, you are correct. Do you think they realize how clearly they can be seen? Surely he would not put his hand there if he did."

"I am afraid, my dear, that anytime a man gets a chance to put his hand there he will. I am not sure the presence of the angel Gabriel would stop him."

"So I should expect you to put your hand there?"

"If presented with the opportunity."

The clock from the hallway struck. Oh dear, Annie would return at any moment and it would not do for there to be four Graces. She glanced at Mark from the corner of her eye. This was the moment. What was she going to do? She should make an excuse and depart, never to be seen again. She would not go without her kiss. She deserved that, at least. "I am feeling a little faint. Perhaps you would escort me to get some air?"

"Out there?" He looked toward the terrace.

"There are too many people. I fear it may be hotter

than in here. Perhaps there will be a quiet room off the main hall, a parlor or sitting room?"

Mark offered his arm again and his companion strolled beside him as they made their way around the edge of the ballroom and out into the hall. It was amazing being at a masquerade, the anonymity that allowed those things that otherwise would have been questioned.

"I do not know your name," he said as they left everyone else behind and walked toward the dark back of the house.

She stopped near a closed door, slipping away and pressing her back against it. He heard a click as she pushed down on the handle. The door eased open a crack. Only blackness lay beyond. "Do you need to?"

The door opened and she slipped through.

He followed. "It would seem the natural thing. Should I light a lamp?"

"I think not. Darkness allows even more freedom than masks. I can only hope we are alone."

He laughed. "Yes, I do hope so. This is not a moment to be shared."

The door clicked behind them as he pulled it closed. "Perhaps I should open the curtains—let in just a touch of moonlight."

"No."

"Why? It is a bit off-putting to not even know what room we are in."

He heard her breath catch. "I believe I heard somebody say there was a conservatory that overlooked the back garden. This must be it."

"Well, don't you think we should see so that we're

sure not to land upon the harpsichord? I can only imagine the noise that would make."

"We'll just have to feel carefully."

He felt a whisper in the air and then her hand upon his face, her fingertips tapping lightly across his cheek below the mask. And then his lips.

Her touch ran across his lower lip and then across his other one. On the third pass she ran right across the seam and he opened his mouth, pulling her fingers in. "I begin to see why you are so fond of the dark."

"Actually I've always been slightly scared of it, but here now it feels like an old friend."

Mark reached out to stroke her cheek. That was definitely not her cheek, but interesting, very, very interesting. He stroked again.

She slapped at his hand. "I believe there is an order to these things."

"I've never heard that. I've always thought one should let things progress as they happen."

"I definitely believe in an order. That"—she slapped his hand again—"is definitely skipping ahead."

"And you don't like it?"

"I wouldn't say that, exactly, but I do think I want other things first."

"Like what?" He leaned forward, pressing against her hand, which still lay cradled against his face.

"Kissing. I believe you promised kissing."

"I am not sure it was a promise—but yes, I do see your point." He could feel her breath against the side of his face and he turned, following it. Nuzzling first her cheek, beneath the edge of the mask, and then her lips, he found his way across her face. Her lips were full and soft, magical. He knew them so well.

He pressed forward, running his tongue across them as he knew she liked.

As he knew she liked.

And then he knew. Darkness and his senses had combined to tell him what his eyes had not. "Bella? I should have known. I did know. But, damn it, I convinced myself otherwise. How can you possibly be here, Bella?"

Her mouth moved from his, but not far. Only the sound of her heart was audible, or perhaps it was the beat of his own.

Seconds ticked by.

"How, Bella? How did you get into Lady Richard's masquerade? Why did you come?"

Chapter 24

She had thought blackness was her friend. Instead it had been her undoing. All those years of fearing the dark had not been without reason. The moment their lips had touched she had known her mistake. She would have known the feel of his lips anywhere, the taste of his breath, the brush of his stubble.

"Yes." It did not answer any of his questions but it was enough.

"You must have known I was coming. Was this a plan to teach me a lesson? You pretend to leave me and then tease me? What more do you want that I have not given you?"

Marriage. But she did not say it. Even within her own mind the word was almost forbidden. If he had not called her his wife earlier she would not be thinking it now. "If I had set out to teach you a lesson you would have failed. I left you this morning and tonight you were already looking for my replacement."

"I was hardly looking for a replacement for you at the Tenants' masquerade."

He should not have said that. Isabella's hand rose, ready to slap him. How many times did he need to show how little respect he had for her? Before she had become his mistress he had never treated her so poorly.

"I am sorry." His finger skimmed her cheek as if feeling for a tear.

"For what?"

"Too often my words move faster than my brain. I only meant that if I had been looking for replacement I would not have chosen a masquerade. I am rather fond of faces."

It sounded good, but she did not believe him entirely. He might prefer faces, but he had also meant he would not seek a new mistress among society. "If you remember, you first met me in the dark."

"And then I asked if I could light a lamp."

"So it is only my appearance that draws you."

He pulled her close, the speed pushing the air from her lungs. Holding her tight, their bodies so close as to be almost one, he whispered, "I cannot see you now and I am sure that you can feel just how much I desire you. And don't ask if it is your body or your voice that I want. I desire them both—but the truth is I desire all of you. We are standing here, in pitch blackness, in the house of a man I barely know, arguing in a fashion that makes me want to scream, and I am harder than I have been in my whole life."

He certainly was. Well, she couldn't speak to his whole life, but as she rubbed herself along his length it was clear he was rather fond of arguing with her. She leaned against him, feeling the hard plane of the breastplate against her chest. She ran a hand over the smooth leather, feeling the artificially well-defined muscles. "You don't need this, you know. Your chest is quite fine as it is." She couldn't wait to feel him, skin to skin.

"It was not my choice of costume. I would have

much preferred to be without the nonsense of costume altogether."

"Should I help you off with it, then?" She ran her hands up his chest and felt for the straps and buckles she'd seen at his shoulders.

"That was not quite what I meant."

"So you don't want me to?" Her hands moved across the top edge of the armor, feeling for the warm skin beneath.

"I did not say that. You must do as you will."

"Ah, the choice you do give me."

"Do you really wish to argue now?" He shifted a leg between hers, letting her ride upon his thigh.

Isabella moved hard against him, trying to ease the pressure growing within. He smelled so good, tobacco, brandy—and man. Combined with the champagne she had consumed it was enough to leave her quite intoxicated. "No, arguing is not what I am thinking of at all."

The thin silk panels of her dress slid open as his hands tightened about her waist and slid down to her hips. "What are you wearing beneath this thing? I could swear that is your skin I feel. I've never known any fabric to tempt my senses in such a manner."

"Nothing."

His gulp was audible. "Nothing?"

"I tried to wear a chemise, but it showed through."

His fingers explored further, sliding completely between the panels to caress her bare thigh. "You are almost naked."

"Yes." She bent her head forward, licking at the salty sweat on his neck. His tendons strained with his excitement.

"I don't know that I like that."

Daringly she slid a hand down his chest and over the firm bulge so evident beneath the leather and linen of his short toga. "I think you like it very much. Yes, very much indeed."

This time she drew a groan from him as she pressed firmly, wrapping her fingers about his thick length. "God, that's good. I will embarrass myself if you are not careful."

"Shhh, you don't want anyone to hear and investigate." She gripped him more tightly, moving her fingers along his shaft. "And you, what do you have under your skirts?" She paused and allowed a small giggle to escape. "That is one question I never thought I would ask."

"I can't say I ever thought to hear it pass your lips either." His words ground out as her hand continued to move. "And I do have on my smallclothes. Divers was ready to send me out bare assed, but I refused. I could only think of what might happen if a breeze arose. There are some secrets a duke must keep."

She knew he strove for humor, but that word, *duke*, stood between them. She did not need the reminder. Refusing to let it intrude, she licked at his neck again, bringing her mouth close enough to nip him slightly. Moving her second hand to join the first she slipped them both under his skirts, seeking the fastenings that held him concealed from her direct touch. The darkness pushed back inhibition, but it also made some things rather difficult.

He pulled back from her touch. "You too." His hand quickly rose to her left shoulder, his fingers pulling loose the single pin that fastened her costume. The pin dropped to the floor with a small clatter as her dress fell to her waist, held only by a thin gold belt of chain.

Then his lips were on her, sucking, laving, devouring.

She met him fully, no longer the meek miss he had first met.

This would be their last time and she meant to make it a time to remember.

The darkness of the room made her aware of each sensation, the rug beneath her toes, the gentle tickle of her gown at each shift in position, the roughness of the hair on his legs as they rubbed against her own—as they slipped between her own—the tightness of the chain at her waist as he pulled to free it, the night air cold against the moisture he'd left on her breasts. And those lips, his lips—hot, wet, plundering—leaving her no recourse. Her head fell back, her whole being focused on those inches where mouth met flesh. All faded from her world as he continued his attack. He caught a nipple between his teeth, pulling, nipping just hard enough to make her cry out.

She brought her own hand to her mouth, biting down hard to silence the gasps that grew loud and heavy. Her other hand tangled in his hair, the waves silky beneath her touch, unsure whether to push him away and grant herself the chance to breathe or to pull him tighter and drown in the sensations that he caused.

"You taste of honey. You've never tasted of honey before." His voice was raspy. She could hear his arousal in it, gauge just how far he'd come and just how far he had to go. It was not nearly far enough. He was sending her on ahead of him.

That would never do.

She pulled back on his head, bending to bring her

lips near to his own, tasting herself upon his breath. "I used a different lotion. Do you like it? It leaves behind a sheen, as if I'd dipped my breasts in gold. My nipples shone bright before I dressed."

"Let me open the curtain. I need to see you. I'll do anything, just let me see you."

"No, you will have to imagine how I looked fresh from my bath, covered with gold, my hair damp about me, curling in every direction."

"You are killing me."

"I know—and you love it. Are your eyes closed, are you dreaming of me, of what I looked like? I promise you it was even better." She kissed him gently on the mouth, but as he tried to capture her lips, she moved upward, raining kisses upon his bristly cheeks until she came upon his closed eyelids. She kissed each one soundly, tasting him as she went. "You did close your eyes. You are thinking of me."

"I am always thinking of you, even when I should not be."

"Well, right now you definitely should be." She slid her hand down from his hair, caressing the hard sinews of his neck, the muscles of his shoulders, the curve of his back, his high firm buttocks—they deserved an extra squeeze. He moaned as she slipped her hand beneath his skirts again, into the tight linen of his undergarments. Her hand came forward, around him, encasing him. "I like it when you think of me. Would you like a reward?" She moved her lips back to his mouth, finding his tongue, sucking it deep into her own mouth, biting at its tip, squeezing, pulling back, releasing—imitating that other action he liked so well.

His penis jerked hard beneath her hand. He understood her exactly.

But then his own hands were on her back, on her waist, lower—slipping between her thighs. He sighed against her mouth as he felt her dampness, the stickiness that already marked her wants, her needs. She squirmed, unable to hold herself still as his fingers found the spot.

Oh, and he knew it. He targeted it again and again, clearly enjoying her helplessness.

But she was not that helpless. She moved her own hand, stroking with all the expertise that he had taught her. She knew just what he liked, the slight cupping over the top, the long pull, the extra pressure along the bottom. She knew and she used it, pushing him farther and farther along the road they both longed to travel.

There was nothing but sensation, taste, touch, sound. With her eyes blinded by dark her whole world was he. The feel of him. The feel of him touching her.

She'd never heard the sound of a day's growth of beard moving against skin. She heard it now.

Never felt the breeze as clothing brushed along her flesh. She did now.

Never tasted the man beneath the smoke and leather and brandy. Now she thought she'd know him anywhere simply by the taste of him in her mouth.

And she knew his forehead, his shoulder, the back of his knee—all by touch. Blindness took her to places that she'd never been.

She moved her hand again, reveling in the velvet of his skin. His whole body jerked. He was getting close. She loosened her grasp, but just a bit, laid kisses upon his neck, wished she could touch his chest, feel his bare skin against her fully.

"I need to be in you—now." It was both a gasp and a prayer.

He was going to die. Here and now, surrounded by black, he was going to die. Die of pleasure. His mind was still filled with the vision of her polished in gold, her nipples gleaming. The tighter he closed his eyes the stronger the image grew. She was his queen and he wanted only to adore her.

And the taste. The taste of honey. He'd been fond of the sweet before, but now, now he wanted it with every meal until the end of his days. There could be nothing better than this. Sweetness. Woman. He wanted more. He was tempted to pull her to the floor, to bury his face between her legs, to bring her all the pleasure she was bringing him, to taste her honey, to— He couldn't wait another moment.

It had to be now.

He slid his hands up, pulling her gown with them. Settling them firmly, he lifted her, pulling her against him until he felt her core. He shifted his hips forward, until he was poised just where he wanted to be.

"Now." He wasn't sure which one of them had spoken, but in the black it didn't matter.

He thrust up, pulling her down and entering her in a single move.

He stopped then, caught in the pleasure of that second, that moment.

He felt her weight, the strain on his legs, and cared not at all. Only one thing mattered, the warmth, the homecoming, the ultimate perfection.

"I need to move." This time he knew it was she who spoke.

He lifted her again, settled her back down.

"No, I want to move. That's you moving," she said.

"Demanding, aren't you?"

"Of course. I learned from you."

He chuckled. Even now he could laugh at the joy she brought him.

How to set her down? He refused to be separated for even a moment.

Was there really a harpsichord in the room? If the cover was down it would be perfect. If it wasn't—well, that could be disaster. He could only imagine the noise—and the aftermath.

He stood still, shifting his hips only enough to keep her gasping.

He debated. "How about against the wall? I should be able to find a wall."

"It will still be you moving. I want my turn."

"How about you have your turn next time?"

She stiffened slightly, her muscles tensing about him. "No. It must be now."

He managed to bend one knee, lowering her feet to the floor. Her arms wrapped tight about him, she buried her face against his chest.

He would never be quite sure how, but they made it to the floor still connected. He held himself above her, glad he could feel soft carpet below. He would have hated to lay her on hard wood, or icy marble.

Her feet pushed hard against the rug, lifting her hips, grinding against him. She'd wanted to move and it was evident that she was not going to wait. Setting the pace, she lifted and settled, working for her own pleasure, but also for his.

If there had been any light to see it would not have mattered. He was beyond sight, caught only in feeling, the feeling of her. He heard her gasps, felt her tightening, her flexing. Her breasts were damp beneath his chest, the nipples teasing him to taste again.

He found her lips again instead, drawing her into a deep, soulful kiss, a kiss that spoke to all that could not be said.

She squeezed tight, her mouth opening beneath him, allowing him freedom to plunder as her body arched up, squeezing him tighter than ever.

She was so close, but so was he.

And then there was only swirly color, prisms of light that shone even in the darkness, filling his senses.

He cried out once, and then again. Her name. Bella. His Bella.

He felt her come apart beneath him.

And then it was done.

He held himself a moment more before collapsing, twisting to pull her atop him, before allowing his body to relax.

It was over. She'd given herself this one last time and now it was done. His heart beat steady against her ear. The sound of comfort—even if the leather breastplate was not. Stirring, she rearranged herself so her head was cradled in his arm. They were lucky no one had heard them. Neither of them had been careful or silent at the end.

She kissed his shoulder, soft, gentle, wishing there were words to portray the way she felt, full of joy and sadness, bittersweet in a way she could not remember.

"You never answered," he kept his voice soft. "Was it all a plan to make me realize how much I needed you? You pretend to leave and then come back in this delicious fashion."

She wanted to ask if he had realized he needed her. If she knew she was needed it would make leaving both harder and easier. It would mean something to know that she was valued, that she had not just been a conquest for him.

But it was time for truth, at least as much as she could tell. "No. It was no game. I really did leave. It never occurred to me that I would see you here, that we would meet up here."

"Then why did you not avoid me during the dancing? You could have lost yourself in the crowd."

"I should have, but I could not. At first I did not believe that you did not recognize me. I knew instantly that it was you."

"I should be ashamed of that. It sounds false now if I say that on some level I did recognize you—but in truth I must have. Nothing else could explain what happened. It is not the way I behave."

"Strangely I believe you. Whatever it is between us, it is strong, uncontrollable. I could no more have not come with you than I could have stopped breathing."

"Then we are together? You will come home with me? We will go back to the way things were—or start again if you like."

She could not impose upon him the trust she'd have to demand, the protection, the compromise of his position in society. She could not believe he would—or even necessarily should—hide what she'd done.

"No. This is the end," she answered. "It is why I could not resist. When you came to me across the dance floor, it felt as if the fates were offering me a gift, a gift I could not refuse."

"I do not understand."

"I am not made for the life you offer me." She shifted up and laid a kiss upon his mouth. His tender lips softened beneath hers, and then pulled away.

"I offer you everything."

"Except what I want, what I need."

He pushed to sitting, and then stood. He walked slowly across the room. She heard the light scratch of a finger as he ran it against the wall, seeking the curtains. Suddenly there was light, not much, but enough. The pale moonlight shone through the window, filling the room, driving their isolation away.

He turned back to her, his costume fallen into place. Only the mask was missing. It lay scowling on the ground beside her.

She traced its brow line with a finger. "I wish I could take what you offer—or explain to you why it could never work."

"Why don't you try?" He walked back to her, standing above her like a conquering king. Her mind formed the image of them, the proud Roman warrior and the half-dressed maiden supine at his feet.

She sat up, pulling her knees to her chest, but not trying to restore her gown. "What if I had a child? I know some mistresses do, but I cannot imagine such a life. I would want more for my baby."

"There are steps we can take to prevent that."

"But they are not reliable—they help, but nothing prevents a child that wants to be born. And even if it did work, do you want to leave me without the chance to hold my own baby, to never know the joys of motherhood?"

"We discussed this in the carriage, before you

agreed to be my mistress." He shoulders pulled back. He had returned to being the duke.

"Yes, and we did not resolve it then. You merely said you would take care of everything. And now I ask how? I gave in to you because I felt I had no choice—and I will admit it was what I wanted, the chance to lie in your arms, to know all the pleasure I would find there. I just never imagined how all the rest of it would feel. How it would feel to see how the other servants look at me, to know what your valet thinks, to have him drop a purse to pay me for my services."

"I realize now I did not handle that well. I can do better." A bit of Mark peeked through; she could hear the man beneath the façade.

She pushed to standing, imagined herself a brave goddess queen with her mortal lover. Her breasts stood bare and she made no move to cover them, let him look—and remember. "I do believe you. I believe you would try, but there are too many problems. What will happen when you marry? I know you want to believe it will not make a difference, but how can it not? How can it be fair to me—or to her? How will I feel when you hold your child—yours and hers—in your arms and I will know that it can never be me?"

"I will let you go when I marry. I will see you well settled. But that will not be for years yet."

She filled her chest, watching his eyes follow the rise of her breasts. His desire fed her strength. "So I shall be discarded later? Besides, I do not believe it will be years. Do you think I do not hear the whispers? They are not always quiet. There is pressure on you to wed. There is no heir to the duchy. If you die then it will revert to the Crown. Nobody wants that, not even the king, I daresay."

"You are right about that—but I can delay them. You are what I want."

"But not enough to marry."

"You know that is impossible."

She did know it, knew it better than he did—it was just not for the reasons he thought. He could not marry a nursery maid, but Miss Isabella Hermione Masters would have been a suitable bride—not a good match by any means, but an acceptable one. "Yes, I know. But I do not feel your regret, as you will feel mine every time we are together. And over time that regret may grow to resentment, anger, even hatred. Neither of us wants that, I am sure."

He did not answer. Not a flicker of emotion showed upon his face.

She turned from him then, picking up his sword and mask and placing them on the harpsichord's bench. She retrieved her own mask, debating whether she would wear it again. She only needed to slip upstairs—while letting Mark believe she had departed. The servants had seen her face already and had not realized her identity. She should be as safe as ever.

She glanced about. The pin to hold her dress was nowhere to be seen.

Chapter 25

She was going to leave him—again. Mark felt as if a small piece were being ripped from his chest, a piece he could not live without. He could function, but not live.

He was not sure why this was so much worse than believing her gone earlier, but it was. This was final. If she left now he would never see her again.

He had to say something. "Of course I regret, but what good does it do to talk about it? I do not make a habit of considering the impossible. Can you not take what is possible?"

"I wish I could." She held her dress up, peering down at the floor. "Damn it. I cannot find the pin. I can't leave with my dress about my waist. And you have me swearing. I never swear."

"Come here. Maybe I can tie it." The last thing he wanted was to enable her to leave, not to mention that he could happily have kept her near naked forever, but it was the gentlemanly thing to do. Unfortunately the silk did not agree. It twisted from his fingers, unknotting itself and sliding loose again. The fine weave refused to stay tied.

"Do you have a pin? You must have something," she asked, her voice laden with worry.

"No, normally I'd have a pin in my cravat, but obviously on this occasion I don't. What about an ear bob? I am sure you were wearing some earlier."

"They're attached to the wig."

He considered for a moment and then pulled the heavy ruby ring from his pinky finger. "Here. I'll see if I can loop it through this and make it stay."

It was done. A few twists through the ring and it held. Perhaps not for long, but hopefully for long enough. He might regret covering her, but he did not wish to share her glory with any other man.

Her hand rose and touched the ring, caressed the knot. The ring had been his father's, the ruby brought from India decades ago, but he would not regret it. It would be one last gift he could give her. She might not appreciate its value now, but hopefully if she ever did need money again, she would use it.

"Before you go, tell me, is there anything you need? I could write you a reference or get Mrs. Wattington to. Or funds? Do you need more money?"

"Now you are prepared to offer these things? Why not before?"

"I should have, but I did not. Do the whys matter now?"

She nibbled at her lower lip. "No, I suppose they do not. And no, I do not need anything from you."

"What if you are already with child?"

Her face froze. He could see that she had not considered the possibility. "I will let you know. In those circumstance I might need aid and I would not be too proud to ask."

"Is it pride that stops you now? I cannot bear to think you might need me and I might be unable to help."

"There may be some pride, but truly my problems cannot be solved by you."

"Do you have a place to go, people who will care for you?"

He could tell she did not want to answer.

"Yes," she said at last. "I have found an old friend who has offered to help."

"And this friend can help you, solve your problems?" He could only hope the friend was not a man.

"No, my problems are beyond help."

"What are these problems that you think a duke cannot solve?" He felt affronted that she did not consider him capable.

"They do not matter between us."

"Are they part of why you leave—is it not just me, my inability to make you happy?" Gad, he sounded an insecure fool.

She walked toward the door, placed her hand upon the handle, easing it open. The light from the hall lit her like an angel, reminding him of their first encounter weeks ago. She had not donned her mask. Lifting the silver confection, she stared at it a moment and then looked out into the hall. Then she fitted it over her head, the blond wig covering her red-gold curls. It felt as if she removed herself from him with that simple gesture.

She stepped out the door and he thought it was over.

Then she stopped, turned back to him, her lips stiff beneath the mask. "Do you remember that ride in your carriage, that first hour, when you bargained with me to be your mistress?"

"Of course."

"Do you remember offering to protect me from anything?"

"I meant it. I still would."

"Only that wasn't all you said."

"I—I don't recall."

"You said that you, the duke, Strattington, could protect me from anything, that you would protect me from anything—because it wasn't like I'd killed a man."

"I remember."

"Well, that is the problem."

"I am lost again."

She looked him straight in the eyes, the bright candles of the hall lighting her blue eyes despite the shadow of the mask. "My problem is just that—I did kill a man."

She shut the door with a decisive click, leaving him to the twilight of the conservatory.

She wanted to lean back against the door and collect herself, but she dared not. She had told Mark her secret, seeking to offer his bleakness some comfort—if her confessing murder could be considered comfort. For the first time she had seen Mark and the duke as one man, and she had given him the only gift she could.

It would take him a moment to recover from his shock, but then he would be after her, wanting to know more, wanting to see if he could be all-powerful, if he could solve this problem too. No, she needed to be gone, to lock her dreams deep in her heart and keep them there.

She would be happy in the country with Annie's children to care for. It might be that she would never have her own, but at least she would not have to pretend to have all she wanted as Mark left her bed to head home to his wife.

She walked swiftly down the hall, head bowed as she let her thoughts run free. If she took the small corridor to the left she could sneak up the servants' stair and hide herself safely above.

She gasped when strong fingers reached out and grabbed her arm. Turning, she found herself staring at Caesar's robes. Why was everyone fascinated with the classical world this evening?

Caesar was tall, with thick dark curls standing out about a hard face hidden only by the smallest of masks. "You're heading the wrong way, my lady. I suggest you join our guests in the ballroom. You would not want anyone to wonder about where you had been."

"But I am not—"

"Don't bother with the different voice, Georgiana. I've observed your compatriots and it is very clear they are not you. Now go, before I decide to see just who is still waiting in the conservatory. I do not wish a scene—not the night before the coronation, not when the king could arrive at any moment."

Caesar stared down at her coldly, his eyes drawn to her kiss-swollen lips. He was clearly Lord Richard, Annie's husband. She was about to clarify that she was not Annie when she stopped, considered. If he knew the other two Graces were not Annie, and she denied it also, then what would he think? She lowered her head, staring at his sandals. "Yes, my lord," she answered softly.

"See that you do that, then. We will talk later." He turned and left, the leather of his soles slapping against the floor.

She was about to give a soft sigh and make a dash for the servants' stair when another voice spoke, a low, harsh whisper. "You'd think a man would know his own wife, wouldn't you, Miss Masters? I don't see a resemblance between you and Lady Richard, but then I've been looking for you for a long time."

She started to turn, but a hand came down on her shoulder, stopping her. "No, don't turn. I've had my agent talk to you before this, but I think it is time I made myself clear. I want the letters you took from Foxworthy and I will not wait much longer. I do not care what you need to do to get them. You have shown yourself most ingenious. I am sure you will find a way. You were given until the day after tomorrow and you had best meet the deadline. If I fear that you will run again—and I will know—I will take no time before spreading word of your deeds to all of London."

"I am still not sure which letters you mean." Did he hear the desperation in her voice?

The gentleman, and she was sure he was one, gave a soft sigh. "That is why I have come to address you myself. You must give me everything that you retrieved. I can find what I seek."

"But it is all junk. If you told me what I was looking for I could be more sure of having it for you."

Could you feel debate and consideration? The man's hand twitched upon her shoulder and her gaze dropped down to his long, lean fingers, a heavy ring, a fringe of lace with plum-colored edging.

"Bring it all. This is the last warning you will get. I have been far too generous already."

"And if I do not bring it?"

"Then I will make sure that everyone knows what

you have done. Do not think Strattington will protect you then. He will cut you from his life in the blink of an eye. I will make sure the authorities take you and that you hang."

Before she could even ask, "What authorities?" his fingers squeezed even tighter.

"And do not try to run again, Miss Masters. I am getting very tired of chasing."

"Where do I bring the papers? I cannot just walk around with them at all times."

"I will let you know—you can be sure I will find you. I seem to have a talent for it. And now, Miss Masters, I suggest you head down that hall, as you so desire, and flee upstairs to your room. Do not look back. It would so complicate matters."

She thought she'd killed someone. Mark was sure she hadn't actually done it. Bella could barely bring herself to swat a fly. He couldn't imagine the circumstances that would bring her to commit murder. He'd killed men in the war and could remember each one of them. Necessity could force actions that one would otherwise not take, but he could not imagine Bella—no, not Bella. . .

He had to find her. If she told him what had happened, he could help her, then she could stop running.

He might not be able to marry her, but this he could do. He'd set his investigators to proving her innocence—if there was anything to prove. He still couldn't picture a circumstance that would lead his Bella to end a life.

He grabbed his mask and toy sword, staring at the latter with distaste and then dropping it back on the floor. Pulling the mask over his face, he followed her. She would not escape him. He needed to be sure she was safe, not running forever.

He yanked open the door—and stopped.

Caesar stood without.

"Lord Richard, can I help you in some way?" he asked. Damn it, he didn't have time to greet his host, not now. He had to find her or she'd be gone. If she was back in the ballroom with the other Graces would he ever find her? He'd sensed her before, but would he really be able to tell?

Lord Richard spoke, each word ice. "I do not know who you are and I do not care to know. I would, however, suggest you leave my home immediately or I will have you tossed out like the refuse that you are."

"Now, hold on—"

"I have been informed that the king is on his way here—anonymously, of course. If it were not for his arrival you can be sure I would not leave you unbloodied." Lord Richard turned and was about to walk away.

"Stop, this is no way to treat—"

"I have said I do not wish to know you, sir. Please be gone."

"But I need to find—"

"Do you not listen?" Lord Richard looked like he would spit. "I do not care what or who you need to find. If it is my wife you are looking for, then I would suggest you think again, unless you wish to meet at dawn."

"But I don't know your wife. I've seen her, of course, but I do not believe we've ever had a proper introduction."

Lord Richard glanced past Mark into the dark of the conservatory.

"Apparently some things do not require an introduction. And if you truly do not know whom you just—just fucked, then I suggest you be more careful in choosing your companion for the evening. Not all husbands would be as understanding of their wives' lovers. Now, be gone."

Isabella stood there shaking. Her hand shook. Her legs shook. Even her toes were quivering. It was all too much for one night. First Mark, then Lord Richard, and now the man with the purple lace. He was different from any of her previous pursuers. This man knew exactly what it was he wanted. And when he'd threatened her she'd had no doubt that he meant it. He had spoken with absolute authority. He clearly was the mysterious employer, and whoever he was, he was used to power. The memory tweaked at her mind. There had been something familiar about him, but what?

Her feet moved forward a step. She had to move. It would not do if Mark found her. She could not involve him in this mess, not if there was someone with power who cared about Foxworthy. Mark cared so much about becoming the perfect duke. He was willing to give up anything to achieve it. She would not ruin it by involving him in scandal.

"Isabella. Isabella, is that you?" The soft voice spoke from the direction of the ballroom.

She'd wondered what else could happen. Now she knew.

Could she run? Physically run away? She'd never seen her sister move at anything faster than a saunter; perhaps she could escape. No. There was nowhere to go. If she went in the opposite direction, she'd run into Mark—or the man who'd just threatened her. She couldn't push past Violet, not with her husband, Lord Peter St. Johns, behind her. Besides, if she left Annie's home and ran from her sister, she truly would be out of options.

Slowly she turned. She could still bluff, pretend.

One look at Violet's face told her otherwise. There was no doubt, no question, only joy.

"Isabella, it is you. Don't even try to pretend. Nobody walks like you do when you're nervous, landing high on the toe and then lowering yourself slowly to the floor. You've done it since you were a child. And your hair is showing beneath your wig. You should have taken more care." The angel wings of Violet's costume flitted lightly as she stepped forward.

Isabella looked past Violet. Lord Peter stood just behind her, the look in his eye informing Isabella that she had better not disappoint his wife.

Isabella glanced about. She could not be found by Mark now. Trying to remember the layout of the house, she chose a door and opened.

"Come, sister. Let us talk." She held the door wide for Violet and Lord Peter.

Mark sat in his carriage across from the house. She had to leave sometime. The clock had rung three a while ago and still Bella had not emerged from the front door. He'd seen one of the other Graces leave, slipping out as if hiding, but he had known instantly it was not Bella. Bella was at least an inch shorter, not quite as full of figure—and, well, he didn't know how else he'd been sure, but he had known deep it his gut. It was not Bella.

No, Bella had not left yet—unless she'd been under

a heavy cloak and domino. He'd seen several people leave so attired, and short of accosting each one he'd had no choice but to let them go.

Where was she?

What if she truly was Lord Richard's wife? No, that was nonsense. Lady Richard was not a nursery maid, even a well-educated one, and while she had been gone from London for years she had returned long before Isabella.

So who was she? He'd forced himself not to wonder since their first conversation in the carriage. She'd agreed to be his mistress and in return he promised not to pursue further inquiries. He'd assumed that the men searching for her were from her family. Now it seemed more likely that they were involved in the "murder" she claimed to have committed.

Before he could consider further there was a knock on the door and Douglas climbed in.

"What are you doing here?" Mark felt no need to be polite.

Douglas reached behind the carriage's cushions and pulled out a flask. He took a good swig. "It's going on four in the morning and you have not returned home. You were not quite yourself when you left this morning. I merely thought to see if you needed a second. Are you dueling in the morning? My life could use the excitement."

Mark grabbed the flask from Douglas and took his own swallow. "I was almost called out, but managed to avoid such unpleasantness. Divers would have been most displeased if I got blood on my clothing."

Douglas snorted. "You will not convince me that you'd care if you got blood on the finest of your brocades, not to mention that thing." He gestured at

Mark's costume. "Sandals. A duke in sandals, is that the impression you really want to leave?"

"No one recognized me—well, Bella did, but that hardly counts."

"Bella was there? At a society ball?"

Running his fingers through his hair, Mark answered, "I haven't figured that out either, but yes, she was there. And there is more to the story. I think I know what she was running from, why those men were pursuing her."

Douglas leaned back, taking the flask with him. "And does this explain why you are sitting in the dark of night in your cold carriage instead of home in your warm bed—or in hers?"

"I am waiting for her."

"And she's keeping you waiting? At what time exactly did you plan to meet?"

A sigh could not begin to express his feelings. "She doesn't know I am waiting. She ran off on me again. She left after telling me she'd killed someone. She tells me something like that and then expects me to ignore it."

Douglas leaned forward and stared out the window toward the Tenants' house. "Perhaps she doesn't expect you to ignore it. Perhaps this is her way of asking for help."

"I had not considered that. It is odd that she would say it and run, although she does seem to like to run. I gather she always runs from her problems."

"You'll need to work on that. It's hard to solve a problem if you can't find it. Are you sure she hasn't left?"

"As sure as I can be. It will be hours yet before the

party ends and I fear I am doomed to sit here for all of them."

"I can wait instead of you. With the coronation tomorrow you had best get home and get some rest."

He had not even thought about the coronation. Mark had watched the flurry of activity as the king slipped out anonymously with only three or four carriages of followers, but he'd not considered the next day. "Damnation. I know you are right, but I fear that you'll miss her. She's dressed in costume—as is everybody else." He gestured out the window at what he thought was a shepherd.

"I can get considerably closer than the carriage can. Plus nobody will notice me." Douglas looked down at his dull pants and scuffed boots.

Mark didn't like it. He didn't like it at all. It was, however, the logical thing. "If you see her come out, follow her. I must know exactly where she goes."

Chapter 26

Isabella stared about her old bedroom. She had never imagined being in it again, the dainty, sprigged curtains and the tall windows overlooking the back garden, the high narrow bed in which she'd dreamed of a perfect future. It was not her childhood bed. The room had been hers for only the occasional visit to London and for the brief months of her season before everything had gone wrong.

Still, it was more her room than any room she'd ever had, besides the nursery back in Dorset. But that room had always seemed to belong to all the children who had come before her. This room had been hers.

Masters had allowed her to choose the furnishings and even to choose which room of the house she desired for herself. The spreading tree that stood outside the window and the smell of summer roses had made the choice an easy one.

If she opened the window it would smell of roses now.

Still, she did not do so.

It was enough that she was here, in her brother's home.

She flopped onto the bed, falling back across the mattress.

Masters was not yet home, but he would be at any

moment. Isabella was not sure she was ready for him.

Violet had sent a messenger to him at first light the morning after the masquerade, despite Isabella's pleas that she not do so. Violet was convinced that the two of them must talk, must work out their differences. She swore that Masters had changed since his marriage. She had begged Isabella to do this one thing for her, to try and reconcile with their brother.

Isabella had reluctantly agreed. After all the worry she had put Violet through it seemed a small price to pay—plus it had gotten her into Masters's house and into this room.

Unfortunately, or perhaps fortunately, the coronation had required his attendance and the dinner afterward had gone well into the night. He'd been called away first thing this morning and now Isabella, having been deposited at his home by Violet, was forced to wait for his return.

She'd met his new wife. Clara seemed very nice, far better than he deserved. It was almost enough to make Isabella wonder if Violet was right. Could he have changed? She did not hold out hope.

So why was she lying on her bed staring at the ceiling instead of searching for the papers she needed? Why was she not even considering fleeing?

She'd promised Violet she'd stay, but she'd broken promises before.

She should at least look for the papers. Nothing was gained by prolonging the inevitable—and once her brother was back, who knew what would happen. Her room was much as she'd left it, but it had clearly had a good cleaning. She'd probably left stockings draped over chairs and hairpins scattered on the floor when she left.

Pushing up on her elbows, she pursed her lips and considered.

She'd left the papers in a trunk on the bed—a trunk that had been moved. Had it been emptied? If so, what had happened to its contents?

She walked over to the dresser and began shuffling through the orderly piles of garments. It was surprising that Masters had kept them.

Nothing.

She searched through her wardrobe. No papers. No trunk.

Nothing.

Under the pillow. No. Although she couldn't imagine the maid putting them there.

An ache began to grow in her gut again, not that it had ever really left. It was unbelievable that she'd ended up here, in her old room, when she'd thought coming back here to retrieve the papers impossible.

And now she couldn't find them.

She sat at her writing table and began to shuffle through the drawers and compartments. She never kept anything personal there, but a maid might have thought that was where they belonged.

She was going to start swearing, using all the colorful words she pretended she didn't know.

Could the maid actually have thrown them out? They had looked like nothing more than bits and rubbish, but surely a maid would ask before disposing of them. But Isabella hadn't been here to ask. Would a maid have asked Masters? And if so, what would he have done?

She worried at her lower lip. It would be too cruel to be forced back here, forced to face her brother, and to still not find the papers that might end this whole blasted thing.

She tapped her heel against the floor. It had seemed a brilliant move to persuade her brother's wife that she needed a few hours to collect herself and rest before seeing Masters. Clara had been all too ready to spend the morning chatting while they waited, but Isabella had not felt quite up to that task. Clara might be lovely, but until things were straightened out with Masters she did not want to form any type of relationship with his wife.

And then she saw it. Neatly set beneath her bed was her trunk, the trunk she'd thought to take with her when she'd run away and then fled without. It had taken only a few minutes for her to realize that she'd never be able to handle the trunk herself. She'd packed a small valise instead.

Could the papers still be there?

She walked over and knelt beside the bed, knees shaking.

Pulling out the heavy leather and wood trunk, she said a silent prayer. *Please, let this be it. Let this one small part of my problems be over.*

Mark stood across the street from Lord Peter St. Johns's house and stared up at the handsome façade. What was Bella doing there?

Perhaps she knew one of the maids or another of the servants?

No, she had been escorted here by Lord Peter himself. That did not sound like she was a member of the staff.

Could Douglas have followed the wrong Grace?

That was distinctly possible. It certainly made more sense than that Bella had come to one of the most elegant homes in London by invitation. Lord Peter was the brother of the Marquess of Wimberley and you couldn't move much higher than that.

Unless, of course, one was a duke who kept company with the king. Mark grimaced at the thought.

What a farce yesterday had been. It had felt more like a play than a coronation. He understood the importance of production, but surely the king would have been advised against such obvious wanton spending. The public was already outraged enough at the king's debts without the public reminder of how quickly he could incur expenses. Had it really been necessary to have a raised platform to walk on all the way to Westminster? And the crown—the single blue diamond at its center could probably have fed half the city.

And that was not even considering the spectacle of barring the queen from the whole affair. There had actually been prizefighters stationed at the door to bar her entry to the ceremony. That was not something that would be forgotten soon.

And it had all kept Mark from pursuing Bella. That had been the true hardship of the affair. He might even have survived the codpiece and pantaloons if she'd been there to laugh with him.

But she hadn't been. She'd been here.

At least he hoped she was. It seemed so unlikely.

He considered the high windows and gracious proportions, the delicate flowers blooming along the short path to the door. The house had belonged to Lord Peter's wife before their marriage and it still retained a feminine touch.

It was odd that Lord Peter had not sought a new home upon his marriage. There had been stories about the wife, if Mark remembered correctly. He didn't know the details but he believed she'd been rather notorious in her day—not exactly a courtesan, but as close to it as a woman could come and retain her respectability. Their marriage had been quite shocking.

He hadn't heard anything about her since he'd returned to Town, however.

Could Bella be visiting the wife? He wished he could remember more. If she'd actually been a courtesan then maybe Bella was looking to her for advice.

No, Bella had said she'd met an old friend. Lord Peter's wife was supposed to be years older than he. That would make it unlikely that she'd been friends with Bella. Which led him back to Lord Peter. What exactly was the man's relationship to Bella?

Mark swung his walking stick against a low garden wall, enjoying the jarring of the hit. He'd much rather it had been Lord Peter he struck.

Isabella stared down at the pile of things before her. It made no sense. There was nothing here that anybody would want. She'd hoped for something she'd missed before, but none of it seemed of value.

She picked up a few notes marking gambling debts. There were more of them than she had remembered, but they were not for outlandish amounts. Still, perhaps they were for enough that some might have trouble with payment. The man had called them letters—could he have meant vowels, IOUs? It didn't seem likely, but she put them neatly aside.

Next was a pile of scribbles. Perhaps a code? Could

Foxworthy have been a spy, or known of one? No, she could not imagine that they were anything but somebody's odd and senseless jottings.

There was half a map. She had not remembered that. A spot was circled. Buried treasure? She examined it closely. No, more likely it was the direction of a cheap but fashionable tailor.

A recipe for sugar biscuits. She could not even begin to guess why Foxworthy had that. Again, it could be code, but why somebody would disguise code as sugar biscuits she could not imagine.

She picked up the last papers. Love letters. She remembered these well. Even at seventeen she had not been able to picture penning such overwritten drivel. The woman who'd written them went on endlessly, describing the muscles on her lover's shoulders and how his shirt pulled across them. Isabella had spent plenty of time admiring Mark's shoulders but she'd never have called them *broader than a stallion's withers and harder than cannon's ball*. What woman would even be thinking of cannonballs and the male body? And that didn't even get to the description of the lower body. She couldn't imagine thinking of Mark as having *a hard iron sword that pierces my most tender places*. That just sounded painful.

And purple ink. Who used purple ink?

It was almost the same color as the lace on the man's cuffs.

She stopped breathing. Her mind filling with the impossible.

What if they were not a woman's letters?

What if they were his? The handwriting did look masculine. She had heard rumors of such relationships, relationships that a man could hang for. It seemed unbelievable. How would such a thing even work? Could it be true?

If it was, now, that would be something Foxworthy could have used for blackmail.

Something that was worth almost any price to get back.

But who was he? She could not get past the feeling that there was something familiar about him. He was not somebody she knew well, but she was sure they had met—and recently. It was not a comforting thought.

The letters were easily tied together into a small bundle and she pushed it down the bodice of the dress Violet had loaned her. The dress was loose and the papers hardly showed. It seemed she was forever running away, leaving her clothing behind. She was sure that somebody would bring her the things she had left at Annie's, but it was unclear when.

Annie might be furious with her over the misunderstanding with Lord Richard. She could only hope that he had figured out she was not his wife. Although if Annie had taken a lover, as she'd planned, it might not matter what he thought.

That, however, was a worry for another day.

She patted the papers. For now she only need figure out how to deliver them.

There was a tap at the door. Masters must be home. She hoped that Violet was right and that he had changed. It took courage to call out to him to enter.

He strode in stiffly, and stood looking down at her as she knelt beside the bed. His face was as expressionless as ever. She'd sometimes wondered why it didn't crack.

He had not changed at all.

And then she saw them. Tears. There were tears in his eyes.

"Isabella, oh Isabella. I could not believe it when Violet said she'd stumbled upon you. Do you know how hard I have searched for you? I had begun to despair that I would ever find you. Even when my agent said you'd been involved in some scandal with the Duke of Strattington, I could barely believe it. And now you are here."

Isabella didn't think she'd ever heard so many words from her brother at once, at least not addressed to her. "Yes, I am here."

Masters stood staring down at her. Having finished his speech, he clearly did not know what else to say.

She did not know either. The trunk still lay open beside her so she shut it—the top closed with a bang—and shoved it back under the bed. Bracing herself on the rail of the bed, she stood as gracefully as she could manage. "You kept my things," she said.

"Yes, they have been here, waiting, since you left."

"Did you really think I would come back?"

"I hoped you would."

It was too painful. She turned and walked away from him, staring blankly into the dark fireplace. Remembering all she'd been through in the past years, she found it hard to even contemplate forgiving her brother. "Why would you hope that? It is not as if you cared for me. You could not have cared for me and tried to force me to marry Foxworthy."

Masters's boots tapped as he took a step toward her and then stopped, hesitated. "I did care. I just did not know what to do. You saw the papers he had—you are the one who retrieved them for me. They clearly said our father had committed treason. Foxworthy would have ruined us all. It was selfish of me to give in to his demands, but I truly thought it would be better for us all—not just myself. I could not imagine what would happen to you if it all came out."

"Probably about what happened to me anyway. I would have been forced to seek employment and fend for myself. It has mostly not been so bad." She avoided thinking about these last most wonderful and most horrible weeks.

"Was it wrong of me to try and save you from that?"

She turned back to him. "And to try to save yourself?"

He looked straight at her. "Yes, and to try and save myself—and Violet. I saw no other choices at the time."

"You could have talked to me about it."

His gaze wavered, but did not drop. "Yes—and I should have. If you've met my wife, and I believe you have, you will know that I have been informed of that many times. And we will not even begin to discuss my conversations with Violet."

"I was quite surprised when she insisted that I come and talk to you. I did not think the two of you spoke."

"That is my Clara's doing. She is a great friend of Violet's and between them they managed to persuade me of the error of my ways."

If she'd been unsure of what to say before, she was speechless now. Her brother still walked like himself, still held himself stiffly, still kept his face blank, still spoke in the same carefully modulated tones—but his words, his words were not those of her brother.

And yet. . .

"I do appreciate what you say," she said, "but it does not change things. What happened happened."

"It does not have to be that way. You are home now."

A while ago she'd been thinking of this room as close to home. Now it felt anything but. "But not to stay. I intend to go to the country with Annie, with Lady Richard Tenant. I will act as companion to her and governess to any future children."

"No." Now, that sounded like her brother.

"I do not see that there is a choice. You seem to forget that I killed a man. You may not have been there, but surely Lord Peter and Violet informed you of the situation."

"Foxworthy was stabbed after you left. Violet reported no knife wounds. Foxworthy must have still been alive when you left."

"Is that what Violet said? I can assure that he was very dead when I left. I have wished that what you say was true, but it is not. I killed him. Do not doubt that."

Now Masters did turn away. He went and stared out the window, but she doubted that he saw the sunny, flower-filled garden. "It does not matter. No one knows. We will pretend it never happened."

Isabella patted the papers held tight in her bodice. Was it possible? If she managed to return the papers, maybe it could all be hidden away. "And where will you say I have been these last years? I am sure my absence has been remarked on."

"We have said you were in the country."

"And I am sure everyone believed that."

"They claim to have. No one has questioned me."

"Not to your face. I am sure rumors abounded when I left and did not return."

"Nonetheless, once you are safely here, back in the bosom of your family, we can launch you again, find you a good, steady husband. Once you are wed any rumors will stop."

"You want to marry me off again?" She truly could not believe him.

He turned from the window. "I am afraid I phrased that badly. Yes, I do think you need to marry, but to a man of your choosing."

Her mind filled with an image of Mark and her dream cottage. "I do not wish to wed. Not now. Probably not ever."

"What has you acting like a cornered tomcat?" Douglas settled in the chair across from Mark and swung his boots up onto the table.

"It's a fine thing when a man can't have peace in his own library," Mark replied.

"Perhaps I should have said growling like a bear."

"Do you want me to run you through?"

"I might be scared if you threatened to shoot me. We both know that I am the better swordsman." Douglas leaned forward, picked up Mark's glass, and sniffed it. "If you're drinking brandy of this quality, and still grumbling, it must be bad. You still can't find her?"

"It could be something else, you know."

Douglas just raised a brow and set the glass back on the table.

"Yes, it's Bella. Are you sure it was her you saw

with Lord Peter St. Johns? There has been no sighting of her in days. She can't simply vanish into his house."

"I've a feeling that girl can do just about whatever she wishes. You find her a nursery maid, make her your mistress, and now she's moved in with a marquess's brother. Next she'll be marrying one of the highest lords in the kingdom."

"Lord Peter is already married. Bella wouldn't stay with a married man." Mark knew he was growling again. "And if she's his mistress now, she'd have been better off staying with me."

"I do not believe she is Lord Peter's mistress," Douglas replied, his voice calming. "It is his wife's home. I cannot imagine any wife would allow a mistress under her roof."

"Then what is she doing there, assuming she even is there?"

"I don't know. Are you sure she hasn't left?"

"It is impossible to tell. None of the descriptions of women who have left the home sound like her, but she could have altered her appearance. I don't know whether to instruct my men to look for a maid, a mistress, or a Greek goddess. It does rather complicate matters."

"And what of the murder she claims to have committed? Have you found out more about that?"

Mark pushed himself up to standing and paced back and forth across the worn carpet. "No, damn it. All I can tell you is that Isabella Smith seems not to have existed for more than a couple of years. I believe I have found the first place she was employed and am waiting to hear. She must have arrived with some type of reference. Nobody would have hired her otherwise."

"That is true. So if you find out who gave her the reference you can find out who she is?"

"It is at least a step in the right direction."

"And what will you do when you find her?"

Finally a question he could answer definitively. "I will claim what is mine."

Chapter 27

"So you must tell me all. Are you really living with your brother again?" Annie burst into the parlor at an hour far too early for guests. Masters's butler followed behind, his glance apologetic. "I didn't think you were ever going to speak to him again. I was tempted to skip the coronation yesterday to come and talk to you. I couldn't believe you left Violet's home and came here."

"It's a long story." Isabella rubbed at her temple. "I agreed to meet with Masters to make Violet happy and to get into the house. There was something I needed to retrieve from my room. But—but when Masters started to talk, things changed. I feel like I suddenly have the brother I always wanted, one I can depend on."

"So you've told him everything and he's going to help?" Annie asked as she took a seat across from Isabella. She leaned forward eagerly.

Isabella pulled in a slow breath and considered what to say. "Masters knew about Foxworthy already—or at least most of it. Violet told him. He also wondered if Foxworthy hadn't still been alive when he was stabbed. It all sounds strange to me. Foxworthy was dead when I left. I have no question. He seems to think that I can just come back to the family and rejoin society."

"He's probably right about that. If you don't realize it, your family is already more than slightly scandalous and yet they are accepted. I don't see why you should be any different. And it's not like anyone has even mentioned Foxworthy in years. I can't believe that anyone cares anymore." Annie sat back.

But Annie didn't know about the man who wanted the letters. He was supposed to contact her today, the day after the coronation. Isabella refused to even think about the future until he was taken care of. Would he leave her alone once he had the letters? "I still think I should just fade into the background and come to the country with you. I will live a quiet, unremarkable life and no one will ever need think of me again. I can visit my brother and sister occasionally to be sure they know I am happy. I do not want to give them more worry. We are all having dinner tonight. I wish you could see Violet with her niece and nephew. It is the family I have always wanted."

"But don't you want your own family, your own children? What about Strattington? Why don't you just marry him?"

Leave it to Annie to cut to the heart of the matter. "He still doesn't know who I am and I have no intention of telling him. He planned to return to his estates after the coronation. I doubt we will meet again. I will be in the country with you if ever he should come to London again."

"I still don't see why you don't just tell him. It seems a simple thing to me. If he wanted you enough to make you his mistress, surely he would want you enough to make you his wife."

"I wish it was so simple. Dukes do not marry their mistresses. And the type of wanting that a man has for his mistress is very different than the type a man has for his wife. Besides, Mark—Strattington—is trying to be a proper duke and I would only bring scandal. Can you imagine the whispers if he married his mistress?"

"Poppycock. Nobody but me knows you were his mistress. I am certainly not going to tell anybody. And he thinks you are a maid. If he knew you were the granddaughter of an earl everything would be different."

Isabella was not so sure. "Miss Isabella Hermione Masters was of barely eligible birth to marry a duke at the age of seventeen. The best that could have been said of the match was that nobody would actually laugh at the idea. Now I have a mysterious past—even you thought I'd had a baby—and a scandalous family—you said that yourself. I hardly think I am duchess material."

"I still think—"

"And I am a murderess. Whether or not it is ever proven, there might still be rumors. I don't think I could place that burden on Mark. Some dreams do not have happy endings." She had told him the truth and now hoped to never see his face again, except in her dreams. Annie's plan might be wonderful, but it was also impossible. "Now, I am going to change the subject. Tell me about what happened at the masquerade. Did your plan work? I had a slightly unpleasant run-in with Lord Richard. Did he tell you about it?"

"I shouldn't let you get away with this. I have much more to say about your life." Annie leaned forward again. "But in truth, I do need your advice."

Before Annie could say more there was a tap on the door and Masters's butler entered. "The Duke of Hargrove is here to see you, miss."

"Doesn't he mean the Duke of Strattington? Why would Hargrove be here? My brother-in-law never pays calls. He expects the world to come to him. Why on earth would he be visiting you?" Annie asked.

Before Isabella could answer, Hargrove strode into the room. He frowned at Annie. "Lady Richard, don't you have other errands you should be running?"

"You'll never believe who wrote Isabella's first recommendation." Mark collapsed into a chair by the hearth and stared at Douglas.

Without his asking, Douglas poured him a large glass of brandy and brought it over. "I must confess I couldn't even begin to guess. The king himself?"

"Almost as unlikely. My dear aunt, Lady Smythe-Burke. It was apparently glowing and spoke of Miss Smith's fine character and respectability. It sounded as if they'd known each other for years."

"Perhaps they had. Your aunt does keep a wide variety of friends."

"But a nursery maid?"

"You've said she started out as a companion. Perhaps Lady Smythe-Burke employed her?"

"It seems unlikely. The only servants my aunt takes interest in are her handsome footmen. She's always insisted she did not want a companion and she certainly has no need of a baby nurse or a governess."

"Perhaps Isabella worked for one of her friends. Surely some of them must have companions."

"It is possible, but then why not get a reference from her actual employer?"

"You will have to ask your aunt." Douglas poured himself a glass of the brandy.

"I do intend to, but unfortunately she is out of London until the end of the week. I am undecided on whether to chase her down. I don't want to arouse her curiosity. You know how she is."

"My brother's wife is a lovely girl, but rather tiresome. Note how slow she was to realize the necessity of her departure." Hargrove took Annie's seat without waiting for an invitation.

It had taken Annie a surprisingly long time to leave. She had clearly been trying to understand what purpose Hargrove could have in calling on Isabella. Isabella herself was baffled.

"Perhaps she thought you were looking for her."

"Doubtful. I am never looking for her." Hargrove stared at her hard. She felt like a butterfly, wings pinned to paper, unable to move. "Ring for some tea. I am quite parched." He waved his hand, a strong male hand, the wrist surrounded in lace edged in palest mauve. A slow curl of dread formed in her stomach at the sight of it. "Though once I found where my sister-in-law had gone my course was clear. You do keep making it easy to find you."

He waved his hand again, the lace fluttering about it. Mauve lace.

Mauve, that was a name they had never used to describe that awful bedroom.

She didn't know why she'd had the thought, not now when she was trying to understand why Hargrove was here.

And then she knew. Her gaze moved up from that lace-edged arm to the Duke of Hargrove's face. He was staring at her, his eyes harder than the diamond stone adorning his finger.

Shock took her. She had been right. It had seemed an impossibility, but . . . She had not even been sure such things were real. And then—her chest loosened as if her corset had been unlaced, her lungs filled with air, blood rushed to her brain.

She wished she could pull out the sheaf of papers and wave them in the air. She raised her eyes to Hargrove. Direct might be the best approach. "I believe I have something of yours."

"Do you, now?"

"Do you wish to pretend? If so, you should give up the purple lace. It is rather distinctive."

Hargrove laughed—harshly. "Do you know I hate lavender and mauve? I have tried to develop a taste for them, but I cannot, and now they bring only unpleasant memories."

"Then why . . . ?"

"Because he liked to see me in them. Isn't it strange? Lord William's been dead years now and I still cannot break the habit. It was our special code and it has become part of me."

She had been right. "Is it all coincidence, then, my ending up with Strattington? It seems impossible that I should be with him when you were his cousin's . . ."

Hargrove did not look away. "*Lover* is I believe the word. No matter what society may think, it is the only one that fits. And yes, it is nothing but irony running amok. I find it quite unbelievable that you should end up with Strattington. I search for you high and low and when I find you it is with him. I would much have preferred you anywhere else. He is such an unworthy replacement to my sweet William, no taste, no refinement—and horrible political views. And then he installed you in our house, in our room. I could have killed him for that." The look he gave Isabella made her believe him.

"I can assure you neither of us knew. I imagined it was the old duke who kept the house, not his son."

"Originally it was, but the old man was such a stickler I am not sure he ever used the place." Hargrove tapped a finger on the table. "He certainly never intended it for the use we put it to."

"And the bedroom, that was Lord William's design?"

"Hideous, isn't it? I never understood his love of the color, but it was such an easy whim to give in to. It always made him quite amorous."

That was more than Isabella needed to know. "I still cannot quite believe it at all—and that I should come to stay with Annie, to place myself in your power, that seems almost too great a coincidence."

"I must agree. I was in quite the mood when my man said you had left Strattington and he was not sure where you had gone. You are quite the runner. Then I visit my brother and there you are, just waiting for me. And when you disappeared again—despite my warnings—I had only to wait for Annie to lead me to you."

"I was not trying to run. I had to come here to get what you required. I left the papers here, in my brother's house, when I left."

"So you have them?"

Isabella rose and walked to the writing desk. Did she just give him the letters, or did that leave her without defense? "I am still not sure how you knew I had the letters."

"I watched you take them. I have been waiting for

your blackmail attempt for years—and preparing to do anything necessary to get them back." His hand slipped into the pocket of his coat.

Isabella felt the threat in his words and walked away from the desk. "You were there?"

"I think I mentioned that when we met at Georgiana's masquerade."

"I wasn't sure that was you. Why did you not let me know you were there, at Foxworthy's?"

"I had come to kill the man. It did not seem like the time to renew acquaintances."

"You were going to kill Foxworthy?"

"Damn you, yes. I had it all planned out. The man was going to suffer. And then you came and ruined everything."

"I didn't mean to kill him—although it is hard to say I am sorry when I would do the same thing again."

"If only you could have stayed away. An accidental death was not enough, he deserved to suffer for what he did to William."

And suddenly even the few pieces of the puzzle that had not made sense slipped into place. "You stabbed him. I never understood why everyone thought he was stabbed when I knew that he slipped and hit the mantel."

Hargrove rose to his feet. "Yes, I bloody well stabbed him. I'd have done it a dozen times if I hadn't heard voices. There was little enough satisfaction in it. I wanted to feel him squirm beneath my hand, but I'd have done worse if I could."

He was too near. Isabella could feel the menace leaking from him like mist off a bog. "But why?"

He stepped even closer. "Do you know how my William died?"

"No." She hadn't heard anything beyond that Mark had inherited after the death of both his cousin and his uncle.

"He killed himself, and it was because of me—only it was Foxworthy who drove him to it."

"I am afraid I don't understand." Her back was against the wall. If he stepped any closer they would be touching.

"Lord William and I were happy—or as happy as any two men could be in the circumstances. We knew that we could never be open, but we knew that once he inherited nobody would question us. Two dukes working together to improve the empire. If we met frequently it was only because we had so much to discuss. I was even going to marry that twit Georgiana to lend us respectability. The greatest problem we had was that blasted purple bedroom. He loved it and I felt trapped in a jar of plum jam." He glanced down at his cuffs.

She tried to step sideways. "I don't see what Foxworthy has to do with any of this."

"As I am sure you are aware, Foxworthy was in the habit of collecting bits and pieces of information he thought might be useful. There was a certain measure I wanted to be sure passed in Lords and Wimberley was opposed. Blasted man is too damn persuasive. In any case, Foxworthy hinted that he had something that would keep Wimberley contained. I invited him to dinner to discuss the matter—only after he left did I discover he'd taken William's letters with him. I should have destroyed them when I received them, but I did not. They were a little piece of him that I could keep with me. I could only be relieved that we had kept our identities secret. Even William had the sense not to sign a love letter between two men—still they could have been damaging. It clearly does not take a great intellect to figure them out." Hargrove gave her a dismissing look.

"And so Foxworthy blackmailed you?"

"If only he had. No, he went after William. I don't know how he knew who the letters were from, but he did. William should have come to me, but he did not. Instead he had a 'hunting accident.' He was afraid the old duke would hear. I didn't know what had happened until Foxworthy came to me afterward, still seeking a prize. I should have killed him then."

Isabella tried to put it all together in her mind. It was such a tangle. How could simple feelings end in such tragedy? "So you blame yourself because Foxworthy found the letters at your home."

"I was careless. I will not be so careless again. Where are they?"

It took great effort to keep her eyes from wandering to the desk. She didn't know why she hesitated to give them to him, he certainly had a right to them. "I do not have them with me."

"You lie."

Her gaze shot up to his. She could feel his breath upon her cheek. "I don't know why you would say that."

Hargrove reached out and grabbed her arm, painfully. "I am an expert on lies. I tell so many of them myself."

"That is not reason—"

He cut her off. "Before, when you said you did not have the letters, you spoke the truth—but now—now it is different. You know just where they are. Give them to me."

"Let go of me." She glanced down at his hand. "Then we will talk."

"I think you misunderstand the structure of power between us." His fingers tightened further.

"And what will happen if I do give them to you?"

"Then there will be no need for us to ever speak again. You can run off to whatever bolt-hole you have in mind this time. I am sure you already know where you plan to run—probably to my sister-in-law. I don't even care as long as you stay far from me. I will go on simply being Hargrove. That will be the end of it."

Why did she not feel convinced? "There will never be any mention of Foxworthy again?"

"Why would there be?"

He was lying. She didn't know why she thought so, but she did. She could discern no reason for him to lie. What he said made sense, but . . . "I don't know, but you make it all seem so easy."

"It is."

"A man died. That should never be easy."

"Two men died. Do not forget William." His eyes lost their focus.

"And you do not forgive me for that?" It made no sense. She had not known either man at the time.

"I do not forgive you for killing Foxworthy." His voice grew hard.

"And you want me to pay for it?" She had already paid, lost years of her life, lost Mark. Would there still have been magic between them if they had met for the first time at a ball before the coronation? She rather thought so.

Hargrove released her suddenly and stepped back. His body twitched with emotion. "Give me my letters. Give me something to remember him by."

Chapter 28

His words moved her. With firm, decisive steps Isabella walked to the desk and opened the box. Lifting out a packet of papers tied with a satin ribbon, she turned and held it out to Hargrove.

Hargrove grabbed it with unnecessary haste, paging through the letters quickly. "It looks like they are all here."

"I did not take any out. I do not know if I took them all at the beginning."

Hargrove skewered her with his gaze. "I would hope they are all here, if I were you."

"How quickly your tone changes now that you have what you want." She should have been surprised, but she was not. "I am probably foolish to have given them all to you, but I will not play your game—your game and Foxworthy's. You want to believe that you are different and yet you did everything you could to bend me to your will."

"I did only what was necessary."

"So we are done." She tried to sound strong.

"As long as you disappear again. I do not wish to see you and remember. If you do go with my sister-in-law, I suggest you stay in the country when she comes to Town."

"And if I choose not to go? My brother and sister have indicated they wish me to stay here, to reintroduce me into society." She had not really considered the option until now, but Hargrove's dismissiveness had her dander up.

"You are good at running. I cannot imagine why you would stop now. Society is no place for one such as you."

"One such as me. I am so tired of being described in such ways. I will do as I please."

Hargrove tucked the letters into his pocket. "I think not. I could still start whispers about Foxworthy."

"And I could start whispers about how you know."

"Nobody would believe you." Hargrove stepped toward her.

"Not to your face they wouldn't, but behind your back? Are you sure there are no rumors already? I have always found that very few things stay hidden forever."

"I cannot believe that you are unwise enough to threaten me. Do you really think that anyone would choose to believe you over me?"

"But I do not need to win. That is the glory of rumor and gossip, once it is started people never stop questioning."

"I would not try it, girl. I might be damaged by rumor, but you could hang if I decide to meddle."

That stopped her, but only for a moment. She was so tired of running. "I believe sodomy is also a hanging offense."

Hargrove turned as purple as the bedroom. "Do you really seek to test me? There is no proof. Even the letters were not really proof. No matter how you spread rumor nobody would hang a duke without proof. Hell, nobody would hang a duke with proof."

"And yet you chased me for three years for a packet of letters."

Hargrove did not answer. He glared at her again with his cold eyes. "What do you want, Miss Masters? I would think you would be happy to flee this city and society. I cannot imagine you will have a warm welcome even without my help."

"I merely wish to be free to make my own choices." She walked to the settee and sat, back straight.

"Do you hope Strattington will come to you? He'd never marry you now that he's had you. He's already looking for a bride to enhance his standing. You would only drag him into the dirt. And that's without him knowing your secret. How do you think he would react if he knew you had killed a man?"

"I already told him." And she was glad she had. Mark might not know the details, but he would not be surprised if Hargrove spoke with him. Who was she kidding? He'd still be shocked, deeply shocked, if he knew the whole truth.

"Did you? Is that why he threw you out? How you ended up in my brother's house?"

"No." She was not going to explain to him why she had left, let him know that he had been a large part of the cause.

Hargrove smiled and it was not pleasant. "I am not even going to begin to guess at what you are not saying. Just know that you will be very sorry if you cross me. Scurry away like the mouse you are."

He walked to the door, leaving her staring after him.

Just before exiting he added, "And you never did call for my tea. One would think you lacked all manners."

* * *

"I hear they've chosen your bride already. The Earl of Sangdorn's daughter, although it was a little unclear which one," Brisbane said as Mark entered his library. "The poor man does have seven of them. I do hope it's not the youngest. I believe she's only ten."

"Who is 'they' and why are they choosing my bride?" Mark asked as he took a seat across from Brisbane's desk.

"I've never been clear on exactly who they are, but they do seem to try and control everything." Brisbane took a cheroot from a box on his desk and offered one to Mark.

Mark shook his head. "I may never marry anyone—and certainly not one of the Earl of Sangdorn's daughters."

Brisbane sat up in his chair. "I am not sure you have a choice—the duchy and all."

Running his fingers through his hair, Mark stared down at the floor. "Damnation. Ever since I became a duke I do nothing but what people tell me I must. I am so tired of doing what others say."

A deep laugh filled the room. Brisbane stood and walked around the desk, leaning against its edge. "This is going to sound contradictory, given what I have just said, but I think you've missed the point of being a duke."

Mark lifted his head. "I am not sure what you mean."

Brisbane leaned back, crossing his booted ankles. "A duke does what a duke wants. It really is as simple as that."

Shaking his head, Mark stared at the high shelves of books. "I am so determined to do this right. I've never had any difficulty with doing things well. Everything I've turned my hand to has come with ease. But this, being a duke, I think I'd rather be back in the army taking cannon fire."

"I've never known anything else, so it is hard for me to sympathize. From the day of my birth this is all I have known. Even before my father's death my whole life was spent knowing that this was my fate. Still, I have a difficult time seeing that it could be that troublesome—unless you mean running the estates. That can take time to manage. The rest, though, that is just window dressing."

"The estates I do not find difficult. The principles are the same as they were for my father's much smaller holdings. But everything else—since I have become Strattington all I have heard are rules on how to be a duke. My valet, for example, is always telling me what I need to do and how I need to dress while doing it. And he is only one of many."

"I believe I have already told you that the only thing you listen to your valet about is the tying of your cravat. I cannot imagine why you would care what he thinks of anything else."

"He was with my uncle for years. He knows how everything is done."

"That was your uncle. You are you."

"Everyone says my uncle was the perfect duke."

"And what do they say about me?" Brisbane stood up fully as he spoke, drawing an invisible mantle of authority about his shoulders.

Mark could only stare at the subtle changes in the man. "I believe a drawing of you is posted next to the definition of *duke*. I don't even hear the usual rumors about opera singers. I believe Hargrove made some unsavory comments about your politics, but given the man's own views I assume that is a compliment."

"And am I the same as your uncle?"

"It would be hard to imagine two more different men, except you both have the ability to make it seem like everyone within hearing should do as you say."

Brisbane sat back down on the edge of the desk. "And do you know why that is?"

"That is what I have been trying to learn."

"It is because we are dukes."

"And that is supposed to be helpful?"

"Being a duke means knowing you are always right. Even if you are wrong you are right because you are a duke."

Mark stared up at the ceiling, considering. "I thought being a duke was about being proper, being better, above it all. Everyone has told me how to act, how to behave. I wanted to be sure I did not disgrace myself."

"Being a duke is about not worrying what others think. Their thoughts are not as valid as your own."

"You almost have me believing you are serious."

"That's because I am serious. You are a duke. Society will always think that an opinion you speak is more valid than any other's. I do not say if it is right or wrong, but it is true."

"And yet you say I must marry."

"Even that is not an absolute. I should not encourage such a stance. It does cause turmoil when there is not a true heir, but even that can be overcome. Just be sure that it is what you truly want."

Mark lowered his head and stared straight at Brisbane. "I cannot have what I do want if I marry as I should."

"You speak in riddles, but I imagine I have some idea what you are talking about. Marriage does complicate many things. It can be even worse than leaving a purse in the morning. Is she really worth it?"

"She is what I want. There are other problems to be solved, but I am not happy without her."

"Then go and get her—and marriage be damned."

"That is actually why I came to see you. I had decided to do that already, but I need to find our mutual aunt, Lady Smythe-Burke, first. I was told you might know where she has taken herself off to."

"You had decided that already," Brisbane repeated, smiling. "You might figure out how to be a duke yet."

"You have decided to stay in London, to stay with us?" Violet clapped her hands in joy, a very uncharacteristic gesture.

Had she really just said that? Isabella had come into the dining room ready to announce that she was going to Annie's country estate for a while, that she would wait for Annie to join her, and instead she had said she was staying in London. It had only taken one look at her gathered family to know that she could not leave again.

She was tired of running, of hiding. She would risk whatever was necessary to stay.

"Yes, I don't know quite what my plans are yet, but I am not ready to leave." She pushed aside the image of Mark that suddenly filled her mind. She was sure he had left London already. Such thoughts could not be allowed to interfere.

She would have done almost anything to stay with him, to be with him, but she could not bear the thought of living with him as his mistress, watching him take a wife, father children. No, she would stay here with her family and then perhaps— She didn't even know what *perhaps* was, but it was not running again.

"We will have to have a ball, to reintroduce you to society." Violet turned to her husband. "Do you think Wimberley would host it? If he does then everybody will come."

"That wasn't quite what I meant. I thought I could just live here quietly. I certainly don't need—"

"What nonsense. Of course you do," Masters's wife, Clara, spoke up. "And I am sure Wimberley will do it. His wife does love a good ball."

Isabella drew in a deep breath. She would have to tell her family about Hargrove, tell them about his threats. She could not let them do this unknowingly. If they still gave her their support, then she would be willing to risk it all to stay here, to stay with them—to let them throw this ridiculous party and be done with it.

Masters smiled. "Yes, there is no better way to find a husband than at a ball."

Isabella was relieved that she owned only one of the three sets of feminine eyes that turned on him and glared.

"So who is she?" Mark asked, staring across at his aunt. She had finally returned to Town and he had braved the lioness's den to speak with her. It was a rare man who willingly entered her parlor. He'd heard rumors that they too often left with brides. For having no children of her own, his aunt was a well-known matchmaker.

"Who is who?" Lady Smythe-Burke asked as she took a seat in her normal straight-backed fashion. "I am glad to hear you are getting along with Brisbane. I do sometimes worry that boy is too alone."

Mark was so stunned by the concept of calling Brisbane a boy that it took him a moment to remember his question. "Miss Smith. Who is Miss Smith?"

"Miss Smythe? I don't believe there are any Smythe girls, not for several generations, aside from your sisters, that is. And I assume you do not mean them."

"No, Miss Smith. Miss Isabella Smith?"

Lady Smythe-Burke turned to him with sudden interest. "Oh, I had forgotten about that. Is she back in Town? How delightful. She must be, what? About twenty?"

"Twenty-one, I believe, and that does not answer my question."

Picking up her embroidery and staring at it as if she'd never seen it before, Lady Smythe-Burke avoided his gaze. "And why do you think I know anything about Miss Smith?"

"You did write her a reference."

"It could be a forgery."

"That does not seem likely. Are you saying that you did not write it?"

"No. I wrote it. The girl needed help and I gave it."

"So who is she?"

"I did rather promise not to say. It was the only condition on which she'd accept my help. That family has always been stubborn."

"What family?"

Lady Smythe-Burke set the embroidery back down and stared straight at him, making him feel he had crumbs about his mouth. "I told you, that is secret. Isabella has her reasons for wishing to remain unknown, although if she is back in Town . . ."

Mark leaned forward. "Reasons having to do with the man she murdered?"

He had expected shock, his aunt showed none. "You know about that? Now that is surprising. I didn't think anybody knew about Foxworthy's death besides her family."

"Foxworthy? Who is he? Or perhaps I should ask who was he?"

"A vile little man. And I should not have said even that. Except . . ."

"Except that you actually want to give me enough clues to find her? I am beginning to understand how you work, my dearest of aunts."

"I don't know why you would think that. I am a master at keeping secrets. I shall say no more on the subject." She picked up her needlework again. "I can't even recall starting this piece. Who would decide that all the flowers should be pink? I have always disliked pink. It is a color for silly young chits—and even when I was young I was never silly. I always wore blue. I think blue looks much better on most girls than pink. Pink tends to make one's cheeks look ruddy. What do you think? Oh, don't look at me like that. You're a young man and I am sure you've noticed girls and what they wear. Not the details, mind you, I do understand the male mind. But surely you must have an opinion. I've chosen the most delightful turquoise blue silk to wear to the Wimberleys' ball this Friday. I may even wear a turban with it. Do you think a feather would be too much? Clearly you do. What a shame. I was rather expecting you to escort me. In fact I think I shall insist that both you and Brisbane escort me. I will be quite the most popular of matrons with an eligible duke on each arm."

"I really had not thought to attend."

"Nonsense. The Wimberleys' is a must. You may fetch me at nine o'clock."

"I am still in mourning. I attended affairs before the coronation, but only because the king—"

"Double nonsense. He was your uncle, not your father. I do insist, and if I insist then nobody will say otherwise. I may even insist that you dance."

Chapter 29

Isabella had thought nothing in her life could ever make her so nervous again.

She had been wrong.

The ballroom was beautiful. A thousand candles glittered along the walls and on high chandeliers. Hundreds of deep apricot roses decorated every surface. Crystal and silver shone on tables, and brocade of pristine white draped elegantly to the floor. The Marquess of Wimberley had spared no expense to make this a ball to remember, not an easy feat little more than a week after the coronation. Isabella was still not sure why he was doing this for her, but he was certainly doing it right.

Only she wasn't sure it was what she wanted.

Everybody told her that she must take her place in society. Once she had shown the slightest inclination to accept the idea, they had joined forces against her. Masters had told her he could never be happy if he felt that he had kept her from what should rightfully be hers. Clara, his wife, had confirmed his deep regret over Isabella's disappearance and explained how happy she would be if Isabella had it in her to do this for her brother. Violet had said "nonsense" to that and then told Isabella that she must do it because it was the right thing to do. Lord Peter had simply smiled at his wife and sent a note to his brother the marquess. Before Isabella knew what had happened, the ball had been planned.

Even when she'd told them about Hargrove, they'd showed her nothing but support. She had to admit there had been more than a little anger directed at Hargrove himself. Only Masters had shown any surprise at the nature of his relationship with Lord William. Violet had merely exclaimed, "That explains some things."

And now she was here.

It was time for her reintroduction to society. She began to wish she had run away after all.

"You look lovely." Violet came up behind her.

"I must admit it is one of the most beautiful gowns I have ever seen." Isabella glanced down at the froth of crimson silk. It matched the ring she wore on a long chain about her neck, the ruby hidden by the bodice of her gown. "Are you sure it is appropriate? It seems quite bold. Would it not be better if I were slightly less—less noticeable?"

"The whole point of this ball is for you to be noticed. We want the world to know that you are back among us and that we are proud of you."

But would they be proud if they knew everything? Not just about Foxworthy and Hargrove, but about Mark? It was the one thing she had not told them. "And you think this is the way to do it? There must be hundreds of questions about where I was the last few years. I am sure that almost nobody believes that I just decided to go back to Dorset for a few years halfway through my first season."

Violet pursed her lips. "Yes, I cannot deny there

was some gossip. Mostly it was at the very beginning. I believe the most popular rumor was that you had eloped with Lord Langdon."

"Langdon?" It was true she had flirted with him and briefly pondered him as a suitor, but that was before she had gotten to know him. He had never been a serious contender for her affections.

"I know it was a preposterous thought, but I must confess we let the rumor run free for a while. When Langdon appeared, having spent a fortnight fishing, and the gossip was proved wrong, it made it easier to discount any further rumor."

"And the gossip was proved wrong—I would not have put it past Langdon to let some rumors remain. He always did fancy himself a dashing rake." It was far better to converse here, at the top of the stairs, than to consider walking down to the ballroom below.

"Well . . ." Violet hesitated, and Isabella turned back to her.

"Well?"

"I am afraid that you are correct, he did not quite discredit all the rumors, and so when you failed to appear some small fragments of gossip remained."

Isabella did not say anything; she simply stared at her sister.

"Many believe that you ran off to have a child after Masters stopped the elopement. The rumor is that you have been living as widow in some small seaside town and raising the child." The words flew from Violet's mouth in flurry.

"A secret baby? And you are just telling me this now?" Isabella could not help chuckling. "They think I left because I was with child? Annie said something about that." She didn't know why she found it so funny except that gossip and rumor was supplying her with the one thing she had always wanted and never had.

"That is why it is important that we present you in such style. Wimberley was in complete agreement. Once you are launched and have our support, society will know that this rumor was just as preposterous as all the others."

"But not nearly as preposterous as the truth," Isabella felt compelled to add.

Violet laid a gloved hand upon her arm. "There is no need to think about that. It is over. Things are different now."

That was easy for Violet to say. She had not killed a man. Was Hargrove here? There had been much debate on whether to invite him, but in the end it had been decided it was far better to keep the man in sight. Isabella peered down at the crowd below, entering the ballroom. He had not contacted her since she'd given him the papers. Was he prepared to just let the whole matter rest? Or would he take on not only her, but also her whole family?

She let her eyes focus on the entire crowd. "There are so many people down there. Couldn't we do something quieter? Perhaps a musicale evening? Nobody ever comes to those."

"Isn't this where the conversation started? We want society to see that we are proud of you, that there is nothing mysterious to wonder about. Peter and I faced down rumor and you can too. Here he comes. He will walk you down, and Wimberley will greet you immediately. There will be no room for gossip."

There was always room for gossip. Still, Isabella fixed a smile on her face and waited for her brother-in-law to join them. After all she been through she would not be cowed by a few of society's matrons. She tilted her chin up and waited as Lord Peter held out his arm for her.

He stopped and stared.

This was why his aunt had insisted he come—and no wonder she'd left his side as soon as they'd entered the room.

Mark had always known Bella was a goddess, but as he watched her descend the stairs on Lord Peter's arm his breath was taken away. The deep red gown clung to every curve, slipping over her body like a stream over smooth pebbles. No pebble had ever caused his body to react with such vigor, however. Her skin shone like pearls and her hair swooped in a riot of fiery curls.

His gaze moved to her face. She was unhappy. She did not wish to be here. If she could, she would run. It took only the briefest of glances for him to see all that. He'd seen that expression before and she'd always disappeared immediately afterward. He could not afford to let that happen again, not now, not when he'd finally found her.

She stopped a few steps from the bottom, scanning the crowd. He waited for her eyes to fall upon him, but before they could, Lord Peter said something and she turned to him. Her lips froze into a fixed smile. She nodded, but looked no happier. He leaned toward her, whispered. Her mouth relaxed. She said something back.

Mark wished he could hear the words. They did not look like lovers. He had assumed they were not, but it was good to see their body postures reaffirm the fact. He still had not figured out their relationship. All his sources had confirmed that she'd disappeared from Lord Peter's house just as quickly as she'd arrived. And yet here she was on his arm, acting like she had every right to be there. Although, judging by the whiteness of her knuckles, she was not exactly comfortable.

He tried to remember exactly what Lady Smythe-Burke had said to him. She'd insisted he attend this affair and had brooked no resistance. He'd tried several times to refuse. At first he'd assumed her insistence was another plot to introduce him to marriageable chits. Everyone seemed to think he needed to meet some young thing and start a nursery. He couldn't deny that the duchy needed an heir, but he'd already decided not to marry now—if ever. And he certainly wasn't interested in the children that kept being paraded before him. He wanted a wife he could talk to, someone with a little life experience—

Someone like Bella. She might be young, but she understood how the world worked.

His gaze swept over her again as he had the thought. He'd never been bored talking to her—in fact, even in the midst of some activities that normally did not require talk, he'd found himself as intrigued by her thoughts as by her—well, as by any part of her, including those that were capable of stealing his own capacity for speech.

"Never thought I'd see her again—not in decent company at least." The comment came from his left and he turned to see an older matron, Mrs. Thomas or Thompson, he believed. Her gaze was fastened on Bella and she was whispering loudly to her companion.

He stepped closer.

"I know there was never any proof of the rumor, but it was pretty clear what happened. No young girl disappears back to the country for no reason—and then stays there for years. And I heard she hadn't been seen about Masters's estate, no matter what he may have claimed. The girl was clearly led astray, and I am sure she didn't protest too hard. She is Lady Carrington's sister and blood does run true. The older sister may have trapped Wimberley's brother—I was shocked her stomach wasn't swollen at the wedding. It must be true she's barren. Probably a good thing given that family's behavior. Wouldn't want to risk one of them falling heir to the marquess. The younger sister clearly wasn't so lucky. I am sure there's a brat somewhere crying for his mother."

Mark did not hear the reply to that as his mind strove to make sense of what he had just heard.

Lady Carrington—that would now be Lord Peter's wife, Wimberley's sister-in-law. He tried to remember all he had heard about said lady. There had been scandal attached to her name, several husbands and then several lovers. Nothing, however, that had caused society to truly frown on her.

And Masters—that would be Mr. Jonathan Masters. He'd also been involved in some type of scandal a few years back. Mark had been out of London at the time, but he thought there had been cartoons—something about sex and a library. He'd have to inquire further.

But a younger sister? He didn't remember anything about a younger sibling. And certainly not any scandal. Could Foxworthy's death have been part of it? He'd done some investigating on his own and knew all the details of the death, and that if ever a man deserved to be murdered it was probably Foxworthy. He'd even heard rumors of a redhead being seen fleeing. That was probably Bella. He still couldn't imagine her stabbing anyone, however. Why hadn't she trusted him? He would have helped her, whatever the cost.

"Is that Isabella Masters—the one who eloped with Langdon?" Another whisper came from his other side. Mark could not determine who had spoken.

Isabella Masters. That was who she was. And they certainly weren't talking about murder. And what did Langdon have to do with it? The man was a pompous dolt. He listened further.

"I do believe it is. She always was a pretty thing. It's hard to believe she's had a child, not with that waistline."

"It's the red hair—you always hear about redheads."

"I can't believe Wimberley invited her—family or not."

"I heard she'd kiss any man who wanted—and I am not just talking kissing."

"She had sex in a library—caught right in the midst of it, showing all there was to see."

"No, that was her brother—Masters. At least he married the woman, not that they ever admitted who she was."

"She had sex with her brother in the library? Why did nobody tell me?"

The voices continued to swirl around Mark, but his whole focus had shifted to Bella. She still stood on the stairs, frozen. Color drained from her face as the buzz of innuendo reached her. She stepped back, almost tripping on her skirts. Lord Peter moved his hand over hers, holding her tight.

He whispered something. She did not answer.

And then she saw him. Mark felt the jolt as their eyes met. Her mouth opened. Even across the room, Mark could feel the soft breath that escaped between her lips.

Lord Peter said something else in her ear. Still, she made no response. Her eyes stayed locked with Mark's, begging him for something, but he knew not what.

The entire room seemed locked in the same spell—everybody waiting, but for what?

Would she flee back up the stairs? Would somebody give her a direct cut? And if so, who would be the first? They were a room full of sheep waiting for a shepherd.

Mark started to step forward, then caught himself. He had no standing here.

Wimberley swept across the room, his delicate marchioness by his side. He stopped at the bottom of the stairs, held out his hand in greeting to Bella.

She did not take it. She simply stood and stared. Mark willed her to move, willed her to push back her shoulders and proceed, willed her to realize that whatever came next would not be as bad as this moment, this second.

And still she stood.

The crowd did not breathe. Not a word was spoken.

They all waited.

The marchioness held out her hand also, almost trying to force Bella to action.

There was the whisper of words, but even in the silence they could not be heard.

Bella moved her lips, but no sound came out.

If it were not for the bright color of her dress, she would have appeared a ghost.

He started forward again. This situation could not continue. Bella needed him.

A hand came down on his shoulder. He turned. The Duke of Hargrove stood beside him. "I wouldn't do that. You must remember, you are not a man—you are a duke. A duke cannot risk being involved in scandal. Certainly not with one such as she. Let her family take care of it."

Mark opened his mouth to reply, but Hargrove's next words stole his answer. "And wouldn't it suit your purposes better if she is disgraced? Her family doesn't even know the half of it, do they?"

"I do not know of what you speak" was the best that Mark's brain could come up with. He turned back to Bella, ignoring Hargrove, ignoring the man's cold fury.

Bella's hand was in Wimberley's and he was raising it to his lips, welcoming her to his home. Lord Peter stood beside her, stiff as a fireplace poker.

Where was her sister? Where was Masters? Not enough was being done.

And then she smiled.

She was dying inside. Isabella felt each breath fill her chest and knew that it would be her last. She could no longer force herself to pull in another. It felt as if the very air was filled with the spite she could hear flitting about the room. Each whisper seemed a dart aimed directly at her heart.

Lord Peter's fingers squeezed her hand, trying to give her strength. It was not enough.

Wimberley strode over, ready to take control.

The whispers went on. If it had not been for Lord Peter's firm grip she would have turned and fled back up the stairs to Violet. This was a disaster. There was nothing to win and so much to lose.

And then she saw him. Mark stood across the room attired in full ducal finery. If she had thought him grand before, now he robbed that last remaining breath from her body.

Their eyes met. She could not read his from such a distance. If only it were he beside her instead of Lord Peter. His touch had always given her the strength she so desperately needed now.

Her eyes called to him, begged him to help her. She didn't know what she expected, but something.

She didn't know why she should expect something now, when he had never been there for her before. She stood, not breathing, waiting—let him come, let him save her.

He took a step.

She pulled air into her lungs, felt herself begin to draw strength.

And then he stopped. A hand held his arm, a strong male hand, the wrist surrounded in lace edged in palest mauve.

Hargrove.

Why did he have to appear now?

Now, when she was a single breath away from fainting to the floor in front of all society.

Now, when she was a single breath away from running from the room, never to be seen again.

Now, when she wanted to yell Mark's name, to call him to her, to demand he recognize her for what she was to him.

She wanted to shout at the fates as Hargrove leaned forward and whispered to Mark. Mark glanced at him, and then at Isabella, his eyes full of question.

Her eyes flitted back to Hargrove. His gaze spoke for him. He was not done with her.

Wimberley said something, welcomed her to his home, gave her his approval—and it didn't matter. She could see her path clearly now and she was ready to run down it.

She raised her eyes to Mark, expecting disgust. She saw only concern.

A smile trembled upon her lips.

She glanced back at Hargrove, but he was gone.

Chapter 30

Mark watched her smile catch. It had started out full of strength, but now the doubt leaked in.

It sliced at him like a saber slash against his chest.

"I'll cut her direct if she even tries to speak with me. And she'd better not try to renew her friendship with my daughter. They are much of the same age, you know?" It was Mrs. Thompson again and Mark found himself almost baring his teeth at her. He'd never felt such animal impulse course through him.

"I can't believe she'll have the chance. Even Wimberley can't save her now. I doubt we'll ever be forced to see her again. Surely her family will send her back to the country—this time for the duration. I can't imagine there's even a chance a man would take her now."

"Oh, they'll take her, just not in the way she wishes." Mrs. Thompson spoke in an undertone, but a very loud one. Clearly she wanted her cleverness to be heard.

Bella's hand transferred from Lord Peter's arm to Wimberley's. She took that step forward. Her smile was back, firm and strong, but her eyes were still afraid.

He doubted any but he could read that fear, but he saw it all too well.

She took a step, Wimberley leading her forward.

He could sense the indecision in the crowd. Did they dare turn from her with Wimberley at her side?

"They will not accept her, not young and unmarried. Their worries over how she will influence their own daughters, how she will lure their own sons, will win out." When had Brisbane returned to his side? There was no mistaking that cool, arrogant tone.

"How can they not, with Wimberley at her side?" Mark asked.

"They will manage. Fright will always win over reason."

Mark looked at Bella. The desire to run was back in her gaze. Yes, fright could win over reason—or fright could convince one that it was reason.

Damnation. Brisbane was right. He could see it in every face, see everyone worry that they would be approached first.

"Do you want me to save her?" Brisbane asked. "A duke and a marquess together might do the trick. Or was Hargrove right? Do you wish to give her no choice but to return to you? She might not take you anyway, you know."

It was the single beat of a heart. It could not have been longer. There was not time for an eyelash to flutter or a breath to be pulled in. There was certainly not long enough for a look of scorn to form or a head to turn away.

Mark stepped forward. No, he strode forward.

He cut through the crowd, straight and direct, unmindful of those he brushed past.

He'd had the chance to put her first once before—and failed.

Twenty feet.

This time he would not fail.

Ten feet.

He would think only of her.

Five feet. Never in battle had each bit of distance been so painfully won.

Only of her.

Her head came up. Their eyes met again. He saw shock. Then fear. Then—could that be relief?

Did she trust him to save her? Did she finally trust him?

"Miss Masters," he called, the new name strange on his lips.

Wimberley turned to him. And then Lord Peter. The sister, Violet, was halfway down the stairs, Wimberley's marchioness just in front. He did not see the brother, Masters, anywhere, but it did not matter. He knew what he needed to do.

He watched the words form slowly on Bella's lips. "Your Grace, I did not expect you here."

Wimberley's shoulders were back, it was clear he was ready to protect Bella by whatever means necessary.

Did he not realize that was Mark's job?

Mark stopped a foot away, only just observing the boundaries of propriety. "What nonsense is that, my dear? Not expecting me?" He had raised his voice, to make sure everyone in the room would hear him. "How are we supposed to give your family our news if I am not here? I had hoped to speak to your brother first, but I will not risk losing my claim to any other man."

Yet his tone told that there could be no true competition, he was a man who did not lose—and beyond that he was a duke, a duke who was not to be questioned.

"I am not sure what—" Bella began.

"I do not know what you—" Wimberley was taking no chances.

Mark stood straight, for the first time feeling like the duke he was.

"My dear Miss Masters," he cut them both off. "It is not normally done in such a public manner, but as my future duchess you can do what you wish. I merely thought that we would tell your family of our engagement before the rest of the guests."

He had not just said those words. He had not. Isabella fought to understand.

For a moment it felt like a dream come true. The tone of the crowd's whispers changed. One did not risk the displeasure of the future Duchess of Strattington. They would back off for now—and wait.

But how would they react when they realized it was all a farce? Mark could not possibly mean to marry her.

She focused on Mark's face, trying to understand what she saw there. Anger marked the crease in his forehead. The firm line of his lip bespoke determination. His fingers twitched with barely controlled violence. He was ready to fight, to take on any challenge.

She could feel Wimberley draw tight beside her, the muscles of his arm flexing beneath her touch. Lord Peter had come up behind, his large body prepared to charge to her defense.

Three big, strong men ready to tear one another apart on the dance floor—over her. She ran her fingers across Wimberley's jacket, seeking to reassure. Then she dropped her hand, stepping away from him and toward Mark.

Searching his face, she sought the clue of what she should do next, what she should say. How could she avoid trapping them further, avoid trapping him?

"Do not poke fun at me, Your Grace," she said quietly, seeking to give him an out. "They will all take you seriously."

He dropped his voice to match hers. "And what if I am serious? What if I think it is time we let our intentions be known?"

"You cannot be."

Isabella glanced about the room. Every head was turned in their direction. There was not even the polite pretense that they were not the center of attention. Even the orchestra was stilled, turned to see what would happen next.

Mark spoke loud and clear. "I intend to marry you, Miss Isabella Masters. I want you—no one else. And I have been recently informed that what a duke wants—a duke gets. Questions?" His tone did not invite answer.

Isabella had thought she could feel no more pain. She'd been wrong. The impossibility of Mark's proposal felt like the final straw, that little bit of extra weight that would send her crashing to the floor.

She dropped her eyes, staring at the buttons of his coat. "But you do not know everything about me."

"We must talk further. I know more than you think." He spoke softly, hardly louder than a whisper, but his voice brooked no argument.

"You do?"

"Yes." Mark glanced at Wimberley and then back

to her. "I know about Foxworthy. Where can we have some privacy?"

"Perhaps . . ." Wimberley spoke from beside her, letting the word draw long as if he sought what to say next. "Perhaps, Strattington, you would care to dance with Miss Masters? I had planned to open the affair by leading her in a waltz, but now that you have gotten ahead of me and announced your engagement I can think of nothing more fitting."

She looked out over the empty dance floor. Once the orchestra began it would be much harder for everyone to hear what was being said, and after the first minute other couples would need to take to the floor, granting them some privacy—as much privacy as you could have in a ballroom.

Everyone would still stare at them, but they would at least be pretending not to.

Mark bowed his head to her, the perfect angle for a question one was sure of the answer to. "Miss Masters, would you care for my escort to the floor?" He offered his arm.

It was her last chance to run. She could crash through the crowd, make it to the street. The ring Mark had given her at the masquerade hung on a chain about her neck. It could supply any funds she needed. She could be free—as free as she had ever been. No need to hold her head up, no need to pretend.

Or she could take Mark's hand, dance with him in public, be claimed by him before all society. She did not know his game, could not believe he truly meant marriage, but she did trust he meant well.

She trusted him. She had avoided giving in to her feelings, giving in to her desires, for so long, but she could no longer.

She did trust him.

She lifted her hand, watched it move toward Mark, watched the fingers take his sleeve. She did not feel the thick silk of his coat, although she could see its softness. She did not perceive the warmth of his body, although she well knew his heat. Her hand moved as if by itself, controlled by unseen forces.

They turned as one toward the dance floor. The crowd parted before them. Wimberley gestured and the waltz began.

Mark placed his hand low on her back, brought the other out before him. Her own shaking fingers gripped his waist.

He swept her out onto the floor.

The crowd still did not react, did not indicate what society's decision was.

Once around the floor. Twice.

The first couple joined them. Wimberley and his marchioness. Then Violet and Lord Peter. Masters and Clara. And then finally others. A decision might not have been reached, society might be waiting to know the truth of the situation, but good manners would prevail.

And then she saw him. Just as the swirling dancers filled her view, Isabella saw the Duke of Hargrove again, standing at the side, scowling.

The dance floor was not a good place to talk, but he had little choice. Mark kept his voice quiet, speaking to Bella and only to Bella. "I am going to go right to the heart of the matter. Foxworthy."

"You know I killed him?" Her voice trembled only a little as she whispered, her eyes darting nervously to the edge of the dance floor.

"If we are quiet enough nobody can hear us—and yes, or at least almost yes. After some investigation I assumed it was him you had spoken of at the masquerade."

"I am glad that you know. I have wished so often that I could confide in you, share my troubles."

"You always could have."

"It did not seem that way."

He glanced back at the ballroom. "I cannot claim that my actions this evening demonstrate that I will do anything to protect you. It was only a room full of busybodies that I took on. But Bella, I would slay dragons for you."

She closed her eyes, but he could see her careful consideration in the gentle movement of muscles upon her brow. She opened her eyes and stared at him. "I know. I didn't before, but I do now." She glanced toward the ballroom herself. "And yet I think they are worse than any dragon."

"So speak. Tell me about Foxworthy, tell me why you fled."

She swallowed, looking over his shoulder at the dancers beyond.

He drew her closer, blocking her from all others. "I will protect you, no matter what. Just tell me everything."

She shuddered and he saw her debate, then she leaned forward, whispering the whole sordid story to him, telling him of her family's scandals, of Foxworthy, the man in blue, her other pursuers. She paused, as if wishing to say no more, and then told him of Hargrove and Lord William.

He knew his eyes widened for a moment as she spoke of his cousin, but he kept his face calm. Only when she spoke of Hargrove's continued threats did he allow his lips to draw tight.

He drew her closer, closer than propriety would allow. He would focus only on what was important. "But it was an accident, Foxworthy's death. Surely you do not hold yourself responsible for that?"

She closed her eyes. "During the daylight hours I do not. I know there is nothing else I could have done, but at night, at night I see his face as he lay there on the floor. I cannot forget the blankness of his gaze. He was not a nice man. He may even have been an awful one, if all I have heard is true, but no one deserves that. No one deserves to lie there on the floor like that."

"I do understand. I have killed men—in the war. Each and every time it was justified, I had no choice, and yet it is impossible to forget their faces. It is a burden I carry with me always."

She dropped her head, looking down at her feet. "I have been running from that burden. I did not realize it until this moment. I thought I was running from fear and scandal, but I have been running from what I did. I know there is nothing else I could have done, but at night, at night I see his face as he lay there on the floor. That is when the bad dreams come."

"I would protect you even from those if I could, but if you are like me, you may not forget but you do learn to live with it. You will find new dreams, perhaps a home with children and a meowing kitten. Duchess has not forgiven you for deserting her."

"I did not mean to. I wanted to bring her with me. I hated to leave her, but I could not see how to manage it. I knew you would care for her."

"So you do trust me?"

The music ended before she could reply and their shoes clicked on the marble as they left the floor. The sound was not one she was familiar with. When had a ball ever been so silent?

Mark squeezed her arm in a gesture of reassurance. "Trust me," he whispered.

Before she could answer the yes that was ringing through her mind another voice interrupted. "How touching, Miss Masters," Hargrove said. "What a pity it is not to be. I happen to know the new Duke of Strattington has no intention of marrying you. Shall I tell them why, Strattington?" He spoke loudly so the whole room could hear.

Mark had never felt such violence course through him. "Do you really wish to do this now, here? I would have thought that dawn and pistols were a more appropriate forum."

"Do not overestimate your power, pup." Hargrove pulled his shoulders back. "I have been playing this game far longer than you."

Mark stepped forward. "And look where it has gotten you, arguing over pieces of paper with a mere chit." He sent Bella a look full of apology. "You have them now. Leave her, leave us, alone. I think your time would be far better spent looking over your estate books and counting up the seats you control in Commons. Foxworthy is dead. Let the matter rest."

"Do you presume to tell me what to do?" Hargrove's fists clenched.

Mark looked down at them. "So dawn it will be. Do you prefer swords to pistols?"

Silence reigned again as everyone turned to hear their exchange.

"Are you threatening me, boy?"

"I am not a boy—or a pup. I am the Duke of Strattington and you would be wise not to forget it."

"You are not a duke. Your uncle was a duke. Your cousin would have been a duke. You are nothing more than a placeholder." Hargrove puffed up his chest, stepping toward Mark.

This time Mark did laugh, long and deep. His eyes swept the gathering. All could be won or lost by a tone of voice. "A placeholder. I never thought of it like that—I will not even dispute the term, if it pleases you. But do not forget, I am a placeholder with power. Power I am not afraid to use."

"Hah." Hargrove refused to back down.

"Do you really want to push me and find out? I assure you I can piss as far as the next big dog—and with considerable accuracy."

Isabella's mouth dropped open at his crudity. He did not even look at the crowd.

Hargrove stepped toward him.

Mark matched the step.

"I do not see what you can do to stop me in taking any action I wish," Hargrove said.

Mark stood up straight. He felt power flow into him. For the first time he understood what it was to be a duke. "You are right," he said. "I probably cannot stop you, but I can promise you would live, or not live, to regret your actions."

"Are you threatening me?"

"I thought that we'd already established that. I knew you were older, but had not realized that senility might be setting in."

Hargrove sputtered. The crowd gave a low laugh.

Mark smiled, victory in his grin. "And do not think

my threats are idle," he said. "I do not know when two dukes last met at dawn, but I've never been afraid of risking death. Those years in the infantry do have some advantage. You have not yet told me your preference, swords or pistols?"

Isabella stepped forward, moving between them. "Stop it," she said.

Sweat beaded on Hargrove's brow. It was clear he had never believed Mark would stand up to him. He tried one last time. "I am not going to fight you over a woman of her kind. It's not like you actually mean to marry her. We've all heard the rumors about her."

Mark pulled in a breath. He could feel the crowd consider, think about all the past rumors. Could he have come so far only to lose now? He could see in her face that Bella would not marry him if she thought it would bring him ruin.

She was going to run. Her gaze darted to the stairs and back, her fingers nervously playing with the chain about her neck.

Then her gaze came back to him. He saw renewed strength and something else—something he could not identify.

Her fingers swept lower into the very bodice of her dress. What was she doing?

And then he saw it. The ruby shone bright.

His ring.

His father's ring.

He heard the slight gasp from the crowd.

Even Hargrove had recognized it when they first met.

She pulled the chain from her neck, unmindful of how it caught against her curls. She held the ring out, letting the ruby catch the light, letting it glow with fire. "Would you like to put it on my finger now? I think I've waited long enough for my dreams to come true."

Isabella didn't know how much longer she could go on breathing. She waited as he took the ring, waited for Mark's words, for his commitment.

"Yes. Yes, you have, and yes, I would." He took the ring from her, sliding it off the chain and slipping it onto her finger. It was large, but she did not care.

"Damn you. Damn you both." Hargrove cursed as he turned and left the floor, stomping from the room.

No eyes but hers followed him. Everyone was too intent on what would happen next.

Mark leaned toward her. "You did mention your family is scandalous?"

"Yes."

"Then they won't mind this." He bent forward and kissed her, claimed her—and it was far from a polite society kiss.

Epilogue

Isabella opened her eyes slowly and stared across the pillow at the blue glare across from her. Duchess was not pleased to have been left behind. She lifted a leg disdainfully and began to lick her foot, her gaze never leaving Isabella.

"How did you get here?" Isabella asked, looking about her room in Masters's house. "Is Mark below? Did he bring you?"

Duchess turned her head, clearly unwilling to forgive Isabella for her abandonment.

Isabella scratched her between the ears anyway and laid a kiss upon her head.

Then Isabella bounded out of bed, dressing as quickly as she could.

Mark was here. Had last night been a dream? Could he really have meant all those things he'd said? Could all her troubles really be finished? Could society actually have accepted that they would wed?

She glanced at Duchess. No, not a dream.

Almost running in her eagerness, she sped down the stairs, heading straight for the breakfast room. He might be a duke, but he still had to eat.

There he was, seated beside her brother, a full plate of kippers and eggs before him.

She looked nervously from one man to the other. There did not seem to be any suggestion of bloodshed. Could they have reached agreement? Masters had been plenty mad at being kept in the dark about their engagement.

Masters stood as she entered the room. "You must forgive me, Isabella. I have an early appointment."

Then he was gone, leaving her alone—with Mark.

"I had two early appointments this morning myself," he said, rising from his chair.

"You did?"

"Yes. First I called on Hargrove. I wanted to be sure that the matter was finished. I must admit to some temptation to make sure he was silent—forever."

"I hope you did nothing. I would not want the responsibility of another death. And I think he has suffered enough. Love can make us all act differently than we otherwise would."

Mark nodded. "So I found out. He has had the night to think the matter through. I believe to some extent he now regrets his actions."

Isabella did not want to think about Hargrove. "You mentioned two appointments?"

"Yes, I went to see Mrs. Wattington."

"Mrs. Wattington?"

"I decided to take no chances. She is the only one still left who could tell stories, so I paid a morning visit. She was not amused at the hour at which I called."

"I would imagine not."

"Although her husband was more welcoming."

Isabella could not decide whether to sit. Her stomach was undecided as to whether food was a good idea. "Get to the point."

"Even she came around once I made clear the purpose for my visit."

"Stop delaying."

"I made it known that I would be pleased to become Master Joseph's godfather."

"You did what?"

"It is rather impossible to say bad things about the people who are securing your son's place in the world."

Isabella could see the wisdom of that.

"And," he continued, "it does mean that a certain future duchess will be free to call on them whenever she wishes. It is only natural that you should take an interest in my godson. You may visit Joey whenever you like. Mrs. Wattington has said she would be delighted to meet you—for the first time. She finds it a shame you have never met before."

Tears formed in her eyes. She stepped toward him, unsure what to say. And then she said the only words possible. "I love you, Mark. I didn't get a chance to say it last night, but I do."

He took a half step toward her. His eyes met hers and she could see the words within them. And then he said them. "And I love you, my Bella. I don't know why it took me so long to say it."

She reached out and took his hand in hers, grasping the fingers tightly. "I can never begin to thank you. You bought me Duchess, and then you brought her back to me. And now you have enabled me to see Joey again. The problem with running has always been that I've left so much behind."

"No longer, my love, my Bella. You are done with running." He pulled her toward him until she was in his arms.

For a moment they just stared at each other, eyes saying even more than words.

Then he bent, bringing his mouth to hers. The kiss started soft and then his lips grew more demanding. They moved over hers with such command. Isabella had felt his kiss a hundred times before, but this was different. Could a kiss be softer and more domineering at the same time? This was a kiss of ownership—and offering. This was love.

Next month, don't miss these exciting new love stories only from Avon Books

Holly Lane by Toni Blake

For Sue Ann, retreating to a cabin on Bear Lake was her chance to piece her life back together after a bad breakup. Unfortunately, her ex's best friend, Adam, shows up, claiming *he's* rented the cabin too. So when a sudden blizzard strikes, stranding them, they find they have no problem keeping the cold out . . . and the *heat* in!

To Pleasure a Duke by Sara Bennett

Saddled with the business of a dukedom, Sinclair St. John can't be bothered with the bold and beautiful Eugenie Belmont—or can he? Unable to take his eyes and mind off the temptress, Sinclair can't seem to find the upper hand in this game of seduction. And brazen as Eugenie is, he's about to let her have her way . . .

All About Seduction by Katy Madison

When Caroline Broadhurst's much older husband forces her to take a lover in order to produce an heir, she resists. But when she meets the rugged Jack Applegate her heart is unable to ignore the passion. Falling in love with Jack could be dangerous—especially when a violent secret is revealed, threatening to destroy not only their love . . . but their lives.

Night Hawk by Beverly Jenkins

After bounty hunter Ian Vance's wife was murdered a decade ago, he swore he'd never love again. But when he's forced to rescue prisoner Maggie Freeman, it's her sassy attitude and unyielding spirit that has him thinking differently. Together they try to outrun their pasts, but it's the fire between them that just might save their lives.

978-0-06-200304-1

978-0-06-173508-0

978-0-06-204508-9

978-0-06-194638-7

978-0-06-199968-0

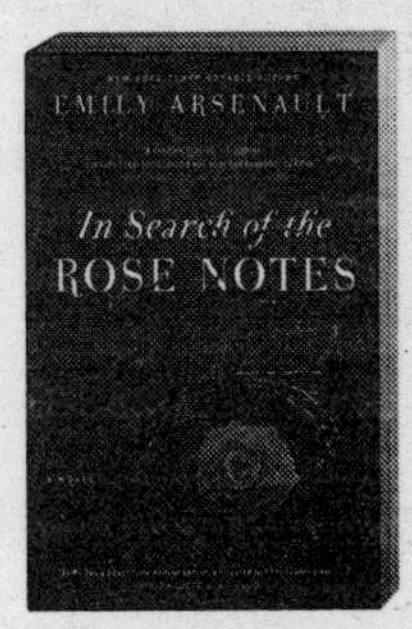

978-0-06-201232-6

Visit www.AuthorTracker.com for exclusive information on your favorite HarperCollins authors.

Available wherever books are sold, or call 1-800-331-3761 to order.

ATP 1011

The Bridgerton Novels

On the Way to the Wedding

978-0-06-053125-6

Gregory Bridgerton must thwart Lucy Abernathy's upcoming wedding and convince her to marry him instead.

It's In His Kiss

978-0-06-053124-9

To Hyacinth Bridgerton, Gareth St. Clair's every word seems a dare.

When He Was Wicked

978-0-06-053123-2

To Sir Phillip, With Love

978-0-380-82085-6

Romancing Mister Bridgerton

978-0-380-82084-9

An Offer From a Gentleman

978-0-380-81558-6

The Viscount Who Loved Me

978-0-380-81557-9

The Duke and I

978-0-380-80082-7

At Avon Books, we know your passion for romance—once you finish one of our novels, you find yourself wanting more.

May we tempt you with . . .

- **Excerpts** from our upcoming releases.
- Entertaining **extras**, including authors' personal photo albums and book lists.
- Behind-the-scenes **scoop** on your favorite characters and series.
- **Sweepstakes** for the chance to win free books, romantic getaways, and other fun prizes.
- Writing **tips** from our authors and editors.
- **Blog** with our authors and find out why they love to write romance.
- **Exclusive content** that's not contained within the pages of our novels.

Join us at
www.avonbooks.com

An Imprint of HarperCollins*Publishers*
www.avonromance.com

Available wherever books are sold or please call 1-800-331-3761 to order.

FTH 0708